Christopher Golden

HARK! THE HERALD ANGELS SCREAM

Christopher Golden is the *New York Times* number one bestselling, Bram Stoker Award–winning author of such novels as *Snowblind, Ararat, Of Saints and Shadows,* and *Tin Men.* He cocreated (with Mike Mignola) two cult favorite comic book series, Baltimore and Joe Golem: Occult Detective. As an editor, he has worked on the short story anthologies *Seize the Night, Dark Cities,* and *The New Dead,* among others, and has also written and cowritten comic books, video games, screenplays, and a network television pilot. A frequent lecturer and speaker at libraries, schools, and conferences, Golden is one-half of River City Writers (with James A. Moore), providing writing workshops, seminars, and editorial services. He cohosts the pop-culture podcast *Three Guys with Beards* with Moore and Jonathan Maberry and *Defenders Dialogue* with Brian Keene. He was born and raised in Massachusetts, where he still lives with his family. His original novels have been published in more than fifteen languages in countries around the world.

www.christophergolden.com

HARK! THE HERALD ANGELS SCREAM

HARK!
THE HERALD ANGELS SCREAM

AN ANTHOLOGY

EDITED BY

CHRISTOPHER GOLDEN

BLUMHOUSE BOOKS | ANCHOR BOOKS

A DIVISION OF PENGUIN RANDOM HOUSE LLC   NEW YORK

A BLUMHOUSE BOOKS/ANCHOR BOOKS ORIGINAL, OCTOBER 2018

Library of Congress Cataloging-in-Publication Data
Names: Golden, Christopher, editor, author.
Title: Hark! the herald angels scream / edited by Christopher Golden.
Description: First edition. | New York : Blumhouse Books/Anchor Books, 2018. |
"A Blumhouse Books/Anchor Books original"—Verso title page.
Identifiers: LCCN 2017025363 | ISBN 9780525433163 (trade pbk.) |
ISBN 9780525433170 (ebk)
Subjects: LCSH: Horror tales, American. | Christmas stories, American. |
Paranormal fiction, American.
Classification: LCC PS648.H6 H37 2018 | DDC 813/.0873808—dc23
LC record available at https://lccn.loc.gov/2017025363

Anchor Books Trade Paperback ISBN: 978-0-525-43316-3
eBook ISBN: 978-0-525-43317-0

Book design by Anna B. Knighton

www.anchorbooks.com

Printed in the United States of America
10 9 8 7 6 5 4 3 2 1

CONTENTS

HARK! THE HERALD ANGELS SCREAM

ABSINTHE & ANGELS

KELLEY ARMSTRONG

A proper reading of Dickens requires absinthe," Michael says as he lifts his glass. "The nectar of the muses."

Ava shakes her head. "There's no way anyone could drink this and still write."

"All those old writers did. How do you think they penned prose like this?" He lifts the book and reads a few lines from the arrival of the first ghost. "Trust me. That required chemical intervention."

"Just tell me our Christmas tree isn't actually on fire," she says.

He chuckles. "Nope, just your brain." He refills her glass. "Unless the tree really is on fire, and *I'm* hallucinating that it's *not*."

She tugs out her gifts, saying, "Just in case," and he laughs and kisses her cheek before he resumes reading.

The absinthe isn't actually so bad. It makes things clearer, sharper . . . and occasionally weirder. Nothing wrong with a little head tripping for the holidays.

Ava takes another sip and rolls onto her side to watch Michael read *A Christmas Carol*. Her favorite holiday story, proving perhaps that she does indeed enjoy the weird. But right now, the words float past, and she just watches him as she basks in the warmth of the fire and the gift he's given her.

Whatever is in the boxes under the tree, they aren't her real presents. This is. Her perfect holiday getaway.

Start with a cabin in the snow. It can't be some resort-property cottage, either. Out here, their nearest neighbor is a mile away. They're even far enough from the road that they'd never have made it without four-wheel drive.

No neighbors. No Wi-Fi. No cell service. Just peace and quiet.

The isolation is Michael's way of making this holiday season easier on her. As a child, Ava had wonderful family Christmases. Even after Dad took off, Mom held it together, especially at the holidays. Now Mom's gone, stolen by cancer two months ago, and Ava's brother, Jory, called last month to say he wouldn't be flying home for Christmas.

So Michael gave her this—a quiet cabin ten miles from the ski chalet where their friends are staying.

It's Christmas Eve; snow is falling; the fire's blazing; absinthe is making her head spin, and her fiancé is reading *A Christmas Carol*.

It doesn't get better than that.

Ava looks out the window. As snow swirls through the darkness, she envisions a moonlight stroll through the woods, the perfect cap for their evening. Maybe even more than a stroll, if it isn't too cold.

She smiles at the thought and sips her drink and watches the dancing snow and imagines endless evergreens laced in white. Their own private winter wonderland. When Michael pauses to turn the page, she thinks she hears . . . music? Singing?

Oh, angels we have heard on high . . .

Angels or absinthe, singing through her veins.

Michael raises his voice to play the part of Scrooge and then lowers it for—

A sharp rap sounds, and Ava jumps, absinthe spilling. Michael frowns at the cabin door.

"Did you hear . . . ?" he says.

She nods, clutching her glass.

"A bird?" Michael says as he gets to his feet.

When he heads for the door, Ava scrambles up and grabs him. "Don't. Please."

He lifts his brows. "Pretty sure it's not the Ghost of Christmas Past. And if it is, it must be for you. I've been a very good boy."

He smiles, and she relaxes her hold on his sleeve. "Just . . . be careful."

He continues toward the door. "Let's lay bets. A bird or the wind?"

The rap comes again, and this time there is no mistaking it for bird or wind. It's three distinct raps, knuckles on wood.

Ava creeps to the side window and peers out. She can see their truck, alone in the lane, covered in snow. She tries to get a look at the front door, but the angle is wrong.

She turns to find Michael behind her, looking out and frowning. The knock comes again. Three raps.

"Don't answer," she says.

"The fact we don't see another vehicle might explain why someone's at our door," he says. "Roadside trouble, and they followed the lights to the cabin. Or hikers who've lost their way. Are we going to leave them out there on Christmas Eve?"

She calls, "Who is it?"

No answer. Michael strides to the door. "Who's there?"

Silence.

"I asked, who's there?" His voice booms through the tiny cabin.

Still nothing. Ava sidesteps toward the front window. All she can see is the falling snow. She cups her hand to the glass and—

A white face appears. Stark white with blackened eyeholes and a red slash of a mouth. Ava staggers back with a shriek as Michael races over. Then he sees what she sees, and he stops.

"What the hell?" he says.

It's a man in an old suit—a jacket and tie. Over his head, he wears a pillowcase painted with a grotesque face. A second man appears beside him, also masked with a painted pillowcase. Beneath it, he's dressed in old-fashioned pajamas.

"Are you seeing what I'm seeing?" Michael whispers.

Ava doesn't answer. She wants to tell herself they *aren't* seeing the same thing, that she's imagining these figures, conjured from her oldest nightmare.

Before Michael can speak again, one of the men presses his pillowcased face to the window and says, "Give us food. Give us wine. Then our song shall be thine."

His voice is eerie and unnatural, wheezy, as if he's inhaling as he speaks.

Ava takes a step backward and smacks into Michael. He wraps his arms around her and whispers, "There are two men at our window, wearing old clothing and pillowcases, right?"

She nods and finds her voice. "They're mummers."

"Mum—?"

"Give us food. Give us wine. Then our song shall be thine," the two men say in unison.

"Mummers," Ava whispers.

"You told me about . . ." He trails off and gives a ragged laugh. "Well, now I understand what you meant, and I don't blame you one bit."

Last year, they'd been drinking with Ava's college friends, comparing Christmas horror stories. It was mostly the usual jokes about terrifying post-Christmas credit-card bills and having to suffer through dinner with drunk relatives. Michael, though, Michael had one-upped them with Belsnickel, the old-world boogeyman from his German grandmother's stories. He did that for Ava, after she confessed to her real holiday fear: mummers. Her friends had laughed and teased her, and Michael had come to her rescue with his story, even if secretly, she suspected, he'd been fighting the urge to join her friends' laughter.

Michael had never heard of mummers—no more than she'd heard of Belsnickel. Michael was from Ontario, where they seemed, thankfully, mummer-free. Ava grew up in Newfoundland, and most of her friends were familiar with the tradition . . . and thought it was cool.

It was not cool. It was being three years old, waking up Christmas Eve to the sound of bells, running to the window, expecting to see Santa's sleigh, and instead spotting a group of passing mummers with their strange costumes and horrifying pillowcase heads. Ava had ducked fast, but not before one saw her. They'd come to her window and crowded in and asked her—in those wheezing voices—if she'd been a good girl. If not, they said, they'd come back. Even after she'd hidden under the bed, they stayed at her window, taunting and tormenting her.

And now there are mummers at her window again. Which cannot be. Absolutely cannot be.

"So I'm going to admit—even at my age—they're kinda freaking me out," Michael whispers. "At three, I'd have pissed my pants." He takes a step forward. "I'll just tell them we're not interested, give them a few bucks for their trouble and . . ."

He stops, finally realizing what she has already.

"What are they doing out here?" he says. "The nearest town is—"

"Ten miles away."

Michael takes a deep breath. He eyes the mummers and then

says, "They must be from one of the neighboring cabins. I'll handle this."

He steps to the window. "Hey, guys. Thanks for coming by but—"

They slap their gloved hands against the glass. Michael jumps, but his shoulders square, as if steeling himself not to inch back.

"I'm having a quiet, romantic Christmas with my fiancée," he says, "which I'm sure you guys can understand. If you want a more appreciative audience, there's another cabin—"

They push their faces against the glass. "Give us food. Give us wine. Then our song shall be thine."

"Yeah, thanks, but no." He reaches into his pocket and takes out a twenty. "I'm going to slip this through, and you guys have a great Christmas—"

In unison, four gloved hands thump the glass. "Give us food. Give us wine. Then our song shall be thine."

Michael adds another twenty and holds the bills up. "You can buy your own." He walks to the window and unlocks it.

Ava struggles against the urge to stop him. But he's being careful, and she's overreacting. It's just a couple of guys from a nearby cabin, who got loaded and decided to go a-mummering, grabbing old clothes and a couple of pillowcases.

Michael eases the window up a half inch and pushes out the bills. One man reaches out . . . and grabs the window instead. He wrenches up, and Ava leaps to help Michael get it shut.

The window slams down, catching the man's fingers. The mummer only withdraws his fingers slowly. Then he stares at them.

Both men stare with their painted eyes, and this close, Ava should be able to see the holes. But there are none. Below the noses, the red mouths have openings, but she sees only darkness behind them.

One man bends, his mask sliding down the glass as he disappears. When he rises, he holds the two bills in his hand. Painted gaze still fixed on the window, he rolls the bills. Then he gives one to his companion. They lift them to their mouth holes and push them through, jaws working behind the masks as . . .

"Did they just eat twenty-dollar bills?" Michael says. "Okay, that isn't a few beers. These guys are on something." He raises his voice. "Well, apparently, we've fed you. Now, if you walk back a few steps, you can grab a handful of snow to wash that down. Then it's time to go and have yourselves a very merry—"

"Give us food. Give us wine. Then our song shall be thine."

"You know what this window needs?" Michael mutters. "Curtains."

When Ava doesn't respond, he turns and says, "Ava?"

She's returning from the kitchen. In her hands, she holds a bag. She opens it to show a bottle of wine and a box of chocolates.

"I'm giving them what they want," she says.

"Okay, but we're not opening that door."

"Of course we aren't." She heads for the bedroom. "Just keep them busy."

She shuts the bedroom door, and outside it, she can hear Michael talking to the mummers. Meaningless patter—asking them where they're from, what they want for Christmas, whether they have family plans . . . acting as if there is nothing odd going on at all. Nothing unnerving. Certainly nothing frightening.

Michael is staying calm, cracking jokes, trying to handle an irrational situation rationally. And so will she. She'll forget the terror of that childhood Christmas Eve, and instead she'll remember the day after it, when two of the mummers came to her house. Without the costumes, she knew them from town—the couple who ran the bakery. They apologized for frightening her. They'd had too much to drink and hadn't realized she'd been genuinely terrified.

Not boogeymen: just regular people who'd gotten carried away with the spirit—and the spirits—of the season.

That explanation hadn't worked for three-year-old Ava. She'd never been able to set foot in their bakery again, and she'd spent the next two Christmas Eve nights sleeping under her bed. Even these days, when she goes home for the holiday, if mummers come to call, she finds a reason to be out for the evening.

But Ava is not three years old anymore, and there is indeed a rational explanation here. If she can't see eyeholes or faces, that's the absinthe messing with her mind. The men didn't really eat those twenties—they just shoved them into their pillowcases.

A couple of idiots who've had too much booze or too much dope and decided to prank the neighbors.

All she has to do now . . .

She opens the bedroom window, drops out the bag, and walks back into the front room, where the two figures stand silent at the window. She strides up to it and raises her voice. "You want wine and food, right?"

No answer. Those unnerving masks stare at her, and as hard as she tries to spot eyeholes, she can't.

Absinthe. Just the absinthe.

"There's a bag beneath the back window," she says. "It has wine and chocolates. Now, if you insist on singing us a damn song, go for it."

Silence. Then they say in unison, "Give us food. Give us wine. Then our song shall be thine."

"I did!" Ava's voice rises. "It's right outside the window." She jabs her finger toward the bedroom. "Go get it."

Neither figure moves.

"Peyton," Michael whispers.

Ava glances at him.

"It's Peyton or Chris," he says. "They're both at the chalet tonight. They know where we're staying, and they were there when you talked about the mummers. They set this up."

He walks to the window. "Peyton sent you, didn't she? Or Chris."

He glances back at Ava. "Maybe Jory. Your brother knows where we're staying, doesn't—?"

The glass smashes. Four hands reach in and grab Michael. Grab and yank him off his feet so fast that he's sailing out the window before Ava realizes what's happening.

She snatches at his feet as they fly through, and she catches one, but the mummers easily rip it from her grasp.

She starts scrambling through the window, screaming for them to stop. She'll give them what they want, whatever they want.

"Give us food. Give us wine. Then our song shall be thine."

Their voices float back as they cross the snow at an impossible speed, Michael struggling and shouting as they drag him behind.

Ava wheels. Her gaze lights on the bottle. Not good enough. She flies into the kitchen and grabs a knife. Then she races out the door.

They're gone.

Completely gone.

Ava can't even find tracks in the snow. She's been out here for at least twenty minutes, walking and listening and trying to hold it together. Every whistle of the wind or cry of a bird has her jumping, knife raised. She's long since lost feeling in her feet, but she never considers going back for her boots or coat.

As she walks, she thinks of earlier, envisioning a moonlight walk in the snow.

The perfect cap to a perfect evening.

She swallows back a gasping sob.

When she hears a grunt, she follows it, expecting to find an animal. Instead . . .

She isn't sure what she's seeing at first. The moon has disappeared behind cloud cover, and all she can make out is three figures standing in the forest. When she blinks hard, she sees white pillowcases over the heads of the two mummers. But it isn't Michael between them. It's a tree. They're flanking a tree, and they're . . .

Give us food. Give us wine. Then our song shall be thine.

One lifts a glass and takes a drink. The other pushes something into his mouth.

Michael. Where is—?

The cloud passes, and the moonlight shines down, and she sees Michael. He's tied to the tree. Bound and struggling, grunting against a gag.

Blood streams down his chest, glistening in the moonlight.

The first mummer presses his glass against a cut in Michael's neck, filling it with blood. The other chomps down on Michael's arm, ripping out a chunk of flesh and gobbling it down.

Ava runs at them, screaming, "No!"

The mummers stop. They just stop. She's twenty feet away, running as fast as she can through the snow, and they just stand there, watching her. She sees Michael's eyes go wide, and he madly shakes his head, howling against the gag, telling her to go, to run.

She raises the knife and charges at the first mummer and—

Ava starts from sleep, gasping for breath, Michael's name on her lips, her fingers aching, as if she's still gripping the kitchen knife.

She blinks and stares at the lights of the Christmas tree. Behind her, Michael is reading from *A Christmas Carol*. A half-finished glass of absinthe rests by her elbow.

She pushes up, blinking harder now, trying to clear her head. The lights seem to glitter and glide, and her ears feel as if they're stuffed with cotton, every sound distorted.

She turns and sees Michael's empty glass beside her. And next to it . . .

Is that the knife? From the kitchen?

She rubs her eyes and sits up. Michael sits cross-legged, his sweatshirt hood pulled up as he reads.

"Michael?"

He turns. His hood falls back, and she sees . . .

A white pillowcase, crudely drawn face grinning at her.

Michael reaches for the knife.

"Give me food. Give me wine. . . ."

CHRISTMAS IN BARCELONA

SCOTT SMITH

There's a moment, toward the end of the flight, when the two of you flare up into the sort of argument you haven't had since your early days together. You're whispering, because of the other passengers, these strangers who started to hate the two of you while you were still taxiing out from the gate in New York, when the baby—*your* baby—first began to cry. As the plane sped eastward across the Atlantic, their hatred for you mounted, the baby jiggling first on Tess's knees, then on yours, then back to Tess's, and so on, all to no avail: the child crying, howling, shrieking, more or less continuously for the entire flight. And now, as you descend toward Barcelona, Tess's whispered assault emerges in a hissing sort of gale. Your response is more guttural—half grunt, half cough— but it amounts to the same thing. Each of you is blaming the other for having suggested this trip, which at one point, though it's difficult for either of you to believe this now, had seemed like such a wonderful idea.

The baby was born the previous April. Such a perfect child. One month in, and he was sleeping through the night. People said he was spoiling you, giving you the wrong impression of parenthood. And it was true: you couldn't understand what all the fuss was about.

For the first six years of your relationship, you and Tess traveled every Christmas. Buenos Aires, Paris, Belize, Prague, Amsterdam, Costa Rica. You both assumed the baby would force an end to this tradition, but as October pivoted into November, and everything about the child continued to seem so effortless, one of you uttered that most dangerous of questions: *Why not?* You're certain it was Tess who said these words, and she's equally confident it was you, and this is what you're raging about as the plane lowers its landing gear and a foggy-looking Barcelona comes into view beyond the window.

The baby flails in Tess's arms. Screaming.

It must be the plane, you think. He'll stop once you're on the ground. And at first it seems like you might be right. He quiets as you make your way along the Jetway to the terminal, and by the time you've reached the baggage claim, he's sleeping on your shoulder. People who weren't on the plane with you—people who don't know any better—smile as they pass: *such a sweet-looking child.* Tess slips her arm through yours, leans her weight against you, travel-tired, conciliatory. You drop your arm over her shoulder, a silent gesture of contrition, and in the same instant, a buzzer sounds, a door bangs, the conveyer belt jumps into motion, and your flight's luggage begins to emerge.

Everything is going to be okay.

Or no, maybe not.

Passengers step forward, one after another, to claim their suitcases, then hurry off toward the exit. The crowd drains away, until it's just you and Tess standing there, your sleeping baby on your shoulder, the same handful of forlorn-looking bags circulating on the belt, unclaimed. You keep waiting, neither of you wanting to be the one to concede what is becoming increasingly irrefutable. Who knows how long you might've persisted in this denial had the buzzer not sounded again and the invisible door banged shut and the conveyor belt shuddered to a stop.

The buzzer, the bang, the sudden silence that follows: some part of this sequence yanks the baby back into consciousness. You feel him come awake, a tautening of muscle against your shoulder. He starts to howl again. Without a word, you hand him to Tess. Then you stride off through the maze of conveyor belts toward an official-looking counter, where a woman sends you to another floor, where a man in turn redirects you back to the original floor, but to a different counter, and finally, after more than an hour of ping-ponging like this through the terminal, you receive formal confirmation: your bags did not arrive.

They could be in Frankfurt.

Or London.

Or possibly Rome.

The only thing that any of the airline's representatives can agree upon is that wherever your bags might be, it's definitely not Barcelona. Off and on, as you wander the airport, searching for assistance, you hear your child crying, somewhere in the crowd.

Invisible, but undeniably yours.

The airline promises to contact you as soon as they find your missing luggage. Someone will deliver the bags to your hotel. This might be later today. Or, more likely, tomorrow. But since tomorrow is Christmas, it might also not be until the day after tomorrow. But since the day after tomorrow is Sunday, it's conceivable that it might not be until the day after the day after tomorrow.

The various representatives assure you they are extremely sorry for the inconvenience. One of them gives you a slip of paper that will grant you entry to the airline's Premiere Access Club. Another hands you two free-drink vouchers.

You text Tess, arrange to meet her at the taxi stand.

The baby is still crying.

Loudly enough, in fact, for the first driver to wave you off.

He's smiling, good-humored, but still: it feels like an affront. His job is to ferry passengers to their destinations in the city, and he won't take you. You start to protest, in English, since you don't speak Spanish, but the driver just keeps smiling, holding up his hands, palms-out, pushing you and your screaming child away from his car. You're saved by a sharp whistle: another driver has pulled to the curb, stepped out of his taxi. He waves for you to approach, opens the cab's rear door, gestures for you to get in, and for the second time since you left New York, the baby falls quiet.

Once again, that thought arises—a pat on your hand: *Everything is going to be okay.*

The driver is a short, voluble young man, with a shaved head, a five-day beard. He smiles in the rearview mirror at you and Tess, says something in Spanish. Tess smiles, says something back, and he laughs, and responds, and you say: "What's he saying?"

Tess ignores you, leaning forward, the two of them speaking rapidly to each other. Tess's gestures change when she speaks Spanish, become more sweeping and exaggerated, like an actress in a silent movie. It seems like she and the driver are talking about the baby, who has fallen asleep now, with his usual abruptness, strapped into his car seat between you and Tess. You shut your eyes.

Perhaps you nod off for a moment, too, because when you open them again something has shifted. The driver has stopped smiling; the tone of Tess's Spanish has grown heated. The way she's emphasizing her words, with hard little finger-taps against the driver's headrest, makes you want to reach for her hand and hold it. When the driver responds, his voice doubles in volume. He keeps looking at you in the rearview mirror, as if you're part of this too, shaking his fist at you. Tess makes a scoffing sound, utters a string of words that even you can tell must be an insult, and then the driver brakes, pulls the taxi to the curb, gestures for you both to climb out. Tess doesn't protest; she pushes open the door, spills onto the street, stands there, staring off, with her arms folded across her chest, while the driver continues to harangue you, urging you from the cab. You fumble with the baby's car seat, unbuckling it, but too slowly for the driver. He starts to poke at his horn in impatience, short bursts—a man slapping his palm against a door.

From your pre-trip web browsing, it seems clear you're not in the same neighborhood as your hotel. There's an edgy, industrial feel to the buildings. Tess appears to know where you are, or at least which direction you need to head in, because she's already in motion, striding up the sidewalk with an air of assurance.

You follow her, the baby's car seat clamped under your arm. Somehow the child has managed to sleep through all of this commotion—the raised voices, the horn, the jostling as you wrestled him out of the cab.

Tess stops on a corner, allows you to catch up.

There are so many questions you could ask her at this point.

You could ask: *"Where are we?"* Or: *"How far to the hotel?"* Or maybe just: *"Are you okay?"*

You could tell her that you love her.

Or you could even say nothing at all, just put your arm around her waist, kiss the top of her head.

Only an idiot would ask, with a peevish, aggrieved tone: "What did you *say* to him?"

You're an idiot.

Tess turns, crosses the street, starts up the next block.

You hurry after her.

Perhaps it's not as far as it seems. Perhaps it's only a mile or so that the two of you walk like this, Tess ten strides ahead of you. But it feels much longer. A blister begins to form on your left heel, and you start to limp, possibly with a slight degree of exaggeration, though for whose benefit it would be hard to say, since Tess doesn't glance back.

Not once.

It's almost noon when you reach your hotel.

Both you and Tess had hoped to sleep on the flight over, but the baby's distress had made this impossible. Aside from your brief head-bob in the cab, you've been awake for twenty-five hours.

Tess has an email from the hotel, which seems to assure the two of you that you'll be allowed to check in early. But when she shows the email to the woman at the front desk, the woman points out that this isn't actually what the email says. The email assures the two of you that the hotel will do *everything possible* to enable an early check-in. But if there are no rooms free, then obviously there is *nothing possible* to be done.

There are no rooms free.

You and Tess take this news surprisingly well. The woman behind the front desk has a kind smile. The baby is still sleeping. There are comfortable armchairs in the lobby. Complimentary tea and coffee is available. Doughnuts, too.

Tess settles into one of the chairs. You pour a cup of tea, wrap a doughnut in a paper napkin, and bring both to her—a peace offering she accepts with something that isn't quite a smile, but close enough to feel like one. You sit across from her, a low table between you. The baby is in his car seat, on the floor at your feet. You feel the same thought stirring—*everything is going to be okay*—but this time you have the wisdom to resist its lure. You've learned your lesson; you're not going to hex things again. Pleased with yourself, you settle more deeply into the big chair, and as you lift your foot to cross your legs, the toe of your shoe nicks the car seat, jostling the baby awake.

The open mouth, the sharp inhalation . . .

In the instant before the baby begins to cry, you glimpse Tess, staring at you with a look of loathing.

The lobby has a high ceiling, a marble floor: the child's screams echo off the hard surfaces, doubling and redoubling. You take him out of his car seat, bounce him on your knee. You can sense people turning to stare, and you make a show of checking the baby's diaper. Five minutes pass. When you see the concierge start in your direction, you know what he's going to say. There are the other guests to consider. If you can't quiet your child, perhaps you could find somewhere else to wait until your room is ready?

This is how you end up out on the street again, with the baby in a pouch on your chest. Tess remains in the lobby, sipping her tea, nibbling her doughnut, dozing in her armchair. If it weren't for the blister on your heel, you probably wouldn't harbor any ill feelings over this arrangement. You'd feel chivalrous. But there *is* the blister on your heel. There's also the weather, which has turned wet: fifty degrees, with a misty drizzle that seems to carry a faint smell of sewage.

You're worried about getting lost, so you walk in a manner that always keeps the hotel in sight: you circle it, never straying more than a block or two away. The rain gradually soaks through your shoes. Your socks. Your blister tears open, and your limp grows proportionately more dramatic.

After nearly an hour of this, the baby is still crying.

You reenter the hotel, pushing through the revolving door, and find Tess standing by the elevators with an impatient expression. She's holding a key card in one hand, a half-eaten doughnut in the other. "Where have you *been*?" she asks. "I've been *texting* you." She utters these words with an air of exasperation, as if she assumes you must've spent the past sixty minutes sipping whiskey in the hotel bar.

The fury that her tone elicits in you is too intense to permit speech, and this is an excellent thing—a blessing. Nothing good would come from you being able to put your feelings into words at this moment. Nothing at all.

Your room is ready.

You tell yourself that this is the only thing that matters, and then you climb onto the elevator with Tess and your wailing baby.

The door shuts. The elevator begins to rise.

You don't speak.

Both of you seem to sense the wisdom of this strategy.

Wordlessly, you enter the room, which is smaller than you expected, even though you were expecting it to be smaller than you'd expect. Tess takes the baby from you. She sits on the edge of the bed and tries to feed him, but he has no interest. He just keeps screaming, making the room feel even tinier than it already is.

You gingerly remove your shoes and socks and inspect your blister. It looks pink and damp, but like nothing at all really, and the gap between how it feels and how it appears seems unjust to you.

Tess sets the baby in his car seat, tries to rock him, tries to play peek-a-boo, tries pursing her lips and making funny noises. You should be helping her, you know. But how? You pull off your clothes and step into the bathroom and turn on the water in the tub. There must be a way to switch the water from the tub's faucet to the shower nozzle, but you're too tired to solve this puzzle, so you take the path of least resistance and close the drain and begin to draw a bath.

You can hear Tess on the phone, ordering room service, in Spanish. She has to raise her voice to be heard over the baby's cries, and it makes her sound angry. You're certain the two of you will find a way to reset things—you always do—but you wish it involved a less mysterious process, wish it was like rebooting a computer: a button pressed, a click, a whirring, and thirty seconds later, everything is fine again.

What is the opposite of vigorous? Weak? Feeble? Frail? Whatever it is, that's the word to describe the hotel's water pressure. The tub is filling slowly enough that you fear it might be leaking. You keep thinking you should get out and unpack your clothes, but then you remember that your luggage is in Frankfurt. Or London. Or possibly Rome. And each time this happens, you feel the same jump of anxiety.

The doorbell rings. Room service has arrived.

Tess brings a plate into the bathroom for you, then a plate for herself, then the baby in his car seat. The baby continues to howl. Tess has ordered you both turkey sandwiches. You eat yours in the tub, with the plate balanced on your upraised knees. Tess lowers herself onto the closed lid of the toilet. The baby thrashes about in his car seat on the floor between you.

When you finish your sandwich, there's still only two inches of water in the tub. You give up on the idea of a bath, turn off the faucet. And it's as if the spigot controlled more than the tub, because when the water stops, the baby's crying does, too. You and Tess sit, watching your son, both of you afraid to move, or speak, or breathe. The child stretches his arms, settles more snugly into his blankets, opens and shuts his mouth in a fishlike manner, then closes his eyes and falls asleep.

Tess smiles.

You smile back.

"I'm sorry," she whispers.

You nod. "Me too."

This would be the moment to have that thought again—*everything is going to be okay*—but you're too tired to indulge it. Instead, you climb out of the tub. Tess hands you a towel, and you pat yourself dry, careful not to make any noise, lest you disturb the sleeping baby. When you turn to leave the little bathroom for the only slightly less little bedroom, Tess bends to pick up the car seat. You give a vigorous shake of your head, and wave her off, worried she'll rouse the child.

You lie down on the bed together, spooning, your chest to Tess's back. You're naked. Tess is still in the clothes she wore on the plane; there's a faint smell of sweat to them. You're curious about the taxi—what happened between her and the driver. You know better than to ask again, though. The time will come when this might be possible, but it's still a long way off. You think about reaching to unbutton Tess's blouse, weighing the prospect of sex, here in this tiny hotel room, on the day before Christmas, in Barcelona, with your baby sleeping so peacefully in the bathroom, and then you hear Tess begin to snore, and you shut your eyes, and press your face into her hair, and breathe in, and think: *Everything is going to be . . .*

Then you, too, are asleep.

You wake to the sound of Tess singing, softly, in the darkened bathroom. You lie there on the bed, coming back to yourself, listening:

> *Gone away, is the blue bird.*
> *Here to stay, is the new bird.*
> *He sings a love song,*
> *As we go along*
> *Walking in a winter wonderland.*

You turn on the bedside light, and she falls silent. You can sense her watching you through the half-open door, but the bathroom is too dim for you to make out her expression. "How is he?" you ask.

"Hungry."

"Feeding time at the zoo?"

"He's a bottomless pit tonight."

You pat the bed. "Bring him out."

"Can't."

"Because?"

"Every time I try, he starts to cry again. You didn't hear?"

You shake your head. "Slept right through. What time is it?"

"Quarter after eleven."

"Shit. We'll be up all night."

Tess laughs—you've always loved the sound of her laugh. "Yeah. We're all fucked up, aren't we?"

"And what's going on with our little man?"

"Not a fan of travel, apparently."

"Maybe he sensed how small this room was gonna be."

"Or that they shut down room service at eleven."

"You're kidding."

"Afraid not."

You close your eyes, knowing what this means. You'll need to get dressed again. You'll need to put on your damp socks and shoes and head out into the night, to forage for food. It's Christmas Eve, but this is Barcelona, so there's bound to be someplace open. You can ask at the front desk. You can get them to change your dollars into euros. You can see if they have any Band-Aids for your blister.

"Sweetie . . . ?" Tess says.

"On my way."

And you roll off the bed, stand up, reach for your clothes.

The woman at the front desk does indeed have Band-Aids; she gives you four of them. You use your credit card to get euros— three hundred—and then ask for directions to a 24-hour convenience store. The woman takes out a map of the area and highlights your route for you in yellow.

You head across the lobby and sit in one of the armchairs. You pull off your shoe and sock and apply all four Band-Aids to your blister, one on top of another. You can feel people staring at you as you perform this operation, but you don't care. You'll never see any of them again. This is one of the great pleasures of traveling.

The rain has stopped; the night air has grown crisp, though it still retains that faint smell of sewage. The streets around the hotel are empty, but you can hear a crowd caroling in the distance— drunkenly, it seems. You can recognize the song, even though the carolers are singing in Spanish: "Rudolph the Red-Nosed Reindeer." You don't want this tune to get caught in your head, and your desire for this not to happen is enough to ensure that it does, so you find yourself half humming it as you make your way to the store and enter what could easily be a Walgreens or a Duane Reade anywhere in America.

Tess made you a list. You check the items off as you drop them into your basket: deodorant, diapers, toothpaste, two toothbrushes, floss, more Band-Aids, crackers, cheese, a comb, a bag of carrots, a carton of milk, skin lotion, a chocolate bar, baby wipes, cornstarch.

You hand your credit card to the cashier. You say, *"Feliz Navidad,"* and when the cashier responds with what seems like a full paragraph of Spanish, you smile and nod and pretend you understand.

Then you're heading back to the hotel again, through the quiet city streets.

Your blister has never really stopped hurting, despite the quadruple Band-Aids, and it prompts you to make a stupid mistake. You second-guess your map and attempt a shortcut via a warren of narrow lanes, one of which turns left even though you're certain it ought to be turning right, and when you try to retrace your steps, nothing looks quite like it did on your way into the neighborhood, so you blunder about, taking one turn and then another, confident that eventually you'll find your way back out to the wide avenue where you began.

It's in this fashion—meandering, limping—that you come upon the old woman.

The street has opened into a small plaza. There is a dry fountain in the plaza's center, with a statue of what appears to be an angel, head bowed, wings folded, hands clasped in prayer. Wooden tables are arrayed around the fountain, as if for an outdoor market. The old woman is the only person in sight, though. You can't tell if the market was held earlier today, and she's stayed here late, or if it will begin tomorrow, and she's arrived early. She's dressed in a dark blue parka, with a black scarf over her white hair. She's short and plump, and the thick parka seems to exaggerate both qualities, making her look nearly round—so much so that you can imagine her rolling off across the plaza, like a ball, if someone were to push her.

You approach her table with the intention of asking for directions, nothing more. You have the suspicion, even from a distance, that she might not speak English. But it doesn't matter. You'll show her the map you were given at the hotel. You'll point to the wide avenue. If she can get you there, you're certain you can find your way back to the hotel.

The woman is bent forward, arranging her merchandise on the table, a dozen wooden boxes. They look handmade, smaller than shoe boxes, but not by much—like tiny pine coffins. A piece of paper is taped to the front of the table, and it says: "100 Euros."

The woman smiles as you draw near, and you see that she's missing her two front teeth. It gives her an impish air, likable but a bit untrustworthy, as if she might tell you a funny story while she's picking your pocket. You have your shopping bags in one hand, your map in the other. You're about to extend the map toward her when your gaze catches on the boxes. Each one holds a different figurine. You see a bearded man in dark trousers, a white smock. You see a camel. A young woman in a coarse brown dress, a yellow shawl across her shoulders. A donkey. A lamb. An ox. A king with a scarlet robe and a golden crown. A Roman legionnaire. And a pink-faced baby.

That's the one that triggers recognition for you: the swaddled baby.

It's Christ, of course. These are crèche figures.

The woman watches as you bend to look more closely. The figures appear to be handcrafted, and quite old. The fur on the animals is worn in spots; Joseph's trousers are torn at the knee. The old woman looks Middle Eastern to you, and you wonder if these boxes might be heirlooms. You picture them wrapped in burlap and straw, smuggled north across the Mediterranean from some war-torn land. One hundred euros seemed extravagant when you first approached, but now you're not so certain. That's how it happens, so simply, so quickly. You know you're going to buy one of these figures from the old woman; it's just a question of which. Because that's another thing that has gone missing in your luggage—your Christmas gift for Tess. You can easily envision how happy she would be to own one of these creatures. It will be the perfect way to jar your visit here back onto its proper path.

You set down your shopping bags. You take out your wallet.

You know you're supposed to bargain. But it's late, and you're hungry, and this old woman is selling things you assume she must hold very dear, and it's Christmas Eve, and you have the money, so you remove two fifty-euro notes from your wallet and set them on the table. Then you point at the ox. "May I see that one, please?"

The woman answers in a language you don't recognize. All you can tell is that it's not Spanish. She senses your incomprehension and begins a complicated pantomime, pointing at her watch, gesturing at the surrounding plaza, then the wooden boxes, widening her eyes in an exaggerated expression of wonder, and gradually you start to grasp that she wants you to wait till midnight, that something extraordinary will happen then, something that only occurs on Christmas, and when Christmas is over, it will be over, too, until the following year, when it will happen again, and so on, through the unfolding years, on Christmas, every Christmas, but only then.

Or no, maybe not—maybe you're misunderstanding her altogether. The only thing you know for certain is that she wants you to be patient. She insists upon this. She won't be swayed.

You check your own watch. It's four minutes till midnight.

You can see no harm in waiting, though you'd prefer if she'd just go ahead and sell you one of the figures, which seem wonderful enough as they are, without the supposed intervention of midnight, a moment that you suspect will amount to nothing whatsoever, or something silly, perhaps, a joke whose meaning you will likely fail to grasp.

The old woman removes the ox from its wooden container, sets the beast on the table before you, upright on its hooves. You're wondering what might be unfolding back at the hotel room, if the baby is asleep again, or crying ... you're wondering if you should just summon an Uber to take you the rest of the way ... you're wondering if one hundred euros is an excessive sum to pay for what after all is really only a worn-looking stuffed animal ... you're wondering if you should pick the Roman soldier instead, or maybe the camel, or the plump Magus with his gold crown, and then you hear the bells begin to toll.

Church bells, near and far, all across the city.

It's midnight in Barcelona.

There must be a church just a street or two away, because one of the bells stands out from the rest, echoing across the plaza. You count each strike of the clapper as it rings the hour. In the silence that follows, you turn to the old woman, waiting for her to reveal her Christmas miracle. She is smiling down at the ox with an air of expectation, and you follow her gaze. The little figurine is standing there, unchanged. You're thinking that maybe you will try to bargain after all—or perhaps you should forget the whole exchange, take back your money, pick up your shopping bags, and head off across the plaza—when the astonishing thing happens.

The ox moves.

No, that's not it—it doesn't merely move. It moves in a way that only a living thing would move. It moves like a creature waking from sleep. It shakes itself and snorts and lifts its head to look at you, and you can see the instant when it registers your presence in its eyes. For a long moment, you're too stunned to react; you simply stare. Then you reach a hand to touch the thing, and it shies away from you, its hooves making a clomping sound against the wooden table as it retreats, and the old woman gives a pleasure-filled laugh. She scoops up the ox—it struggles against her grip, swinging its wide horns—and then she sets it back into its box.

All in an instant, the creature goes still again. Lifeless. The magic undone.

Yes, that's the appropriate word: *magic*.

Because you know immediately that this is what you're witnessing—you have no doubt. You've stumbled upon some ancient enchantment here among the narrow streets of Barcelona's old city. Witchcraft. Sorcery. Something you'd never believe could exist. Something you'd scoff at, even, if anyone ever told you the tale. But you're not scoffing now. You heard the creature snort. You saw it move.

And you want to see more.

You point to the figures in the boxes, and the old woman lifts them out, one by one, to set them on the table. There's that same pause with each creature, that same feeling that this time the magic won't take hold, nothing is going to happen, and then, just when you're falling back into a comfortable state of unbelief . . . the same awakening. The donkey is so vigorous in its movements that it almost gallops off the table. You catch it at the last instant, and there's the shock of its warm body, the tautness of its muscles, its breath hot against your hand.

Alive.

Each of them: undeniably alive.

Mary looks frightened; she cowers backward, makes a whimpering sound, pulls her shawl around herself. Joseph, for some inexplicable reason, keeps sneezing. The infant Jesus begins to cry— howling, screaming—sounding eerily like your own child, crossing the Atlantic. The Roman soldier scowls and paces; he draws his sword and tests the blade with his thumb, then slides the weapon back into its scabbard and paces some more. The camel lies down and refuses to rise again. The Magus looks about with a haughty air, offers a tremendous yawn, then folds his pudgy arms across his chest.

After each demonstration, the old woman catches the figure in her hands, drops it back into its box. Instantly, the creatures resume their doll-like stillness.

The old woman does her pantomime for you again, pointing at her watch, gesturing around you at the plaza, pointing once more at the watch, and you nod—yes, yes, yes—you understand, only on Christmas, every Christmas, from midnight to midnight. You empty your wallet onto the table: three hundred euros. You hesitate over the Holy Family, feeling an obligation to choose them, but there's the cowering to consider, the sneezing, and the crying. You think of your son, growing up with these mysterious beings. Which of them would give him the most delight, coming to life each Christmas? Which would give a young boy the greatest pleasure?

You point to the Roman solider.

The donkey.

The ox.

The old woman takes your money. She covers the three boxes with their wooden lids. Then she pushes them toward you, one after the other. She watches as you set them into your shopping bag. You thank her with passion, saying thank you and *gracias* and *merci* and *grazie,* and then, when this doesn't seem sufficient, miming your gratitude for her, bowing, touching your heart, your lips, your heart again, and the old woman smiles her toothless smile and bows back and sends you off into the night.

In your excitement, you forget to ask for directions. But it doesn't matter. You hurry from the plaza, turn a corner, head up the block, then round another corner, and there, in the distance, you glimpse the rooftop of your hotel.

The baby is back in his car seat, in the darkened bathroom, asleep.

Tess has changed out of her travel clothes and taken a shower and pulled on one of the white terry-cloth robes the hotel has provided. She's wide awake and so focused on discovering what sort of food you managed to procure—the cheese and crackers, the baby carrots, the milk, the chocolate—that she doesn't seem to notice the three wooden boxes.

Not wanting to get crumbs in the bed, you agree to sit on the floor. When Tess vanishes into the bathroom to fetch two plastic cups for the milk, you arrange the wooden boxes on the carpet at your feet. Tess returns, sits down beside you, and you eat the cheese with the crackers and crunch your way through half the bag of carrots and drink the milk. It's only when she's unwrapped the chocolate bar and snapped off a piece and begun to nibble at it that she acknowledges the boxes' presence. "Looks like you went a bit beyond the list I gave you," she says.

"I did indeed."

"Three little coffins?"

You smile, savoring the moment before the revelation. "No matter how long you live? What you're about to receive? Will be the best present you ever get. I guarantee this."

You tell her about your attempt at a shortcut home. You tell her about the winding streets of old Barcelona. You tell her about the tiny plaza, the old woman behind her table. You tell her about the figurines and how the woman mimed out the wonder that was to come. You tell her about the tolling bells and the miracle that followed.

Tess doesn't believe you, of course. Which is what you wanted. Because now you can take the lid off one of the boxes and lift out the figure within and set it on its feet and watch her face. It's the Roman soldier. In his sandals and greaves, his armor and tunic, with his sword in its scabbard, his helmet on his head. There's that moment of stillness before anything happens, and this time it seems to stretch even longer than in the plaza—so long that you begin to fear you've made a terrible mistake, you've been swindled, you're a fool—and then the soldier takes a dozen quick strides and stops to draw his sword and checks its blade with his thumb and scowls and slides the sword back into his scabbard, and Tess lets out a yelp of astonishment and reaches to grab your hand.

You were right about her joy—Tess seems breathless with it. Panting. Giddy.

You lift all three figures from their boxes and let them range about on the carpet. The soldier paces and scowls, drawing and sheathing his sword. The ox walks a slow circuit, as if plowing a field. The donkey is more puppy-like, gamboling back and forth between you and Tess.

Tess calls the soldier Brutus; the ox, Somber John. She tries out a series of names for the donkey—Randy, Tigger, Goofus—before finally deciding on Pip.

She keeps laughing. Clapping her hands.

You don't want to admit this to her, but as you sit there, watching the three creatures, you begin to feel a sense of disappointment. You keep hoping the soldier might speak in Latin or sing a song or do anything, really, besides pacing and scowling and repetitively testing the keenness of his sword with his thumb, but apparently this is all the creature is capable of. The ox is even worse. "Somber" seems like a generous appraisal on Tess's part. If it were your decision, you'd call him Sullen John, because he moves about on the carpet with a brooding air of hostility. You picture your son, in the years to come, struggling to play with these creatures. Once the shock of the magic wears off (and it does—that's the startling thing—it wears off with alacrity), you're forced to confront how boring most living things are, even things one wouldn't normally expect to be alive. If technology were at work here, rather than enchantment—if these creatures were tiny robots, for instance—they'd probably be designed for a far wider range of activities. The ox might play music and do a dance. He might heave himself up onto his hind hooves and walk. The soldier might turn cartwheels or climb onto the ox's back and ride it like a horse or maybe even learn to say your name.

Perhaps you should've picked the camel instead.

Or the portly Magus.

Well, at least there's the donkey. The donkey is worth every euro you spent—all three hundred. He's a playful, happy creature. Smart, too. Somehow he figures out what the belt does on Tess's robe, and he keeps trotting up to her, gripping the terry cloth in his teeth, rearing back to yank it loose. When the robe falls open, Pip tosses his head with pleasure and makes a hee-haw sound and gallops in a tight circle. Tess gives a gleeful hoot of laughter—loud enough for you to worry she might wake the baby—then pulls the belt tight and waits for Pip to try again.

An hour passes in this manner. Two.

Soon your son will rouse himself and demand to be fed. You wonder if he'll allow you to tour the city while you're here. You picture yourself at the Sagrada Familia or Park Güell, the baby howling in your arms. Perhaps the three of you will end up spending the entire trip in this tiny room.

Dawn is starting to break beyond the room's single window when Tess yawns, stretches, snatches up Pip, sets him back in his box.

"Merry Christmas," you say.

Tess smiles, leans to kiss you. "You're right. Best ever."

"I feel bad about the ox and soldier, though. I wish I'd chosen better."

They've both wandered off somewhere, and you get on your hands and knees, peering under the bed for them.

"I sort of like the ox," Tess says. "He seems so sad."

You can see him, almost as far beneath the bed as it's possible to go. You have to get on your belly and wiggle forward, stretching, before you can reach him. He tries halfheartedly to gore you as you grab him—just as he had with the old woman in the plaza.

Behind you, you hear Tess's voice: "Why a soldier?"

"I don't know. It seemed like the sort of thing a boy would like. I would've, I mean. Growing up." You're wiggling backward, Somber John writhing in your hand, working to free himself from your grip. The carpet under the bed is dusty, and you keep feeling like you're about to sneeze, but then it doesn't happen.

"No," Tess says. "Why would there be a soldier in a crèche?"

"You know. The whole Herod thing." You're free of the bed now. You set Somber John in his box. Instantly, the life goes out of him.

"Herod?"

You nod. "The Magi tell Herod about a king being born, in Bethlehem. And Herod panics. He sends his legionnaires to kill all the babies there."

Tess is holding the soldier's box. Staring at you.

You gesture at the box. "Find him?"

But she's already on her feet, heading for the bathroom.

And this is what you will always remember.

Always.

This instant . . . right *here*.

The dreadful, drawn-out pause before Tess begins to scream.

FRESH AS THE NEW-FALLEN SNOW

SEANAN McGUIRE

Where the *fuck* is the babysitter?"

"Language, John." Antonia Daniels somehow managed to make even criticism sound vaguely bored, like she couldn't imagine she had to lower herself to correct the behavior of others. Her attention remained fixed on the silver oval of the hallway mirror as she adjusted the sleek coils of her hair.

"I can watch the girls," said the lanky teenage boy in the living room doorway. He looked anxiously at his mother, then over at his pacing father. John Daniels was not, and had never been, a patient man. If something didn't break his mood soon, he was going to ruin date night.

When date night got ruined, Mom was disappointed. And when Mom was disappointed, everyone suffered. Andy was only sixteen, but he had long since figured out that keeping his parents smiling was the key to a happy life.

"You will do no such thing, Andrew," snapped his father. "Your little sisters are not your responsibility. Babysitting is for flighty girls who need to learn skills for their futures, and who don't have your brains or advantages."

Andy didn't say anything. This wasn't a winnable fight.

"She'll be here any minute," said Antonia, finally turning away from the mirror. She looked perfect. She always looked perfect. As a Realtor, looking perfect was one of her best methods of clinching a sale. "Really, John, calm down. We have plenty of time to reach the restaurant."

Andy swallowed a derisive laugh. Mom was the one advocating calm, but she would be the one who took it out on the rest of them if this night didn't go as planned. Almost on cue, the wail of his youngest sister blared from her bedroom upstairs.

"Great, and now the damn baby's awake," said John venomously.

"I'll get her," said Andy. This time, neither of his parents moved to stop him. Without a babysitter, it was him or them—and no matter how much his father tried to write off childcare as women's work, he would sooner allow his teenage son to do the job than lift a finger to do it himself.

The air seemed to brighten and grow sweeter as Andy pounded up the stairs, away from the cloud that always hovered over his parents in moments like this. They were going out because it was almost Christmas, and because their social capital depended on people seeing them as good, kind, and loving. The sort of folks who would sit down for a good meal once a month as a treat, while their perfectly cared-for, pampered children enjoyed a little rec-reational naughtiness under the eye of a well-paid local babysitter. That didn't mean they enjoyed each other's company, or the neces-sity of putting on a show.

The baby's room was at the far end of the hall. He paused, know-ing she would continue to wail until he reached her, to stick his head into his middle sister's room. Chloe was sitting on the floor at the foot of her bed, hair in her face as she hunched her shoulders and tried to focus on her book.

"Hey," he said, voice hushed.

She looked up, and for a moment, she reminded him of nothing more than a startled fawn standing at the edge of the woods, entire body vibrating with the readiness to run. She tilted her head, ever so slightly, toward the floor, and he nodded, pressing a finger to his lips. Her nod was vigorous, almost violent.

"Soon," he said, and moved on toward Diane's room.

As expected, the baby was standing in her crib, a bar grasped tight in each pudgy hand, her face screwed up into an expression of anger and misery.

"Aw, pudding," he said, and scooped her up. She kept wailing. A quick check confirmed the reason why: she had soiled her diaper, leaving her sopping wet.

"That has to be uncomfortable," he said, bouncing her as he walked toward the changing table. Diane answered with another wail. "Don't you worry. We'll get you fixed right up."

Midway through changing Diane's diaper, he heard the door slam. The tension left his shoulders in the same moment, leaving him more relaxed than he'd been since his father had announced that they would be auditioning a new babysitter. According to the cartoon cat clock on Diane's wall—"Just the thing for a model nursery," claimed his mother, who always liked her house to look like it was ready to go on the market—the sitter had been two minutes early.

Not that that was going to save her. She was never going to work in this house again. She definitely wouldn't be getting a tip.

"Hello?"

The voice was sweet and female, with some unidentifiable

accent—Eastern European, maybe, or Russian. Andy relaxed a little more and took his time getting Diane's new diaper on. The babysitter was in the house. Things were going to be okay.

Dry and diapered, Diane clung to his shoulder as he walked back down the hall to the stairs. Chloe was peeking her head cautiously out of her room. He motioned for her to follow, and she did, creeping along at his heels. Her steps were soft as ever, measured so as not to make too much noise.

Their mother *hated* it when she made noise.

The babysitter waited at the bottom of the stairs. She was tall and slender, with white-blonde hair that fell most of the way down her back. She was wearing a thigh-length blue sweater dress spangled with silver snowflakes, and just looking at her made Andy feel faintly grubby, like he needed to take a shower long enough to strip off the top layer of his skin. She looked up at them as they descended. She smiled, and he realized he couldn't tell whether or not she was pretty: something about the shape of her face seemed slightly off, like she had been assembled in a dark room by someone who wasn't entirely sure what a teenage girl was supposed to look like.

"Hello," she repeated, without the questioning lilt. "You must be the children. My name is very difficult to pronounce in this country: you may call me 'Raisa.' I would prefer it. You are . . . ?"

"I'm Andy, and this is Diane," said Andy, holding his baby sister up for the sitter to see.

"I'm Chloe," said Chloe. She narrowed her eyes. "We're not stupid. We can learn your name."

"I'm sure you could, really I am, but we have so little time together, and do you really want to spend it on a tongue twister?" Raisa smiled like the sun reflecting off new-fallen snow. "Let me be simple for tonight. If we meet again in the future, then I can be complicated. Now. You." Her eyes went to Andy. "You seem grown for a sitter. Are you my responsibility, or no?"

There was a snare buried somewhere in that question: Andy could feel it tickling the back of his neck, even if he couldn't quite see it. Quickly, he reviewed the responsibilities of the babysitter. She was supposed to make dinner—fish sticks and tater tots. She was supposed to supervise the younger children, which technically meant playing board games with Chloe and reading picture books to Diane, but functionally meant watching television more than half the time. When a sitter never stayed long enough to develop a routine, they would usually default to the lowest difficulty.

But Diane didn't *like* having books read to her by strangers, and when he told the sitters that he wasn't part of their job responsibilities, they had a tendency to view him hanging around to keep an eye on Chloe as some weird form of hitting on them. He was exhausted from waiting for his parents to explode. Maybe it would be nice to have someone in charge of him for the evening.

"Yes," said Andy, pulling Diane a little defensively closer. "We all are."

The sitter looked at him, and for a moment the hallway lights shining in her eyes turned them entirely opaque, like clouded ice, stealing all their color away. Then she moved her head, changing the angle of the light, and they were bright and blue again. She smiled. She seemed to always be smiling.

"Three on one? Oh, won't this be a lovely night!" She clapped her hands. Andy jumped a little. Diane pressed her face into his shoulder. "Your parents have left me a list. Who wants fish sticks?"

All of them, it turned out, wanted fish sticks. Even Diane, who had reached the stage where she was happy to wrap one chubby fist around a breaded prize and gnaw at it with more enthusiasm than skill. Andy deftly took over getting her settled in her chair while he watched the babysitter out of the corner of his eye, noting with some relief that she actually seemed to know how to handle Chloe. His mother had a tendency to hire sitters based more on how they'd look to someone watching from the street than their experience with children. His life had been a succession of short-term sitters who didn't know which end of the baby was which.

Chloe shyly began telling Raisa about the book she was reading, some magical adventure with horses and secret princesses and evil overlords who needed overthrowing. Andy tuned her out, focusing on Diane, who had somehow managed to pull her shirt off without unfastening the straps holding her in the chair.

By the time he was finished getting her sorted, the fish sticks were ready. Raisa brought them to the table, along with the tater tots, the milk, and a still babbling Chloe, who was now exploding into joyous narrative. Someone who wasn't Andy was *listening* to her, paying *attention* to her. Andy smiled at the sight, while his heart ached like it was being squeezed. She was nine years old. She deserved better than a house filled with chilly silence and unexplained rules.

"Now then, eat quickly and without getting tartar sauce on the ceiling, and you shall have a story after we are done," said Raisa, clapping her hands in almost childish glee. "I have a lovely one for tonight. You would be sorry to miss it."

Andy blinked at her before he grinned. Noticing his expression, Raisa raised her eyebrows questioningly.

"What? Have I said something wrong?"

"No," he said. "You're just the first sitter we've had who wanted to tell us a story."

"Then you have had very poor sitters in the past, and I am sorry," she said.

Andy didn't have an answer for that.

Somewhere, their parents were eating steak and lobster and fiddly appetizers, sipping champagne and smiling at each other like lovesick teens. Somewhere, the "in" crowd was murmuring about how in love they were, and by extension, how much they must love their children. Somewhere, the polite fiction of their family history continued.

But in the house, which felt warm and safe for once, without the constant, looming shadow of their parents waiting to fall on them for the slightest transgression, Raisa washed the fish stick off Diane's fingers and pressed a kiss to the burbling toddler's forehead, blowing on the still-baby-fine hairs that grew there. She helped Chloe carry the dishes to the sink, and kissed her too, high on the crown of her head, where her hair was parted.

Andy grinned as she approached him. "What," he asked, only half-kidding, "do I get a kiss too?"

"Of course, silly boy," she said. "They are for all my charges tonight. When the North Wind blows, he blows for all, not only for the privileged." She leaned in and kissed his forehead.

Her lips were cold.

"Come now," she said, dropping back to the flats of her feet. "Your sisters are waiting."

Andy, who hadn't noticed when she took Diane from her high chair—which was alarming; he usually kept track of Diane no matter what, even when he was at school and she was in daycare, or with her nanny—blinked.

"Yeah," he said, and got up and followed her.

Chloe was already in the living room, perching on the absolute edge of a couch cushion with an awkward look on her face, like she was waiting to be thrown out. Andy smiled at her. She smiled unsteadily back, relaxing only when he came and sat beside her, flopping all the way into the corner. Chloe wrinkled her nose at him.

"We're not supposed to wrinkle the upholstery," she said.

"I'll clean it up before Mom gets home."

"Yes."

They both turned to stare at Raisa, Chloe guilty and Andy wary, twisting his body so as to shield his sister as much as possible. Their sitter looked sad, and oddly disappointed, like she had expected better of the world.

"This," she said, using a wave of her free hand to encompass the living room. It had been decorated for Christmas on the first of December, when a huge production had been made of the delivery of the tree. Everything was perfect, and why wouldn't it be? None of them had been using it since the holiday season had begun. Their parents and their rules had seen to that. Still, Raisa looked confused and kept frowning sadly even as Diane began chewing on a hank of her silvery hair. "This is not for you? This is not for the warmth and coming-together of the season?"

"We're not supposed to be in here without an adult," said Chloe uncomfortably. "We break things."

"Do you, now? I doubt that very much. You are both old enough to know better, and this one," Raisa gave Diane a bounce, "is too small to make it in here unescorted. Unless you are in the habit of winding her up and letting her dance among the ornaments, I feel you have given me an excuse."

"Our father paid a lot of money for these decorations, and we have to keep them nice for company," said Andy.

"Ah. Company. Yes, I suppose company is important, when one has so few friends." Raisa continued bouncing the baby as if she hadn't just said something unbelievable, while Andy and Chloe stared. After a moment, she appeared to notice them and asked, with faint concern, "What is it now?"

"Do you know our parents?" asked Chloe.

"Oh, I do," said Raisa. "I know everyone. But I promised you a story, didn't I? Yes, a story, and you are all my responsibility, have all accepted food from my hands and kindness from my lips: you should all have the chance to hear it before our time together ends."

She sat cross-legged in the middle of the living room floor, the baby in her lap, Diane still chewing on the sitter's flaxen hair. Andy suppressed a shiver. It felt like the heat had been turned down. He wanted to check it—Dad would throw a fit if he came home to a cold house—but he didn't want to move. Something about their babysitter, the way she sat, the way she held herself . . . he didn't want to leave until he'd heard the things she had to say.

"You know of Santa Claus, yes?" she asked, and then she grinned, sudden and bright and beautiful. "Of course you do. All good children of the world know Santa Claus. But did you know that he is not the only open hand of Winter? The world knew, you see, that humans would be small, fragile things compared to the sturdiness of a bear or the wildness of a wolf, and so when it came time to decide who would watch over them, the world set so many guardian spirits to their care that it became necessary to divide things among them. Winter watches, and Winter rewards not only through Santa Claus, but through a hundred of his cousins, a thousand of their families."

"Is Winter a person?" asked Chloe shyly. She was still young enough to be enthralled by a story, no matter how cold the room was—although maybe Andy had been wrong about the heat. It was starting to feel quite comfortable now.

"Winter is an idea, and an idea shared by everyone in the world becomes alive, in its own way," said Raisa. "Bears and wolves thought of Winter. Trees and flowers thought of Winter. And now, humans think of Winter, and the Winter continues, and flourishes, and changes to be what they believe."

"Winter is a season," said Andy. "It's not a person. It would exist whether anyone thought about it or not."

"But the planet had to think of Winter before we could have it; do not look upon your grandmother's children and claim that just because you've never met them for yourself, their gifts are any less good." Raisa's tone was mild, but the warning it contained was unmistakable. "Shall I continue?"

"Please," said Chloe.

Andy said nothing.

Raisa smiled. "Very good," she said. "So you know of Santa Claus, and you know that Winter has many hands, many faces. Now, allow me to tell you of Snegurochka—the Snow Maiden. Her grandfather is a man called Ded Moroz who walks through Russia when the wind howls and the snow comes down. He is like your Santa Claus. He gives good gifts, and Snegurochka follows behind him, peeping in windows and seeing what is done with his generosity."

"That's a little creepy," said Andy.

"Perhaps," said Raisa. "But if your little sister gave her favorite doll to a child who asked for it, wouldn't you want to be sure that child was not going to scribble on it with crayons or cut off all its hair? Wouldn't you want to know it was loved?"

Andy said nothing.

"Snegurochka loves all the little children, even as her grand-father does. She has no parents of her own. Ded Moroz made her from the enchanted snow that fell in his garden, and what sad-dens her most of all is parents who do not care for the things they have. She does not look for letters written to ask for toys or trin-kets. She does not look for letters at all. She looks for . . . other things."

"Like naughty kids?" asked Andy sarcastically. He should have known that a first-time babysitter in a home this impeccably main-tained, with employers who paid as well as his parents did, wouldn't be looking to tell them a nice little bedtime story. It was going to be another morality play about how kids who didn't listen would be punished.

He had only known Raisa for a few hours, but he still felt disappointed and oddly betrayed. He had already been thinking better of her than that.

"No," she said, with a crisp fierceness that made him sit up a little straighter in his seat. "Children are . . . There are bad children. I won't lie and claim to you that such things do not exist; you would laugh at me. But children are like snow, fresh and new-fallen, waiting to be sculpted by their parents. Molded into some shape that will see through the winter. Snegurochka does not look for letters or for naughty children in need of punishment. She looks for tracks in the snow. Snowmen sculpted without kindness, without care for their form. She looks for children who are suffering, for parents who do not understand that they have been given a great and precious gift. She looks for children who could be great, if only the snow that made them were melted down and given to someone else for safekeeping."

Chloe inched a little closer to Andy on the couch and said nothing.

Bouncing Diane to keep her quiet, Raisa leaned forward and asked, in a conspiratorial tone, "Would you like to hear the story now?"

"Yes," whispered Andy.

"Once upon a time," she said, "there was a family that lived in a beautiful city, very far from the winter woods. They had everything they could possibly want, but they were not happy. They could have been, if they had been willing to see how good their lives were. They had a house with a strong roof and thick walls. They had food to fill their bellies, and warmth to fill their nights. They had each other, and while that was not the greatest gift of all—do not ask a starving child to choose between company and a crust of bread, unless you are willing to accept whichever he should choose— it could have been enough to soften the sting of living in a cold world. It could have been enough."

Raisa looked at each of them in turn, even Diane, who had quieted and was staring at the babysitter with wide, rapt eyes.

"The children were good, because they were still children; they had not yet had enough time to be spoilt. Fresh as the new-fallen snow they were, and held fast to each other, because they had nothing else to hold to. But the parents . . . ah." Raisa made a clicking sound deep in the back of her throat. "There is a special place in hell for people who bring children into this world solely for the sake of seeming better than they are. These parents were not cruel in a way that any outside the house could see. They did not strike with hands or withhold food. The roof was strong for parent and child alike."

"So how were they bad?" asked Chloe, in a meek voice.

"They withheld love," said Raisa simply. "They refused to treasure what had been given to them. Maybe it was not their fault: maybe no one had treasured them. Maybe the Snow Maiden, so busy, trusting in people to tell her when she was needed, should have come a generation, two generations, three generations before. Maybe if she had come when they were being sculpted, she could have melted them down and reshaped them into people who would be better for their children. But she did not. She was far away, doing other things, and they had been allowed to grow to adulthood, to become frozen in the forms they knew. This is the secret, children: all things are limited, even impossible things like Ded Moroz or Snegurochka. Because she did not stop their parents from freezing, these children, these precious, precious children, were left to grow in a house that was warm, and clean, and beautiful, and knew nothing of love."

Andy said nothing.

"But she is always listening, Snegurochka, the Snow Maiden, she is always looking for the good, unfrozen snow. The snow that can still be melted cleanly down and reshaped into something else." Raisa smiled down at Diane. There was ice in her eyes. "This family, it had been as it was for many years. Long enough for the children to have had teachers who noticed 'they are so sad.' Long enough for the parents to have spoken a little too freely in the company of others, after they had been drinking too deep of their sweet mulled wine. They thought they were clever, hiding their children away behind walls of manners and appearances. They did not count on hiring a babysitter who remembered Snegurochka."

"You?" asked Chloe, eyes wide.

Raisa shook her head. "No, sweet girl. Not I. Another, whose grandmother had been born far away from here, who had seen a family visited by the Snow Maiden when they failed to live up to the standards of the Winter. She looked on these children, and her heart broke like a mirror. She stayed with them as long as she could, and when her services were no longer needed over some minor infraction—"

"Tasha ate an apple from Mom's table arrangement," whispered Andy.

"—she went home, and she wrote a letter to Ded Moroz. She asked him to send his granddaughter, to let Snegurochka judge for herself what was to be done. The Snow Maiden does not look for letters, you see, but she listens when her grandfather speaks. She always listens. So she came to see if there were children who needed to be released. To be melted back down to clean, clear water, and allowed to fall a second time, in a second home, as fresh as the new-fallen snow."

A key turned in the front door. Raisa turned her face toward the sound, already rising, holding Diane out to Andy. He took her as he stood, Chloe hurrying to smooth out the wrinkles in the couch upholstery.

"Remember," said Raisa softly. "You said that you were my responsibility."

The door began to open. Andy glanced at the clock and blanched. It was after eleven. How had so much time gone by? He couldn't remember wasting that much of the evening. He couldn't—

"Did the damn heater break? Why is it so *cold* in here?"

"Where the hell's the babysitter?"

Andy turned. His parents were in the living room doorway, both frowning, looking none the calmer for their night out.

"Well?" demanded his father. "Where is she?"

Diane screwed up her face and began to whimper. Andy bounced her in his arms, automatically trying to soothe her.

It was the wrong move. "Oh, God," said his mother, stepping forward to sweep the baby into her own arms. "You threw her out, didn't you? Nothing is ever good enough for you, I swear."

Diane, who had already started to learn that upsetting their mother was not a good idea, quieted, although her whimpers continued.

"Yes," said Andy, through the fog of slow horror that was beginning to cloud his mind. He felt Chloe move closer to him, hiding herself from their parents' wrath. "I'm sorry."

"Antonia." John touched his wife's arm. "At least we didn't have to pay her."

Antonia shot a look of pure fury at him before snapping, "Apparently *your son* didn't think it was important for the baby to have her bath before he threw the sitter out. I'll be in the bathroom." She turned on her heel and stalked away, carrying Diane with her.

John remained in the doorway for a few beats more, looking at Andy and Chloe. Then he turned and walked away. The heater came on a few seconds later.

Andy felt Chloe's cold arms lock around his waist, felt the wetness seeping from her cheek and through his clothing. He raised his hand, looking at it dispassionately. It looked the same as it ever had, save for the faintly translucent tips of his fingers. They were beginning to drip on the carpet, fat, painless droplets, like tears. It didn't hurt. The Snow Maiden was kind, after all.

From the bathroom—from the direction of the tub filled with hot, soapy, unforgiving water—he heard his mother start to scream.

Andy closed his eyes and waited for the thaw.

LOVE ME

THOMAS E. SNIEGOSKI

*A*lthough *it's been said, many times, many ways* . . .
  Flynn Townsend heard the holiday song drifting through
the Target parking lot and fought the reflex to finish the
lyrics.

He didn't care much for Christmas songs; didn't think too kindly
of their season either—just another way of separating people from
money they didn't have. A big rip-off.

"How long you been out?" Cindy asked before taking a long
drag from her cigarette, her dark, stringy hair whipping around
her face in the cold wind.

"Week," Flynn replied, noticing the gray now streaking his ex's
hair. He took a pull on his own smoke.

"What do you want?" Cindy asked, an edge of impatience to
her voice.

"How is she?"

"Good, has a cold, but otherwise she's fine." The woman pulled some strands of hair away from where they had stuck to her thin, angry lips.

"It's school," Flynn said. "Bein' around all those other kids, she's pickin' up all kinds of—"

"What do you want, Flynn?" Cindy demanded again before he could finish his sentence. "You said this would be quick."

"Yeah, yeah," he said. He avoided her eyes, poking at the filth-encrusted snow with the toe of his sneaker as he began, "I was thinking—"

"No," Cindy firmly interrupted.

This time he looked at her. "No?"

"Whatever it is, no," she said with finality. "I'm done ... *we're* done with you and your shit."

"That's a little harsh." He finished the last of his cigarette and flicked the filter into a nearby snowbank. "I was only hoping that with Christmas and all ..."

"Excuse me?" she said, dropping the remains of her butt to the slushy ground and stomping on it with her boot-covered foot. "You think that just because it's Christmas you can come waltzing back into our lives—our daughter's life—and fuck it up some more?"

"Hey, it's different this time. I'm lookin' into some stuff, hopin' that—"

"You're always hoping, Flynn," she interrupted again. "Hoping that the next time you fuck up you won't get caught is more like it."

"When did you become such a nasty bitch?" he asked with a scowl, feeling his anger surge like scalding vomit in his throat.

"Oh, I don't know, maybe when my husband and the father of our child got himself arrested for breaking and entering again and sent upstate for two more years." She paused for a moment, as if thinking, then nodded. "Yeah, I'd say it was right around then.

"I'm done." She turned toward the store's entrance. "Don't fucking call anymore."

"Wait." Flynn reached out and grabbed her arm, pulling her back.

She looked at him sharply and, sensing the potential for greater trouble, he released his hold, throwing up his hands in surrender. "I just want to make it up to you and Meg," he said quickly. "Please."

"Make it up?" she repeated incredulously. "Are you fucking kidding?"

"I'll get a job by Christmas Eve," Flynn said. "I can prove that I mean what I say, that I'm gonna clean up my act for you and Meg. Just give me this one last chance to be the man you used to think I was," he said.

She stared at him fiercely. "I'm fucking freezing."

"Please," he begged again.

She abruptly turned to the store entrance, and he felt his heart sink.

"Christmas Eve," he heard her say as the automatic doors slid open and she went inside.

"Christmas Eve," he repeated, not exactly sure how he'd fulfill his promise.

But he was filled with a new determination nonetheless.

The skinny guy with the malformed arm cackled hysterically as he leaned back in the red vinyl booth.

"Oh, you kill me, Flynn," Dougie said. "And by Christmas Eve?" He cackled some more before breaking into a nasty cough.

"I hope you fucking choke," Flynn said, pulling his beer mug closer.

"I'm sorry," Dougie said, sitting up straight again. "I can't help but laugh at the stupid shit you get yourself into."

Flynn said nothing as he lifted his mug and drank.

"Seriously," Dougie said, reaching with his clawlike appendage to pull his own drink closer. "Why do you do this to yourself?"

"I want to see my kid again."

"Yeah, that's all well and good," Dougie began. He used his good arm to lift the mug to his mouth and took a long drink before smacking his lips and continuing. "But do you seriously think anybody's gonna hire you? You're less than a week out of county, for Christ's sake."

Flynn remained silent, not wanting to acknowledge that his annoying friend was probably right.

"Hey, I've got an idea." Dougie snapped his fingers. "Maybe Santa's hiring," he said before bursting into hysterical laughter again.

"You're a fucking riot," Flynn said. He took one last gulp of his beer and slammed the mug down on the tabletop. "I'm getting out of here."

Dougie managed to get control of himself as Flynn began to rise. "Wait up," he said. "I actually do got an idea."

Flynn stopped and glared.

"I'll fuck up your other arm if you're dicking me around," he threatened.

"Nice," Dougie said. "Seriously, sit down, I want to run something by you."

Flynn was torn. Dougie's ideas seldom amounted to anything good, but he was desperate, so he sat.

"What?"

Dougie stared at him as he drank more of his beer.

"What?" Flynn repeated, louder this time.

"I'm not sure I want to tell you now." Dougie shrugged. "That shit you said about my arm . . ."

"I'm gone," Flynn said, ready to leave this time for sure.

"All right, all right!" Dougie looked around and leaned forward. "I've been hearing about this place—building on Stewart Street, business below, apartment above."

Flynn didn't like where this was going, but listened anyway.

"Business was a junk shop, antiques and shit. Owner croaked, guy's old lady didn't want to keep it open, shop shut down. Word on the street is that there was some pretty valuable things in the shop, and that wifey took 'em upstairs for safekeeping."

"Hey, man, I just got out of jail," Flynn said, picking up his mug and downing the warm dregs, more spit than beer. "I promised I'm not goin' back."

"And that would only be the case if you got caught," Dougie said. "How hard would something like this be for someone with your talents? You can do shit like this in your sleep."

Flynn shook his head. "Doesn't matter, I'm done with that life."

"Okay," Dougie said, sitting back. "Just lettin' you know what's out there."

"You're not gonna convince me," Flynn said, shaking his head. He knew he should just get up and leave, but he remained.

"Not even trying," Dougie said. "You told me no and I respect that." He motioned for the bartender with his spindly arm. "Just let me know how it works out for you."

Flynn sat on the bus, heading back to the fleabag hotel he was staying in. He'd lost track of how many applications he'd completed that day without even a glimmer of hope that anyone would call him back.

And now he found it particularly cruel that a water main break caused the bus to detour down Stewart Street.

"Shit," he cursed beneath his breath, realizing where he was and trying to keep his eyes on the filthy floor of the bus. But he couldn't do it. He lifted his head and allowed himself to gaze through the window as the bus slowly made its way down the traffic-clogged street.

There it was. The old sign hanging over the doorway said REED'S ANTIQUES, and his eyes focused on it as if he'd been searching for it his whole life. He saw the old building in all its glory—the antique store with its metal shutters drawn, and the dim lights from the two-story apartment above. The apartment where treasure was kept.

Treasure. What am I, a fucking pirate now?

The bus continued on its way, but Flynn could still see the building in his mind's eye. He tried to push it from his head, to turn his thoughts to his current plan of action, but the sad realization that he didn't have one dragged him back to the building and its potential.

Flynn pulled the cell phone he'd bought for ten bucks from a guy outside the liquor store from his pocket and checked it for messages. One message from one of the places that he'd filled out an application with would have been more than enough— something ... anything ... a sign that things would turn out all right.

But there weren't any messages, and he felt his resolve begin to crumble.

The weather had turned nasty, a mixture of snow and rain, and Flynn was soaked through to the skin as he entered Gower's Pub. He tried to convince himself that he was only stopping for a cup of coffee—even though he knew that Dougie was almost always there at this time of day.

He stood in the warmth of the doorway, suppressing a shudder that ran up his spine to the base of his neck. A few stools at the bar were occupied, but most of the tables were empty.

Most.

Dougie sat by himself at a table in the back, playing with his phone.

For a brief second, Flynn thought he would just turn around and head back out into the storm, but then Dougie lifted his head and saw him. A huge smile spread across his face as he waved Flynn over with his clawlike hand.

"Can I get a coffee?" Flynn said to the bartender as he passed on his way to the table.

"Flynn!" Dougie said, slipping his phone into his jacket pocket. "How goes the job search?"

There was a smirk on his friend's face that Flynn wanted to slap away.

"It goes," he said, pulling out the chair opposite Dougie and sitting down.

The bartender brought his coffee and placed it in front of him.

"Thanks, Phil," Flynn said. He reached out and grabbed a few sugars from the cup in the center of the table, tore them open and poured them into his coffee as Dougie watched. "Bus took a detour down Stewart today," he said, slowly stirring his drink.

"You don't say. How fortuitous."

Flynn set the spoon down. "Fortuitous," he repeated. "Do you even know what that word means?"

"I know what it means for you," Dougie said with a smile that reminded Flynn of a shark he'd seen on television the other night.

Flynn silently drank his coffee. It was old, burnt, and scalding hot, but he drank it anyway, knowing he deserved far worse for being so fucking weak.

"What do I need to know?" he finally asked.

Flynn stood across the street from the shuttered antique shop, feeling as though he'd already been there.

Dougie was an observer. He could look at something and see all its weaknesses and strengths and the opportunities it could provide. That and his connections made him especially good at casing joints for break-in. He took great pride in his work, as well as a 20 percent cut of the profit. His information was that good.

Flynn already knew there was no security system, that the old woman lived alone with no children, no pets, nothing that would prevent him from getting in, taking what he could find, and getting out. He wasn't too keen on the fact that the woman would be home, but sadly that was his specialty.

The Creeper was what they used to call him, given his unique ability to get inside a place where the owners were home and pick it clean with no one the wiser.

Flynn considered his options once more as he stood in the cold rain on the dark, deserted street. He should forget the whole thing and go back to his room at the flophouse. But that meant facing another day of filling out pointless applications and enduring the suspicious looks of managers, all the while no closer to being able to spend time with his daughter.

His choice was obvious.

Without further hesitation, he crossed the street and walked quickly down a narrow alley to the back of the building where a set of old, wooden stairs led to the apartment above the store. Flynn glanced up and down the alley, looking for signs of life but saw none.

Dougie's info was good. It always was.

Flynn felt himself settle into the familiar Creeper mode. Cautiously, he made his way up the steps, careful to stay on the sides where they were strongest to minimize creaks and groans. The lock on the door at the top was simple, and it was less than a minute before Flynn had it picked and entered the warmth of an open foyer, facing an ornate wooden staircase. He stood silently, listening to the sounds of the building around him. There was a steady hissing from an old steam radiator against the wall, but no other sounds.

Maybe this was his lucky night, and the old lady had gone Christmas shopping.

It was when he placed his sneakered foot upon the first step that the music began to play.

Said the night wind to the little lamb . . .

The song wafted down from a room at the top of the staircase.

. . . do you see what I see?

Flynn froze, a surge of panic coursing through him.

"Hello?" called a woman's voice over the holiday song. "Are you down there?"

He held his breath, foot still upon the step. He thought he heard another voice, high-pitched like a child's but unintelligible.

"Please come up. I . . . I need your help. Please."

Flynn's every instinct screamed for him to get out of there, something wasn't right—but still he remained.

"You came to steal from me, I know," the woman called out. "Everyone in the neighborhood knows about the poor old lady who lives alone above the antique shop and the valuables she's hidden." She laughed strangely then. "Valuables," she repeated.

Flynn felt a sudden chill that had nothing to do with the weather and immediately went for the door. He was done. This was his last chance, and he couldn't let it go.

"You can have anything that you want," her voice drifted down the stairs accompanied by the strains of "Frosty the Snowman."

His hand was already on the doorknob, about to turn it.

"Anything," she said again. "Just please help me."

Flynn turned back toward the stairs again. That tiny voice chattered excitedly before the old woman shushed it quiet.

"I know you're still there," she called to Flynn. "I promise, anything you want, but you must come up and help me."

This was not at all how Flynn had imagined the job turning out—people never parted willingly with their belongings, but if she really needed help, maybe he could still come out on top.

"Okay," he called up the staircase. "I'm coming up."

He began to climb the stairs, no longer concerned by their squeaks of protest under his weight. He thought he heard the old woman sob beneath the strains of Handel's "Messiah," and utter words that could have been "thank God."

He reached the top of the stairs and stood, searching the darkness of the hallway for signs of the woman. "Hello?"

"I'm in here."

Flynn turned toward the sound of her voice and saw a faint glow coming from underneath a partially closed door. Cautiously he pushed the door open and stepped into the dim light of a sitting room of sorts. An old record cabinet sat against the wall to his left, Handel's most famous composition sounding slightly static as it blared from the cloth-covered speakers. Directly across from him a large, well-worn sofa and an overstuffed wingback chair sat before an ornate fireplace where a burning log cast the only light in the room. A large curio cabinet stood against the wall to his right. Through its dusty glass doors, he could just about see a shelf filled with fancy baby dolls, all staring out at him. They were kind of creepy, but he bet his daughter would love them. Every surface in the room seemed to be cluttered with objects of value—tin toys, crystal vases, a vinyl folder that was likely full of old coins. The place was a gold mine, and Flynn wondered how he was going to carry it all out.

He heard a scuffling from the corner behind the door and stepped further into the room to see an old woman turn from a small table beside an artificial Christmas tree. She was slightly hunched with thick gray hair wild upon her head. She wore a heavy cardigan sweater, slightly threadbare at the elbows. She shuffled toward him holding a plate of cookies, then stopped abruptly, her eyes, large behind the thick lenses of her glasses, wide with surprise.

"You're not who I thought," she said, a slight tremble in her voice, either from fear or the advancement of years. Flynn couldn't quite tell.

"Excuse me?" he said, feeling a sudden urge to flee.

"You're not the man I was seeing from my window," she said, moving past him and placing the cookies on a stack of newspapers atop the coffee table between the sofa and the chair. She turned back to Flynn, pulling her sweater tighter around her as if cold. "Skinny man, something wrong with his arm."

Dougie, Flynn thought, watching the woman closely, wondering if he should just cut his losses and run.

She shrugged. "Doesn't matter," she said with a sad smile. "You're here . . ."

With those words, she picked up the plate of cookies and thrust it toward him with one hand, holding the front of her sweater tight about her throat with the other. "Cookie? I made them myself."

They were Christmas cookies shaped like gingerbread men, candy canes, and Christmas trees.

Flynn reached for a Christmas tree as the plate began to shake in the woman's hand. She seemed suddenly unsteady.

"Do you . . . do you need to sit down?" Flynn asked, taking the plate from her.

"I should, yes," she said, sinking down into the wingback chair.

"You're welcome to sit." The old woman nodded toward the couch as she began to stroke her left arm and shoulder.

Flynn placed the plate of cookies back on the table and turned to the sofa. He had to move piles of magazines and crossword puzzle books to clear a space.

"My husband would never ask for help," she then said, staring into the fire. "Even when he began to realize what it was doing to him."

"Was he sick?" Flynn asked. He could feel sweat beginning to drip down his back but wasn't sure if it was from the heat in the room or the strangeness of the situation.

The old woman turned her eyes to him. "Eventually," she said, continuing to stroke her left side as if attempting to massage away pain.

He ate his Christmas cookie as the woman silently watched him, the "Messiah" still playing behind her. The cookie was actually quite good, but he was becoming more and more unnerved.

"So," he said, finally wiping the crumbs from his fingers and leaning forward on the couch. "You said that you needed help with something."

The old woman smiled dreamily. "If only someone had asked that question when Philip was still alive," she said. "That was my husband's name—Philip."

Flynn nodded. "And he wasn't big on asking for help."

"No, not like this. He said it was his responsibility; he had found it and it was his burden. He gave it all he could," she said wistfully. "But just couldn't give it anymore." She looked as though she was going to cry.

"I'm sure he did," Flynn said, trying to sound sympathetic although seriously beginning to wonder if the so-called riches in the room were worth the oddness of the situation.

"He didn't know what was going to happen when he passed," she said. "He thought it would just leave . . . maybe go back to where he'd found it."

Flynn cocked his head, totally confused now. "Where he found it? I don't . . ."

"Philip was a picker. He loved the lifestyle," she said. "I didn't care for it, so I'd stay here to run the business while he drove off somewhere to search through old dusty barns and abandoned houses. The things he'd come back with." The woman chuckled, shaking her head.

But her amusement was short-lived as she rubbed at her chest and shoulder. It must have been a trick of the light from the fireplace, but Flynn could have sworn that something moved beneath her thick sweater.

"I thought it was the ugliest thing he'd ever brought home," she continued. "And he brought back some real whoppers, let me tell you. 'Betty, you just don't know what's good,' he'd say to me.

"We'd laugh every time he said it, and then he'd take whatever it was down to the store to sell."

Betty paused, her expression pained.

"But he didn't bring *that* downstairs," she said. "He kept it with him . . . said it was special. Found it in an old orphanage in Kentucky. He didn't find out until later that forty children died in a fire at that orphanage."

Her hand stopped massaging her arm and this time Flynn was sure he saw something move beneath her sweater.

"Betty, what . . . ?" he began.

But she continued with her story as if she hadn't heard him.

"No matter how ugly I said it was. No matter how much I said it bothered me, it never found its way down to the store. He always had it with him. It was just strange at first, but then I began to see the changes in health, and I'd hear him speaking to it in the middle of the night." She looked at Flynn then, her watery eyes huge behind the lenses of her glasses.

"Saying that he loved it."

"What, Betty . . . what did he . . . ?"

Before Flynn could finish his question, it crawled from beneath her sweater, furry paw pushing back the lapel. Its button-like eyes fixed upon him.

And it spoke.

"Love me," it said in a high-pitched, childlike voice.

Flynn recoiled at the sight of the oddity.

Betty's sweater fell open. Her pale skin was marked by angry red welts where the black-furred *thing* held on to her. It looked like a toy, a stuffed animal, but it was somehow alive.

"Love me," it said in an angry, catlike hiss.

"It needs constant attention to survive," the old woman said, her voice sounding very tired. She shifted in her overstuffed chair and exposed her left breast, a nearly airless balloon. "Constant love," she continued, pushing the thing's head toward her scabbed nipple.

"What . . . what is it?" Flynn asked. He couldn't take his eyes from it as it suckled, its fur-covered fingers kneading the mottled flesh of her chest.

Betty placed an age-spotted hand gently on the back of its head. "A toy," she said, the words so incredibly heavy with emotion. "At least that's what Philip thought it was . . . what we both thought it was."

The thing lifted its fur-covered face to gaze up at her.

"Love me," it said.

She pushed it tighter against her, wincing as it eagerly continued to . . . what? . . . feed?

"So many die unloved," Betty said, still staring at the horrible thing that clung to her. "Have you ever thought about that?" She paused and turned her eyes on Flynn. "I don't know your name."

"Flynn," he said uncomfortably.

"Flynn," she repeated dreamily, then smiled and nodded. "Before Philip . . ." She paused again, her gaze upon the stuffed thing harder, angrier—meaner. "Before he died, he was trying to find out what it is."

She was petting it now, and it emitted a strange, gurgling purr.

"He had some wild theories: the love-starved spirits of dead orphans, the forever playmate of a powerful witch's daughter still seeking love after its mistress's death so long ago, a fallen creature of Heaven desperate to find its way back to the Creator through the love of His chosen creations."

Flynn could only stare. The stories were fantastic, unbelievable, but so was what was right before his eyes.

"Sounds pretty crazy, but how else do you explain it? You should have seen what it did to poor Philip."

She was crying now, tears streaming down her withered cheeks as she stroked the black furred head of the stuffed animal.

"The love he gave it . . . was forced to give it," she said. "It was never enough, even though he tried so hard to satisfy it."

The thing's muffled growl filled the room and she cried out in pain. Flynn actually made a move to go to her, but she shook her head slightly, and he sat back on the edge of the sofa.

"He gave it everything he had in him," she said, slowly, lovingly petting the thing's head. "He actually believed that once he ran out of love, it would begin to feed on his soul." Betty's voice shook, and she seemed to be trembling. "He was so scared."

She sniffled, and Flynn suddenly realized that the "Messiah" had ended as her words hung menacingly in the silence.

She looked at him again. "He was in such pain. I couldn't bear to see him suffering. He held on for as long as he could, and when he couldn't take it anymore . . ."

Betty looked down on the thing, and it turned its black, wide-eyed face up to hers.

"Love me," it said as their gazes locked.

"And I've done that," she told the horrible thing. "But I'm afraid I've just about reached the end."

She lifted her head and looked around the room. "I'm not as strong as Philip was. I started talking about his things, and how valuable they are. I knew someone would come eventually." She sighed heavily. "And here you are."

"And here I am," he repeated softly, suddenly ashamed.

"I'd hoped that it would be someone horrible," she said.

Flynn looked down at his hands, and then at the floor.

"How do you know I'm not?"

Betty laughed, making him look up. There was nothing humorous about the sound.

"I guess you're right," she said. "A good thought to have. It'll make it easier." She moved to stand, and the thing on her chest began to growl. "Yes, yes, I know you don't like to be disturbed," she said to it. "But the record is over, and we need more music."

Betty managed to stand with a grunt of exertion. She swayed for a moment, steadying herself by holding the back of the chair before shuffling over to the old console stereo.

"You mentioned needing my help," Flynn said as he watched her put the vinyl record back into its sleeve and take out another.

"I did," she said. "Yes."

He heard the sound of the record dropping as the arm moved over, and the needle touched the vinyl with a crackling hiss.

As "Silent Night" began to ring out through the speakers, she turned, gun in hand, pointed directly at Flynn.

He jumped as if shocked with electricity. "Hey, wait a minute now," he began, raising his hands in a feeble attempt to protect himself.

"I'm such a coward," she said by way of explanation. "I can't bear the thought of my soul being eaten. I saw what it did to my strong, strong Philip, and I can't ever imagine going through something like that."

She stepped a little bit closer, gun still pointed at him.

"Which is why I wanted someone to try and steal from me, but in reality I'd be giving something to them."

The truth suddenly hit Flynn like a shovel to the back of the head.

"No," was all he could muster as the hand that had been petting the suckling creature gripped the fur at the back of its neck and pried it away with a terrible ripping sound.

"I'm sorry, Flynn," she said, and there was true emotion in her voice.

"Love me! Love me! Love me!" the furred thing wailed as it squirmed in her grasp, its tiny claws ripping at her sweater and the paper-thin flesh beneath.

Flynn screamed above the wailing of the creature and "Rudolph the Red-Nosed Reindeer" blaring from the old stereo and took a step to sprint for the door, when—

Betty flung the toy. It snarled and snapped as it flew, bouncing off Flynn's leg before thumping to the rug.

Flynn stumbled back as the thing scrambled to its feet and started back toward the old woman. Betty began to back away, waving the gun.

"For what it's worth, Flynn," Betty cried, as the toy began to climb her bare legs, "I'm truly sorry."

Then she placed the gun barrel against her temple and pulled the trigger, setting the side of her head on fire as the bullet tore through her skull and exited the other side in an explosion of blood, brain, and bone.

"Oh God, oh God," Flynn gasped. He found himself heading toward the woman as she toppled backward into the stereo, causing the needle to slide across the surface of the LP with the most horrible of sounds.

But the stuffed animal had already crawled atop her chest, hovering over her blood-spattered face. "Love me," it demanded, jumping up and down in an odd parody of resuscitation. "Love me! Love me!"

Flynn began to back quietly toward the door as the creature turned its attention to him.

"Shit," he muttered. He made a run for it, but the toe of his sneaker caught on the leg of the coffee table, sending him crashing to the floor. He landed hard on his chest, knocking the wind out of him. For a moment he lay there, struggling to catch his breath, until he heard the soft patter of stuffed paws running toward him.

He pushed himself to his feet and lunged for the door, almost there when it landed on his back.

"Love me," it commanded.

He felt needle-tipped claws sinking into his jacket and the skin beneath. Crying out, Flynn struggled to pull it from its perch, but it held fast. He crashed to the floor, frantically rolling back and forth.

"Love me!" it screeched.

Flynn became like a wild animal, scrambling to his feet, ripping off his coat and the thing that clung to him and tossing them to the floor. He could feel the rivulets of blood streaming down his back as he threw his full weight down onto his coat and the thing trapped within.

A log within the fireplace suddenly snapped like the crack of a bullwhip, and he cried out in surprise, glancing toward the burning embers as they swirled above the burning logs before being sucked up into the flue.

Fire, he thought. *Maybe . . .*

Quickly he snatched up his coat, wrapping the writhing nightmare all the tighter as he stumbled toward the fireplace. So desperate was he to get there that he forgot Betty's body and tripped over her legs. He fell to the floor face-first, the impact knocking the coat from his grasp.

The nightmare was free.

"Love me!"

It sprang at him, and Flynn caught it. It felt warm in his hands, strangely alive, but boneless. All cloth, fake fur, and stuffing.

It clawed at his hands and wrists, tearing painful, bleeding furrows in his skin, but he held on tightly, carrying the thing toward the hearth.

Toward the fire.

The creature wailed.

"Love! Love! Love meeeeeeeeeeeeeeeeeeeeeeeeeeeeeeeee!"

Its cries were painful, like knives to the brain, and Flynn winced, resisting the urge to drop the furry terror and clap his hands over his ears.

He reached the fireplace and kicked away the metal screen before it. "This is how much I love you," he grunted as he tossed the thing onto the burning logs.

It wailed as its fur began to smolder and catch.

Flynn watched as the toy burned, kicking up embers in its furious panic. After a moment, he reached down to pick up and replace the screen in front of the hearth, but the toy was faster, and surprisingly stronger. It hit the screen at full force, knocking Flynn back.

"Love me!" it wailed as it tried to scale the screen, to crawl upon Flynn, to burn him as it burned.

Flynn dropped the screen and grabbed a metal poker from the stand beside the fireplace. He swung it hard, swatting the flaming toy across the room, where it hit the wall and fell to the floor.

"Love me!" it demanded as, unbelievingly, it began to crawl back toward him, its smoldering fur setting tiny fires wherever it touched.

"No!" Flynn screamed, not wanting to hear its horrible voice any longer. Fire alarms began to ring as he strode toward it, lifted the poker, and skewered it.

"Love me! Love me! Love me!" the creature cried over and over again as it struggled on the tip of the poker.

Before it could free itself, Flynn returned to the hearth, tossed the burning stuffed animal back into the fire, and quickly sealed it in with the metal screen. It wasn't long before it was nothing more than black ash and a fading scream, pulled up the flue, dispersed into the cold winter's night.

Flynn continued to stand there, trembling, half expecting to hear the cries of *Love me* coming from the fire. But it seemed to be gone, and after a while, he was able to step away, although he did keep an eye on the smoldering fire just to be sure.

The fires set by the creature's burning body were beginning to spread. It was only a matter of time before the whole place went up. For a moment, Flynn considered trying to snuff out the flames, but remembered Betty's body on the floor. *Better that it all burn,* he thought, making his way toward the door.

And then he stopped. To have gone through what he had, and not have anything to show for it just wasn't right, but he'd have to be quick.

His eyes fell on a large pillow on the sofa, and he reached for it, tearing away its cover to use as a sack. He walked quickly about the room, randomly tossing things into the pillowcase. The binder of coins, some tin toys, and then he found himself in front of the curio cabinet, the baby dolls gazing blankly at him through the dusty glass. His daughter would adore them. He opened the case and gently placed the delicate toys inside his sack.

Flynn was ready to go. The fires were growing quickly, and he was beginning to choke on the wafting smoke. It wouldn't be long before someone on the street would notice. He headed for the hallway but stopped to look down on Betty's body. The lenses of her glasses were spattered with blood, but he could see that her eyes were open, staring at him.

He couldn't be angry with her. Desperation made people do terrible things.

As he turned to leave, he kicked something with his foot and looked to the floor. Betty's pistol—he hated the things, but every buck would help with his new life, and he was sure that Dougie could find a buyer with little effort.

Flynn picked the gun up, slung the pillowcase over his shoulder like Santa Claus, and quickly made his way down the stairs and out into the cold, cold night.

He was two blocks from the building before he heard the sirens.

Like ghosts wailing in the night.

Flynn didn't know how long he'd wandered the freezing cold, early-morning streets, lost in an odd kind of feverish funk. His eyes darted to the shadows around buildings and homes, any patches of darkness that could have hidden something black and starving for affection.

Love me.

He heard the thing inside his head as if it were still clinging to him. The punctures and scratches on his body burned, so much so that he considered the idea of a hospital visit but then thought better of it.

Shivering in the early-morning cold, Flynn hefted the stuffed pillowcase from one shoulder to the other. His injuries were throbbing with the beat of his heart, and he felt incredibly warm yet so very cold.

He knew that he was sick and began to wonder, to hope that what he had seen on Stewart Street had been nothing more than a fucked-up fever dream. But the sack stuffed with treasures on his back told him otherwise.

As he shambled slowly down the street, he realized that he was nearing the darkened tenement where his ex-wife and daughter lived. He approached the building and stumbled up the stairs to push the buzzer. His entire body was trembling now, wracked with feverish chills. He pushed the buzzer again, leaving his finger there until—

"Who the fuck is this?" Cindy's voice blared from the speaker.

Always the sweetheart, he thought, leaning heavily against the wall.

"It's me," he said, barely able to keep his eyes open.

"Flynn?" he heard her ask. "What the fuck? You've got a lot of nerve coming here at this hour and—"

"I'm good," he told her, preparing his story—readying the lie.

"What do you mean you're good?"

"Did what you asked. Can I come up?"

"You got a job?"

He didn't confirm or deny, doing everything in his power to stay on his feet.

"Can I . . . ," he started to say when the door buzzed loudly.

He pushed the door open into the lobby and stopped before the stairs that would take him up to Cindy's apartment, not sure he could make it. Flynn leaned against the wall and looked up.

Betty was standing there, completely naked, the black furred stuffed animal suckling on her ancient breast.

"I'm so sorry, Flynn," she said to him. "So, so very sorry."

And then it all went to black.

Flynn awoke with a start.

It took a moment for it to sink in, for the synapses in his brain to fire enough for him to put it all together and remember where he was.

He was lying on the couch, heavy blanket draped over him, staring into the multicolored lights of a fake Christmas tree stuck in the corner of the small living room space. His pants were gone, and his shirt had been removed.

"You were bleeding," Cindy said, coming out of the kitchen with two mugs of steaming coffee in her hands. She was wearing a heavy blue terry-cloth bathrobe.

Flynn winced as he slowly sat up. "Yeah, fell down the stairs at the place I'm working," he said, making it up as he took the offered mug of coffee.

"And where's that?" she asked, wedging herself into the space next to him. She reached out a cool hand and placed it on his brow. "You were burning up when you got here. Could barely get you up the stairs."

He remembered seeing Betty and the thing at the top of the staircase and shivered. "Yeah, must've picked something up at work."

"Yeah, where is that?" Cindy asked, eyeing him with suspicion over the rim of her mug.

"Warehouse off of Sixteenth," he said. "Car parts and shit."

He looked at her, hoping that she didn't see through his lie. As long as he made it through the day, he would fix it later.

"You really did it," she said, seeking confirmation.

"I really did," he said. The words tasted bitter. He didn't like lying to her, but he didn't have a choice.

"I didn't think you'd pull it off," she said. "I'm proud of you."

"Yeah," he said, forcing a smile. "You're going to be saying that a lot now."

"Oh yeah?" she said, and smiled at him the way she used to look at him a very long time ago, before Meghan was born.

Meghan.

He felt suddenly foolish, the entire reason that he'd done what he'd done the previous night having slipped his mind.

"Where is my little girl?" he asked, looking around the room.

"She's in her bedroom, playing," Cindy said.

He looked for his pants and found them slung over the arm of the couch. "I want to go say hi," he said, putting one leg into his pants, and then the other. His cuts and scratches stung like hell, a reminder of what he had been through, and the reason he needed to see his daughter.

"Sure," Cindy said. "She was all excited to see you this morning."

Flynn walked barefoot toward his daughter's room.

"Yep, all excited to see her daddy—until she found that bag full of toys."

Bag full of toys.

Flynn stopped and turned to smile, remembering the collectible dolls that he'd taken for her.

Then he remembered the gun.

"She's got the bag?"

"Yeah, why?" Cindy said. "It was full of toys. Those were for her, right?"

Flynn ran from the room, bounding down the hallway.

"Meghan?" he cried out, trying not to sound upset. He didn't want to scare her, to startle her if . . .

"Daddy?" he heard his daughter's tiny voice call out as he entered her room, almost tripping over the pillowcase lying crumpled upon the floor. He could see the gun's barrel sticking out through the opening and breathed a sigh of relief.

"Hey, baby," he said, squatting down to pick up the pillowcase, shoving the gun down inside.

She was sitting with her back to him over in the corner, in one of her tiny play chairs in front of a plastic kitchen play set.

"Whatcha doin', sweetie pie?" he asked her, breathing a sigh of relief.

"Playin' with my baby," the little girl said. "This baby needs lots and lots of love."

She started to turn in her chair, and that was when he saw it, covered in black fur and clutched tightly to his daughter's chest.

"Love me," the thing said, turning its hateful gaze to him.

"Oh God . . . Meg," Flynn cried, stumbling toward his little girl.

"Love me," it said again, in that most terrible of voices.

As it turned its face to his baby girl's chest.

And began to feed.

NOT JUST FOR CHRISTMAS

SARAH LOTZ

Jake was early. He sat in the car for a few minutes, semi-hypnotized by the Christmas lights twinkling through the windows. They gave the house a homey, welcoming glow, which made him feel lonelier and more like an outsider than usual. Amira had gone all out with the decorations this year. An ostentatious wreath hung on the door, and he could make out the gaudy limbs of a giant Christmas tree in the lounge. Someone must have helped her haul that inside—someone who wasn't him. Never mind. She'd come around. By this time next year at the very latest, he promised himself, he'd be back where he belonged.

He opened the boot and took out the aerated box containing his secret weapon—the weapon he hoped would help rectify his mistakes. It wasn't heavy, and the contents shifted inside it as he shoved it under an arm to ring the bell. Amira had changed the locks when she kicked him out, and he had to wait in the cold for her to open up. Her face carefully blank, she stepped out of his reach when he lunged in for a kiss. "Come through," she said to him as if he were a stranger. The twins were in the den, lost in whatever VR game was flavor of the month, and barely murmured "hi, Dad" when he greeted them. The house smelled of spice and slow-roasted meat. He knew she had her parents coming for Christmas dinner tomorrow. He wasn't invited. He was lucky to be here now.

She glanced at the box. "What's in there, Jake?"

"Surprise for you and the kids."

"Do we really need any more surprises from you this year?"

Don't take the bait. "Let's go into the kitchen and I'll show it to you first. You're going to love it."

He placed the box on the butcher block and lifted the lid. The bundle of fur inside it uncurled, shook itself, and stared up at them with bright button eyes.

Amira was speechless for a second, then: "A puppy? What the hell, Jake? I can't believe you—"

He cut her off before her indignation reached boiling point: "It's not just any old puppy, Mira. It's a Gen."

"A Gen? You got the kids a *Genpet*? How did you . . . They cost a fortune!"

"I sold my mountain bike to pay for it." Not entirely true. He'd downgraded his state-of-the-art mountain bike to a cheaper model, but she didn't need to know that. Not until he was safely back in the house, feet under the table. But it *had* cost a fortune, as had the special food it needed, which ensured it only excreted odorless pellets. No pooper-scooper needed—the genetic engineers had thought of everything. The puppy yipped. He picked it out of its box and placed it on the kitchen floor. With its round button eyes and large, out-of-proportion paws, even he had to admit it was ridiculously cute (and he loathed dogs). It sniffed at his shoes, cocked its head, and let out a soft woof. It resembled the Labrador puppies that toilet paper manufacturers used to put on their packaging.

Amira's eyes softened. But she wasn't that easy to win over. "I thought Gens were banned," she said. "Wasn't there a court case—"

"PETA lost the case. Gens are totally legit now."

"We don't have the space for an animal, Jake."

"It's a *Gen,* Mira. It'll never grow up. It's engineered to stay this small and cute forever." Well, not strictly forever, although Genpets were tweaked to last almost thirty years ("with a Genpet, your child won't experience the heartbreak of death!" went the advertising slogan).

"Hmmm." The puppy yawned, showing off a pink tongue and white baby teeth. She smiled. "Aw. It *is* adorable."

"And it'll get the kids away from their screens, teach them some responsibility."

Amira gave him a sideways look. "Yeah, because it's the kids who need to learn *that.*"

He bit his tongue. "So what do you say? Shall we give it to the kids?"

She glanced down at the puppy, then smiled again. "Okay." As she bent to pick it up, the dog froze, mid-woof, as if it were having some sort of petit mal seizure. "There's something wrong with it, Jake."

"It's just updating. They implant something into their nervous systems to help control their behavior." He dug out his phone and clicked onto the Genpet home page. "Look, you can download apps for it. You can get updates, teach it to do tricks, that kind of thing. Takes all the work out of having a pet."

"But I thought the point was to teach the kids some responsibility?"

The twins appeared at that moment, saving him from answering. They let out identical screams of glee when they saw the puppy.

"No way!" Caitlin threw herself on the dog. It didn't snap at her or try to run away. "You're the best, Dad!"

Jake even received a hug from Carl. He'd missed the twins. He could have fought for shared custody, but he'd learned from bitter experience that his studio apartment wasn't suitable for kids (another selfish decision, according to Amira). No, he would wait. Amira would forgive him eventually.

"What are you going to call it?" he asked them.

"He looks just like a teddy bear," Caitlin said.

It did. "Then let's call him Teddy," Amira said.

"Teddy!" the kids yelled in unison.

Amira allowed Carl and Caitlin to stay up late playing with Teddy. Jake downloaded a "sit and roll over" app, and the twins watched the Gen practicing its tricks until all three of them were exhausted. As both wanted to sleep with Teddy, they sprawled across the bed Jake used to share with Amira, the puppy squeezed between them. Amira took a pic and shoved it up on her Instagram and Twitter feeds. Within minutes, it had thousands of views. Most of the comments were along the lines of <CUTE!!!> and <A Gen!! I'm sooooooooooooo jealous!!!> but there were a few snarky messages: <Gen Pets are CRUEL & UNNATURAL>; <u know these gen pets are made just so that they can infiltrate yr homes and then steal data that is sold so that companies know what advertising to target to u>; <messing with nature is just wrong. And what about traditional pets? What happens when they die out?>

"Just ignore them," Jake said to her. "They're just jealous."

It had all gone so well, he dared to hope that Amira would offer him a glass of wine. She didn't, but she gave him a warm hug when she saw him out.

He drove home through the quiet streets feeling more at ease than he had since Amira caught him with the intern. Would Teddy make up for his mistakes? He honestly did regret the years of self-ishness, leaving her alone with the twins every weekend so that he could go mountain biking with his mates (and the other extra-curricular activities that he didn't really want to dwell on). He thought the dog just might help bridge the gap. *Genpets, bringing families together.*

He used Teddy as an excuse to return two days later. The kids were out in the front yard playing with the puppy. It was the first time he'd seen them unglued from their screens since they were toddlers.

This time, Amira let him kiss her on the cheek when she let him in. "They're *loving* Teddy, Jake. They're walking him every day and feeding him and cleaning up after him. It's so good to see them outside for once."

"They're going to love what I've brought them even more. I've got a surprise for you all."

"Another one?" No sarcasm this time. They shared a smile. *You're almost there,* he told himself.

He called the kids inside and downloaded the app he'd pur-chased into Teddy's home page. It had cost almost as much as the Genpet itself, but that's what an overdraft was for.

Teddy froze while he updated and then said, "Hello! I'm AddNameHere. Can we go for a walk?"

Amira gasped, and the kids squealed. "OMG, Dad! Teddy can *talk?*"

"Yup. It's a new add-on they've just developed."

The dog's words didn't quite match its mouth movements, so watching it speak was disconcerting, like cheap CGI, but that didn't matter. And sure, the voice was childlike and accent-less, and more saccharine than he'd like, but judging from Amira's stunned reaction, that didn't matter, either. He added its name to the home page, and Teddy paused momentarily while this new information trickled through to the software embedded in his cortex.

"Hello, Caitlin and Carl Tillman-Khan and Amira Khan and Jake Tillman. Thank you very much for making me part of your family. I love you!"

Amira blinked. "How does he know our names?"

"He's Wi-Fi enabled. I've linked him to our devices."

"So awesome, Dad!" Carl hugged his legs.

Teddy rolled onto his back, exposing his belly. "Teddy needs to poop! Teddy wants to go walky!"

They all laughed.

That night he didn't go back to his apartment.

Amira wanted to take things slow, which was fair enough. All that mattered was that the cold war between them was over. Every weekend Jake was invited to join Caitlin, Carl, and Amira on their outings with Teddy: picnics, walks around the park, and hikes through the woods. He couldn't help but feel smug. This new screen-free family togetherness was all down to him. His only concerns were that Teddy's conversation skills were sorely limited and dull (they mostly involved pronouncements about walks and food), and as Genpets were becoming more and more ubiquitous, he was worried the puppy would lose his edge. Everywhere he went he spotted Genpets in handbags, Genpets in the backs of cars, Genpups for the sight and hearing impaired, Genbunnies gamboling in front yards. The world was awash with kittens that wouldn't stray and puppies that wouldn't chew furniture and shit everywhere. He'd heard that PETA had successfully blocked horses and exotic pets from being Gennified for now, but it was only a matter of time before there were talking tarantulas and ponies. It was amazing how quickly a talking dog could become the norm.

On Valentine's Day he rocked up to the house clutching twenty red roses. Amira took them from him distractedly. "We've got a problem, Jake."

"What kind of problem?" He swallowed nervously.

She called Teddy's name, and the puppy came bounding up to her. "Listen," she said to Jake.

"Hello, Amira Khan," Teddy said. "Are you still considering size six Louboutin shoes snakeskin? Hello, Amira Khan, you won't *believe* what David Hasselhoff looks like now!"

"What the *hell*?"

"Teddy's spamming us. Someone must have hacked him. He's been trying to sell the kids *Minecraft* updates all day."

Teddy snuffled at Jake's shoes. "Hello, Jake Tillman! Are you still considering Ibis Ripley 29 LS Mountain Bike with a Boost 148 option?"

"See?" Amira said. "He's got access to our browsing history, remember."

Jake had reason to feel uneasy, but it was too late to do anything about it, for a second later Teddy trilled: "Don't forget to renew your DeviantTeenPorn premium subscription, Jake Tillman. Underage Scandi Babes just for you!"

Amira's face shut down. He tried to convince her that he wasn't actually signed up to a dodgy porn site (he was) and had only clicked on it out of boredom, but she refused to listen.

"Get the dog fixed, Jake. Take it to the vet. And do it before the kids get back from soccer."

Cursing the dog, and himself, he did as she asked. He wasn't the only one who was having issues. The vet's waiting room was packed with punters and their malfunctioning Genpets: a kitten that mewled the soundtrack to an upcoming HBO series over and over again; a golden retriever pup that jabbered on about "half-price sheds at bargain prices," and a bunny that squeaked about the top-five celebrities who'd had botched plastic surgery.

He kept Teddy sealed safely in its box. Christ knew what else it might dig up from his history. The Genpets' owners all avoided one another's eyes, and Jake's attention drifted to the posters on the wall. One blared: "Genpets: THE DOWNSIDE. What you need to know." Another poster entreated people not to dump their old faithful traditional pets in favor of Gens. It showed a forlorn golden retriever cowering by the side of the road, fur matted and ribs visible.

He was called in to the examination room. The vet resembled Gillian Anderson, and he squirmed as he opened the box, steeling himself for whatever embarrassing nugget Teddy might reveal. Teddy didn't disappoint: he cocked his head and said, "Jake Tillman, are you still considering hot Asian girl will do anal?"

"Oh dear," the vet said, not bothering to hide a smirk. "He was hacked, was he? We're seeing a lot of these." She looked at Jake shrewdly. "You have insurance?"

"Is it going to cost a lot?"

"Oh yeah. When Gens go bad, they cost a fortune to fix." He realized she was enjoying this. She was probably one of those anti-Gen campaigners.

While Teddy babbled about cut-price Danish furniture on eBay and Nissan 350Zs for sale on Autotrader (the vet's browsing history was clearly less compromising than Jake's), she checked Teddy's vital signs and placed the dog inside a machine that resembled a pet-size CAT scan. "These days I feel more like an IT guy than a vet," she murmured, adjusting its settings. The machine whirred and clicked, and then she said, "All done. He's back to normal."

"Will it happen again?"

The vet yawned. "Dunno."

"You think I could get my money back from the company I bought it from?"

She laughed. "Good luck with that. You might want to purchase a stronger firewall, though."

When he left, his bank account was firmly in the red.

Back in the car, Teddy rolled around on the back seat "Teddy want a walk. Teddy want a walky, Jake Tillman."

"Okay, okay."

He stopped at the park and stormed around the playing fields, the wet grass soaking his shoes. Teddy's little legs had to work overtime to keep up with him. He crossed paths with another couple of Genpet walkers. Neither the pets nor the people looked like they were enjoying the experience. What was the point? Gens were cute but annoyingly predictable. A dark thought came drifting in. He could chuck Teddy out of the car en route back to the house. Tell the kids he ran away. No. Genpets couldn't run away. They were genetically engineered not to stray. Anyway, it would be a waste: Teddy was fixed now. It would all be fine.

The year wore on. Porn-gate had been a major setback, and Jake was back to square one as far as relations with Amira were concerned. Plus, his plan had backfired. The kids were now bored of the talking dog. Teddy had become a background ornament to them, like a chair, or their parents. Sometimes he didn't see the kids for weeks at a time—Amira always had an excuse.

He found himself googling adventure holidays, as well as other, darker things. Depressed, he put on weight. He spent his days at work and nights slumped on the couch stuffing his face with junk food. His mountain bike sat gathering dust in his locker.

Amira's call came on one of his rare days off. "Come and get it, Jake. Come and get it now."

"Come and get what?"

"The dog. The bloody dog, arsehole."

She hung up.

The car wouldn't start on the first try. It needed a new starter motor, but he was still paying off Teddy's vet bills. And he'd missed the boat as far as pet insurance went. There were rumors that the Genpet corp was heading for bankruptcy; there were only so many class actions it could field.

Amira was waiting for him in the doorway when he climbed out of the car, Teddy in her arms. The dog looked as innocent as always.

"What's the problem?"

He'd barely finished speaking when Teddy blurted, in his cutesy kid's voice: "Teddy wants a walky, Amira Khan. Teddy wants a walky *now,* you motherfucking piece of shit."

Jake barked a laugh. He couldn't help it.

"It's not funny, Jake. It's been hacked again. They think it's PETA this time."

Teddy stared straight at Jake, raised an ear, and said, "Your mother sucks cocks in hell, Jake Tillman."

"Jesus."

Amira bundled the dog into his arms. "That's nothing. You should hear what it's been saying to the kids. I want it out of here *now.*"

"But . . . I can't afford to get it fixed again."

"Not my problem."

She slammed the door in his face.

Christmas came around again. Amira had decided to take the kids to her parents, so he was alone. Alone except for his foul-mouthed, four-legged companion. Teddy's verbal diarrhea was no longer even vaguely amusing. Still, it could be worse. There were reports of far more insidious hacks—Gens turning on their owners, nipping at them, trying to smother small children, or having explosive digestive problems. But he needed to get rid of it. The last woman he'd "invited" over had left after twenty minutes, tiring of Teddy's nonstop abuse. He'd put Teddy on eBay, but there were more than a million Genpet ads on the site—pages and pages of cute baby animals that would never grow up and no one wanted—and some of the owners were even offering to pay people to take their Gens. A pet shelter was out of the question. They were overflowing with the traditional pets people had dumped when they'd upgraded their "household pet experience." Jake slumped on the couch and cracked a can of lager. Next to him Teddy wagged his tail and chirped, "Want food, cunt-face. Want food *now*."

Did he have it in him to stave in its head with a brick? No. Teddy might talk like a pissed-up sailor, but it still resembled a puppy. He couldn't do it.

There was only one option. It was time to set himself—and Teddy—free. "Teddy want a walky?"

The dog jumped onto his lap and danced in a circle. "Yes, yes, yes, yes, you cum-sucking whoremaster! Teddy wants a motherfucking *walk*!"

Jake put Teddy on the front seat of the car, then ran back up to his apartment to retrieve his mountain bike and bike rack. It was sleeting when he pulled out onto the motorway, the sky a moody gray. The temperature had dropped.

After two hours of navigating slippery main roads, Jake took the old familiar exit and weaved down country byways riddled with potholes. Next to him, Teddy was silent and still. It was updating again. At least the dog was quiet.

As Jake drove up the rutted track that led to the forestry area, a sleek 4x4 barreled toward him, forcing him to swerve into the tree line. The driver waved apologetically. He looked as guilty as Jake felt. Jake checked the time. Three p.m. An hour or so before it got dark. The woodland's parking lot had an aura of neglect, and there was a wisp of what looked like police tape tied to a tree, as well as a couple of signs warning hikers and mountain bikers to keep to the trails. Odd. It had been months since he'd been here. He used to spend hours exploring the trails on his mountain bike— the one he'd downgraded to pay for the Genpet. He hoped it was far enough from home to confuse Teddy's tracking system.

He put Teddy in his backpack ("it's fucking dark in here, Jake Tillman!"), strapped it onto his back, and got moving. Within minutes his thighs were burning. He ducked off the path and headed deeper into the woods, crisscrossing an old logging road. His spirits lifted as the endorphins kicked in, only to dip again as a splash of red in the sleet-covered ground caught his eye. A frozen deer carcass, ribs protruding, lay curled at the base of a tree. He shuddered as he whipped by it—foxes must have eviscerated it.

He went on a bit farther, but the shadows were growing, the pine trees around him sucking up the remaining daylight. Here would have to do. He stopped, propped the bike against a tree, and tipped Teddy out of the bag.

Teddy swore, woofed, and trotted to the nearest stump to sniff around it.

"Bye, Ted," Jake whispered. He jumped on his bike and pedaled away. He peered behind him. Teddy was running after him, its little legs going like pistons. "Jake Tillman! Fucking wait!"

Shit. He pedaled faster.

He didn't see the tree root. There was a *thunk* as the front wheel caught it at an awkward angle, the handlebars skewed out of his hands, and then came a kaleidoscope of images: trees, his knees, the ground, and then, nothing.

When he came to, it was fully dark. He sat up carefully and vomited. Gingerly, he touched his limbs. His face was wet, and he could taste blood. Phone, he needed his phone. There was no pain. He had the cold to thank for that.

He sensed, rather than saw, movement around him. He blinked frantically, and gradually his eyes adjusted to the gloom. The shadows around him shifted, and he smelled something—a fetid feral odor—over the low hum of the pine. The shadows shifted again. Something was moving toward him. Several somethings. And now he could hear a low grumbling sound. A primeval fear woke in his gut. He dug in his jacket pocket again for his phone, finding it this time. He jabbed at it, the screen lit up, and he waved it in front of him, catching the gleam of several pairs of eyes. And then he knew. The things approaching him weren't foxes or badgers. They weren't Genpets. These were the fully grown dogs that had been dumped after Gens came on the market. The feral dogs like the one he'd seen on the poster in the vet's waiting room. Adrenaline surged, but his body didn't seem to want to work properly. This was bad. This was very, very bad. An old slogan from his youth came wafting into his head: "A dog is for life, not just for Christmas."

They were closing in. "Nice doggy," he said lamely. The phone slipped out of his hand.

Then: "Hey! Cunt-Face! Where the fuck you been? Tired, Jake Tillman. Teddy's *fucking knackered.*"

A flicker of hope flared. "Teddy! Go get help!"

But Teddy wasn't engineered for reconnaissance or protection, and Jake didn't stand a chance. As the first one came for him, he thought he heard a sound he'd never heard from a Genpet before. Teddy was laughing.

TENETS

JOSH MALERMAN

Christine and David argued as they pulled into the Chamberses' drive and Christine said that all couples argue on the holidays so could they please just end it and get over it and put a smile on as they entered the party? David said yes, of course, we will, we always do, but it's a damn strange thing to suddenly get over, a damn strange thing, indeed. Then the argument started all over again, right there in the circle drive, with Christine saying they don't know one thing about this Michael guy who Adam had invited and could they, Christine and David, please either give the guy a chance or ignore him entirely? The last thing she wanted to be thinking about at a holiday party reunion was cults and cult leaders and what all that means and how sad it was if you really broke it down. But David continued to break it down. A cult means lies, he kept saying, and lies mean brainwashing and so Adam had invited a kind of monster to the Chamberses' holiday party and what in the world was Adam thinking? What kind of mood would this set? Christine took the opportunity to touch up her face and hair. She lowered the passenger side visor and made small adjustments to her eyes as David went on about this Michael and how he wasn't just once the leader of a cult, he was a "failed cult leader." Christine bristled at the words (even though she'd heard them a dozen times on the drive), and in the mirror she saw her eyes as the kind of eyes that could be fooled into believing something impossible. She had to turn away from her reflection. And while the moment *had* chilled her, she really just wanted David to stop talking about it. To stop worrying about the "vibe" this mystery Michael was "guaranteed" to project.

But of course David went on.

What kind of cult was it? How *big* was it? Had anybody . . . died?

And the whole thing about Anne and Hank Chambers not knowing that Adam was bringing him, that was too much to think about right now, too. Why hadn't Adam told them? David didn't know. Hadn't asked. Christine *almost* said, *Well, what's the difference? All religions are cults anyway.* But it felt wrong to say something like that at this time of year. Like she'd be tying their arms behind their backs before sending them into a party of old friends, university alums, a bright and energetic set that was difficult enough to keep up with on an average night. No need to make things more difficult.

In the end it didn't matter what Christine did or didn't say about religion. David said it anyway. He said: On one level I guess it's not that big a deal, but I worry that I've talked myself into that. Then Christine said: Well, you're certainly talking. She closed the visor and turned to face him, David, her college sweetheart, her Merrick University beau, who had gained some weight and gone a bit gray at the temples but was still cute as Patrick Dempsey to her.

Ready? she asked, tightening her scarf.

Beyond the car window, snow fell. A snow so white it warmed Christine's heart and told her, yes, yes, despite the crazy idea of

Adam inviting a . . . a criminal? . . . to the holiday party, it was winter, pomp and glory, time for drinks with old friends.

And wasn't it just like the old Merrick set to somehow involve a philosophical dilemma at a seasonal soiree?

David turned the car off, got out, and went and opened Christine's door for her.

They walked the stone path to the Chamberses' front porch, holding hands, their black coats collecting the soothing, uncluttered flakes.

Anne and Hank Chambers were very good at hosting. Especially with the set they'd invited this evening. Ten years ago the sprouting, opinionated lovers were the mutual hub of the intellectual wheel at Merrick University, and neither had been willing to relinquish that power in the decade following. One way of maintaining was to host. But never to over-host. It was a challenge they both enjoyed, one of the many things they had in common.

As Anne uncorked white wine in the kitchen, Hank came through the swivel door to tell her that someone was ringing the bell. Must be Jane and John, Anne said, silently acknowledging how aware she was of her guests and their behavioral patterns. The invites said the party started at seven o'clock, but of course nobody was there quite at seven. Kevin Bloom showed shortly after, as expected, usually, if not always, the first to arrive. After Kevin came the Younts, Darla and Berry, as flatly conservative as ever in their gray pantsuit and mauve turtleneck, respectively. Anne was certainly keen enough to note that, at these reunions, most of the old gang wore clothes they might have back at Merrick, as if proving to the rest that they hadn't quite lost their university charm. Not old yet, Hank called it. NOY. But some *had* lost a particle of that magic dust. Christine and David, for example. Always bickering and then adoring, bickering and adoring. Sustaining that level of energy would be enough to add paunch and wrinkles to just about anybody. But the fact that they were consistently an hour later than party invitations stated told Anne that they were more regulated than even they knew. And here they were already in the living room, eight sharp, a mix of concern and eagerness in their eyes.

Perhaps they were keeping a secret? Anne didn't mind if they were. Everybody had secrets, but the way David avoided Anne's eyes suggested the secret had something to do with her.

Jane and John, Hank said, sticking his head into the kitchen. He smiled and Anne winked and then she followed him out of the kitchen and into the foyer to greet the two. By the time the hosts reached the new arrivals their hands were extended and the handshakes became hugs. Pop music from ten years gone came from the living room record player and Anne winced a bit inside, preferring modern music always to that of the past. We've got to move on, she often told Hank, whether we want to or not. But she kept her mouth shut. Best to host, never to over-host, and besides, there was hardly ever an element to a party of her own that Anne Chambers wasn't easily able to predict.

Did you hear about this Michael guy? John asked Kerry by the speakers in the living room. This guy Adam invited? I did, Kerry said, running a hand through his thinning fair hair. The look on his face told John enough; Kerry had indeed heard about the cult stuff. What do you know? John asked. Well, Kerry said, I heard he ran a . . . group . . . out in Michigan's thumb . . . he was in charge . . . a number of young girls. Young girls? John asked, incredulous. Someone's gotta warn Hank and Anne, right? But Kerry only shrugged. I don't know. A side of me rather likes it, he said. Then he winked and John had a glimpse of the long-ago Kerry, the university prankster, the young man who snuck into the classrooms the night before and wrote things like *DON'T TRUST MISTER OLIN'S OPINION ON MAILER* on the black-board. What I wanna know, Kerry said, is why Adam felt the need to invite someone outside of the old gang? John held up a finger like he always did when he was about to make a point. Jane didn't go to school with us, either, he said. Kerry understood. The old gang was always bringing new boyfriends and girlfriends to these reunions. This was common stuff. Kerry said: Remember that one fella Marcia brought? The one who brought his own bottle of Early Times whis-key and drank the entire thing and didn't seem drunk at all? John said yeah, he remembered that guy. Then Kerry said: But this *is* different, of course. The guy presumably has a pretty big past. John nodded and Kerry could tell John was holding back a little more information, a nugget, something Kerry didn't know.

What is it? Kerry asked. What do you know?

John looked over his shoulder, saw Jane coming from across the room, then whispered to Kerry: Adam said the guy could really use a *friend* right now.

A friend? Kerry laughed. Shouldn't he know how to make those ... whether they want to be his friend or not?

When Jane caught up to them she asked what they were gig-gling about and John said, aw nothing. Old times.

That's the doorbell again, Anne said to Hank. And though he couldn't hear her over the lively chatter in the living room (the party was proving to be energized; ever a validation, ever a relief to the hosts), it was clear what she was saying. So Hank excused himself from a good conversation with David and made his way through the dozen or so friends, who all seemed to have needed this very thing, this night out, this holiday party at the Chamberses'. Marcus and Wendy certainly needed it (their little boy was asleep at home), and yet they were a little piqued (first time hiring a sitter, first time out without the little one). Hank smiled at them as he passed, then had to duck some tinsel hanging from the ceiling (but not *too* much decoration; never over-host). He stepped around the "holiday tree," which did its best to represent all the holidays without being tacky about it. Marcy Ryan and Ryan Mills were cheers-ing in the foyer and Hank made a mental note that the two singles made an interesting-looking pair. Who'd have thought it? But oh how things changed over the years, oh how things looked different.

At the door, Hank switched his whiskey from his right hand to his left and turned the knob. He saw Adam and another guy, a guy Hank didn't know, standing on the welcome mat, both with their shoulders covered in thick white snow. The stranger had a deep, distant stare, an observation Hank didn't feel particularly proud to have made, as the man's depression would have been obvious to a toddler.

Adam, Hank said, reaching out and pulling his old friend into the house. Despite Adam being the most liberal of the liberal gang, often proposing juvenile theories, Hank had long had a soft spot for him.

And who is this? Hank asked, extending a hand to the stranger. But the stranger only half nodded and looked at Hank's hand as if it were made of something he wasn't allowed to touch. *DAMAGED* was the word Hank silently used to describe the stranger because there could be no doubt that the slumped posture, the short but unkempt hair, and the obvious unease spoke of depressed depths and probable regrets that Hank had only read about in nonfiction essays.

This is Michael, Adam said. A friend of mine. He was alone tonight, so I said, come on, are you kidding, you're coming with me, you'll love the old gang.

Hank closely watched Michael's reaction to Adam's brief introduction. He noted that Michael seemed to endure it.

Adam's right, Hank said. Come on in. We won't bite. And while we're intellectuals with strong opinions, he parodied, fear not, we're easily persuaded.

Anne spotted the stranger straightaway, caught his name from Kerry, and made a point of introducing herself. It was unexpected, to be sure, Adam hadn't told her he was bringing a guest. She didn't mind at all. Maybe it was a date? You never knew exactly where Adam stood philosophically, politically, even sexually, which was partially the reason she and everybody else enjoyed him as much as they did.

You're Michael? Anne said, extending a hand. You look thirsty.

Michael avoided eye contact and sheepishly shook his head no. No thank you. Anne had a sudden vision of a puppy. Or, perhaps it was a dog, yes, full grown. An animal who felt tremendous guilt for what it had done.

How do you know Adam? Anne asked, but Adam answered for him.

Michael and I met at a prisoner rehabilitation meeting in the Ontario Room at the Hyatt on Third.

Ah, Anne said, so you fancy yourself a reformer like our dear Adam does?

Michael looked particularly distraught by this comment and Anne had no choice but to look to Adam questioningly. Sometimes a host had no choice. Adam smiled but Anne detected some of the other Adam in there; the run-down, possibly binged-out, exhausted Adam whose eyes didn't quite sparkle the way they had at Merrick U.

Well, make yourself at home, Anne said. And be sure to get me if you find you're thirsty after all.

Then Anne walked away, but not before noting his white button-down shirt tucked into his blue jeans. His black shoes. His slouch. The word *sad* came to mind and Anne supposed maybe the man was just that.

Michael took a seat on the couch. For Anne the image was interesting, if not striking: the lone stranger sitting solo as the old gang talked and moved in quick rapid gestures around him.

The music continued to provide energy. The familiar conversations lifted and lowered, lifted and lowered. And, walking through it all, Anne noted how Christine was watching Michael. Then she realized that almost everybody was unduly focused on the stranger. Why? What did they know that she didn't? Clearly the man was damaged in some fundamental way. He hadn't been able to look Anne in the eye. Didn't shake hands or want a drink.

Need anything? Hank asked her, heading toward the kitchen. Yes, Anne said, following him. I need to know why everybody is looking at us like we're the only ones not in on a secret.

Hank looked at her questioningly. Then, as Anne passed him and entered the kitchen first, Hank looked to the troubled new-comer Adam had brought and saw he was sitting on the edge of the couch, rocking subtly back and forth, his eyes on the hardwood floor. Michelle, who was always looking for party romance, made to talk to him and Michael looked up at her and the Christmas lights above the mantel hit his eyes in just such a way that Hank saw they were wet. Not crying. But wet.

Hank followed Anne into the kitchen and saw her talking to Kerry by the sink.

What do you know? she was saying. And Kerry kept saying he

didn't know anything, until Anne said you're lying and you're not doing a good job of it. Then all of Anne's smiling and reasonable veneer took a hit as Kerry told her that he'd heard the guy Adam brought had once led a cult in the thumb area of Michigan. That the cult had grown large enough to concern the State of Michigan and that the guy, Michael, had "done some time" for it.

Anne looked to Hank and saw her own astonishment in his eyes.

Done some time? Anne asked Kerry. Hank placed a hand on her shoulder and Anne gently removed it. Yeah, Kerry said, sipping his fourth gin and cranberry juice. He was in jail for four years. That's just what I heard.

Who told you that? Hank asked. Then Kerry said Roger told him and that Adam had told Roger and oh you know how information travels through the old gang. Hank smiled and fanned a hand to suggest he wasn't going to let this ruin his night. But then he actually thought about what it meant, what a cult leader must do, the impetus to coerce people, to get them to do things for you, the lies and false ideology that must have been tossed around like truth.

Hank looked at Anne and saw she was looking to the kitchen door. Adam was standing there, smiling his easy-free smile, saying, What? What's up, Anne? Why are you looking at me like that?

You brought a fucking *cult leader* into our house?

Anne had decided this wasn't over-hosting.

Kerry sipped his drink.

Oh come on, Anne, Adam said. You're better than that.

Excuse me?

We don't judge people. We never have.

What exactly did this guy do, Adam? For Christ's sake he looks shell-shocked.

He is. He has no friends. His family disowned him.

What did he *do*?

Adam looked to Hank, then back to Anne. He smiled the smile of the deeply frustrated and composed himself enough to continue.

Michael was put away for all the wrong reasons, Anne. He and his followers—

Followers, Anne repeated.

The record came to an end in the living room and was quickly replaced with music from the same era. Music from the past.

I mean, yeah, Adam said. He had followers, Anne. He actually . . . led a cult. Yes.

I'm going to ask you one more time, Adam. And please, be open with me. What did your friend do to go to jail?

Adam hesitated and for the first time all evening his real face showed through the many expressions he'd been wearing.

I didn't ask him.

Anne looked to Hank. Hank kept his eyes on Adam.

Okay, Hank said. So you're trying to help him out.

Yes.

You're trying to be his friend.

I am his friend. Yes. His only friend.

Hank looked to Anne.

Let's not let this rule our night. We have guests. Friends of our own. A houseful.

Anne made to say something but stopped. It seemed, to Hank, that she was about to ask Adam to leave.

Then Adam said: We've always been open-minded, haven't we? Come on. How much can we have changed in ten years? The guy is *down*. I mean you can see for yourself he's . . . he's a mess. Obviously, he made a mistake. And obviously he's living with it. Let's celebrate the holidays and let Michael see that there's still some joy in this life. That's what I wanted to show him tonight. You know? The guy hasn't seen joy in like . . . four years.

How long ago did he get out? Anne asked.

Ten days ago, Adam said.

Silence in the kitchen. The sounds of a holiday party beyond the kitchen door. Distant now. The image, too, of a dangerous man seated on the edge of the couch.

Ten days, Anne repeated. I just . . . don't know.

Don't know what?

But Anne didn't answer. Rather, she was imagining desperate families, young girls, broken men and women who had come to this man Michael looking for some kind of answer to questions Anne couldn't invent on her own. And what had he given them? What had he given them instead that had sent him to jail?

If you're uncomfortable I can take him someplace else, Adam said.

Anne continued to stare into the probable recent past.

Don't worry about it, Hank said. It's the holidays, after all. The right thing to do is to . . . welcome him.

Anne didn't argue. She couldn't find it in herself to demand the man leave. It was over-hosting. It was inconsistent. It was . . . unlike the old gang.

Thank you, Adam said. And hey, unless you're staring at him, you won't really even know he's here.

Laura and Steve left when they heard that the newcomer Michael had gone to jail for presumably persuading people to do things they didn't want to do. Or worse. Who knew? Steve heard about it from David over by the sliding deck door, as a pop song ten years old played crackly through the Chamberses' speakers. Often, Steve hid little things from Laura that might upset her. Other times, like when he was three drinks deep, he blabbed. Sometimes he got a big response from her. He got one here. Laura smiled at first, disbelieving, then asked *what* a few times, then grew cold and couldn't stop pivoting to look at the guy. He was sitting on the edge of the couch, hands on his knees, staring at the hardwood floor, making a face that said, *What can you do?* Or, perhaps, *What have I done?* Or, perhaps, *How did I get here? Where did everything go?* Finally Laura couldn't take it. She couldn't stop imagining young girls and guys, lost teenagers, listening to whatever implausible poisoned philosophy he'd once fed them. She imagined a farmhouse, an empty warehouse, a church. And in every vision the lost teenagers walked in a row with wide, blissful eyes and the man Michael (who was sitting *right there*) wore a robe or wore nothing at all and told them what to do. She kept imagining young men and women on their knees.

It was, Laura thought, somewhat like being privy to the bad stuff about a person long before that stuff was made public. Like when the neighbors say *he was a nice guy* about a local who went berserk and now they're reconciling images of him alone, planning, with that friendly face they'd seen on the street. And while Laura understood that the Merrick University gang had long prided themselves on being open-minded, this was simply too much.

She asked Steve if he was ready to leave. Then she demanded they go.

Darla and Berry left, too, which to Anne made a bit of a dent in things because a party of chitchatters needed the quiet ones if they wanted somebody to talk to. Hank told her not to think about it. Called it a "weird night." Then he squeezed her arm gently because it was their way of saying don't worry.

But Anne worried.

A lot of the old gang worried. Adam introduced Michael to all of them, as they came close to the couch. But once word had spread about who Michael might've been and once everybody's imaginations had pictured the worst possible scenarios (brutal, idiotic, *sad* scenes) they all gave the couch some distance, forming something of a semicircle, as though Michael could suddenly reach out and convince them of something impossible.

Anne and Hank noted how the conversations were getting louder. How some of the guests (many) kept looking at the solitary man on the couch, the hard stare in his eyes, like he was currently reliving every beat and breath of his days as a leader of the lost. Hank turned the stereo up a notch, hoping to combat the rising tide of edgy opinions, the drunk lift of familiar voices, slurred and blurred.

But the mood would not be abated.

And Greg Henderson was the first to crack.

It was no surprise to Anne, as Greg had long been the most volatile drinker in the Merrick gang. His nose was always red, his body always bloated. He'd been eyeing Michael with disgust for many minutes.

Hey, you.

He was bending forward, his bulk testing the seams of his gray suit. He was close to spilling his martini on the hardwood floor at Michael's feet.

Hey, you, he growled. What were your tenets?

Half the room got quiet but the whole room was paying attention. Kerry actually turned the radio down.

Hey, you. I'm talking to you. What were your tenets, buddy?

Hank crossed the room and Greg turned slightly to face him. His saggy jowls and watery eyes made him look something like an old English bulldog. Like he was saying: *This is my bone, Hank.*

Michael looked up into Greg's eyes.

Kerry turned the radio down even more.

Adam intervened. He said: Michael's had a rough go of it recently, Greg. Leave him be.

A rough go, eh? Greg said, still bent at the waist, his hands on his knees, the drink tipping toward the floor. I hear you led a cult, buddy. What did you get those poor people to believe in?

Michael looked to Adam.

I'm right here, Greg said. I'm the one asking you. Surely you've got answers. A man like you. What were your tenets, buddy?

Again, Anne imagined a guilt-ridden dog. Bowed and beaten.

Then Michael spoke.

We believed in loyalty.

His voice was quiet, each syllable an Everest to climb.

Bloated Greg, still leaning, smiled and shook his head. Loyalty, he repeated. Young girls? Old people? Huh?

Women, Michael said. Yes.

Greg made a sudden move toward him. Michael flinched back. Then Greg smiled disgustedly and rose to his full height.

You're garbage, Greg said.

Hey, Adam barked. Michael is rehabilitated. You have no right—

Fuck off, Adam, Kerry said.

Hank stepped toward the couch. Like he was going to smooth this over. Like he was going to fix this.

What did you go to jail for? David suddenly asked.

Even Hank paused and waited for the answer.

The old gang from Merrick U. Always better to talk things out, to say them out loud.

Answer him, Beth slurred.

Michael didn't look anybody in the eye when he said: I punished a man for leaving. For being . . . disloyal.

How did you punish him? Christine asked.

Torture? Kerry asked.

Greg moved fast back to the couch and this time planted both hands on either side of Michael so that his palms sunk into the leather.

Quit the vague speak, garbage man. We're smarter than the poor souls you fooled into sucking your dick. What did you do to the man who expressed his disloyalty? How did you *punish* him?

Adam reached for Greg and Hank held Adam back.

Then Greg slapped Michael and Hank let Adam go and Adam grabbed Greg and threw him hard against the wall. Greg's arm cracked against the record player and the music came to a violent stop.

Only there *was* music. Music did remain. Music after all.

Carolers outside, down the street it seemed, their voices floating upon the cold white air, bringing back, if only momentarily, the spirit of the holiday reunion to begin with.

Michael bent an ear in the direction of the singing and brought a hand to his red face.

Then he started sobbing and every guest at the party imagined the stranger beating an old man near to death. Cutting him with unwashed knives from a farmhouse sink.

Anne told him he had to get out. Get out now. Adam, she said, take this man out of my house *this minute.*

It wasn't the first time the old gang had seen Anne angry. There were times at the university. But it had been long since then.

Go on, Kerry said. Take him home, Adam.

Michael rose, stiffly, like an aged and beaten man, and the guests inched away from him. His eyes seemed to be peering through old filthy glass.

The carolers' voices rose outside.

That was our main tenet, he said through his tears. That if you ... left for any reason ... even if they dragged you away ... even if you didn't choose to leave ... you'd be punished.

Jesus fucking Christ, Greg said.

I'm sorry, Adam said. He reached for Michael, to comfort him.

Get out, Hank said.

Then the doorbell rang.

Anne answered the door. It was the carolers of course. They'd made their way up the street and were eager to sing for the Chamberses' house. At the sound of spry female voices, the old gang slowly shuffled into the foyer. *What we must look like,* Hank thought. He wondered if the eight young women on the front porch could detect the mood, if the mood had seeped out the open front door.

They started singing "Away in a Manger" and their voices did something for the mood straightaway. Put a dent in the horrible vibe Adam had brought with him. And yet, there was an edge to the singing. Something thirsty in the timbre. It sounded to Anne like they were perhaps too forceful. She wondered if it was because they felt they needed to over-sing, to make the people in this house feel a holiday spirit that had been bled.

But Christine detected something else yet. Something behind the big white flakes, the earthy voices.

The eight young women on the front porch wore matching brown dresses that flowed like desert sand and Christine wondered how? How could they be wearing only dresses in all that cold? How could they stand barefoot outside?

They sang "Away in a Manger" and Christine started to feel cold inside. She wanted Anne to close the front door. Some of the carolers had dirt in their hair. Some had bad teeth. Wide-eyed and wide-mouthed they sang. And they all seemed to be looking at the same person within the foyer of the Chamberses' house. They all seemed to be looking past Anne and Hank, Jane and John, Kerry and Greg and Adam.

Christine turned slowly to see Michael at the back of the pack, a horror in his eyes that suggested a stronger imagination than her own. As if he was picturing things she could not.

"*Away in a manger, no crib for a bed,*" the carolers sang.

"*Be near me, Lord Jesus, I ask you to stay,*" they sang.

Christine saw it as two of the young women turned from looking at Michael and smiled as they sang. As if they knew him. As if they'd found something. Something they were looking for.

"*Bless all the dear children in your tender care,*

And fit us for heaven, to live with you there."

GOOD DEEDS

JEFF STRAND

I just wasn't feeling the Christmas spirit this year, even after chugging a quart of eggnog. I'd put up the Christmas tree, hung the stockings haphazardly over the chimney, gobbled a dozen candy canes, and bought new lights to replace the tangled ones, but nothing was working.

Was it because I couldn't get my drum set to make a *rummy tum tum* sound? Or was it because my wife had left me three weeks ago and taken the kids? I wasn't sure. Either way, as I stood in line on Christmas Eve to buy a couple of last-minute gifts, I was more Ebenezer Scrooge than Clark Griswold.

A little boy stood in front of me. Every time he fidgeted, a cloud of dirt came off his clothes. Poor little orphan. He held a pair of shoes.

When it was his turn at the register, he took a handful of pennies out of his pocket and began to count them out, one at a time. This was going to take years. I sighed with frustration.

"Son, there's not enough here," said the cashier.

Of course there wasn't. That was an eighty-dollar pair of shoes, minimum, and the kid had set down maybe thirty cents. He was trying to act like he was some toddler who didn't know basic math, but I'm sure he was in fourth or fifth grade, so there was no excuse for the whole handful of pennies thing.

The boy looked crestfallen. "But I want to buy these shoes for my mama."

Oh, he had a mother. So he wasn't an orphan after all. I didn't have to feel sorry for him anymore.

"Daddy says that she's running out of time," the boy continued. "You see, she's been dying of cancer, and today she got hit by a car, so she's going to meet Jesus from one or the other tonight, if the brain aneurysm doesn't take her first. And these shoes would fit her perfectly, because it says they're size seven and my mama is size seven. I can't have my mama meet Jesus in hospital slippers. I just can't."

The little boy began to weep.

"Be that as it may," said the cashier, "those pennies don't even cover the sales tax. Maybe your mama could meet Jesus in something from the clearance aisle?"

The tears made little clean trails in the dirt on his face. "I just want her to look beautiful."

"If she's in the final stages of cancer, new shoes aren't going to do the trick. She could have passed while you are here standing in line. How are you going to reconcile the guilt if your mother dies while you are trying to scam your way into a pair of shoes? Your intentions are good, son, but I'll be honest: you didn't think this through."

The little boy looked back at me with his wide, soulful eyes. "Mama always made sure we had a nice Christmas," he said with a sniffle. "She never cared about herself. She'd say that the best present we could get her was to buy something for ourselves, which we did. I just want *her* to have a good Christmas on the night she goes to Heaven. Without these shoes, she'll die screaming, I know it."

And as I stared at that boy, something happened to my heart. No, it wasn't a cardiac arrest; it was . . . the Christmas spirit. This was what it was all about. This was why Christmas was the champion of all December holidays.

"I want your mama to look beautiful, too," I said. "And I'm going to pay for those shoes."

The cashier shrugged. "That'll be $139.57."

"Oh, no, no, no," I said. I knelt down beside the boy. "I know you love your mama, but I'm sure there are shoes that will make her very happy for about half this price. Go find another pair. Get them quickly," I said.

He left. It did briefly occur to me that I could hurriedly pay for my stuff and get out of the store before the kid came back, but I decided against it. Instead, I stood there feeling great about my generosity.

The replacement pair was $99, which seemed pricey for shoes that were basically just going to be lying around in a casket, but the people behind me in line were getting annoyed, so I paid for them without protest.

"Merry Christmas," I told him.

"Thank you, mister," said the little boy. "Now my mama will be beautiful. She won't be disrespecting Jesus anymore. Thank you so much." He hugged the box of shoes to his chest and ran out of the store.

I began to cry. I'd never known I was such a wonderful person. The world was a dark, ugly, selfish cesspool of misery, but I'd done my part to shine a ray of joy upon it. With only a credit card, I'd made the universe a better place.

The man behind me was crying as well. "I'm going to call my mother," he said, taking out his cell phone.

"Could you do that after you pay?" asked the woman behind him. "Some of us don't have all night to wait in line."

The man glared at her. "I waited for him to buy shoes for the cancer lady, so you can wait for me to make a damn phone call. God, you must be one of those 'Happy Holidays' people."

I ignored the grinches and walked out of the store with smiles flowing through my arteries. I'd saved Christmas! Maybe not for the entire world, but regionally, I'd shown that Christmas *could* be about kindness and compassion and benevolence.

As I walked to my car, I whistled a merry tune.

It was a catchy tune, made up on the spot.

Maybe it could be an actual song.

Maybe it could be a song about . . . me.

If my selfless act could touch my own heart, maybe it could touch the hearts of millions! "Santa Claus Is Comin' to Town" could bite my ass. I was going to write this song tonight!

I sped home. Yes, I ran a stop sign and caused an accident, but the joy I'd bring to humanity would outweigh a hundred car accidents. I couldn't stop crying tears of happiness. I bet that little boy was putting those shoes on his mother's withered feet at this very moment.

When I got home, it occurred to me that I didn't have time to write, record, and distribute a song in time for Christmas, since that was tomorrow. It would have to be a holiday classic for next year. That meant I didn't need to do any creative work tonight; I could sit at home and bask in my glory.

The next year, on December 23, I wrote my song. It was called "A Precious Young Child's Wish for His Terminally Ill Mother to Have New Shoes to Die In, and How I Granted That Wish One Magical Christmas Eve." It's not my place to say that it was a masterpiece, but I will say that I cried the entire time I was writing it.

"What's wrong?" asked my new wife, Candi, walking into the garage.

I strummed my guitar. "Listen to what I've created," I said.

I played her the song. By the end she was weeping.

"Did it fill you with the Christmas spirit?" I asked.

"So the kid's mom died?"

"Well, presumably, yeah."

"I thought there'd be a twist ending where Jesus healed her."

"No, it's not a song about Jesus. It's a song about me. Those are tears of holiday joy, right?"

"They are tears of being completely bummed out. That song has literally ruined my day. Why did the father let that kid go out by himself on Christmas Eve? Maybe the last conversation his mother ever had was with the police about how her son had been abducted!"

"This isn't a song about child abduction," I assured her. "It's a song about the true meaning of Christmas."

"Lingering death?"

"The death doesn't happen until the song is over. It's supposed to be heartwarming."

"It's the opposite of heartwarming. I can't even cope with it right now. I just ... I can't ... I don't know what to ... I can't ..."

Candi took out a gun, shoved it in her mouth, and pulled the trigger.

I shouted something very un-Christmassy as a significant portion of my wife's brain splattered against the cement wall. Her knees buckled and she fell to the floor. I stood there, gaping, watching the pool of blood expand.

I didn't even know she owned a gun, much less carried it around with her while we were relaxing at home.

This was not at all the reaction I'd been going for.

I felt a little silly calling 911, since, let's face it, even the best-trained paramedics can't do much for somebody who's blown their brains out. But I was pretty sure it was the law.

While I waited for them to arrive, I tried to figure out why the reception to my song had been so poor. It seemed pretty goddamned inspirational to me. Did Candi have psychological problems she hadn't divulged before our wedding? We had a prenuptial agreement but it had never occurred to me that she should sign an affidavit of mental health.

If I seemed dispassionate about the death of my bride, I should point out that we'd been married for less than three months. That's not enough time to get truly invested in a marriage. I was glad I'd found this out about her before I got too used to having her around.

The paramedics, of course, asked if I knew why Candi had taken her own life, and I told them about the song, and they seemed to think there was more to it than that, and I agreed.

There was a lot of paperwork. But I wasn't a murder suspect or anything, and I had some free time the following evening. Despite the unwelcome response from my wife, I was proud of the song and wanted to play it in front of an audience to gauge their reaction.

To clarify, I was not a professional musician and I apologize if I gave that impression. I was just a guy who liked to write the occasional tune on his hand-me-down guitar. I knew a place that had an open mic night (by which I mean they left a microphone unattended and you could get in a quick song or two before the bouncers dragged you away) and I was anxious to give my musical gift to those who would cherish it.

I walked into the bar. It was filled with the kind of people who would be in a bar late on Christmas Eve without being Jewish. These dozen or so people needed me. It was time to squeeze the lemon of Christmas spirit over the halibut of their loneliness.

"Hi," I said, standing in front of the microphone. I'd learned from previous experience that it was best to skip an introduction or lively banter and just go straight into the song.

I played like my soul depended on it.

When I got to the part where I paid for that little boy's shoes, yeah, I wept. Not a day had gone by for the past year where I didn't think about what I'd done for him, and it always filled me with deep emotion. I thought about how happy he must be, even with his mother presumably long-dead and buried. Hell, it had brought a tear to my eye on my wedding day, which Candi thought was me being sappy about our nuptials.

I finished the song and stood there, basking in pride.

"What the hell was *that*?" asked a large man seated on a stool.

"That was a true story," I said, though to make the song more dramatic, I'd given the mother kidney stones as well.

"That sucked away my will to live!" the man told me. He lifted his shirt, revealing both his enormous gut and a revolver tucked into his jeans. He took out the gun, pressed it against the side of his head, and pulled the trigger. Red goo sprayed all over the counter and the woman next to him. He tumbled off the stool and landed on his head, making the exposed portion of his skull even larger than it already was.

"He's got the right idea," said a blond woman, breaking her wine-glass against the table and then slamming it deep into her throat. There was no shortage of spurting blood.

Another guy picked up the first man's revolver and flipped out the cylinder. "He's got five bullets left," he announced. "Line up. First come, first served."

Several people got up and hurried over to him.

"Wait!" I said as he shot the first person in line. "This isn't—" *Bang!* Another one dead. "—necessary! Why are you—" *Bang!* One more body dropped. "—doing this? My—" *Bang!* Another corpse. "—song was an inspiring tale of Christmas generosity! I don't get why you're all killing yourselves!"

"Sorry," the guy with the gun said to the last person in line. "There's only one bullet left, and I need it for myself."

"Well, couldn't you beat me to death with the gun first?"

"It'll hurt."

"Not as bad as I'm already hurting."

"All right, yeah, sure."

It took about three minutes to beat the man to death, during which time I kept protesting on deaf (well, mangled) ears. Why did they feel this behavior was necessary? Even if they didn't like the song, why be so extreme about it? I'd heard plenty of songs that I didn't enjoy, and you didn't see me putting a bullet through my head. Honestly, it was ungrateful and rude.

An elderly woman stepped over the corpses and shook my hand. "I don't care what they thought. It was a lovely song. That poor woman might be burning in hell if it wasn't for you."

"I know, right?"

"All my life, when children have asked me for money, I've told them to fuck right off. But you've taught me that there's a positive side to charity. Thank you."

She gave me a hug, which I'll admit went on long enough that it started to get creepy. Finally she broke the hug and walked out of the bar, some brain matter trailing behind her shoe like a piece of toilet paper.

"What did you think?" I asked a man who sat alone in a booth.

"Oh, I'm not into violent death," he said. "I just took a whole bottle of sleeping pills. Hope they kick in soon."

I left the bar, feeling that my first public performance of the song had gone below expectations. Was it really such a bummer? Did people not understand the message of personal awesomeness? If somebody else had written this amazing song, I'd rush right out to buy the single from iTunes, if it weren't readily available on a file-sharing site.

It saddened me to think that my hard work and life lesson might go to waste, but I could not in good conscience continue to perform a song that made people kill themselves after they heard it. I'm not trying to be a social justice warrior, but I believe that even *one* grisly death over a song is too many.

I vowed to never play the song again. If I could sacrifice money for shoes, I could sacrifice my art.

I didn't call the police. I should have, I know, but I wasn't up for another round of questioning. What if they decided I was some thrill-killer who made the murders look like song-related suicides?

When I got home, I sat next to the Christmas tree. I hate to sound maudlin, but I missed Candi. I knew she would have wanted me to open my presents from her, so I did. One of them was a pair of socks, which reminded me of the shoes I bought for that little boy, and it made me cry again.

I fell asleep in my chair, though I kept being woken up by fireworks, or something that sounded like them.

The next morning, my cell phone rang. The display said "Ex-Wife."

"Hello?"

She was crying. "That song!"

"Which song?"

"The one that was uploaded to YouTube last night! You were singing it in a bar! Everybody killed themselves after hearing it!"

"Not everybody. One old lady had very nice things to say about it."

"I've never been so depressed. Not even the sight of our beautiful innocent children happily opening their Christmas presents can cheer me up. Good-bye."

There was a bang as she set off a celebratory firework.

Somebody had uploaded the video to the Internet? It seemed

like there could be quite a downside to that. I'd dreamed of having a viral video, but I couldn't help but feel that maybe a cat video would've been better right now.

I turned on the news. "—thousands of unexplained suicides," said the announcer.

They were unexplained ones, so this wasn't necessarily my fault.

I switched to another station. "—apparently after hearing a terrible, terrible song," said a different announcer.

Well, damn.

They cut to the video of me performing the song, which struck me as a mistake.

Okay, this was not going to be my merriest Christmas ever. Legally I didn't think they could hold me liable, but with thousands of deaths across the nation, I was sure some lawyer would try to find a loophole.

I was screwed, all because I tried to do something nice for somebody.

Thanks for nothing, Jesus.

And that little boy sucked. Dying mama this and dying mama that, while not giving a rat's ass about those of us who stood to suffer from his self-centered footwear fetish.

I could hear sirens in the distance.

Yep, I was boned.

I figured I could buy myself some time by playing the song for the officers that tried to break into my house, causing them to commit suicide before I could be apprehended. But I couldn't sing forever.

Though I *could* play the video on a loop . . .

As it turned out, that wasn't very effective, and only about eight cops killed themselves before I was taken away in handcuffs. You may think that they didn't blame me for the holiday carnage, but that's because, unlike me, you haven't had every last drop of optimism squeezed out of you. Oh, they blamed the hell out of me. I could've gone on an ax-murdering spree in a Santa suit and had less negative energy thrown my way.

So, yeah, my good deed landed me in prison. I don't expect you to sympathize with my plight if you're one of the many people who lost friends or loved ones during the mass Christmas suicides of last year, but I'll bet the rest of you are shaking your heads right now at how badly I was treated.

Anyway, I hate to end this on a cynical note, but if you're ever doing some last-minute shopping and a dirty little ragamuffin kid asks you for shoe money, kick him in the face and run. Trust me. Good deeds just aren't worth it.

To those of you who haven't quit celebrating, merry Christmas.

IT'S A WONDERFUL KNIFE

CHRISTOPHER GOLDEN

Cassie hated Christmas parties in L.A. It wasn't just the weather, though she'd grown up in Wisconsin, where snow days were more plentiful than holidays and ugly sweaters were more than just ironic fashion statements. She remembered building whole kingdoms out of snow, sledding down streets closed off to traffic, and those first romantic snowstorm kisses with her high school boyfriend on a white Christmas Eve.

Still, it wasn't the weather that put her teeth on edge at an L.A. Christmas party. It was the fakery. The festive decorations, the ornamentation, the wreaths and bows and cheery Christmas music, the unneeded scarfs and crystal punch glasses full of eggnog. So fucking fake, like so much of this city, like the smiles on these faces. Even the house they were all meandering through, this mansion in the hills, surrounded by trees and green lawns and enough land that it was hard to imagine she was still in L.A.... Even the house seemed like a set on some studio back lot, like they were all extras in some faux 1950s holiday film.

James Massarsky had come up in Hollywood the way few people did these days. He'd quite literally started in the mailroom and worked his way up through the industry to become head of a studio. After a few glory years followed by one catastrophic summer box-office season, he'd been bumped out to make room for the next scapegoat, put out to pasture with a producing deal. In time, he had become an independent producer with more power than most of the studio heads he worked with. Massarsky got movies made. He got shit done. But he'd earned his reputation as a ruthless, narcissistic shitbag.

Nobody cared. His reputation, his behavior, his divorces and scandals . . . they didn't matter. The crowd at his Christmas party laughed and drank and sang along to holiday tunes. They kissed beneath mistletoe and paused to watch curved-screens silently showing scenes from the greatest hits of both animated and live-action Christmas films. On one sitting-room screen, George Bailey stood up to Mr. Potter, and Massarsky's guests watched without a trace of irony.

"Now, this is just a crime," his voice said, silky and low, as his hand glided along her back and he smiled down at her, like he knew something she didn't.

"If you mean the Pink Martini version of 'Little Drummer Boy,' I agree."

Massarsky frowned in confusion. When he laughed, she wasn't sure if he'd noticed the song playing over his sound system or if he simply discarded any human dialogue that diverged from the script in his head, as if original thoughts did not compute for him.

"I mean a beautiful girl like you without a drink in her hand," he replied. "I don't have a pink martini, but I'm sure I can get the bartender to make you one." He guided her into the corridor with that hand on her lower back, steering her. "Or anything else you'd like."

Cassie smiled. She had no choice. It was why she'd come, after all. Just like the rest of them. She'd been in L.A. for four years, been to hundreds of auditions, scored a few commercials and sitcom walk-ons, and finally starred in an indie film about lesbian parenting that got her nominated for best actress at Outfest. Massarsky wouldn't have seen it, but it made her feel like a real actress and it nudged her up a few notches on casting sheets.

Still . . . *Girl*.

The word did not surprise her. Twenty-six years old, but to men like Massarsky, she'd always be a girl.

"Don't you want to put your purse down? I've got someone checking coats and things."

Cassie smiled, slinging the straps of her purse a little higher on her shoulder. "It's part of the ensemble. The designer who loaned it to me made me promise to keep it with me, show it off."

Massarsky chuckled. "Don't you love this town?"

"More than anything."

She let him guide her to the vast living room, where furniture had been rearranged to make room for the bar. The windows were open to let fresh air circulate. Snowflake decorations were everywhere, but it was seventy degrees even up here in the hills. Christmas in Hollywood.

"I'll have——" she began.

"Can I suggest something?" Massarsky interrupted, and he didn't wait for her reply, looking to the bartender. "Pomegranate martini." He glanced at her. "You'll love it."

Cassie didn't tell him she'd had one before and had not, in fact, loved it. She took the offered glass and sipped from it and smiled, and when he put that guiding hand on her back again and steered her away from the bar and deeper into the house, she went along.

The walls were decorated with decades' worth of photos of Massarsky with actors and politicians, the famous and the powerful. Always just him and those celebrities. In some of the framed photos, it was clear there had been others in the picture, people whose hands or arms or shoulders remained but who had been cropped out because their presence did not contribute to his legend. This was the kind of man Cassie had come to celebrate Christmas with.

"I didn't catch your name."

"Cassandra Ochoa."

"Oooh. Exotic," he said. "I like it."

She wondered if men like James Massarsky could tell a real smile from a fake one, and realized they probably didn't care. As with a woman's orgasm, the pretense of a smile was enough to reassure him.

"You're an actress?"

"Isn't everyone?"

"But are you a real cinephile? A real movie lover?"

"Of course."

"Old movies are my passion. I collect mementos from my favorites, oddities and props and rare photographs."

Cassie smiled shyly. "Honestly? That's half the reason I came. My agent and her husband were coming and invited me. Normally I like a quieter Christmas with family, but that's hard these days. Kind of grim in this town. I'd read an article in *Variety* about your collection and it just fascinated me. Is it true you have the tooth De Niro had knocked out filming *Raging Bull*?"

Massarsky grinned like a schoolboy. "I know, weird and gross."

"No, it's cool," she said, and touched his elbow the way she knew a thousand other actresses must have.

Balding, sweaty upper lip, pot belly, hairs growing inside his ears, Massarsky either didn't see how repulsive he'd be to most young women or he didn't care. When Cassie had arrived, she had assumed the latter, but now that she'd been in his presence for a few minutes, she had changed her mind. He had an air of confidence, a swagger more appropriate for a leading man than an obese producer careening ungracefully toward his sixtieth birthday.

And yet . . . something about his excitement, the sparkle in his eyes when he thought about his collection, made him seem human, like in that moment Cassie could imagine the little boy he'd once been. If nothing else, his love of movies was sincere.

He looked at his watch—only men his age still wore watches—and gave her a conspiratorial look. Late as it was, people had continued to arrive, and the boisterous laughter and chatter of his guests nearly drowned out the Christmas music pumping from the speakers.

"I keep the room locked up during parties," he confessed, with a boyish shrug. "A lot of one-of-a-kind items in there. But if you'd like a tour . . ."

Cassie felt a little thrill travel up her spine. "I'd love it." Even her smile was genuine, and tonight, in the Hollywood hills, that was nothing short of a miracle.

"At some of these Christmas parties, I've taken little groups in with me, but then people get pissed that *they* didn't get a tour. Half of them couldn't give a damn about the collection, but they feel slighted or they're trying to curry favor."

Massarsky paused, eyes narrowing with suspicion. "What's your favorite old movie?"

"You mean aside from *It's a Wonderful Life*?"

"You're saying that because it's Christmas."

"I'm not. That movie makes me cry every time I watch it," Cassie said. She wasn't lying. Maybe he saw that in her eyes. "But if you mean something else, I guess I'd say *The Children's Hour* or the Gable version of *Mutiny on the Bounty*."

He smiled. "The Gable version." With a snobbish roll of his eyes, he nudged her back. "Come on. Later on, I'll show you the reel I have from the original version of *Bounty*."

"The Australian thing with Errol Flynn?"

Massarsky beamed. "You really do know your old movies. Most people know nothing about *In the Wake of the Bounty,* but I'm not talking about that. The first version was Australian, but—"

"The silent version?"

Massarsky stared at her. "Wow. That's . . . I don't know that I've met more than one or two other people who know that movie exists."

"It doesn't. I mean it did," Cassie clarified, "but it's lost. Like thousands of others."

"Correction," Massarsky said, "it *was* lost."

Cassie let her mouth drop open in a little O of wonderment.

"This way," he said.

She hoisted the straps of her purse higher on her shoulder and let him steer her into a darkened side corridor, around a corner, past a pair of French doors that opened into a sunroom, and then up three steps into another corridor. She sipped her pomegranate martini and only grimaced a bit when she swallowed.

Massarsky tapped a code into a keypad beside the door and Cassie heard the lock click. He opened the door and stepped inside. Motion-sensor lights flickered on.

"You wanted to see De Niro's tooth," he said.

She grinned. "That's so nasty, keeping his tooth."

"It's Hollywood history, honey."

Cassie took his arm and smiled up at him. "Show me."

The lights were low and warm, with individual illumination in most of the cases and small lamps above rare posters and artwork on the walls. The poster for *Revenge of the Jedi*—the original name for the third *Star Wars* film—hung on the wall, and she pretended that she hadn't seen it before. It was very rare. In the condition it was in, she figured it must be worth at least five thousand dollars, but compared to the truly unique props and other items in his collection, the poster was unremarkable.

Massarsky showed her De Niro's tooth. It had yellowed, but it looked like there might still be a bit of blood on it. When he brought her over to a small case holding the prop gun that had killed Brandon Lee on the set of *The Crow*, Cassie got a chill. There were other unsettling souvenirs as well. The glove that Harold Lloyd had worn to hide his missing fingers in the 1920s, after he'd picked up a bomb he'd thought a prop while shooting publicity photos for *Haunted Spooks*. The dress Virginia Rappe had died in. A portion of the Fokker D-VII that stunt pilot Dick Grace crashed filming 1927's *Wings*.

"Dick Grace. That was a crazy one. The guy broke his neck and crushed four vertebrae, and he was back to work like a month later," Massarsky said, beaming. "They don't make men like that anymore."

"At least he lived," Cassie replied. "Some of these are pretty grim."

"That's half the fun for a collector. The macabre stuff always goes for top dollar. That and the erotic. I had one guy try to sell me a half stick of butter he claimed was from the filming of *Last Tango in Paris*. I've been known to have a kink or two, but that seemed pretty disgusting to me, not to mention impossible to prove."

Cassie wrinkled her nose. "We all have a kink or two. I'm glad you didn't buy that."

Massarsky hadn't missed that fact that she'd agreed with him about people and their kinks. He slid his arm around her and they proceeded through his little Hollywood museum more intimately after that. When they paused in front of a baseball bat from Walter Hill's *The Warriors* and the actual sword from John Boorman's *Excalibur,* he put a hand on her ass and she did not remove it.

"You have another sword. What's that one?"

"Oh, you spotted that?" He turned to look toward the far corner of the room. "You told me you didn't like the gruesome ones."

"I said some of them were pretty grim. I didn't say I wasn't . . . intrigued."

A shiver went through her, something dark and delicious. He must have seen it in her eyes, because he inhaled deeply and his smile widened.

"Okay. It's a great story. Maybe not the best story I've got, but fucking tragic," he said as he guided her, hand at the small of her back, toward that far corner. "You ever heard of *They Died with Their Boots On?*"

"Of course. Errol Flynn and Oliva de Havilland. God, she was beautiful."

"She was."

"So the sword is from that?" Cassie asked as they stopped in front of the glass case. The light shone up through the case, gleaming on the blade within. She tucked a lock of hair behind her ear and turned toward Massarsky, shifting her purse straps on her shoulder again. "So what's this tragic tale that goes along with it?"

He glanced at his watch, a look of pleasure crossing his face.

"Am I boring you?" she asked, putting just the right touch of petulance into her voice.

"No, no. It's almost midnight. I've got another story for you. The best one. But okay, first . . . The movie's this bullshit version of General Custer's life, right? Great movie, but they played it like a biopic and it's not that at all. Anyway . . . do you remember the big cavalry charge?"

"Vaguely, I guess. I saw it years ago."

Massarsky's smile dimmed a bit. "Doesn't matter. Point is, during the charge there were accidents. Horses went over. Three riders were killed, including an extra named Jack Budlong, who was riding right next to Errol Flynn when he fell. The guy's going down and in that split second, he tosses his sword to have his hands free, try to break his fall."

"Don't tell me."

"The damn sword landed handle first, stuck in the mud, and the poor bastard impaled himself on it. Killed almost instantly."

Cassie put a hand to her mouth in a flutter of scandal and horror. "Oh my God. That's awful."

"I know. Great, right?"

"And that's *not* the best story you've got in this room?"

"Nope. I've got a handful of things in here connected to accidents and famous deaths, but only one actual, real-life murder weapon."

Her mouth went dry. She wetted her lips with her tongue and watched him notice. Her face flushed and she let out a small, nervous laugh. "Show me."

Massarsky reached out and touched her face, moved the same lock of hair she'd shifted before. He pressed himself against her. If he'd been a younger man, she was sure she'd have felt an erection, but there was nothing. Not yet. He bent to kiss her and she let it happen, let his lips brush hers for just a second before she bit him. Just a playful nip.

He drew back, eyes wide as he prodded his lip, then glanced at his fingers. No blood. Not this time. Cassie let him see the danger in her smile and Massarsky nodded in approval.

"I did say we all have our kinks," she reminded him.

He grinned, then glanced at his watch. "We'll get to your kinks. But I promised you this story. I'll keep it short. The clock's ticking."

"What does time have to do with it?" she asked.

Massarsky turned toward another case, two down from the sword that had killed the unlucky horseman. This case was smaller, and empty.

"There's nothing in it," Cassie said.

"That's not strictly true."

She moved closer and realized he was right. At the back of the case was a small wooden object, some sort of display stand—though there was nothing on display. Flat on the bottom of the case was a photo still from *It's a Wonderful Life,* a shot of a very scruffy, wild-eyed Jimmy Stewart.

"Were you robbed?" she asked, turning toward him. "I mean, I told you it was my favorite, but what am I missing?"

Massarsky's eyes clouded. "I've been robbed, yeah. A few years back. But it wasn't this case. Inside this case is the greatest thing that's ever come into my collection."

"You said a murder weapon. I see a photograph."

He stroked her neck, ran his hand along her back and over her ass. "You'll never believe me." His voice deepened. "Not at first."

Cassie sighed impatiently and glanced toward the door. He saw that, too. For a man with his reputation, James Massarsky seemed to notice a great deal, even if his attentions were mainly focused on his precious collection and wanting to fuck her.

"This is your favorite movie," Massarsky began. "So I know you remember this scene."

"Of course. This is in the alternate reality, where George Bailey was never born. He and Clarence go into the bar, but it's like a nightmare version of what it used to be. Even the bartender's horrible. The angel orders a Flaming Rum Punch. I remember that because I tried it once."

Massarsky looked impatient now, glancing at his watch again. "So here's the story. The girl who played Violet, Gloria Grahame . . . rumor had it she was sleeping with a guy named Tommy Duggan at the time, and got him a job as an extra on the film. He's in the background in a few scenes, just barely there. No lines, nothing, but if you had a picture of Duggan and you freeze-framed your way through the picture the way I have, you'd find him. They mostly cut him out."

"Cut him out? An extra? Why would they bother?"

Massarsky grinned. A shark's grin. For the first time, she was nervous.

"This scene . . . they shot it on Christmas Eve. Trying to get it in the can before they broke off for the holidays. They were shooting late. Understand that Duggan had a reputation as a tough guy. Maybe he did some work for organized crime or maybe people just didn't like him. Either way, in the midst of that crowd scene, when they're all jammed around George Bailey and Clarence the Angel, the camera drifted past Duggan and then he was out of the frame. It was midnight when that happened. Exactly."

Cassie felt her throat tighten. Her heart had begun to race. It seemed colder in the room than it had before.

"What happened at midnight?"

"Someone stabbed Duggan in the back, nicked his spine and punctured a kidney and twisted it. Thing is, in a room full of people, everyone was focused on the main actors, so nobody saw who did the deed. There were four or five people close enough to Duggan to have stabbed him and the police had suspects, but they could never prove a thing. Duggan fell on his face with the knife sticking out of his back. A dozen people were staring at him, saw the blood starting to pool. The guy playing Nick the bartender started swearing—Henry Travers, who played Clarence, remembered that. They were staring at that knife . . . and it just vanished."

Cassie shuddered and stared into the case. She wanted to touch the glass, reached out to do so, but then hesitated. Massarsky kept these things sparkling clean and she didn't want to mark it up.

"That's not possible," she said, though she knew her voice sounded hollow.

"I didn't think so either, but I've shown this case to people on Christmas Eve at least half a dozen times. They all see it. They think it's some kind of trick, some fucking smoke and mirrors David Blaine bullshit, but it's real."

Cassie frowned. "Go on."

"We've got maybe a minute before midnight. When the clock strikes twelve on Christmas Eve, you're going to see that knife appear, right there in the case. For sixty seconds, exactly. One minute. And then it's gone for another year."

Entranced, she stared into the case. "Where did it come from?"

"I've heard a dozen stories, most of them about magic and deals with the devil, but it's all just mythmaking as far as I'm concerned. Maybe one of those stories is true, but I'll never know which one. And it doesn't matter. The best part of the story is the murder of Tommy Duggan."

Cassie exhaled. Reached back and took Massarsky's hand. "You show this to people every year? And it's really there?"

"Not every year. Not last year."

"What happened last year?"

He squeezed her hand. "I met someone who . . . distracted me before midnight."

Cassie grinned at him. "Bad boy, James. You find yourself a distraction every Christmas Eve? Is that all I am?"

He moved closer to her, kissed her neck from behind. "Of course not." This time she thought she did feel something stirring against her back. Maybe his age hadn't completely unmanned him yet, or maybe it was the Viagra talking.

"Actresses, I bet," she said. "You make them promises, right? Isn't that the game?"

Massarsky stopped kissing her neck. "I help people out some-

times. Have a little fun along the way. I can see you're not naïve.
You're too pretty not to know the way this town . . ."

"The way this town what?"

But Massarsky had stiffened, and now he shifted her aside.
"What the hell?"

He glanced at his watch, then into the case. He put his hands
on either side of the glass, peering inside. "What the hell?" he said
again.

Midnight, she thought. "Maybe your watch is wrong."

"I set it just for this," he sniffed. "Down to the fucking second."
Baffled, he stared at the glass case. At the little wooden display
stand, upon which nothing at all had appeared.

"I expected smoother moves from a guy with your casting
couch history," Cassie said. Smirking, she stepped back from him.
Reaching into her purse, pushing aside her cell phone.

Massarsky huffed. He scratched his head and stared at the case.
"Get the fuck out," he said, without bothering to turn. "You were
interesting. Most don't know movies like you do. But now you're
just getting on my nerves."

Cassie drove the knife into his back. Stabbed deep and twisted
the blade before sliding it out. He cried out and dropped to the
floor, reaching around for the wound as if there was anything he
could do about it. Flopping, twisting, he started to swear at her,
and she stabbed him in the gut. Blood poured onto the floor, pooling around him. Cassie stepped carefully, avoiding the blood, trying
to keep as clean as she was able.

He stared at the knife in her hand.

"I stole it last year, since you're wondering," she whispered. "You
were fucking my friend Anita over by your precious De Niro tooth.
At midnight. You didn't get to tell your story last year. But I'd heard
it before, the year before that, when I was heavier and blonder, and

you had half a dozen people in here for your midnight story. You barely noticed me."

"Fucking bitch," he slurred. "Fucking . . ." Massarsky drew a deep breath, preparing to scream for help.

Cassie stabbed him in the throat. Blood burbled up through his lips and ran down over his chin. She smiled.

"Three years ago, it was my sister Cori in here with you. Oh, the promises you made, just to get her to open her legs. She had stars in her eyes when she came home. She told me about your collection, about this knife, called it magic. Told me you'd promised to do some magic for her career. And you did. The cell phone video you made, the one you showed to all your fucking cronies, it got her all sorts of offers. The kind of offers that made her take all of the pills in her bedside drawer. Your little game killed her. The magic you promised her."

The knife disappeared, right out of her hand, blood and all.

She didn't need it anymore. Massarsky's eyes had already gone glassy. His chest had stopped rising and falling. She went to the little bathroom at the back of the room and washed her hands, then checked her clothes and shoes and legs for blood. Most of Massarsky's friends would know his habits, know not to come looking for a while after he'd taken an actress to see his collection. They all played the game. Still, she had to hurry.

Where the knife had fallen, she had no idea. Next Christmas Eve, it would appear again, likely on the floor. But only for a minute.

She paused on her way out, just beyond the expanding pool of blood, and peered again into the glass case. For the first time, she noticed the little bone-white card set into the nearest corner, just below and to the right of the photo from the movie. She saw what Massarsky had printed there and a quiet laugh crossed her lips, followed swiftly by a whimper, as tears began to spill from her eyes.

Backing away, covering her mouth to keep from screaming, she rushed to the door, peered into the corridor, and slipped out. The words written on that bone-white card stayed with her as she fled, and she knew they always would. Massarsky's sense of humor made her wish she could kill him again. But the words on the card had been accurate, she couldn't deny that.

1946, it had said. The year of the film's release. And then four words.

It's a Wonderful Knife.

And it was. Oh, it was.

She retraced her steps to the sunroom and pushed through the French doors. The room had been decorated with ribbons and Christmas knickknacks and the largest gingerbread house she'd ever seen. A massive wreath hung on the back door, and when she unlocked the door and yanked it open, the bells on the wreath jangled merrily.

Cassie froze, hung her head, and couldn't stop the smile on her lips as she drew the door silently closed.

Every time a bell rings, she thought.

Then she darted across the lawn, pulling off her shoes as she went, laughing to herself even as she wept for Cori. She could almost hear her sister's voice in her head.

"Attagirl, Cassie," she said aloud. "Attagirl."

MISTLETOE AND HOLLY

JAMES A. MOORE

The children were happy. That was what mattered.

Deanna watched her boys run around with the other kids on the snowscape that had replaced their usual day-care playground.

Jeannie looked her way and said nothing, but that look was there, just the same. Deanna knew it wasn't intentional, but her sister kept casting pitying glances at her, as if she might be too fragile to survive the day.

"Stop it, Jean."

"I'm not doing anything." Her tone made a lie of her words. She'd been busted and she knew it.

"I'm fine, okay? It's been almost two years."

"I know. And I don't mean to, but it sucks, Dee. It sucks a lot."

That was the truth of the matter. Almost two years since the nice men in uniforms had arrived at her door and told her that Matt was never coming home again.

She couldn't remember the words. She could only remember the way it had felt when she'd opened the door to the men in their formal Navy blues. The light had been too bright. That was a thing. The sun had been blasting off the field of fresh-fallen snow in the yard and she'd had to squint. Still, as soon as she'd seen them, she'd known why they were there and she'd forgotten all about the brightness of the day.

There'd been words. Oh, so many words. Expressions that were polite and firm. These men did not offer tears. They offered sympathy, but she'd had no doubt they made the same condolences a dozen times a week. For a moment she'd felt pity for them. How horrible. What a miserable job, to go door-to-door and tell people that their loved ones were coming home in boxes and being buried with full military honors. What a miserable way to spend a work-week. How, she wondered still, did it feel? How did they go home and not become roaring drunks?

She thought about that a lot, especially when she was settling back for a glass of wine and contemplating going for the pack of cigarettes she had hidden behind the family portrait over the mantel.

She still hadn't broken and gone for one of those cigarettes, but they were there as a constant temptation. That was her daily victory march for a while. Her silent mantra: *Only one glass of wine and I still haven't broken into the Pall Malls.* Whatever worked to get you through it without breaking into tears, or screaming at the kids when the worst of the loneliness came along.

The sensations swept through her again. Her stomach fell away. Her heart hammered steady as ever but too damned loud. The tears were the absolute worst, of course. There were the boys to consider and they never needed to see Mommy crying. Too young, and she wanted them to be kids for as long as they could, because that meant she was still a young mother and not a middle-aged widow.

She *was* still young. That was what everyone said. Thirty-five wasn't so old. It just felt that way when she rolled out of bed and saw the empty spot on Matt's side. She still didn't sleep on that side. Part of her sleeping mind and heart insisted that he would be coming home.

Closed casket funeral service, of course. Even with the morticians doing their very best, there was no way she would have let the children see their father that way.

She had not spared herself the same fate. She'd needed to see him. She'd needed to *know*. There could be no doubt at all, no false hopes, and so she looked at the remains when they came back. They'd done their best with wax and makeup and a military-cut wig to hide the fact that most of his forehead and skull were still lost somewhere in the Middle East.

There had been a time when she believed in the war. She thought they were over there doing good. God knew she and Jeannie had argued the benefits of war versus the virtues of peace on a hundred occasions. All of that changed after Matt died.

What good was a war that left her without a husband and her kids without a father?

"You still there, Dee?" Jeannie looked at her with a half frown. Her brow was wrinkled up like she was concentrating.

"Yep. Just trying to figure out what's left to do."

"Well, we've got the worst of it, don't we? The packages come home with me and I'll get 'em wrapped in no time."

"You're a lifesaver," Deanna said.

"I am not a little candy with a hole in the middle." She looked down and poked herself in her perfect, flat stomach.

Sometimes she wanted to punch her younger sister on general

principles. Perfect hair, perfect smile, perfect body, perfect social life. Most times Deanna was okay with that, but the last twelve pounds refused to go away, no matter how many classes she took or miles she jogged.

Jeannie continued, "I mean, belly button, yes, but it doesn't go all the way through."

"Really? That's the best you've got?"

"There are kids present." Jeannie winked.

As if that were their cue, the boys all called out at the same time and came trotting through the snow, smiling their beautiful smiles. They had their dad's smile. Every last one of them. How had that happened? She didn't know but she looked away from them for a brief second to close her eyes. It was one of those days. The tears were closer than she wanted to think about.

Jeannie must have seen it, or sensed it, or whatever it was that little sisters who became aunts did. She called out to them and moved closer, squatting so she could capture two five-year-olds and one three-year-old in her arms. "Baby boys," she cried out, a perfect smile on her face. "Who has hugs for auntie!"

Not nearly for the first time, she thanked any gods that might be listening for her sister.

"You have your hands full, don't you?" The voice was pleasant and completely unknown, smoky and sultry in the way of the very best jazz singers. Deanna turned her head and looked at a woman a few years younger than she, with dark, wildly curly hair, perfect Irish skin and the bluest eyes she'd seen in a long time. The woman was wearing a black, fur-lined coat that probably cost as much as a car. She had a perfect smile to go along with a model's body. Model's height, too, though that might have been the heels on her boots. How the hell could anyone walk in high-heeled boots? Deanna would have hated the woman on sight, but she was smiling too brightly.

"You better believe it." She found herself smiling right back, the dreaded tears suddenly pushed aside by a stranger's smile.

Shelly, the woman who owned and operated the day care, looked over from where she was herding a gaggle of heavily bundled charges and offered a quick wave. Her cheeks were rosy from the cold air, but she, too, looked immensely happy.

It was the holidays, and sooner or later it seemed the Christmas spirit bit almost everyone.

Almost everyone. *Fake it till you make it.* That was her motto and she was sticking by it. So far it had done her pretty well.

"Dee, meet Ella." Jeannie's voice was warm and happy and— looking at the woman and then at her sister—Deanna knew instantly that they were an item.

"It's nice to meet you, Ella." She smiled and she meant it. Anyone who made her sister happy was good news. One of them needed to be filled with cheer. Deanna had spent ten wonderful years with Matt. She'd hit the jackpot. It was time for Jeannie to do the same, whatever she needed to get there.

"You good from here?" Jeannie looked her way as all three of Deanna's children adhered themselves to her legs.

She looked at her sister and then at her sister's friend. Jeannie had plans. Ella had the same plans. She nodded her head. "Yep. You guys go have fun. I'm baking some cookies for my kiddies when I get home." All three of her sons let out happy cheers at the mention of cookies.

For once, just for a moment, Jeannie's look of pity was gone, replaced by a different sort of expression—one set aside solely for Ella.

That, in itself, was something of a holiday miracle.

———

Deanna called Jeannie at nine that night, and despite the temptation to torture her sister over the amazing woman she was with,
she said nothing at all about Ella.

Jeannie took care of that in seconds.

"What did you think of Ella?"

"You mean aside from hating her for looking that good?"

"I know, she's stupid gorgeous, isn't she? And smart. Who knew
smart could be so interesting? She's studying ancient religions,
with an interest in the roots of modern Wicca and witchcraft. She
wants to be an anthropologist or archaeologist. One of the two."

"Smart *and* she looks like that? I think there should be laws. She
should have a tax levied against her or something." Wine made her
think she was funny. That thought made her snort and chuckle.
"Seriously, where did you find her?"

"She just came into the store one day, looking for pastries
because she was hosting a book club at her place. We got to talking.
Next thing I know, I'm in a book club."

"You? Seriously?"

"I can read."

"Yeah, I know. You just don't." Her wineglass was empty. She
looked at the bottle and decided against. Happy sister or no, distracted or no, it was best not to take chances.

"Well, I do now. At least one book a month." She laughed as she
said it.

"Good. You should expand your horizons."

That one was a little too close to the subject at hand for Jeannie.
"So. I got the packages finished. You want me to keep them in the
car for now?"

"You okay with that? They're probably not going to start looking
for a few more years, but just in case, you know?"

"They can't find them in my trunk. None of the little boogers
knows how to drive and I always lock up."

"You're the best." Deanna sighed and thought about how lucky she was to have an awesome sister. The little blessings. They were what made the days tolerable. She closed her eyes and smiled and for a moment she could almost feel his breath on her neck, smell his cologne as it sighed softly away from his warm body. God, how she missed him.

The tears tried to come around again and she shook them away as Jeannie started talking. "So me and Ella are going shopping again tomorrow. No stuff for kids. Serious stuff, like shoes and dresses. We might even go nuts and look at hats. Wanna come with?"

There was not enough time in the day. She shook her head. Still, her mouth had a mind of its own. "Yeah. I can spare a couple of hours. Especially if this is an excuse to go out for lunch." That was the good thing about being a teacher. She had lots of time off for the winter break. The pay could be better, but Uncle Sam still reimbursed a bit every month to make up for taking her husband.

"I think we can squeeze in time for lunch."

"Perfect." They worked out the details, Deanna making a note to take the kids to day care, and then Jeannie was saying good night and Deanna was walking over to the front door to make sure everything was locked up properly. On a whim she opened the door and checked to see if any more snow was falling.

No snow. But there was a set of footprints that walked across the front yard, meandering along from the mailbox to the stairs. The footprints were heavy and the tread was definitely from a boot. They walked all the way up to the door, and then faded into a light marking of water where the snow failed to reach.

By rights she should have been chilled. The fact that the boots had the same sort of tread that Matt's boots in the closet had—she certainly knew them well enough and had held them a hundred times since he passed—gave her a sense of comfort. She let herself have the thought that Matt was looking out for them.

Sometimes she had the most amazing dreams about him: long, wonderful conversations that she never remembered clearly in the morning. Was there a heaven? She had her doubts. Was there an afterlife of some sort? She thought maybe yes. Maybe he came to her in her sleep sometimes, and said hello. Like the footprints in the new-fallen snow, she found that notion comforting.

Still, when she slept that night and Matt came to visit, he was not happy and loving and warm. Instead he was angry and drunk and stank of alcohol and something darker.

Sometimes, when she slept, her mind reminded her that Matt wasn't always loving. Sometimes, just now and then, he'd been a complete bastard. When he was alive he could apologize and make it right. In her dreams, the bad ones, he never ever said he was sorry.

The air was cold and just right for staying buried in the blankets when she woke up, but Deanna had no desire to stay there. "Kids will wake me soon anyway," she whispered to herself.

The house was still dark, but it was New England in December, and that meant the sun came up later than most people woke up anyway. No luck. The alarm clock on the nightstand said three a.m.

Her mind was too active for sleep and she knew it. So Deanna carefully slipped out of bed and moved her feet into her fuzzy slippers before shuffling as quietly as she could toward the kitchen, stopping only long enough to make certain that all three of the boys were sound asleep. They were.

The wind outside howled around the edge of the house and the windows shook.

Once again she found herself looking out the window, this time in the backyard, to see if more snow was falling. Nothing. Just the wind and skittering gusts of old snow captured and hurled through the air.

The water met the electric kettle and she poured a pack of instant cocoa into her favorite mug. Hot chocolate, just the thing to promote a good night's sleep. That was her theory and she was sticking to it. The water was ready in no time and she poured and mixed and then shuffled over to the seat nearest to the table. Cookies were close enough to grab and so she did. Three of them, which she drowned in hot cocoa before eating. Really, she knew the reason that last dozen pounds refused to leave her alone.

When she closed her eyes she could almost hear Matt calling her piggy. He'd only done that once, when she was eight months pregnant. That had been their first serious fight in over a year. He'd meant it as a joke. Hormones and a body swollen by not one but two children sitting inside her and beating the hell out of her internal organs had guaranteed she didn't take it that way.

Very late at night and early in the morning, those were the worst times. She still missed him, only sometimes she hated him, too. He'd been the one who'd decided to reenlist. He'd had choices. He had plenty of choices and some of them paid better. Civilian work for the military almost always did, but he insisted. His duty to God and country.

The tears didn't threaten. They came out full force and Deanna shoved the palm of her hand against her lips and her teeth to suppress the noises of her angry, bitter tears. Angry because he'd left her, whether he'd meant to or not, and bitter because as much as she wanted to hate him for leaving and for hitting her those rare times when he had—and for leaving her without a husband and without a father for their kids—she still missed him and loved him so goddamned much that it carved a hollowed core where her heart should have been.

Every man she'd flirted with, every one of the four men she'd tried to date, had been compared against Matt and they always fell short. She didn't know if that was her over-romanticizing their love, or if he'd really been that amazing despite his flaws. But next to Matt they were all just pale, shallow imitations.

The tears were hot and they stung her eyes and she had trouble catching her breath.

And then the tears were gone again, just that fast. It was almost always like that.

"Fuck. I hate the nights most of all."

The cocoa went into the sink. She'd deal with the cleanup tomorrow. Well, later today, after the sun rose and the kids were packed up and off to day care.

Outside the wind wailed with an all-too-human sound of tragedy. Deanna looked out the window again and saw a ghostly white shape in the snow. It seemed to look at her for one second before dissolving into nothingness.

Just her imagination, of course, but sleep did not come back to her easily, but eventually it showed itself, and she drifted off into a dreamless stupor.

The thing about kids is, you want them to be happy. Happy kids mean happy mom. So she smiled and made pancakes with chocolate chips and she set them up with hot chocolate (lower temperature, of course, to avoid burning tiny mouths), and after breakfast she drove them to the day care. By the time she dropped the munchkins off she was in far better spirits.

After that she pulled out all of the old decorations for the artificial tree—she preferred real ones, but the cost was insane and the thought that one of her boys might manage to drop a real one on his head terrified her. The fake tree weighed fifteen pounds. The real ones, on the other hand, could crush a little life. Maybe that was paranoia. She'd lost Matt. Jeannie always joked about her treating the boys like glass.

Was it ever likely to happen? No. She anchored even the fake one at three points, but why take the chance?

The decorations were laid out, box after box. She looked them over and had the exact same problem she did with almost everything. Memories, memories, memories. Matt was everywhere. She loved that. She hated that. No tears. She had a lunch date. So instead she set down the Hallmark ornament that her parents had given her to mark her first Christmas married to Matt, and she grabbed her coat.

Fifteen minutes of rocking out to Christmas songs had her waiting for Jeannie and the supermodel to show up at their agreed-upon too-trendy restaurant. She was early. They were punctual.

Ella was dressed in another outfit that screamed of money and a heightened fashion sense. Jeannie was dressed like Jeannie, in painted-on jeans and a blouse that managed to hug all of her curves in the best possible way. She made a note to cut back on the cookies, but even as she scolded herself, she knew it would do no good. Chocolate chips were just too damned tasty.

She hugged both of the women and felt a sense of awe at her body's reaction to Ella. Some women just exuded sensuality and her sister's new friend was one of them.

Despite a small blush, she was happy to see both of them and they sat at a booth and ordered the sort of food that no woman would ever consider getting on a first date with a potential partner. There was no guilt involved and the banter was good.

Deanna thought about what Jeannie had said and asked, "So, you're studying witchcraft and religion in school? Jeannie said you were thinking about becoming an archaeologist?"

Ella smiled at her and shook her head. "Close. I'm studying

anthropology and comparative religions with an emphasis on dru-
idic lore and the foundations of modern Wicca."

"Jeannie's way was easier to say."

Ella's smile was pure seduction. "That's one of the things I like
about your sister. She's easy."

Jeannie looked away, blushing. Ella winked.

Jeannie said, "Anyway, we were discussing boots."

Deanna looked at her and smiled. "We were?"

"We are now . . ."

Deanna smiled and let herself relax.

Somehow they wound up doing wine with the meal and then
with dessert. Not enough to get drunk, but one more glass than
Deanna should have done. It was that same old problem: wine
made happy and wine made sad and sometimes it was challenging
to know where to stop.

Everything was fine until that damned song came on.

The first chorus of "I'll Be Home for Christmas" was all it took
for Deanna to get sniffly. Jeannie got that look again and even that
made the situation worse. She couldn't get angry with her little sister when she was the one who was starting with the waterworks.

Without a word spoken, Ella reached over with a handkerchief
and—in the process of moving in—shielded Deanna from the
view of everyone around them.

Deanna nodded her thanks as she dabbed at her eyes and shook
her head, embarrassed.

"Don't be. Don't be embarrassed. You've earned the right." Ella's
words were unexpected. Deanna looked at her sister, part of her
horrified.

Ella continued: "I asked. She told me. We were talking about
old lovers, and well, once upon a time with Jeannie and Matt. Old
water under the bridge, Deanna." Perfect. Her sister's new special
someone knew that she'd stolen Matt from Jeannie forever ago.

One more reason to feel horrible. As if reading her mind, Ella said, "All it means is that I know you lost someone. You have every reason to cry and not be worried about the tears."

Jeannie was looking at Ella, horrified, worried and probably just a little scared, too. Deanna was not known for liking it when people aired her private business.

Deanna nodded. Really, what was Jeannie supposed to do if someone asked? Lie? Hardly. She offered a weak smile to her sister and Jeannie returned it gratefully.

"The thing is, I know he wasn't that good a guy," Deanna said, surprised to find herself sharing so openly with a woman she barely knew. "There were times I even maybe hated him a little. But he was mine, and I was his, and I miss him all the time."

Ella shrugged and smiled. "I miss smoking, even knowing it was never any good for me. What you're going through? I wouldn't wish that on my worst enemy."

Ella leaned over and gave her a quick hug. The contact was warm and bordered on sensual. It was also a wonderful distraction that only lasted for a few seconds.

"So. Are you still up for shopping? Or would you rather go home?" Ella looked at her and stared into her eyes and Deanna had trouble remembering the question.

Still she managed to choke out, "Shopping, I think. But no more wine."

"There's a Starbucks down the street. Cappuccino and chocolate for you."

A few minutes later, lunch paid for by Ella amid a few protests that were ignored, they headed for the coffee shop.

Ella asked, "Would you really want him back? Even at his worst?"

Deanna looked at her and nodded her head. "Isn't that horrible?"

"No. That is human. We always want what we can't have." Ella smiled and looked at the windows of the coffee shop. They were festooned with Christmas lights and promises of endless goodies past the front door.

Jeannie ran ahead to open the door for them and Ella looked at Deanna as they moved toward the open warmth and the smell of coffee. "Still, it's almost Christmas. Who can say what sort of miracles we might yet get out of this old year?"

Deanna did not find the words very comforting, though she was sure they were meant that way.

Later that night, after the boys were fed and they'd all watched the animated version of *A Christmas Carol* with Mr. Magoo and then *Rudolph the Red-Nosed Reindeer,* while decorating the plastic tree, Deanna tucked her little ones into bed and settled on the couch. More hot cocoa and a few cookies—fuck her weight. It was a crisis day. She'd actually cried in public.

Ella had given her a small package, wrapped in festive red paper and sporting a blue bow. She'd said, "A little something. Nothing fancy. I made them myself, but Merry Christmas."

She thought of the other woman and again had that mix of lust and confusion wash through her. Not even a little gay, but maybe she was, after all. Normally, if anything like that had come up, she'd have called Jeannie and discussed it. This time? Not a chance. The one time they'd locked horns over a guy, it had been Matt. He had dated Jeannie for a few weeks before they both knew it was over, and somehow along the course of those events he'd started giving Deanna the eye. Damn, but he was so cute. Sculpted marble, that man had been. With a perfect smile and those eyes . . .

That had been a dark point in the relationship between the two sisters. They'd gotten over it eventually, but still. Even today they didn't mention it very often.

Because she was in a mood, and because she now felt obligated to buy something for Ella, Deanna opened the package and looked at her gift. If they truly were handmade, then Ella had insane skills. It was a set of earrings and a simple choker necklace. All three had the same design for a centerpiece. It was a figure that could have been a man, poised with one leg bent and resting on the other. Both arms were held up in celebration, the head tilted so the face was pointed almost straight up. The form was made entirely of carefully crafted holly and mistletoe leaves and berries.

They weren't exactly festive, but they were oddly beautiful and the craftsmanship was undeniable. Looking carefully, she could see the skeleton of the man's shape made of gold wire filigree. Each piece was handmade. She looked at the sculpted foliage carefully and saw the flaws in the tiny leaves. No two were alike. Even the tiny berries were hand painted and attached.

She set the earrings down and slipped the choker in place. It nestled perfectly against her throat. Deanna smiled and considered what to get the woman in return. She was still thinking about it when she drifted into a deep sleep.

Matt, so damned handsome in his dress blues, smiled at her as he came through the front door amid a howling flurry of snow that stuck to everything and accumulated instead of melting.

Behind her, Deanna heard Matt screaming, his words slurred and spewed angrily. Something crashed to the ground and all three of her sweet boys cried out in fear.

He came closer still, and his handsome face shifted a bit, changed in subtle ways. His smile was certainly frozen in place. His gums were the wrong color, a dim gray, and as she looked at his lips she saw the broken threads, pulled apart when he moved his mouth. The same was true of his eyes. At first she thought they were fine, beautiful, but as he came closer she saw the cotton ticking that had replaced them, and the dark threads that had kept his eyelids sewn shut.

The sounds behind her grew louder. One of the twins let out a scream of pure fear. The other gasped in pain. She couldn't make herself turn around, couldn't get up to see what was happening to her boys. She was frozen, staring as Matt came closer and closer, his white teeth clenched together in his perfect smile. His forehead was wrong, held together by mortician's wax and more stuffing, but she could see where the makeup was peeling back, could look into the deep dent where his skull had been before he died.

She didn't know which was worse, the feelings she was experiencing or the fact that she knew she was having a nightmare and couldn't break free of it.

Matt placed his lips against her earlobe and hissed the words, "I've missed you so much, baby," against her flesh. His breath was frozen and the words tickled her skin in a sick parody of the passion they used to share.

Even as he was whispering in her ear, she heard him screaming at their youngest to shut his fucking mouth if he didn't want his tongue pulled out.

Deanna woke up with sweat covering her skin. Her breath came in fast, panted gasps, and her eyes rolled in her head as she tried to tell herself it was just a dream.

The choker around her neck still felt perfectly comfortable, but she could feel her pulse bouncing the odd mistletoe man with every beat of her heart.

It was late, she knew that, but she did not know the time, only that her fresh hot cocoa had grown a skin and was tepid.

Christmas Eve.

By this time tomorrow, she'd have set out all the presents.

Deanna looked at the tree, at that first ornament that reflected the year she and Matt got married, and felt a chill ripple up her spine.

Did she love him? Yes. But she was glad he was gone. The anger she'd looked past a few times had been much worse his last time back in the country. His temper around the boys had been horrible.

He'd never actually hit them, but she'd been afraid he would every time they were around him.

He'd known it, too. He'd looked at her with wounded eyes when she'd tensed up as their baby boy toddled over to see his daddy.

The winds outside slammed into the side of the house and shook the whole place.

Snow. They were expecting snow.

Deanna looked out the front door's window and saw the snow whipping frantically in the air, writhing and dancing and creeping closer to the house. She thought of Matt again and shivered. For a moment she considered whether or not she might have a fever, but then shrugged the notion away.

"Just bad dreams," she said to herself.

Would she want Matt back? In the depths of the early morning, with hours to go before the sun rose, she could not say for certain.

When she woke up, exhausted after only a few hours of actual sleep, Deanna did her best to smile as she got breakfast for the boys. They made her happy. They filled her with good cheer.

Her youngest was particularly quiet throughout breakfast and finally she looked at him and asked what was wrong. He picked at his food and stared down at the table more than he looked at anything else.

"Hunter? Are you okay, baby?"

He looked her way and nodded but he looked miserable.

"Tell me what's wrong." She squatted next to his chair until they were the same height.

Hunter leaned in close and whispered, "I can't tell you."

That earned him a small, confused frown. "Why not, baby? You know you can tell me anything."

He leaned in closer still and she had to strain to hear his whisper. "Because Daddy said he'd steal my tongue if I spoiled the surprise."

Could she have screamed just then? Hell yes. Damned skippy. It was an effort not to back away from her baby boy. Sometimes she was surprised Hunter even knew who his father was. The last time they'd seen each other he had barely been a whole year old and just starting to walk with his lumbering, jerky steps. Remembering his serious face at that age, her heart filled with love for her baby boy and broke a little that he would never really know his dad.

"It was just a bad dream, baby boy. Don't you worry about any of that, okay? Daddy isn't here and even if he was, he'd never hurt you that way." Little white lies. She wanted to make sure her boys stayed happy for all of their lives. That was the job of a parent, wasn't it? Happy, healthy children?

Relief changed the shape of her son's face. Of *course* his mother was telling the truth. What was it her dad used to say about kids? Oh, yes: *Mother is God to child.* Gods do not lie. Not when you're three.

He hugged her hard, his tiny arms moving around her neck. He said something, but she couldn't make out the words.

"I love you, Hunter. Okay? Mommy loves you so much."

She didn't cry, but it was close.

It was always close.

No day care that day. She was sort of handicapped but in the best possible way. There were treats, and in no time her baby boy had forgotten all about his nightmares.

Deanna remembered them, of course. That, too, was part of being a parent. Keeping the nightmares at bay.

Jeannie showed up just around lunchtime and borrowed Deanna's keys for exactly long enough to transfer all the presents from her own trunk to her sister's car. While she did that, Deanna made coffee and grilled cheese sandwiches with crisp bacon. Decadent, but screw that, it was the holidays. She made a promise to include dieting in her New Year's resolutions.

While they ate food and drank much-needed caffeine, Jeannie chatted about what was left to do in the day. The next afternoon they were supposed to meet at their parents' home for dinner. "Why is it called 'dinner' when we don't have it at dinnertime? Shouldn't it be called Christmas lunch?" Jeannie's brow was wrinkled with her deep thought expression again. Of course that same expression covered almost everything but her little sister's smile.

"I think it's one of those traditions that was lost over the centuries, you know? Just something that started out and now nobody understands it." She smiled at her little sister. "That, or it's a good excuse to nibble all the livelong day."

"I think it's the nibbles." Jeannie looked at Deanna's neck for a long moment. "Cool necklace."

She'd forgotten it was there and for just a moment Deanna felt a flash of guilt, though she had done nothing at all wrong. Her fingers touched the small figure of a man made from holiday greenery.

"Ella gave it to me." She shook her head and leaned in to whisper. "Which kind of makes me feel like an asshole, because I didn't get her anything."

Jeannie's smile was slightly frosty. "Oh. Well, that's very pretty."

"What did she get you?"

"Nothing. Not so far at least. But we're supposed to meet up tonight for a drink after dinner."

"Well, maybe I can get something set up for her and you can give it to her for me? I can't imagine I'll see her before Christmas." She brushed aside her sister's cold expression. She had done nothing at all to promote the gift. She'd only met the woman twice, for Christ's sake. "I think it's a pity gift, because I was bawling my eyes out yesterday. Still, I should get something for her, shouldn't I? Don't you think?"

Amazing how a few words could change a perspective. Jeannie warmed up again, having an excuse for why the woman she was interested in was giving her sister presents. That old scar about Matt was still there and apparently it was still tender. That was okay. Any grief she received over that was probably well deserved.

Jeannie reached over and ran her fingers across the tiny man on the necklace. "That's beautiful."

"It is. I can't imagine what she's getting for you. If this is an example of her work, it must be something special."

Jeannie smiled. "Well, I told her what I want. You never know."

Before Jeannie left, Deanna ran back into her bedroom, grabbed the wine and cheese sample, and wrapped it. Because she actually had a lovely wicker picnic basket, she went ahead and slipped the wrapped package inside of that and handed the entire affair to Jeannie. The tag on the basket said *To Ella and Jeannie! Merry Christmas!*

Jeannie gave her a peck on the cheek and told her she'd see her in the morning. The plan was to go together to their parents' house, the better to face their passive-aggressive mom and dad as a united front.

It was the holidays. Best to be prepared for the emotional bloodshed.

After the munchkins were all tucked away, Deanna went out to the car and pulled out all of the packages Jeannie had stowed away for her. She thanked God for her sister again, and then started placing the gifts. There were a few in there with different paper and labeled for her. Jeannie was the best.

She put her presents for Jeannie under the tree as well. They'd do an exchange before going to their parents' house.

The winds that had been snapping around the house all day

were continuing and as they shook the structure again, the lights flickered for a moment.

Perfect. Just what she wanted for the holidays. A little blackout or two, to keep things properly edgy. The lights on the tree flickered once, then again, and then faded to black. Out on the street the lights were gone, too. The world fell to complete darkness.

Thirty seconds later, as she was reaching for her phone to try the flashlight function, everything came back on.

Outside the winds were shrieking again. Deanna looked at the phone for a second and then sent Jeannie a text message: *Power outages. Yay.*

Jeannie texted back: *Nothing here. You okay?*

Yeah. Didn't bother the kiddos. So we're good.

There was a long silence and then: *See you in the morning. Will bring coffee.*

She was about to text back a snarky comment about her Mr. Coffee working just fine when someone knocked at the door.

Nine o'clock at night and someone was knocking. If it was carolers, she might have to throw a pitcher of cold water at them.

A peek through the window showed nothing, but Deanna answered anyway. There was no one at the door. She frowned. No footprints at the door, either. Obviously it had to be the wind.

That didn't stop the shivers. For a second she felt a deep and unsettling wave of déjà vu. *No,* she thought. *Last time there were boot prints. Military-style, just like Matt's.* Oh, yes, there it was, goose flesh all over her back, neck, and arms.

That last Christmas together, Matt had been at his worst. Home for three weeks and everything started out so nicely. He was happy and he was smiling, even if he was a little quiet. He held his baby son in his arms for the first time ever and he cried a few small tears, smiling the whole time.

But by the end of his stay, the anger had shown up. What was he angry about? Everything, she supposed. He was angry because he was stationed in the Middle East. He was angry because he'd missed his son's birth. He was angry because all three of his sons were too damned noisy for his liking. He was angry, he was broken, and he was okay with making sure she knew about it. He only slapped her once, that was at the end of his stay, but she couldn't really call the time they'd shared in bed lovemaking so much as angry sex, as if hammering her into submission was a required part of consummating their relationship.

Maybe it wasn't rape if she said yes, but that didn't make it any less painful or humiliating.

She thought about that and headed for her bottle of zinfandel without any conscious thought. She'd have the cocoa before she went to bed, naturally, but for now it was time for Mother's Little Helper.

Deanna set down the glass and recorked the bottle. She was heading back toward the sofa next to the Christmas tree when the lights went out again.

Naturally, she'd left the damned phone on the table in front of the sofa, right next to her cookies.

When the front door opened, she looked toward it and saw a silhouette that looked far too familiar. It was there one moment and gone the next.

Deanna's heart twisted in her chest, a sharp pain that was followed by a surprising well of cold. The last time she'd felt anything like it was when—

Matt! Oh, God, Matt!

—they'd told her that Matt would not be coming home.

Her phone rang and she stumbled toward the sound, fumbling and smashing her toes into the corner of the table in a flare of hard pain.

The screen said it was an unknown number.

"Hello?" Her voice was barely above a whisper. Her mind was already playing enough tricks on her that she'd had to suppress a scream as she answered.

Ella's voice was an unexpected but pleasant surprise and she felt relief wash through her. Someone comforting. Someone sane. "Do you know what your sister asked for? For Christmas, I mean?"

"Ella? I've got a power outage here. I think someone broke in."

"No one broke in." Ella's voice was reassuring.

"How do you know?"

"Because you can't break into your own home."

"What do you mean?"

"Jeannie got drunk last week and told me about Matt. She wished there was a way for you to have your husband back."

"Ella? What the hell are you talking about? Matt is dead."

"I know, honey. I know. But that doesn't mean you can't have him back."

Deanna shook her head. That feeling in her chest moved to her stomach and became a snowstorm deep inside of her. The air howled again and the snow swept through the open door. Enough. She couldn't let all the heat out, so Deanna moved toward the door and fumbled with the phone, trying to find the flashlight function.

Ella's voice sounded wrong as Deanna finally reached the door and closed it, remembering to lock it this time around.

Ella said, "Christmas is a time for miracles, Deanna. I've been known to help work those miracles from time to time."

The phone went back to her ear. "Seriously, Ella, what the hell have you been drinking?"

"Nothing. I'm just laying here in bed and thinking of how I can make my special girl happy. You hurt her a lot when you stole Matt away. I have to go. Jeannie's going to wake up soon." There was a pause and then, "I don't think she even wanted him, but you took him, for better or worse. I guess you'll find out once and for all which one it really was."

The phone call ended.

Deanna stared hard at the screen as if it might have answers for her.

In the preternatural silence of a house without power, where almost every hum was silenced, she heard the breathing that came from the short hallway that led to the bedrooms.

In the darkness, Matt's voice sounded completely wrong.

"Merry Christmas, honey. I came home, just like I promised I would."

The wind howled and the house shook. Aside from that, there was only silence.

SNAKE'S TAIL

SARAH LANGAN

(STORY CONSULTATION BY CLEM AND FRANCES PETTY)

This happened.

You won't remember it. You never do.

Look. It starts in that little town on the bay. Quiet, right? You might even call it sleepy. Those are fishing boats. That's the factory. Chain stores and homegrown ones, too. When it's overcast, fog rolls in like wet campfire smoke. We navigate by that lit-up church spire. Tallest structure in three counties. At midnight, its tolling bells turn into a pretty "Ave Maria."

You probably don't want to believe this, but all Gods are the same. Sure, some come from virgin births, some burst from their fathers' heads, some just *happened,* like stars or the big bang. But once you get past that superficial stuff, the stories blend. Crucifixions, crusades, female rivalries, children who overtake their parents, resurrections, and eternal life: they all satisfy the same need for meaning from nothing, for parents we can blame when we've steered our own ships off course. We make them, obviously. They exist because of us. Not just the stories; God, itself.

The thing people really hate remembering, even as they celebrate a guy nailed to wood: all Gods demand a sacrifice. They're so fucking hungry.

It always happens at the same time. People all over the world have given up and this surrender hits an event horizon. Think of a star whose gravity finally overcomes its mass, drawing inside itself and then exploding from supernova to black hole and back in time again, to a star. The future is a funnel that reverses, pulling its children in first, spitting them out in reverse. You make this happen. Every one of you.

Think I don't know you, specifically? I do.

It's Christmas Eve. The night's thick as velvet punched with holes for stars. Agnostics, Chaotic Naturalists, Jews, Islamics, Catholics—it doesn't matter, they acknowledge the day. Presents are left under trees and in stockings. Some wrapped with ribbons, some shoved naked with no care at all. A sorry few have no presents or trees at all. It turns midnight. "Ave Maria" plays. Then, it begins. The star collapses.

It happens. To the good, to the bad, to the ignorant, to the wise.

This time, a mom named Laurel Frances notices first. She's checking on her youngest, whose asthma hasn't lately resolved with simple inhalers. Laurel peers into her daughter Izzy's night-light-illuminated bedroom. "Ave Maria" finishes its last chime. The child lay with her nose and chin just poking out from a Celestia Pony comforter purchased at Target, her breath rattling like a water-clogged leaf blower. Laurel gazes with an aching heart, for this sickly child is her joy. The impossible one, who came in older age. Yes, the clock chimes, and by the time it stops resonating, the child is gone.

Disappeared from her bed.

Laurel searches under the sheets. In the closet. Under the bed.

She opens the window and gapes into the dark, calling the girl's name until her husband arrives, disheveled from sleep and too many glasses of the neighbor's merlot.

What do you do when such a thing happens? Do you run from your house? Go screaming into the street? Do you search under nooks and behind locks, like the item that is missing is a precious nugget of platinum?

Laurel Frances flips the mattress. Tears apart the room. "Where's the baby?" her still-drunk husband shouts, and how can she explain? He's only recently confessed to his affair, his plans to move out and sue for custody because he believes Laurel's sadness has made her *unfit*. Will he not imagine that in her desperation, she's been the one to hurt their child? What if that's exactly what she did, and she only imagined the child's disappearance because she's gone mad? Isn't that the only logical explanation? She climbs out the child's window and scales down while her shocked husband gapes. Then she runs screaming down Poplar Street until a squad car picks her up with bloody feet.

"Izzy! Izzy, where are you, baby?" she cries. She does not stop crying this entreaty. It repeats inside her like a car alarm for the rest of her shortened life.

Little Izzy Frances isn't alone. Three other children go missing at the stroke of midnight, Christmas morning. Police are called. They come to homes. Detective Patrick Clement wonders at first if it's a kids' prank. These post–high school grads without jobs or college get weirder and more reckless every year. They tear down signs and huff paint because they can't figure out how to make good meth. Maybe they've turned to kidnapping. So he listens closely to Laurel Frances's story, along with the others'. "You're sure they disappeared? Right in front of your eyes?"

All nod.

Detective Clement does what he always does. Every time, I fool myself into imagining he remembers this from before: this is the eureka moment. "What would make children disappear into thin air?" he whispers. Then he returns to the mundane. The idea he's got is too crazy. He's got to pull anchor and let it go.

He orders a roadblock to keep strangers from escaping with kidnapped children. He calls reinforcements from other towns and these quickly arrive. The clock chimes one a.m. By now the town holds a peculiar charge. You can stick out your tongue and feel the electricity. Some part of their DNA remembers. Knows the unknown. People wake to sirens and the frantic shouting of children's names followed by commands like *Answer me!* And *Where are you?* And most frequently, *Please come home.*

They do what they've always done when they have the feeling of unease. They check on their tribe. Oliver Dodd is watching his blond son. He lay over his covers, the radiant heat turned too high. Long limbed and impossibly agile. Varsity, and just a sophomore, at that. A scholarship, surely. Then a good job in a big city far from here. The boy will have all the things Oliver does not, and this will validate him in ways his own life has come up short.

The chime's echo fades. The boy disappears. No smoke. No dispersion of air. Just, gone.

This goes on.

The clock strikes two. More missing.

At three, eighteen more children go missing and the entire town is awake. Those directly affected, and even some who are not, walk over dark roads in slippers and robes. Make frantic calls. Punch trees. Tear clothing. Pray to God. Pray to Satan. Pull their heirlooms from hidden safes and offer them to police as bribes. Wonder if this is their fault. If it is worth looking, when something inside them tells them that the loss of their children is inevitable.

The FBI arrives. Helicopter searchlights shine through windows and overhead.

At four, 116 more children disappear. There are too many witnesses to discount. This is happening. The most-searched term in North America: "The Rapture."

By five in the morning, most children have been corralled by their parents into single rooms, where they're held like tethered balloons filled with helium. A few are taken to boats on the bay. Some are taken around police barriers and through still-dark and snowy woods. Fewer still are ushered to basements, lambs' blood smeared on doors, and held tightest of all.

Just one, smothered.

"You should have called me!" people scold the smothered child's father. As if, in that hysteria, they'd have answered his calls. As if they had not known he was the nervous sort, whom they should have checked upon.

Abnegation. Abnegation. Abnegation.

The child's name was Tobin. He had patched black skin. I remember this, because you refuse. You. Yes, you. I'm looking straight through this page. I see you.

At six, Sherman Duffy is making early breakfast. The whole family sits on bar stools at their marble-island kitchen, mom worrying over teenaged Natalie, nanny Esmerelda holding both baby twins. Sherman knows harm will come knocking. But he doesn't want to think about it because something in the pit of him, a thought worn so deep from so many repetitions that it becomes a hole, knows the outcome. He cracks eggs inside toast with holes in their middles. Smiling, smiling, he pours mimosas for all, including sixtysomething Esmerelda, whose family still lives in Ecuador. For Sherman is a generous man.

The sound in the Duffy kitchen is hushed; they've heard the sirens and the stories. They know what has befallen so many friends. Soft, dutiful chatter about cinnamon or sugar, whether they ought to still go walking today, given the police.

The children go missing. The twins, the teen daughter. All gone.

Sherman has prepared himself so deeply that he's already mourned their loss. He plates his toast and eggs, begins to eat while his nanny faints and his wife draws a knife across her throat.

At seven chimes, the National Guard arrive. Sometimes it's sooner, other times they don't come at all. This time, it's at seven chimes. Cars and trucks and yes, tanks, clog the streets.

Fewer children go missing. Only nine.

A little before eight in the morning, Detective Clement learns that some parents have planned a mass suicide. They intend to feed their children rat poison. So Clement herds every man, woman, and child before the church's clock tower. Some are forced, weeping and raging. Most are happy for the company. Fellow witnesses.

"Keep calm!" Clement orders through his megaphone. All the while, he's looking at me as if he recognizes what I am. By now, he should. We've played our same roles so many times that there is no longer a number, just a circle—a snake biting its own tail.

"Your children will be found!" he cries. "We have to work together!"

The clock chimes. Two hundred thirty-six children evaporate from the crowd. First they are there. Then, they are not. It's a funny thing, witnessing something like that. Those people who have faith, lose it. Those people who have none, find it.

We're held in the town square. Surrounded by police. It's determined that all of the missing are under thirteen years old. It doesn't matter whether they're from the town or just visiting for the holiday. The children within the borders, within the woods, are gone. All that are left are 128. Lucky 128. The clock strikes nine.

None go missing.

A buoyant joy fills them. Spared! They've been spared! It's over! Parents embrace. The local bakery hands out warm biscuits and bagels. Those who've lost begin to feel it more keenly. Those who haven't begin to trust they might not. Bloody-footed Laurel Frances breaks into spontaneous song: "Ave Maria."

> *The murky cavern's air so heavy*
> *Shall breathe of balm if thou hast smiled*
> *Oh maiden, hear a maiden pleadin'*
> *Oh mother, hear a suppliant child*

The rest of the people join. The square ignites with elegiac music—a song originally written about the Lady of the Lake, hiding in a Goblin's cave, and is now a prayer to the Virgin. They come together, these myths of fantasy and these people singing. For a moment I think they might remember that this is not new. That time is going in reverse.

The clock strikes ten.

No more go missing. The tenor changes. Now the parents of survivors become smug in their hidden grins, in their pats on backs, and *I'm so sorry*s. Now, they believe that others have done something wrong and they have not.

The clock strikes eleven.

None go missing.

We stay in the square. More biscuits and now coffee, too. The bereaved begin to blame themselves. What have they done to incur God's wrath? And on Christmas! The clock strikes noon. "Ave Maria" plays. The rest disappear. All 127 of them. Every child under thirteen.

All, except me.

It's in the news. It doesn't affect you. You see it in a Facebook stream and wonder if the story's real. Later, you hear from some vicarious account that a friend's cousin's kids went missing in that old waterfront town. But it's as unreal (or as real) to you as Russian spies and American occupation by foreign governments and starving refugees and oil wars and it bothers you until more bizarre news happens that you also aren't sure whether to believe or what, if anything, can be done.

You move on.

Consider Prometheus. For man, he steals fire. With fire, man might transcend his maker. As punishment for man's ambition, Zeus sends Pandora's Box full of plague and strife. He ties Prometheus to a rock, eats his regrown liver every day for eternity. Consider, overwhelmed by his own momentousness, man dreamed God. Why then, does he do this to himself?

Abnegation.

As the only child to remain in my town, I'm interviewed by lots of news outlets, then trapped inside a hospital where they lock the doors behind them when they leave. They tell me they're afraid I'll be stolen, too. But this isn't true. They blame me.

It's my fault, obviously. Yours, too. And even as I tell you this, I know you'll forget. It's your nature. You can't stand still, and so you take the easiest path you can find, having no idea it's a circle.

A new thing happens. I love it when new things happen. The crackpots decide our town is filled with Satanists. They figure the parents struck a deal, sacrificing their own kids. So vigilantes break into the church steeple and smash the bell, hoping to set the children's captured spirits free.

We never hear "Ave Maria" again.

Weeks and then months pass. They let me out of the hospital. The town becomes a graffitied graveyard of flowers and wreaths and empty boxes buried under salty ground. I'm asked to speak at some of the memorials and I do so. I talk about Lucy, whom I earned a karate purple belt with, and I talk about Dan, who licked his ice-cream sandwiches instead of biting them. And I talk about Danica, who in second grade used to spit on me when the teacher wasn't looking. I don't mention these things, or the fact that I've known the infinite incarnations of these people, and with each occasion, have grown to love them more deeply. Their flaws and efforts and failure and mess. I do not explain that my heart is broken. I only say they'll be missed.

My parents believe it is their piousness that saved me. They don't know that I'm not their child, but a changeling swapped out at birth by hungry Gods. For school, I'm bussed to the next town over. The kids keep their distance, as it's rumored I'm dangerous—a Typhoid Mary of evaporated children.

On the first anniversary of our town's missing children, I'm asked to give a speech, and this is what I say on Christmas Eve, in front of our church:

Dear friends,

What? Oh, yeah. I can speak up. Sorry [nervous laugh]. It's hard. Which I guess is stupid to say. I mean, it's hard for all of us. We keep having to go through this. It's like that first time you pick a bathroom stall. You always go to the same one after that. It doesn't occur to you to do something different.

Sorry. Okay. Is this loud enough? Okay. Don't worry. You're happy you didn't hear what I just said. You never remember, anyway.

Well, I guess I should say something. I keep feeling like it's a test, you know? Like old biblical times. You need to rise up and become better than what's happening to you. That's what all those stories are always about, you know? They're not about sacrifice or blood. They're about evolving. We used to be apes. But we haven't changed since then. It's been too long. I'm sorry. That's stupid. You don't want to hear that. I know what I should say. What? Okay. Is this loud enough? . . . [laugh]. Anyway. I want to say I'm sorry. I know you think I should be with them. So, sorry. Sorry I'm not dead.

I get booed off the steps. Somebody shoots a BB gun. Hits me in the cheek.

Detective Clement helps me into a squad car. Takes me to his house, where there are empty bottles everywhere. Gin man. Maps, too, marking the names of every child and where and when they went missing.

I'm supposed to be nine years old. They all know this can't possibly be true. But they pretend, because it's not polite to accuse a child of the uncanny. Pretending makes them forget. "Are your parents hurting you?" he asks as he bandages my cheek.

Always, it's him. Different body, different gender, different color, but always the same soul. He asks because he's trying to understand why I seem like such an alien. I take his chin in my fingers. "I like the feeling of skin," I answer. "I like being alive. I like breath and I like heat and I like cold."

He stares, breath stopped and literally frozen. Abnegation. Abnegation. Abnegation.

"They don't hurt me," I say.

He nods and takes me home.

That night I sneak out to the craggy rocks. I scatter salt throughout the inlet. Nineteen bags of it.

The next morning, we hear the news that it has happened again, in Des Moines, Iowa. These kids didn't go missing. They just never woke up. Still bodies: warm, breathing, unmoving. Thirty-four thousand and seven sleeping beauties.

Only one child remains in Des Moines. A changeling, like me.

I'm asked to help them sort their grieving. This is the speech I make:

Dear Iowans,

They told me it's Iowan. I hope that's right. A terrible thing has happened. But not just to you. To everyone. I hope you solve it before the world falls apart and you all die so very horribly and painfully and slowly. Oh, okay. Yeah. Can someone help me?

A fight breaks out. Somebody shoots somebody else. So they put me in a car and send me back east. I stop making speeches.

And you know? Pretty quickly, people who weren't directly affected forget. You might wonder how that happens. But then you might open a history book from just this cycle alone. You might consider all the people who've died from murder and the wars nobody wanted to fight and the global warming nobody admitted was happening. And it's not just like, hey, generation to generation, people forget what their parents learned. It's the same people, forgetting, over and over again. Every five minutes.

Abnegation. Abnegation. Abnegation.

So anyway, at my new school I'm attacked by a girl with red hair. The Brillo-y kind, as if she's descended directly from Norsemen. She's my locker neighbor and she's always seemed normal. Even smiles once in a while. So, who knows? Anyway, one day her whole face breaks into crazy rage, like the inside of her is kindling lit on fire and for a moment, she *knows*. She knows everything. And I fucking love her because it's a total surprise.

But then she makes it small. Gives it logic. Tears it into pieces and pushes all the blame on me. Abnegation. "You brought the wrath of Jesus!" she screams. Then she slams my face into the water fountain and breaks my jaw.

I eat through a straw for nine months and in the end give birth to a new face. Not my first. The teasing is so bad I drop out. It's not like they can kill me. You could drop an anvil on my head like a Road Runner cartoon. You've done it, actually. You, I mean. YOU.

I stay in that town with my arrogant parents, and like so many humans around me, wish I'd been switched into someone else's crib. These people I'm trapped at dinner with are ridiculous. We still attend the same church with the broken bell every Sunday. By then, people have stopped looking at the oddity. The survivor. They look away.

Abnegation. Abnegation. Abnegation.

Did I mention? This is traditionally the time people stop having babies and this iteration is no different. People stop having babies. The ones in their bellies stop growing. They fossilize and harden into stone. The rest just don't quicken. The streams blame this on bad diets and original sin. Lesser theories involve mercury levels in seawater and the sea monster Leviathan. Nobody's sure when it started. Nobody's sure it's true. Even the women with eight-month-old rocks in their wombs deny it is happening.

Can you guess what I'm about to say? Abnegation.

The next year on Christmas Eve I sneak out again and scatter salt. One of them has risen, tiny bubbles bleeding up. Izzy. The asthma must have made her good at breathing through water. I climb in, swishing through rocks and a watery field of our town's slumbering children. Izzy struggles to surface, her hair swaying like a mermaid's. It's so dark that the water seems bright. I want to ask her why she's struggling. Why she keeps trying when it always ends the same. So I do it. Even though I've never done it before. I pull her up and ask her.

But she's three years old. She doesn't understand. I kiss her before I let her slide back into the wet bed. This is new, too. Then I empty a whole bag of salt over her to keep her from rising back up. We lock eyes as she sinks to rest with the others.

News is already arriving by the time I get back before dawn that Christmas. Eighteen towns affected, all with just one survivor: the changelings. Disappearing children; sleeping children; catatonic children. More than a million in all.

They interview the survivors, but soon tire of these. They can't remember anything we tell them. Next they talk to the parents and the scientists and most especially the preachers shouting fire and brimstone. The streams and the feeds and the checkout counter speakers shriek words of fear and shame and the people worry themselves sick until they get tired of worrying and forget.

Can you forget something like this? Forget the threat looming over you? Forget your own children? Yes, of course you can. It's what humans do, and every time they do it, their Gods grow just a little hungrier.

The fourth year. I bring salt to my sea. More of my town's children have risen. Their skin has softened to the consistency of tissues and the air bubbles stay small, dreamers flitting through dreams. I salt. They fall back down.

Clement stops me on my way back. He's not a detective anymore. Lives like a hermit. It's not new, seeing him. He follows me everywhere. "That's where the bodies went?" he asks as he points at the sea, and I have to admit, the hairs along the back of my neck stand right up. He only figures this out 2 percent of the time.

"Yeah," I say. "They get restless."

"Why do you keep them here?"

"I tend them. For our cycle." Then I point at the horizon, which has become a gravity rainbow. Fragmented colors of unequal distribution, pulling us into each other.

He doesn't understand any of this, but he hears it. He doesn't forget it. This is progress. I think next time, he'll remember more. I always think this. But very incrementally, it is true. He's so drunk the realization fades. He bends over and vomits. Steaming stuff on a cold winter's night.

I finish going home. It's Christmas Day.

By noon, all the children in the world are gone. They are lost to sleeping sickness, disappeared under oceans and streams and inside mountains. You'd think the adults who remain would be shocked. But like cattle they've warmed themselves with indifference.

Abnegation. Abnegation. Abnegation.

The Gods are so hungry they rise up.

They are spiders and krakens and sloths of many mouths. Martyred women and soldiers and warriors. Every nightmare you can think, all dreamed by their makers. It takes six days and seven nights to slaughter every last adult. They catch those on ships. They catch those in houses. They take those in stores and in woods and under cave walls.

They take my human parents while I watch. Split them in two, then feed on their insides, snouts rooting like pigs for truffles.

At last, they surround me and all the other changelings. Like every time before this, I spread my arms wide. They make it slow. They make it hurt. They peel off my fingernails. They chew up my toes. They strip away my skin in seams: arms, legs, cheeks, back. They take turns feeding off my muscles. They peel back my bones and feed on my organs and heart.

The Gods, the humans, and the spirit, united in a perfect trinity. Sated, we return as one to the core of the earth to rest another two hundred thousand years.

I tell you this every time, and you never remember. I am your abnegation. Your mess. Your frailty. Your forgotten memory that haunts you. It is your nature to deny. To refuse. To blame. To create fathers for yourself that do not exist except in your imaginations. You do not understand that it is you humans, in your apprehension and your magic, that are the only God.

The rainbow inverts. The black hole pulls through to the other side.

At last, the children wake from hidden lairs and hospital beds. This sleep has washed them ignorant. They do not remember words or their parents or their names. They will start over. Begin again. And again. And again. And again. Cattle for their own creations.

❦

THE SECOND FLOOR OF THE CHRISTMAS HOTEL

JOE R. LANSDALE

haven't mentioned this to anyone because I know how it might sound, having to do with what some might call a ghost. I am not a religious man, but I think there may well be some things we don't understand beyond this life, though I doubt they have anything to do with the common concepts of heaven and hell.

Some of us may die and merely cease to be, and some of us may remain hung between life and death, caught in a kind of limbo, captured there by intense emotions and events, retaining the dregs of life, but not life as we would want it.

And sometimes those things reach out.

This happened ten years ago, when I was seventy. Robert was the same age. He wrote me a letter suggesting we meet for Christmas Eve dinner, which was coming up within the week. It sounded like a glorious idea. There were no wives or children in my life. I had ended up that way by choice, and early on it seemed a great idea to be a playboy with no plans for children, but if I could go back in time I would alter that. It gets lonely without kin.

I had not seen Robert in some time, and we were no longer the friends we had been, and if I am being completely honest, we were probably never great friends, just friendly, so I was surprised by his invitation.

I wrote him and agreed, and met him on the decided day at a downtown hotel. It was an old hotel, and Robert's family owned it. They had been hotel owners all his life. They had a chain of them, many of them boutique or old classic hotels. They had become quite well-off in the business, and when they retired, Robert took over. He had to travel a lot, examining the hotels to make sure everything was functioning properly.

We sat in the back of the hotel restaurant and dined quietly amid canned Christmas music, multicolored lights, and decorations. The place was nearly empty, people having gone off to parties or to be with their families.

We talked about this and that, recalling things that had happened to us, as well as things that involved old school chums, as they used to say.

After dinner and dessert, we lingered over coffee, and it became obvious that we really had little in common but our school and business experiences.

Just as I felt I had come up with an exit line, Robert said, "Do you remember that old hotel my family owned where we spent Christmas Eve and Christmas so many years ago?"

"It was an unusual place, out in the woods, down by the river. Not very large."

"That's the one. At one point it had been the location for a river stop, back when steamboats worked the water, and later on the hotel was built there. I forget when my family bought it. Very boutique. Only catered to a handful of guests, reservations only. Not too many rooms. It was full for several years, and then finally we closed it down when people quit making reservations. The highway was replaced by an interstate farther north, so there was no longer traffic coming near it, and it kind of faded. In its time we certainly had fine Christmas parties there. My parents really knew how to throw one."

They did indeed. I had only been invited once. I partied in the downstairs lobby with Robert and guests at the hotel, and some like myself who had been invited for the party, but not the Christmas Day festivities. The place was well decked out then, lots of lights and green boughs and colorful decorations. A Christmas tree that stood at the edge of the reservation desk rose up so high anyone on the second floor could have leaned over the railing and touched the glowing, silver star at the great tree's tip.

I remembered that party primarily because I met a pretty girl there, and we shared a Christmas kiss at the edge of the stairs. It was nothing more than a party kiss under mistletoe, but even to this day I remembered it. She was such a beautiful and unique-looking woman, the memory of the event was cut into my brain.

"You know," I said, "I haven't thought about that hotel in years. Do you still own it?"

"I do, but it won't be around for much longer. I'm having it torn down, and then I'll look for someone to purchase the land. Hotel has gone to seed. I could repair it, but I think the time for that place has come to an end. My family had Christmas there for years, and me and my younger sister used to call it the Christmas hotel. I have a lot of fine memories, but toward the end, some not so good."

"How say?" I said.

Robert paused, sipped his coffee, and let the question ferment for a bit. Finally, he placed his cup carefully on the saucer. "I suppose I actually invited you here to tell you the story, and perhaps gain your support and assistance, because you were there one year, and you met what I believe to be the catalyst of this story."

In that moment I was no longer ready to leave. I was intrigued.

"It was the next Christmas, the one after the party you attended, that something peculiar was discovered about room twelve on the second floor, the top floor of the hotel. I don't know if you ever went upstairs or not."

"I didn't," I said. "I was only in the lobby, downstairs, for the party. I met a young woman there."

"Amelia," Robert said.

"Yes. You remember her, too?"

"I certainly remember her, and every male there most likely remembered her, for she was indeed a beauty. Wore those big, gold hoop earrings, a red blouse, a short blue jean dress. You know, I believe she was barefoot."

"Hair tumbling down like an ebony shower, skin like coffee and cream," I said. "Read that somewhere in a book, and liked it."

"Accurate description of her, no matter who said it or when. Anyway, she came back the next year as well, dressed the same way, and that's when the peculiarities began."

"How so?"

"Other than her first name, no one knew who she was or how she was invited, or if she was invited, but she showed up those two years in a row, and it's presumed she drowned in the river behind the hotel."

Hearing that news, it was as if that magical kiss beneath a sprig of mistletoe had been taken from me. In my mind Amelia was still out there, as she had been that night, young and beautiful. The idea that she might have aged wasn't something I could wrap my head around, and the idea that she drowned long years ago behind the hotel was impossible to grasp. I recalled how she moved, and how the men there that night watched her, unable not to, and I remembered one young man making a crass remark as she walked by. That had made me angry. He treated her like she was a bus he meant to catch and had missed.

Other than that, I couldn't recall much about the party. I didn't even remember seeing Amelia again that night. But that kiss stayed with me.

"I hadn't heard about her drowning," I said.

"It was in the news for a few days," Robert said, "but it was merely a suspicion. Truth is, no one knows exactly what happened to her, and I can't even say for certain she has anything to do with the story I want to tell you, so you have to keep that in mind."

I poured myself another cup of coffee and decided to nibble on a piece of bread my diet didn't need.

"Tell me about it," I said.

Robert stared at his cold cup of coffee, as if he might fish his memories from it, finally lifted his head, and began.

My sister and I always called it the Christmas hotel, because of the parties there. These days it's in ruin. I have been out there most every year, even after its closing. I always unlock the door with a head full of fond memories, but once inside they fade.

First word of strangeness in the room, discomfort on the second floor, came many years back, the Christmas after Amelia's disappearance. The hotel was still in business then, of course. A young married couple rented number twelve and left in the middle of the night. I don't know what their exact complaint was, but I was told they found the room "unsavory," and couldn't sleep for things going on up there.

The room was fine the rest of the year, no complaints, but come Christmas Eve, no one could make it through a night. This seemed ridiculous to me, and I thought it best to discover what was causing the problem, so I set about spending Christmas Eve in the room.

Keep in mind this was some years ago, and I was young and strong and willful. I felt that though others had vacated the room, I would not and that I would deduce the problem and see that whatever was causing the disturbance was repaired. A board nailed down, a creaky wind-rattled window fastened shut, what have you. Simply put, I felt the problem with the room was a natural one, perhaps compounded by the guests having indulged in too much Christmas food and liquid cheer during the annual parties.

Before I tell you about that night, perhaps I should preface a bit, and this is where you can make up your own mind about how much Amelia has to do with this, if anything at all.

On the night she disappeared and was assumed drowned, she was seen with two young men on the stairs, laughing, engaging them the way she engaged every male there, and then there were no more memories of her.

At some point in the night she disappeared and was not seen again, though her clothes were found on the river's edge, and that led to the belief she drowned, perhaps having gone skinny-dipping, encouraged to do so by excess alcohol.

The police were called out the next day, but Amelia was not found. As no one actually knew her, or even knew her last name, there was nothing that could be done. The two young men said to have been with her on the stairs were investigated, but neither admitted to going upstairs with Amelia and there was no real proof they had, other than a young woman who said she saw them together on the stairs, and knew them, but admitted the next day she was terribly drunk and was one drink shy of being able to see pink elephants carrying umbrellas. So she was a poor witness at best.

The room was looked over, but there was nothing amiss. No one reported to the police, or the hotel, about a missing loved one, so that was it. There was nowhere to go with it. The very next year, Christmastime, the strange events in room twelve began, the ones that so frightened that young married couple, and they continued every year thereafter.

On the Christmas Eve I chose to check it out, I left the party early, about eleven p.m., and with my overnight bag in tow, slipped up to room number twelve. I showered and dressed in my pajamas, then set about enjoying a room service delivery of hot chocolate and a few Christmas cookies.

The lady who delivered the snack had worked with us for some years, and she informed me that, no matter what, she would not stay in that room past the stroke of midnight. She had been at the hotel too long, heard the stories from departing guests, and was certain there was something dreadfully wrong. She was in and out like a postman.

As I ate, the clock ticked its way toward midnight. The time was easy to see, because the room had one of those old tall clocks from another era. It wasn't a clock that banged the hour, but merely a large-faced clock that could be seen even with the light out if the moon was bright and the curtains were pulled back, and that night it was so bright it made the windows glow like lighted frames.

When I finished eating, the clock hit midnight; I distinctly remember that. I got up and went to the window and looked out. The land behind the hotel, and the river beyond, were bathed in silver, and the water seemed especially bright, like a long, wide ribbon.

It was then that I noticed a curious thing, and to this day I have no idea who was responsible for it, or when it was done, but the window was nailed to the frame in several spots, the nails having been driven in awkwardly but firmly. I know because I tried to lift the window, and it wouldn't budge. I remember thinking the next day I would have the nails removed, and the window frame replaced.

I pulled the thick, dark curtains over the windows, blocking out the moon, slipped off my house shoes, turned off the lamp by the bed, and climbed under the covers. I had already decided that for all practical purposes my ghost hunt was over.

I fell immediately to sleep, but not long after I awoke, chilled. It was not cold outside, or hadn't been when I went to bed. You know how it is in our part of the country, but in that moment of awakening, it was as if I had laid down in a snowbank.

I turned on the lamp by the bed, but it had ceased to work. I got out of bed and felt my way to the light switch by the door, but the results were the same. Nothing. The electricity seemed to have gone off, and my first thought was that an unexpected storm had come through and caused the loss of power.

After bumping my shins a few times against furniture, I located my overnight bag, pawed my way into it, and found the penlight I had there. I used it to make my way to the closet where the extra blanket was kept, something to bundle me against the cold.

It was one of those closets that has a sliding door, and when I slid it back, I lifted the penlight. The beam caught something on the top shelf, and it seemed to me in that instant that it was a set of eyes. I jumped back, stumbled against a chair. When I took another look, there was nothing on the shelf other than the blanket I had been looking for.

In that moment I decided no matter how hardheaded I thought myself, the story of something being wrong with the room had gotten to me a bit. I took a deep breath, pulled down the blanket, and made my way back to bed.

I turned off the penlight, placed it on the nightstand, and tried to go back to sleep with the extra blanket over me. This time falling asleep was harder to do. I thought about those eyes I had seen, or believed I had seen. I couldn't get it out of my mind. I kept picking the penlight off the nightstand, turning it on, and poking it in the direction of the open closet.

Could a raccoon or possum have found its way into the closet? Perhaps there was an opening to the attic, and a creature had somehow come in that way. That idea got me on my feet again, and sure enough, when I poked the light back into the closet, I could see there was indeed a trapdoor in the ceiling, but it was closed.

Dissatisfied, I went back to bed.

I finally did go back to sleep, but a little later on I was awakened once more by intense cold, and now there was a smell like dead fish and wet weeds. The air in the room seemed heavy. I literally felt the hair on the back of my neck and arms stand up, and my nostrils quivered against the stench.

Though the curtains were pulled tight, they were abruptly pushed back by something unseen. The moonlight dropped in, filling the room, but there was nothing comfortable about the lack of darkness. Instead, the feeling of unease increased tenfold. I was paralyzed with fear. I lifted my penlight again and poked it at what seemed to me to be the source of the discomfort, the open closet.

From the top shelf of the closet something dropped and smacked against the floor, and then that something began to move toward the bed where I lay.

I couldn't tell what it was, and even with my penlight on it, there was a dimness about it. It came toward me, slowly, squirming and crawling. Its general shape was humanlike, but the face was like a white grub with mashed human features. Bony arms and legs poked out from the bundle, and long fingers scratched across the floor, pulling it forward. Where it crawled it left behind a slime trail, and it made a wet, squishing sound as it came.

I could not move a muscle. It was as if anvils lay across my body, pressing me down. Excruciating moments passed as it neared the bed, and finally it arrived. A fat, wet hand lifted up and clutched at the edge of my blanket. I could see right through the thing, could see the wall and closet beyond. It tilted its head and examined me, as if trying to make out my face, and then, as if disappointed, dropped to the floor at the edge of the bed.

It stood. It was so surprising I think I screamed aloud. I feared that would attract it to me, and I stuck my hand in my mouth and bit down to keep from crying out again.

But it didn't so much as turn in my direction. It trudged toward the window on its sticklike legs. The window lifted without its touch, and it fell through the open gap. Wind blew the curtains, the moonlight dimmed, then brightened, and the bubble of fear that enveloped the room evaporated. I felt the weight lifted off me.

I forced myself out of bed. I didn't use my penlight. The room was bright enough with moon glow and I could see clearly. The floor was spotted with puddles of water, and I could feel the dampness against my feet. I leaned out of the open window, looked down.

The bony thing lay there in a heap. As I watched, it stood and lurched toward the river, its swollen head nodding first to one side, then the other.

Closer it came to the water the less visible it was. Moonlight poked through it, and by the time it reached the bank it was no longer perceptible, at least to the human eye. Yet, I could clearly see footprints being made in the sand by the shoreline, and then the water splashed, as if something heavy had been dropped into it, and finally the room went dark.

And here is an even more incredible part to my story. The curtains were drawn again, without my aid or that of anyone or anything that I could determine. They just snapped closed. The chill left the air, and I swear on everything I love and believe in, when I peeled the curtains back to try and look out again, the window was down and the nails were still driven into the wood; there was no sign that they had fallen out. The puddles on the floor were gone as well.

I stood in the dark for a long time. When I walked back to the bed, I felt as if I had been in a hypnotic state. All the dread I had experienced was gone. A strange calm had settled on me, a kind of drained relaxation that I remembered from my youth after a hard hike or a strong run.

I climbed back in bed, crawled under the covers, and slept soundly until I could feel the warmth of the morning sun cutting through the dark curtains. It was just a room now, and the events of the night before seemed dreamlike, and I considered that was exactly what it had been, or at least I tried to. But I knew better. It had been there, and now the Christmas haunting had passed.

I dressed and went down to the river to look for the footprints I had clearly seen on its bank in the moonlight, but there was nothing there.

As I said, I don't know if any of this actually has to do with Amelia, but she certainly came to mind. Had she been in that room? How did she end up in the river? The thought wouldn't leave me. I took it upon myself to have the river dragged, and brought in divers to search for the remains of a body, or anything that might have belonged to her, though whatever might be left of her would now be fragmentary, and had most likely long been washed out to sea years ago. It was a long shot, but I took it.

Nothing was found.

I hired a private investigator to find the young woman who had seen the men on the stairs with Amelia, and I set him to look for Amelia herself, to find out if she was still alive.

As for Amelia, when it was all said and done, nothing new was learned about her. However, the investigator did find the drunk woman who had been at that party so many years ago, found her easily. She lived nearby, and it turned out she had been a school-mate of my sister. I either had not known that, or had forgotten it. She said she really couldn't remember much about the event anymore, but at the time felt she had seen the three of them going up the stairs. And she provided the names of the young men, which had been forgotten after the initial investigation. She reminded my investigator that she had been drunk beyond reason.

Once we had the names of those men, they were easy to find. One, Jim Warren, was dead, had drowned in his bathtub. He lived far away from here, another state. His death was said to be suicide. He left a note. All it said was "Sorry."

His family said he had been depressed for a long time, had been having financial problems, and was bothered by bad dreams and a pill addiction. Oddly, he wrapped himself in a blanket, covered his face and most of his body with it, and climbed into a tub full of water and forced himself under. It must have taken great determination to drown himself. It seems to me a horrible way to go.

The other gentleman was found effortlessly as well. His name is Wilbert Kastengate, Jr. He is successful and lives in the city. His parents knew my parents, it turned out, and that's why he was present that night. Once he was found, he agreed to talk to me. We met in a restaurant at, as you might have suspected, one of my hotels.

He was a lean man in an expensive blue suit with a head full of thick gray hair. He had held up well, handsome for his age. But when we began to talk about the night of Amelia's disappearance, I saw him pale, and it seemed to me that the years he had fought off for so long came down on him like a whirlwind. He sagged in his chair like a large beanbag.

I went right at him, but he denied going upstairs with Amelia, said he had no idea who Jim Warren was. Not much was gained from the conversation, as far as satisfying my curiosity goes, but

I convinced him to join me later tonight at the Christmas hotel. That was a month ago when he agreed. Meaning, he may or may not show.

Come with me to the Christmas hotel. It is only an hour from here. I want you to see what is there, know that I'm telling the truth, and again, it would be nice to have a friend along as comfort. I know that we haven't been in contact that much, but you and I are about all that is left from those parties years ago, at least as far as people I know go. So, come with me.

When Robert finished his story, he leaned back and glanced at his watch. That was an obvious indicator that I should decide on my course of action for the night.

I could have declined, but the truth was Robert and his story had grabbed me. I had never believed in ghosts, but I had always been amused and somewhat titillated by the idea of them. And, of course, there was my connection with that night, my small but significant memories of Amelia. I was a bit bothered by the fact that he had come to me because he didn't know who else to come to. It was clear he didn't want to go to the hotel by himself.

Still, it was intriguing, and another incentive was to not spend the rest of Christmas Eve and all of Christmas Day alone. Especially after memories of Amelia had been reignited. Her sweet face, the gold hoop earrings, the short dress, that kiss beneath the mistletoe, haunted me.

Robert drove us. It was a chill night, coat weather, the sky was clear and the moon was bright.

"You think Kastengate will actually show?"

"I got the impression he wanted to come, but it may have less to do with my ghost story and more to do with me trying to link him to Amelia's disappearance. Of course, that doesn't mean he's guilty. However, just so you know, I have a gun in my coat pocket. Protection in case Kastengate thinks it might be a good idea to rid himself of suspicion. I know that sounds dramatic, but, it could be like that, I guess."

After that revelation, I was feeling less excited about the prospect of company for the night, and it even occurred to me that I may have been set up. What if Robert thought I was the one responsible for Amelia's death, and this was all a plan to get me alone at the Christmas hotel and finish me off? What if he were responsible, and for some reason thought I might know something, an idea that had festered over the years, and now he had decided it was best I was taken care of?

This was on my mind as we arrived at the hotel, an hour or so before midnight. There wasn't any electricity, but Robert had brought a battery lantern, as well as a flashlight for me and him.

He let us in and we trudged upstairs, Robert guiding, waving his flashlight before us. When we reached number twelve, he paused, sighed, and opened the door.

The door pushed aside spider- and cobwebs, and in the beam of the flashlight dust motes spun about as if in a cyclotron. Robert moved the light about the room, flashed it on the closed closet door, then the bed, which upon closer observation appeared to have a velvet sheet over it; a coating of dust, made shiny in the flashlight beam.

Nothing about the room appeared odd, other than those indicators of neglect. The clock he had mentioned was no longer in the room. Robert moved to the window and opened the curtains, and as he did, dust rose from them in a cloud.

It was not a full-moon night, but the moonlight was strong. It landed on the window glass and turned the panes bright, fell across Robert like a slat of silver.

I walked over and stood by him.

"See," he said.

He was showing me the nails in the window frame, all around it, slammed in randomly. Something done long ago. You could tell because the heads of the nails were rusty and looked like copper in the moonlight.

We stood there for a while and talked, maybe for as long as an hour, enough that I lost my suspicion of him, and as we stood there, car lights flashed and a car turned around a wooded curve and became visible in the moonlight. It pulled up to the side of the hotel, out of sight, and then some time passed and we heard someone on the stairs, coming up. I found that more disconcerting than the idea of a ghost.

The steps ended at the open door of number twelve, and a tall, handsome man with smooth gray hair came into the room. Although I didn't actually know him, and the years had settled on him, I realized he was the man I had seen that long-ago Christmas night. He was the one who had turned his head to look at Amelia, and had made an uncouth comment as she passed. There was still about him an air of arrogance and privilege. The kind of man who had done what he pleased in life and hadn't suffered consequence of any kind.

"You came," Robert said.

"Curiosity," Kastengate said. His voice smooth as honey, his movements athletic. I hadn't realized how old-man-like I had become until seeing him, a man the years were afraid to completely destroy, a man who could still turn a young girl's head.

"I didn't know someone else would be here," Kastengate said.

"A friend," Robert said.

Kastengate smiled. "I don't think you trust me."

"Do you remember this room?" Robert said.

"I've never been in it," Kastengate said.

"Would you mind closing the door?" Robert said.

Kastengate closed it. Robert leaned in close to the window and lifted his arm so the moonlight shown on the face of his watch.

"Five minutes," he said.

"And that's when your ghost comes, huh?" Kastengate said. "Maybe I should have stayed home."

"I suppose it may be more than five minutes," Robert said. "It's five minutes to midnight, but it may be a bit after that. As I remember, it didn't come right away."

"The ghost you told me about?" Kastengate said, and grinned. The moonlight lit up his teeth, but I got the impression that in that moment he had lost some of his cocksureness. He began to look nervously around the room. Maybe not for a ghost, but perhaps by that time he had become suspicious, thought we might have made plans for his demise. The question was, of course, was he actually guilty of anything?

As for the ghost, well, I doubted that. In five or ten minutes it occurred to me we would all look pretty silly standing in a moonlit room with our hands in our pockets. Maybe Robert thought the ghost story would cause Kastengate to admit what he had done. If so, I concluded that was unlikely. But if the story was designed to scare Kastengate, why tell me the same story?

"Five minutes have passed," Kastengate said.

Robert looked at his watch. "Not quite. Please. Stick around. You came, so why not satisfy your curiosity? Sit."

Kastengate remained standing. Robert went to the windows and pulled shut the curtains he had opened. Robert switched off his flashlight, and I did the same. When we came into the room he had placed the lantern on the nightstand, and now he came over, turned it on, and went back to stand between the window and the foot of the bed.

Kastengate seated himself in a chair by the door. He didn't look in the least perturbed. He crossed his legs. Still, he had come, and

that meant something. Curiosity maybe, guilt perhaps, a combina-
tion of the two.

It is impossible to convey the feeling that came next, or to
describe the stench, but the best I can do is to say the air grew
colder and heavier and there was a stink in the room like dead rats
in the walls, and then there was the sound of movement in the
closet, like something heavy turning over.

Robert switched off the lantern, picked up his flashlight, turned
it on, and shined it at the closet. The closet door heaved a bit, as
if something inside was pushing against it. The door beaded with
liquid, and the liquid ran to the floor and into a puddle.

Robert kept the flashlight on the puddle.

Kastengate stood up, let out a loud breath.

The puddle became a solid mass of what looked like molasses,
and I could see a head poking up out of the slimy mess. The head
was dark and rotten like a pumpkin left in the patch beyond its
prime. Hair the texture of matted water weeds hung from its skull.
The damp, dead odor intensified and filled my nose and turned my
stomach.

An arm moved out from the mess, a bony thing with leathery
flesh and long fingers like dry sticks. Another arm revealed itself.
Now there was a whole, but ravaged body lying there in a puddle. It
reached out with its hands, scratched at the floor, and pulled itself
toward the bed.

As I was standing in front of the bed, it was coming directly
toward me. I was frozen in place, but as the thing came nearer, I
stepped back and sat on the mattress, swung my legs off the floor,
and inched to the far side of the bed, which was flush with the wall.
I felt like a sailor on a rickety life raft watching a shark approach.

Robert kept the circle of light on the thing, but he had moved
back to the foot of the bed and had his back against the wall.

It kept crawling until it arrived at the bed. It was so low down and close to the edge of the bed by then, I could no longer see it. After what seemed like an eternity, a bony hand lifted, the fingers rattling together like dry sticks. It clutched at the blanket, and slowly I saw its head rise like a horrid moon, and the light from the real moon filled its dead white eyes.

It paused there, seeming to look for something and not find it. I don't know how to describe it, as the face was so odd, but I got the sensation that it was feeling disappointment.

"Jesus," Kastengate said.

I'm sure he hadn't meant to say that, but as soon as his voice split the cold, dead air, the thing turned its head toward him, and tilted it in a curious manner.

Kastengate stepped backward until the chair against the wall stopped him. He fell back into it, sitting there as if it was his intended plan.

The thing leaned its head forward. Its mouth opened slightly, and I can't say for sure, but I thought there was a kind of smile there, like a gash in a pumpkin. And then, it moved. It covered the distance between it and Kastengate so fast it was as if I were seeing the event on film and frames were missing. It grabbed hold of Kastengate and that caused him to scream.

Perhaps I should have sprung forward to help him, but I did not; even when he cried out to me, and then Robert for help, I didn't move a muscle. Neither did Robert.

The thing jerked Kastengate from the chair and collapsed out of my sight. I could hear it slithering across the floor. I could see Robert's face, as he looked down, watching that thing crawl, dragging its prize with it. He didn't try for his gun. He didn't move.

Then the revenant rose up from the floor like a puppet pulled upright by invisible strings. It was clutching Kastengate by the neck, as if he were a rag doll. There was nothing handsome about him now. His eyes were impossibly wide. His mouth hung open. He was the color of snow.

The window curtains slid back, as if by some unseen hand, and the moonlight shown in again. I could see the rusty nails begin to turn and lift out of the window frame, and as they turned I could feel the hair on the back of my neck stand up like a bed of thorns. The nails rattled to the floor and the window flew up, and then, like a large windblown leaf, the thing and Kastengate were sucked out of the open window and plunged toward the ground.

Robert came unstuck from the wall, eased toward the window. I found the courage to slip off the bed and stand by him.

We looked out and down. The thing rose up and began to drag Kastengate away by the collar of his jacket. It was obvious the fall had cracked his bones in many places. One arm was twisted in a way an arm shouldn't go, and one of his feet was turned at an awkward angle and raw bone glinted from his broken flesh and ripped pants.

"We should help him," Robert said.

I didn't reply, and Robert didn't move.

Kastengate was dragged out of view behind a row of dark, limb-dripping willows and an ancient cypress tree, on toward the river.

We stood there for a long time, then we sat down on the end of the bed and waited until the sun came up, warm and rosy. Christmas Day.

I looked up as the room darkened. The curtains had been pulled across the window again. It had happened so subtly, neither of us had noticed.

I went to the window, moved back the curtains, and looked out at the newborn day. The window frame was shut and nailed down again, as if the nails had never been removed. It was as Robert had described when he had spent that lonely night in the room some years back. I could hardly breathe.

Down by the river, we found Kastengate's jacket, but besides that there was only the rolling brown water. Kastengate was gone.

We drove to a pay phone and called the police. They came out and looked, thought we were suspects in the case. Nothing was ever proven, though if you look up old newspaper accounts, police records, you will see that Robert and I are still under suspicion.

We didn't tell them what we really saw, figuring that would only compound the situation. We said we drove out there under a spell of nostalgia and discovered Kastengate's car, his jacket, down by the river. Neither of us lied when we said we hardly knew him.

Next year we went there on Christmas Eve. Nothing happened in the room that time. I fell asleep in a chair and Robert fell asleep on the dusty bed. When we awoke the next morning, we decided it was over for good. Early the next year the hotel was torn down.

I never saw Robert again, though I heard he died some years back. Went in his sleep.

So now I'm old as dirt, waiting for the shadow, thinking about how one of those men had done himself in by drowning, and how the other was taken away by . . . Well, I can't say for sure, but I have my idea about it. I think justice was paid.

Sometimes, when I lay down, the last thing I think of is Amelia, young and alive, bright and magnetic, dressed as she was that night so long ago on Christmas Eve, those gold hoop earrings shimmering, almost as bright as the light in her eyes and the shine of her smile.

She was and is a dark and beautiful dream.

FARROW STREET

ELIZABETH HAND

For the last seventeen years, she'd spent Christmas with friends in Devon. Her coworkers at the law firm where she was the office manager thought this was the height of luxury, and there were always the same bad jokes about visiting the Queen and London Bridge. In fact she booked her flight months in advance, which made the trip relatively inexpensive, spent a night at a budget hotel in Heathrow, then caught the train from London to Taunton, where Joanne and Chris picked her up. Once they reached Belstone, her costs consisted of a few meals out and the good wine she always picked up at Paddington.

This year, however, she received a phone call from Joanne in mid-October.

"I'm so sorry, Mel—I know this upsets your plans. But it's the baby's first Christmas, and Sarah and Trent really want us there with them. And of course we want to go. Do you think you could rebook and come after the New Year?"

"I'll check it out. And of course I understand, not a problem."

It turned out that it *was* a problem. Rebooking the flight would cost more than the original tickets. If she stayed at home, Melanie would be on her own for Christmas in her shitty little apartment just outside Tyson's Corner.

So she looked online and found a cheap hotel near Bloomsbury. She reserved a room beginning two days before Christmas, with plans to return home before New Year's Eve. Christmas in London! She'd save on the cost of the train ticket and spend her money on meals out and nice wine for herself. Maybe see a show and find a nice place for a traditional Christmas dinner. She packed her carry-on (she never trusted the airlines not to lose her checked luggage), along with the burgundy cashmere sweater she'd worn to the office Christmas party for the last few years; also paperbacks of *A Christmas Carol* and *David Copperfield,* neither of which she'd ever read.

The Buckingham Arms turned out to be a shabby converted row house off Gower Street, not Bloomsbury, one of eight equally dingy hotels with names like Queen's Grove and Royal Stanwick. Inside it smelled of french fries and marijuana smoke. Her windowless room was tiny, a flimsy bed shoved up against one wall. Plywood shelves built into the other wall had buckled from damp. The bathroom had a metal shower stall and a sagging sink, its pipes dark with rust. When Melanie went downstairs to reception and asked if she could be moved to another room, the very young man behind the desk (it was built into a closet) turned from the computer, blinked sleepily, and shook his head.

"Sorry, we're booked up till New Year's."

She stormed to her room and tried to go online to see if she could get a refund from the booking site. But her mobile couldn't get a Wi-Fi signal, and she'd decided against buying a sim card because it was too expensive. This meant another trip downstairs, where the sleepy-eyed boy was now playing some sort of game on his mobile.

"Yeah, I know," he said when she complained about the lack of Wi-Fi. "It keeps cutting out. I think it's because of all the construction."

She gave up, took a melatonin, and went to bed.

She slept fitfully, awakened by people going up and down the stairs. She'd forgotten to put in her earplugs, and she was too tired to search for them in a strange room in the middle of the night. So she buried her head in the thin pillow and tried taking long, deep breaths. She gave up at five a.m., when an endless parade of delivery vans and trucks began in the street outside, causing the bed to shake.

But she was awake now, and it was Christmas Eve. The Buckingham Arms didn't serve breakfast (or anything else), so she dressed, tucked her copy of *A Christmas Carol* into her handbag, and trudged back downstairs.

The sleepy male receptionist had been replaced by an equally young woman with an Eastern European accent, who greeted Melanie cheerfully. "Jet lag? I know, it's horrible—kept me up for a week when my boyfriend and I went to New York last summer."

Melanie gave her a curt nod. "Is there a place nearby that's open for breakfast?"

"Breakfast?" The young woman glanced at her mobile. "At five? Not around here. Maybe if you head to Marylebone, or Camden. I'm not sure if the tube is running this early. The holiday," she added, eyes widening as though confiding a secret.

Melanie sighed. Maybe that explained all the trucks and delivery vans. She headed for the door, halting when the receptionist called after her.

"Wait, I remember—there's a McDonald's two streets over! Or you can go to Euston, I'm sure there's places inside the station. Pret A Manger, I think."

Melanie turned and left without replying.

Outside, it was raining, not hard but a cold steady drizzle. She'd forgotten to pack an umbrella—in Devon it often snowed at Christmas. She pulled up the hood of her wool coat, relieved that at least she was wearing boots, not her best pair but practical, with sturdy rubber soles and pleather uppers. She walked in the direction the receptionist had pointed to indicate Euston. After ten minutes, she still hadn't seen any sign of the station, and halted under the awning of a news agent. The door was locked, but she saw a man inside behind the register. She tapped on the window and smiled. He glanced up and shook his head. She knocked again, louder.

"I just want directions!"

His muffled voice came back to her. "Six o'clock!"

She stood for another minute, trying to will him to let her in, then trudged the way she'd come, turning down the next street, when she recognized the unwelcoming line of down-market hotels. She found the McDonald's a few blocks away. It opened at six, but by now it almost *was* six. So she waited outside until a girl in an orange uniform came and unlocked the door. She had coffee and an Egg McMuffin, and comforted herself by thinking how this would make a funny story when she got back to the office in the New Year. London at Christmas, and nowhere to eat but McDonald's!

She read a bit of *A Christmas Carol* before she set it aside and took her mobile from her handbag. Miracle of miracles, she was able to get a Wi-Fi signal here. She looked up Christmas sights in London, also last-minute tickets. The shows were all sold out, including the long-running musicals she wouldn't have even considered seeing at home. She thought she might go to Carnaby Street and look at the lights, then walk to Liberty and see if she might find a scarf as a present for herself, or even splurge on an umbrella.

But when she glanced out the window, she saw that the rain had grown heavier. Passing vehicles threw spumes of filthy water onto the sidewalk. People hurried to work, an army of black umbrellas and wireless headsets. She consulted her phone again and decided on Covent Garden, finished her coffee, and set out.

The Underground was packed. She stood in the train car, pressed between a heavyset man in a maintenance suit and a woman standing guard over a large suitcase that blocked the aisle. When the doors opened at Covent Garden Station, people flooded onto the platform. Melanie let herself be swept along with them down the passage and into a lift, up a flight of stairs, and finally out into the chilly gray morning. Covent Garden was as crowded inside as the train had been, but here the mood was jollier, with Christmas music piped over the sound system. A group in medieval garb stood at one end of the arcade, attempting to sing "The Wessex Carol" over a recording of "Merry Christmas Everybody." Melanie found respite in a vintage clothing emporium, where she fortified herself with mulled cider and a stale mince pie before once again braving hordes of shoppers.

Still, the prevailing mood remained merry and bright. She spent the morning drifting from shop to shop. When the rain lifted, she went outside, surprised to see how quickly the buskers and living statues had appeared once the weather improved. A Victorian bride was clad entirely in white: even her face was chalked, everything but her eyes, which gazed out at Melanie, a startling violet. Men in bowler hats performed tricks with gold rings and a flaming orb to a delighted crowd of families with children. She returned inside to find the medieval choristers replaced by a group of men clad in vaguely rustic eighteenth-century attire who lustily belted out "Wassail" and then engaged in morris dancing. Melanie watched them for a few minutes, until with a yawn she embarked on another circuit of the hall. She bought herself a forest-green scarf patterned with wine-colored berries that she thought would go well with her cashmere sweater, and continued to sample enough mince pies and cider to keep her sated until early afternoon, when she ventured out into the street intent on finding a pub for lunch.

It was only then that she discovered her mobile phone was gone. Dropped in the crowd, or more likely, pickpocketed. She felt a frisson of terror that candled into rage: how could she have been so careless? She looked around for a policeman or security guard— she'd seen several milling around inside. Now of course there was not one to be found.

She huddled beneath the awning of an upscale designer boutique and tried to calm herself. The mobile was nearly two years old: she'd have traded it in for a new one within a few months. It didn't work over here, not as a phone, and she'd already discovered that any Wi-Fi access would be sporadic. She was old enough to remember a time when people got around relying on maps and friendly strangers, the theft of her phone notwithstanding. She'd have an old-fashioned holiday, and let serendipity guide her through the city. Thank God her wallet hadn't been stolen.

The streets around Covent Garden were thronged, as were the pubs and restaurants. On one corner a half-dozen children dressed like extras from a production of *Oliver!* sweetly sang "God Rest Ye Merry Gentlemen." She briefly considered dropping a pound coin into the cap at their feet, but she saw a small shining heap in there already, and even a few notes. After all, they weren't *real* urchins.

She wandered along the sidewalks, taking little notice of where she turned. The rain had finally slackened, though it remained cold, and she gazed with envy through pub windows at the people who sat inside, laughing as they ate and drank. More than once she passed a group of drunken Santas standing outside a pub as they smoked.

It was nearly three o'clock before she found a pub where she could make her way inside. She went to the bar and ordered a pint and a plate of fish and chips, found an empty table where she could watch the revelry around her. Office parties and another Santa posse, this one made up of tipsy young women who shrieked glee-fully as they tugged at each other's false beards. Melanie took her time over lunch—it was late enough by now that she could think of it as an early supper. The battered fish was barely lukewarm, and the chips were stone-cold. She considered sending it back, but the crowd at the bar was now three-deep. She grimaced and ate what she could, sipping her pint. She'd forgotten that English beer was served warm.

When at last she finished, it was full dark outside. Automatically she reached into a pocket for her mobile, recalled it had been sto-len. Nothing to be done. She elbowed her way across the room and asked the barkeep where the closest tube station was. He shouted directions at her, and she headed off for her hotel.

A different receptionist sat behind the hotel desk, a young black man plumper than the other, with a neatly trimmed Van Dyke beard and red plaid bow tie.

"Merry Christmas," he said as she walked past him. "Enjoy your-self out there?"

Melanie nodded. "Very much."

She knew that to fight jet lag she should stay up until her normal bedtime, but the long day had exhausted her. She took two melato-nin, remembered to put in her earplugs, read a few more pages of *A Christmas Carol,* and collapsed into bed.

Miraculously, she slept through the night. It was light when she awoke and, disoriented, stared at a blotch on the ceiling. It bore an unpleasant resemblance to a face, mouth adroop and eyes too far apart. She took a deep breath and smelled cigarette smoke, also marijuana, and remembered where she was; reached for her phone on the rickety nightstand.

But of course, she'd lost it. She sat up, in vain looked around the grimy room for a clock. She didn't own a wristwatch. There was no window she could peer out, no way whatsoever to guess what time it was. She went to the door, cracked it, and glanced up and down the corridor. A small window at the far end glowed the dull gray of tarnished silver. Morning, probably, though who knew? She showered and dressed and went downstairs to find out.

Yet another receptionist slumped behind the desk, head cradled in her arms, a Santa hat askew on her matted blonde hair. As Melanie approached she looked up, her eyes bleary and face streaked with mascara. Melanie wondered if she was one of the female Santas she'd seen in the pub.

"Can I help you?" she asked. Wincing, she sat up and tugged the hat until it covered her forehead.

"I just wanted to know what time it is."

The girl picked up her mobile and squinted at it. "Half ten, it looks like."

"Ten thirty?" The girl nodded. Melanie gave a little gasp of surprise. "It's so late!"

"Supposed to be somewhere?"

"No. Just I hadn't expected to sleep so late. My mobile was stolen yesterday."

The girl's eyes widened in such horror and pity that for an instant Melanie thought she might hand over her own cell phone. Instead she quickly slid it into her pocket. "Did you report it to the police?"

Melanie shook her head. "What's the point? It was old, anyway."

"You're right about that. The police, I mean." The girl swiveled her chair to gaze at the computer screen.

Melanie went to the door and opened it to look outside, letting in a blast of chilly air. Above the construction cranes and run-down brick apartment stretched an unbroken wall of ashen clouds. The cold wind sent fast-food wrappers and Styrofoam containers tumbling along the sidewalk. The street was empty, except for a black car that had been booted, and also eerily silent.

Frowning, she stepped down to the sidewalk, craning her neck to see if there was traffic on the cross street a few blocks distant. Nearly thirty seconds passed before a single car fleetingly appeared between the rows of buildings.

She went back inside, clutching her arms to warm herself. "It's so quiet out there."

"That's Christmas." The girl glanced up from the computer and shrugged. "Everything's dead."

"I was wondering about that." Melanie looked around the tiny foyer, wishing that another hotel guest would come downstairs. The girl was useless. Everyone here was useless. "Is there somewhere I can get breakfast? Or lunch, actually, it'll probably be noon before I go out. Not McDonald's or, you know, a convenience store. A proper restaurant."

The girl shook her head. "Not on Christmas. Everything's closed. I doubt McDonald's is even open."

"There has to be someplace." Melanie resisted the urge to snatch the Santa hat from the girl's head. "I was in Covent Garden yesterday, there were restaurants that looked like they might be open."

"Really? I doubt it. But maybe." Her tone was dubious. "It'd be expensive—you'd have to find a taxi to take you there. There's not many of them'll be working, either. And they'll all be booked by now."

"What are you talking about?"

The girl sighed, licked a finger, and absently rubbed it beneath one raccoon eye. "You're American, aren't you? Americans always think they'll come here at Christmas and it'll be like the movies. Tiny Tim and big parties, all that. But it's not. The whole city shuts down. No tube, no trains, no buses, nothing. Well, you might find a bus runs every hour or so in the afternoon," she added grudgingly. "But I don't know where."

Melanie gazed at her in disbelief. "But how does everyone get to work?"

"They don't. I told you, everything's closed. I mean, police and hospitals are open, but they'll be short-staffed. In case you planned on getting sick. Or arrested."

"I don't," snapped Melanie. "How did you get here?"

"My boyfriend dropped me off. I have to stay over tonight, there's a room upstairs where staff can sleep. Not that it's your business."

Melanie closed her eyes, opened them to see the girl once more intent on the computer screen. Gritting her teeth, Melanie stood on tiptoe to peer over the desk, and asked, "All right. I'll find my way on my own. Do you have a map there? A city map?"

The girl groaned and hopped from her chair. "All right, all right. Let's see what we can find."

She ducked behind the desk, rummaged around on the floor, and reappeared, holding a plastic bin overflowing with papers. "I think there's a map here."

Melanie watched as she sifted through wads of receipts, business cards, advertisements for cheap mobile phone service and Indian takeaway. The girl tossed a brochure onto the desk. "There's a tube map, but that won't help until day after tomorrow."

"What's tomorrow?"

"Boxing Day. Everything's dead then, too. Wait! Here we go . . ." Triumphantly she held up a dog-eared tourist map and handed it to Melanie. "Will that do?"

Melanie unfolded the map on the desk. "It's dated 1997."

"Really? Well, that's the best I can do." The girl stuffed the papers back into the plastic bin, set it on the floor, and kicked it against the wall. "Not that much will have changed, I don't think. Anything else?"

Melanie glared at her, but the girl had already turned away. "No. I guess this will have to do."

She folded up the map and returned to her room. She took a shower, then pulled on a pair of black pants and her burgundy cashmere sweater. She examined it for pilling—she'd bought it on sale four years ago, but she only wore it a few times a year. The room's mirror was old; much of its silver had flaked away, so that her reflection seemed that of a different woman, one whose face was disfigured by black spots like spreading mold.

The bathroom mirror was a slight improvement. She stood under the fluorescent, dabbed some concealer under her eyes, then sparingly applied a wine-colored gloss to her lips. There was no hair dryer, so she did her best with a towel and a hairbrush. Last of all she put on her boots and hooded coat, made sure her passport was in her bag, stuck the map in her pocket, and headed out.

The wind had picked up. She clutched her hood around her head, walking briskly until she came to the nearest major cross street. Even here traffic was sparse. She waited in hopes of seeing a taxi, stamping her feet against the sidewalk to keep warm. When at last a black cab appeared, she stepped into the road, waving frantically.

It sped past. Melanie swore angrily and started walking again. Now and then she'd check her map, ducking into doorways to keep the wind from crumpling it. The map was useless for the area around Euston Station, which had been completely transformed by new construction. She set her sights on Euston Road, a thorough-fare that, once she reached it, must lead somewhere. Surely she'd find an open restaurant in that part of the city. Worst-case scenario, it would be a better spot to catch a cab elsewhere.

She plodded on for what must have been hours, with no way to keep track of time or how far she'd walked. The only other people she saw were beggars sprawled on the sidewalk and an old woman who, when Melanie approached her to ask for directions, darted across the road. Above her the sky darkened from ash to charcoal. Her fingers grew numb, and her toes. She was famished and also thirsty—who'd have thought to bring a water bottle on a short excursion to find an open restaurant in a major world city on Christmas Day?

It must have been after three o'clock when the light began to fail in earnest. Over the last hour or so, the neighborhoods around her had grown increasingly desolate: Indian takeaways, charity shops, betting parlors, storefronts selling cheap electronics—all shuttered. She hadn't seen another person in an hour at least, or a bus. Some blocks ahead of her, a thicket of construction cranes overshadowed the street. It seemed unlikely she'd find any signs of life there: in fact, it looked downright dangerous.

She froze as an unexpected sound broke the near-silence: a church bell. She held her breath and counted as it tolled five times. As its last echoes faded, she turned in a slow circle, trying to discern from which direction the chimes came.

Not behind her—she definitely would have heard the bells before now. And certainly not from that arsenal of construction equipment. And the opposite side of the road consisted of nothing but block upon block of shabby shops and crumbling council flats.

No, the church must be somewhere not too far from where she stood.

She felt her heart lighten—a church on Christmas Day wouldn't be empty. If she hurried, she might find a service in progress, or a nearby rectory where she could ask for directions. She quickened her pace, and after only a few steps saw a narrow alley to her right. The building on the corner looked like an abandoned warehouse or factory. Past it, she couldn't see any houses, or anything that might be a commercial establishment. But she was certain that the sound of church bells had come from here.

She shoved her hands deeper into her pockets and started down the alley. Beneath her feet, the cement sidewalk gave way to mottled brick, and the paved roadway to cobblestones. A few yards ahead, a hazy glow surrounded a solitary streetlamp.

Melanie blinked and looked up at the sky, where the silhouettes of looming buildings faded into near-darkness. She hesitated, then turned and walked back to the corner, stopping to squint at the sign posted on the side of the broken-down warehouse. Farrow Street.

She consulted her map. She saw no Farrow Street near the road she'd been following, or anywhere else for that matter. Not that it was a very extensive map. She leaned against the warehouse wall, debating whether searching for the church would be a fool's errand. She could try to retrace her steps to the hotel and from there make her way to Euston Station. At this point she'd settle for another Egg McMuffin.

Shivering, she glanced down the alley. Past the solitary streetlamp, on the other side of the road, a shaft of golden light streamed across the sidewalk, burnishing the old brick. The light seemed too bright to come from a residence. A restaurant, maybe, or a pub or bar.

Melanie stuffed the map into her pocket and headed quickly back down the alley, avoiding gaps in the sidewalk where the bricks had dislodged. On each side of the narrow passage rose a deserted warehouse. If there had been any sunlight, these derelict buildings would have blocked it. A tarry substance seeped from beneath many of their windows, staining the walls and in spots covering the sidewalk like black lichen.

As she drew closer to the streetlamp, she saw that it had begun to snow, minute flakes like glittering sand that shimmered in the diffuse pale light. Perhaps twenty yards farther on, the unseen building's buttery glow grew more intense, making the snow flare like a bonfire.

Melanie pulled her hood tighter and ran to the other side of the alley. Her feet slipped on the greasy cobbles, but she didn't care. Already she saw herself sitting at a candlelit table with a steaming plate in front of her, and a glass of wine. Maybe an entire bottle. A few more steps, and she reached the light's source.

Tucked between the warehouses was a four-story house, built from the same old yellow brick as the warehouses and sidewalk. A tracery of ivy covered its facade, rather than the black mildew on the warehouse walls. Stone steps led up to a door painted dark green. To one side of the door protruded a bow window, and it was through its panes that the welcoming golden light fell to ignite the sidewalk and the alley.

Melanie stopped and stared at the house, enchanted. Long curtains had been pulled back from the three windows: she could clearly see a round bull's-eye mirror on the opposite wall, the corner of a white fireplace mantel. A lit white taper in a silver candle holder sat atop the mantel, its flame throwing jagged shadows on the wall behind it. Larger shadows moved about the room, and she glimpsed a blur of crimson, a dress or suit jacket, a shock of dark hair.

As she stared, the door opened, loosing the sound of faint music into the frigid night. A woman in a knee-length beaded shift stepped out and looked measuringly at the sky before glancing down at the sidewalk.

"Oh, hullo," she said. Her close-cropped dark hair had been slicked back, exposing a long white neck and chandelier earrings that flashed scarlet and emerald in the light that spilled around her. "Are you looking for us?"

Melanie shook her head. "I don't think so," she said, then hastily added, "I've been walking all over, trying to find a restaurant that's open. I don't have a phone, so I couldn't—"

"Come on in." The woman cast a swift look over her shoulder, turned back to Melanie and nodded, beckoning her. "Please, you look half-frozen."

Nodding gratefully, Melanie hurried up the steps. The woman moved aside and gestured into the hallway. "Someone will take your coat."

"Oh, no thanks, I'll just—"

"Suit yourself," the woman said.

She peered at the street one last time before closing the door, turned to a marble-topped side table, and picked up an old-fashioned key from a porcelain dish. She locked the door and gazed past Melanie into the living room. "Some of the others are in there, the rest are scattered around the house. Help yourself to anything you want."

"Thank you," Melanie said. She looked down at her plain wool coat and pleather boots. "I don't know if I—"

But the woman was already walking down the hall, toward a staircase leading to the next floor. Melanie watched her go. Music drifted down from an upper room, a fiddle playing a vaguely familiar tune. She didn't know the song's name, but she'd heard it before, probably in an old movie.

She wondered if she should follow the woman upstairs. Instead she took a deep breath and stepped into the living room. A susurrus of conversation abruptly ceased, as a dozen or so people turned to regard her. Most were standing, though two elderly women perched on a settee upholstered in sky-blue fabric. One of the women wore a drab brown sweater and matching skirt, heavy black stockings and chunky shoes, which made Melanie feel slightly better about her own attire.

But many of the other guests appeared dressed for a costume

party. One man sported green plaid knee breeches and an embroidered waistcoat; another wore a baggy herringbone suit, with a gaudy stickpin in his tie and cuff links shaped like scarab beetles. Several of the women wore elaborate dresses that grazed the floor, one with a bustle. Another woman sported a large hat festooned with crimson and white ostrich plumes. A teenage girl with a brightly lipsticked mouth and a blonde pageboy lounged against the fireplace mantel, her tartan skirt falling just below her knees. Beside her, a middle-aged man in an old-fashioned bobby's uniform repeatedly attempted to light a cigarette with a lighter.

"No spark," he said, and looked accusingly at Melanie. "Or butane's gone."

"I'm sorry," Melanie replied. She smiled wanly, waiting for someone to welcome her or introduce themselves. When they remained silent, she went on, "I got lost, and your hostess asked me in. So I'm sorry, I don't know anyone."

She smiled again. The other guests stared at her without speaking. After a moment, the old woman in the brown skirt gave a hooting laugh. No one else spoke.

Melanie felt her face grow hot. She'd always thought people in the United Kingdom were more polite than their American counterparts, but obviously this wasn't the case in London, where rudeness seemed to have become a spectator sport. She'd rather spend the night walking alone in the cold streets than be treated this way.

As she steeled herself to turn and leave, her gaze fell upon the fireplace. Flames flickered behind the screen, and almost without thinking she walked toward it, crouched, and held her hands up to the blaze. Screw these people: she'd warm herself before going out again.

The fire gave off little heat. She was tempted to remove the fire screen so she could move even closer. But that might annoy the others, or cause that awful old woman to laugh at her again. After a few minutes she straightened and turned to face the room once more.

The other guests hadn't moved from where they sat or stood. The bobby still flicked his cigarette lighter. The blonde with the lipstick-red pumps and tartan skirt adjusted a corsage pinned to her sweater, red roses and a sprig of holly.

"We should go up soon," pronounced a dark-skinned boy who looked about ten. He wore a red hoodie and sneakers and huddled on the floor in a corner by the bow window, which was why she hadn't noticed him until now.

"Upstairs?" asked Melanie.

The boy stared past her into the fireplace but remained silent. Was he afraid?

Melanie took a step toward him, then stopped. For the first time, she noticed that there were no electric lamps in the room. Solitary candles or candelabras stood along the mantel, atop side tables and ranged along a shelf above the wood wainscoting. A large oriental rug covered the floor, its pale swirls of mauve and powder-blue and rose counterpoint to the walls, which were painted a deeper blue. Empty or near-empty wineglasses stood on the tables, along with glass decanters that still held a few inches of what looked like red wine. On a low console by the window sat a silver platter covered with half-eaten tarts and a handful of grapes clinging to a desiccated stem. She reached for the platter, glancing over her shoulder as she did.

The woman in the feathered hat was staring at her. Almost imperceptibly, she shook her head. Melanie frowned. The gesture struck her as more disapproving than warning, and she no longer cared if anything she did might be perceived as rudeness. Pot calling kettle black! She was famished. She picked up a grape and popped it into her mouth, grimacing as she bit into it. Sour.

Yet there might be more food in another room. She looked at

the boy sitting in the corner. He seemed by far the most normal-looking person in the room. If she caught his eye, she'd motion for him to accompany her. But he just fiddled with the zipper of his hoodie and gazed fixedly at the floor.

Melanie licked her lips, trying to dispel the grape's acrid after-taste, and crossed back into the hall. From upstairs echoed that same faint fiddle music, the sounds of muted voices and footsteps walking up another set of stairs.

More voices came from the end of the hall. Candles guttered in sconces, the wax pooling in dark streaks on the floor beneath them. Melanie walked past the staircase and several open rooms, all set as for a party with lit candles and trays that held the remains of food, empty wineglasses and decanters. In the dining room, its table draped with a damask cloth and resplendent with silver candlesticks and place settings for twenty, two men in work clothes stood with their backs to her, staring out a window into the darkness. Melanie paused to watch them, clearing her throat in hopes they might turn and see her.

They did not, nor did they speak to each other. She sighed and walked on until she reached the back of the house. She'd expected to find a kitchen here, and maybe a bathroom. But there was only a small, rather utilitarian-looking room, with a single plain wood table, a very small window, and a door that opened onto a set of stairs leading into the basement.

Melanie stood, listening to determine if she could hear any activity from the basement. There was nothing save a draft of cold air with an underlying scent of wood smoke. Of course: back when this house was built, the kitchen would have been downstairs. But why hadn't it been converted since then?

When she'd been researching things to do in London over the holidays, she'd come across an article about Geffrye House, where visitors could tour rooms done up in the style of bygone years

and centuries. The staff wore period clothing and, in the days leading up to Christmas, held holiday gatherings inspired by Dickens's
work.

That must be the sort of place she'd stumbled upon—maybe
Geffrye House itself. Perhaps she'd come across a private gathering, a group of friends or employees who'd booked the building for
their Christmas party. That might account for the cool reception
she'd received, also the matter-of-fact manner in which the woman
she'd first encountered had greeted Melanie.

She stood there musing, starting when once again a church bell
began to toll. She counted each stroke—eight, nine, ten . . .

It couldn't possibly be that late! She walked to the room's single
window and tried to peer out. It was so webbed with filth she
could see nothing. Somewhere outside, the bell continued tolling.
Not until it struck eleven did it stop, the reverberation of its final
note lingering in the room around her like a foul smell.

A sick feeling came over her, the kind of pure, visceral fear she
experienced when encountering turbulence on an airplane flight.
It had been barely past five when she entered the house. She knew
that five or six hours hadn't passed, just as she knew this wasn't a
museum or private Christmas party. She hurried from the room
and back down the corridor, clutching her handbag as she tugged
her coat tightly around her.

The two workmen she'd seen in the dining room stood in the
middle of the hall, gazing at the stairwell, their expressions blank.
The fiddle music had fallen silent. One of the men shook his head.
He headed up the steps, the sound of his hobnailed boots echoing
through the house. The second man stared after him, then glanced
aside at Melanie.

"Almost time," he said, and followed his colleague upstairs.

Throat tight, Melanie nearly ran toward the front door. Several of the other guests straggled from the main room into the

hallway, the boy in the red hoodie among them. She slowed as she drew near him, her lips parted to speak. He glanced up at her, his dark eyes glittering in the candlelight, looked away, and slouched past. Behind him walked the young woman in the tartan skirt. She glanced at Melanie, lifting her hand. For an instant it seemed she might speak.

But her long fingers only brushed the holly leaves, adjusting her corsage before she, too, headed for the stairs.

People now crowded the entry to the living room in their haste to leave. Melanie hesitated, desperately scanning faces. The woman with the ostrich plume hat held up her long skirt and brushed past her, close enough that Melanie caught the sickly scent of tuberoses and lilies, and heard her speaking to herself.

"... to be late. Never, ever ..."

Melanie darted past the others to the front door, grasped the brass doorknob, and turned it. Locked. She twisted it again, harder.

It didn't budge. She turned and raced to the marble-topped table where she'd seen the woman retrieve the key earlier. The porcelain dish was empty. She moaned softly, looked up to see the woman in the brown skirt staring at her with small beetle-black eyes. Once more she gave that harsh hooting laugh and hurried on to the steps.

Melanie leaned against the wall, forced herself to breathe deeply in an attempt to remain calm. Should she scream? Break a window and jump outside? Grab someone and insist they help her?

But when she looked up, the hallway was empty. She caught a glimpse of green plaid knee breeches, the flash of red satin. That was all.

From upstairs the fiddle music began once more, livelier this time. Melanie took a deep breath and walked to the staircase. She took the steps slowly, glancing back and praying that she might see the woman she'd first met. When she reached the second-floor landing she paused. A single candle burned in a blackened sconce, casting a pallid glow on walls papered in a fleur-de-lis pattern. Ahead of her, a corridor only a few yards long led to another stairway. She could hear footsteps from the next floor, a shriek that might have been a whistle, or a woman.

She cast a final look behind her. A feather of candlelight touched the floor at the foot of the stairs and faded into darkness. She turned and walked down the hall to the second set of stairs, placed her hand on the railing, and began to walk up. In the dying gleam of the single candle, she saw that what she had mistaken for patterned wallpaper was a delicate filigree of mold, threadlike filaments that moved as she passed, like maidenhair seaweed, until the encroaching shadows swallowed them.

Above her the fiddle music wavered and swelled, the sound of waves on the shore. With each receding note, the darkness grew, until she could see nothing. She heard a church bell, impossibly distant. She counted each stroke: twelve, one for each step.

She reached the third-floor landing, where a tendril of reddish light seeped from beneath what must be a door. As she approached, it swung open. For an instant, Melanie saw the woman who'd beckoned her inside, now armless, legless. Her beaded shift slid from her like rain, along with her eyes, nose, hair, teeth; and Melanie gazed into a formless face, devoid of any features save a slack, immense mouth surrounded by myriad minute tendrils that rippled softly as they welcomed her.

❧

DOCTOR VELOCITY

A Story of the Fire Zone

JONATHAN MABERRY

1

Destroyer stood back from the canvas and he was a perfect study in total disgust.

From the defeated slouch of his shoulders to the self-defiant turn of his hip to the white-knuckled clutch of his fist around the handle of the palette knife, he was a man who reeked of angry despair. He tilted his head this way and that, trying to find an angle from which the painting looked like it possessed intensity and passion rather than desperation and confusion. The colors and movements he saw looked inflicted rather than wrought.

"Pathetic . . . ," he murmured.

Destroyer's defeated, disgusted posture was at odds with the music playing from the eight speakers mounted high on the walls of the big loft. The song playing was "Videte Miraculum," performed by a local group called A Choir of Ghosts. Beyond the wall of big picture windows the night sparkled with holiday lights in bright primary colors. Everyone seemed to have gone out of their way to be ostentatious with them, draping every window, every balcony, and lining their roofs. It all looked so goddamn cheerful. The Italian restaurant directly across from him had so many lights that it was impossible to make out any details of the building's actual shape. There had to be two or three hundred thousand of them. The less flamboyant French restaurant to the left of it merely had "DITTO" spelled out in white LED lights. It was the only part of the Christmas cityscape that Destroyer did not actively hate. Normally he loved holiday lights, but that was so last year. This year he wanted to burn it all down.

The artist snorted and flung the palette onto a paint-speckled table but kept the knife clutched in his fist, fingering its edge, wondering if there were more constructive uses for it. Such as hacking and slashing the canvas while laughing maniacally. The thought had some appeal.

So did the thought of taking that knife to his own wrists, his throat. Maybe his eyes. Either ending his life or ending his career as an artist. Would either end the pain?

The fact that he could not easily answer that question was the slim tether that held him back from an act of commission.

Destroyer held the knife in his left hand and laid the edge of the blade against his right wrist. The blade looked hungry, felt hungry, as if it—unlike its owner—possessed a true passion, a genuine intensity. It wanted to cut because that would be beautiful to it. The knife would be embracing its own nature, it would revel in the deep and vibrant redness of the ink of his veins. He closed his eyes, looking inward and downward at that possibility. At how easy it would be. At how many problems it would solve. At how much of the pain would drain out of him with his blood.

When Destroyer opened his eyes he expected to see the cut

already made, or at least started. That would have shown some passion or intensity, maybe even artistic integrity. But the blade had not yet taken that first bite.

"Fucking coward," he muttered, at the knife and at himself. He waited for the bellow of rage that surely had to be inside of him to burst out. It did not. Even his words lacked emphasis. He tried to force the tears, but although they stung, there was nothing more.

"Not even that?" he asked, aware of how pretentious the question was.

No, not pretentious. Trite. Obvious. Shallow. An affectation of passion rather than any species of passion itself.

He turned and walked away from the canvas, his feet clumsy even on the familiar floorboards. The night beckoned and he stood for a long time looking out at the darkness. His studio was on the very edge of the Fire Zone. Behind him, out of sight unless he chose to look through his bedroom windows, was the long hill down to the crooked line of Boundary Street. It was always cold down there. The lights never shone as brightly as they should, and even the Christmas lights glimmered with the hopeless desperation of lights on a sinking ship. He seldom went down there. Most of the people in the Zone avoided the place unless they grooved on the rough trade or if they were hunting for some guppies. Among his clique—the Invited, as they called themselves—there were predators who fed on the swimming innocents, or on the bottom-feeders from whom "Boundary" Street earned its name. Not a real barrier, of course, but what did that matter? It was all affectation—social class above all else. Being one of the Invited did not confer an actual invitation to a higher level of understanding. Some people thought that, but Destroyer had been running with the in crowd for so long that he knew the realities.

Becoming accepted as one of the fashionable, intellectual, artistic elite did not immediately confer spiritual ascendency or freedom from emotional entanglements. And it was sure as hell no proof against ennui.

He raised the knife and studied its edge. Most palette knives were dull, but he always kept his sharpened. Another affectation, he knew, because he liked to think that he was using it as a scalpel to cut deep into the flesh of whatever he was painting.

The song ended and a sprightly contemporary holiday song began playing. About kissing by the Christmas tree. Destroyer wanted so badly to throw himself out of the window and end it all with a splash painting on the sidewalk. At least that would make a statement of true drama.

The idea was so appealing. His fist closed around the handle so tightly his knuckles creaked.

"Portrait of a man who could use my help," said a voice behind him.

Destroyer spun at the sound, the knife coming up ready to stab. Then he froze. A man stood leaning against the open door. Tall and slim, with very dark skin, amber-colored eyes, and a smile that was as bright as all the beauty in the world.

"Vee . . . ," said Destroyer, exhaling pent-up breath and smiling. It was his first smile of the day, the week, and a good part of that month. "I didn't hear you come in."

"Hello, my brother," said Doctor Velocity. "I hope I'm not intruding."

"God, no." The artist hurried over to shake the hand of his visitor. "I wasn't expecting anyone . . ."

"Did you forget that we had plans to exchange gifts?" said the doctor. "Christmas Eve and all that."

"Um . . . no, no, it's great," said Destroyer, tripping over the lie but recovering quickly. He waved his friend to one of the big overstuffed chairs positioned haphazardly in front of the windows. Velocity sank down into his usual chair, crossed his legs, and leaned back, face serene. He removed a thin cigarette case from an inner pocket, selected one, lit it with a gold lighter, drew in a deep lungful, and blew smoke high into the air.

Doctor Velocity was nominally a pharmacist but was really an artist in his own right. His greatest skill was not chemistry but psychology and empathy. He listened in earnest and with insight, which most people did not or could not. He understood, too, and was often able to prescribe something—allopathic or homeopathic—with the subtlety of a true healer. He was that rare kind of person who could be "best friends" with virtually everyone he knew, and could be that without artifice. That alone would have made him invaluable, but Velocity was so much more, so many layers deeper.

Destroyer admired him as a work of art among all the other reasons. That the doctor was the coolest of the cool was obvious to everyone in the Fire Zone; even the ash of his slim French cigarette was correctly long and would not fall until his hand happened to pass idly over an ashtray, and then the ash would fall, untapped, into the precise center of the tray. That was part of Velocity's charm, and Destroyer had no idea how he managed it. Art, sleight of hand, or possibly real magic. Anything seemed possible with the doctor. And, for some reason his cigarettes seemed to perfume a room rather than pollute it. They stank whenever Destroyer smoked one.

Doctor Velocity was so beautiful a person that he didn't even need to be good-looking, but just to be that much more beautiful, he was devastatingly handsome. He had high cheekbones, a strong but not overpowering jawbone, and a patrician nose; he had full lips and a high, clear forehead with gently arching brows. Velocity was a tall man, a fact evident even while seated; he had long, strong limbs, thick wrists, big hands, and sensitive fingers. In contrast to Destroyer's paint-smeared smock and corduroys, Velocity was composed in a charcoal suit of some rough weave, a coral shirt, and hand-painted tie, which blended gray and coral with a dozen other sea colors in a lovely, misty pattern.

He was smiling at exactly the correct angle.

Destroyer always felt grubby when he was with his friend, and yet never felt judged.

"I hope I'm not disturbing your creative process," said Velocity, gesturing to the palette knife still clutched in the artist's left hand.

"No, you're a welcome intrusion, Vee," confessed Destroyer. He looked down at the knife, winced, and tossed it onto a table. Then he pulled up a stool and perched on it like a frustrated vulture, exhaling a long and dispirited sigh. "I thought you'd be at Unlovely's tonight," he said. "Isn't Tortureship debuting their new operetta?"

"That starts at midnight, though, and yes, I'm going." The doctor nodded to the big canvas. "What's wrong? The colors won't come?"

"Oh, it's far worse than that," Destroyer said, sneering at the half-finished painting. "You know, I think I've actually used up what little talent I ever possessed."

Velocity laughed out loud and then stopped, his smile fading. "You're actually serious?"

"Very."

Velocity took a slow drag on the cigarette. "Oh, come on, Des, you know how much everyone loves and admires you. Your paintings are hanging on all the very best walls. They're on display in every gallery that matters. No one else in the trade deserves the right to clean your brushes."

Destroyer snorted. "If that's the case, then God help the art world."

"It's not as bad as all that, surely . . ."

Destroyer gave him a bleak stare. "Vee, right now I don't think I could put red paint on a barn. God, it's devastating." He shook his head. Destroyer had a narrow face with a wide, generous mouth, a thin hooked Roman nose, and black eyes buried in deep wells.

When he was in the flush of his passion, he was exotic, intense, even beautiful, but his disillusionment cast his face into ugliness, and he knew it. "Ahh . . . I don't know what's wrong with me these days."

"I thought you were painting your heart out last week."

"Who told you that?"

"A little bird."

"Yeah, well, that was last week, and when I'm painting, last week is a million years ago. Last week might not even have existed. Painting is so right now." He shrugged. "Besides, Oswald played 'Fire Dreams' last night. The live show."

Oswald Four was the Fire Zone's most famous deejay. He was not exactly a musician but instead let the music in the Zone play through him and out of him and out through the ten thousand speakers mounted along the streets and boulevards and parks. It was more of the magic of this place that Destroyer understood on a subconscious and instinctual level but could never explain to himself—or anyone else—in rational terms. It just was. Oswald Four sat in his glass cubicle at Unlovely's, the largest of the dance clubs in the Zone, and took the music played by the most profound of the local musicians and transformed it and elevated it into *Music*. Capital M because it seemed to become alive and self-aware.

Destroyer did not quite understand it all, and he was aware that he could be completely wrong, but it was his theory that in the Zone, the music had been played so long, so well, with such superb artistry and insight that it had actual consciousness. The song "Fire Dreams," recorded by the supergroup Tortureship, had become a kind of anthem for the Invited. It meant something and told a story of profound truth, even if it was different to everyone who heard it. When Destroyer heard that song it awakened something in him, but like insights gained during a psychedelic high, the thing that was awakened was fickle and fleeting and could never actually be captured. Certainly never tamed.

Destroyer said, "I recorded the concert and played 'Fire Dreams' twenty, thirty, fifty times. I mean, of *course,* I could paint."

"Ah," said Velocity, nodding his understanding. "And to-night . . . ?"

"Tonight even that song seems stale, so I'm back where I was before I heard 'Dreams.'"

"Which is where?"

"Which is nowhere. Absolutely nowhere." Destroyer rubbed his eyes, then stared down at the colorful speckles and smears on his fingers. "You know me better than anyone, you know how it works for me. Paint isn't just grease and oil and chemicals. It's alive. Each color is a separate living thing, and when I blend them they tell me their stories, they evolve, they *become* something that even I can't explain. They're sacred to me, if that isn't too corny a word."

"No," said Velocity, "I absolutely understand you. I've watched you work, and I've sat for more hours than I can count in front of the paintings of yours I own. The one of the young woman with the cracked glass . . . ? I know her entire story from looking at that one painting. I know her damage, her history, her terrors, and her loss, but I also know her power, I've glimpsed her inner light, I know what she's looking for, and I know what she fears. It's all there, a story that tells me another chapter every time I look at it. It's never the same painting twice. So, yes, I get that you've conjured some thing alive in your painting, and that is not me being patronizing."

Destroyer nodded and he felt a knife every bit as real as the one he'd been holding twist a slow quarter turn in his heart.

"That's the problem, Vee. Tonight . . . and for the last couple of days, the paint feels dead, Vee . . . inert. I mean, I can apply it to the canvas, but I can't breathe any life into it. Christ, if this keeps up I'm going to spend my retirement at one of those little booths on the boardwalk in Atlantic City, doing insipid sketches of ugly tourists for ten dollars a pop."

Velocity grinned. "Two words: as if."

"Or I'll be dead," said Destroyer.

The room paused as if taking a breath. Velocity studied him. "You're not joking, are you?"

Destroyer shook his head. "I think it's me. I mean . . . there's something just . . . I don't know . . . lacking in me. Something lost."

"Such as what? Inspiration?"

"No, it's more than that. I mean, I know what I want to paint, I can even see it in my mind, but there's some kind of short circuit between mind and hand. I can't seem to generate the emotional drive necessary to transfer what I see to the canvas. Not in any way that isn't inert, ordinary, merely representational. It's like I have something plugging up my emotions. Somebody's torn out all my wiring."

"Ah. So, I can assume your affair with Aztec is over?"

Destroyer gave him a bleak stare. "Aztec . . . ? Over? Dead is the word you're looking for. He walked out on me last week."

"May I ask why?"

"Oh, it's the same old story with him: one day it's men, the next it's women. I mean, I'm liberal, I can understand being bi-curious, bisexual, or even polyamorous, but the man is just plain screwed up. He doesn't know what he wants. I swear, it'll be sheepdogs one of these days."

"You knew he was fickle when you first asked him out, but now you sound surprised, as if this is all new to you. And it's not like he hasn't broken your heart before."

The artist snorted. "The boy's hurt me so many times I could actually qualify for handicapped plates."

"There are other lovers, my brother. Maybe you might want to go out hunting in safer territory for a while. I mean, just until the wounds heal."

"Yeah, yeah, yeah. That's what Kamala Jane's been telling me."

"My little sister is usually right about such things. Wise lady."

"I know. If I was straight, Vee, let me tell you . . ."

"I think you would have to stand in a long, long line."

"Yeah. Maybe I'll just paint her. Again."

"That'd be nice." Velocity took a slow drag on his cigarette. It smelled like incense. "What about doing some cruising? You know, get back in touch with your roots, so to speak."

"Oh, hell, I can always pick up some tender young thing. I'm popular enough to have a different guy up here every night of the week, but it wouldn't be the same. Let's face it, Vee, I've both been there and done that. No, it's Aztec I want. He may be an infuriating, annoying, contrary little son of a bitch, but I want him." He paused and touched his eyes, looking for tears and still not finding them. "I think I love him. Or, maybe I used to. Or something."

Velocity stubbed out his cigarette. "Love," he said with a Gallic shrug, "is never easy."

Destroyer looked at him. "What are you saying? That *you've* been jilted?"

"Everyone has."

The artist gave him a wan smile. "I can't imagine you losing a love unless you chose to end it."

"Oh, hell, Des, I have my scars, too."

"Mmmph. You hide yours pretty well."

"Hide them?" Velocity pursed his lips and gave Destroyer a small shake of his head. "Not really. I guess I've just found my own rhythms and methods for dealing with them. It's more or less a job requirement for me . . . my patients are more comfortable if I'm not bleeding all over them."

Destroyer sniffed. "Yeah, well. For my own part, I feel like I'm bleeding all over the floor. Unfortunately, I can't seem to bleed this emotional gore onto the canvas."

"And how well you phrase it."

Destroyer almost managed a smile. His mouth was stiff, though, and not accepting of it. "It's funny, Vee, how all this works, how emotion inspires or derails the creative process. I mean, I'm enough of an artist to function according to pure technique. I know structure and balance, light and shadow; I can mix paint and shade it to suggest emotion or mood—but all of that is pure technique. It's the spark inside that's missing; the deep, burning fire that makes me *want* to paint, and makes me want to paint something no one has ever painted before, something no one has ever seen. That's art! That's what real art is all about, to take a knife to one's veins and bleed all over the canvas, to breathe onto it, to stir the paint with tears, to weep and rail and rage at each new smear of paint as it's applied. The canvas should cringe, should tremble at your touch. When the process is over you don't just sign your name and step back—you have to wrench yourself away from it and stagger back breathlessly, aware of how close you came to losing yourself entirely within the painting. When you're finished, what remains is something that's not just alive but *immortal*. Something whose energy is so strong that it must exist and must survive."

Velocity's eyes searched the artist's face for long seconds. "And that's what you've lost?"

Destroyer nodded wretchedly.

"Tell me, Des, that painting I have in my study—the view of the ocean as seen from Villa La Estancia? Didn't you paint that after Aztec left you the first time?"

"Yes."

"Can't you summon those same feelings? Isn't this the same thing?"

"No, no, no, it's totally different. When he left me the first time it was the Great Tragedy. You know what I mean: when you're sure you've lost the love of your life, and you stagger around clutching your heart like there was a knife stuck in it, telling absolutely everyone how your life is over, et cetera, et cetera. That's when the whole world burns down to just your life. You're writhing in the flames, and you're so in the moment that you are positive no one else could possibly understand because no one else has ever loved so well and lost so much. Your heart feels like it's sustained actual physical damage, your arms ache to deliver unused embraces, your mouth is swollen with unshared kisses." He gave Velocity a sharp look, catching the doctor's smile. "Oh, yes, it's to laugh. Such drama."

"And this time?" asked the doctor. "It's different because there is nothing novel about the pain, and the drama is trite because it's a rerun?"

"My God, you do understand after all."

Velocity just spread his hands.

The artist grinned and shook his head. "I even halfway believe he'll come back to me."

"Which would do what to your creative juices?"

"Well . . . probably not turn them into *elixir vitae,*" Destroyer admitted with a sigh. "More likely turn them into Kool-Aid, or something equally banal. Life has taken on that bland taste of the expected, and one does not savor the predictable tastes of ordinary things. You don't close your eyes while you explore the taste of a glass of tap water."

"No."

"So, I guess what I'm experiencing, Vee, is that deadly emotional plateau where there are no real highs or lows anymore."

"And you would relish either?"

"Certainly. Relish them; embrace them with every fiber of my being. Intense pain is as much an artistic stimulant as exultation. At this point getting violently mugged would give me something to paint about." Destroyer rubbed his hands over his face. When he looked at them he was not surprised to see how badly they were shaking. "I'm scared," he said.

"Scared of what, exactly?"

"Of being at the end of what I am," said the artist in a small, bleak voice. "Look, you know how I was when I was younger, what I went through. I understand horror. I've seen things in those foster homes far worse than the fangs of any vampire or the claws of any werewolf. I've felt horror breathing on the back of my neck as it held me in its hands and used me, took me, ripped me apart. I know monsters. Real ones."

"Yes," said Velocity quietly. "You do."

"And you know that coming through that changed me. People talk about surviving childhood horrors, but *survival* is meaningless. Living is what matters. I crawled out of a den of monsters and knew that I could have become one of them. Easily. Very, very easily. That's what happens to some people. They feel how helpless they are when confronted by darkness, and they realize how powerful that darkness is. How vast and unbreakable it seems. And for a lot of kids like me it's easier to just become the darkness and allow it to define them because that work is already done and the template seems so unbreakable."

"Some," said Velocity. "Not all. Not most."

"No. Most creep through life wearing the badge of 'survivor' as if it is a medal for a battle won. It's not. It can't be. Most often a person has survived because the monster did not want to destroy them all the way. To kill them would be to empty them of screams, of struggle, of fear and pain, and that's what those monsters feed on."

Velocity nodded.

"I didn't *survive* my childhood. I rose above it. I put one foot on the neck of my monster and used it to boost myself up out of the shit and the shadows and all of the horror."

"Yes you did."

"Which is why I never talk about this with anyone but you. Not even Aztec knows."

Another nod from the doctor.

"My choice was to define myself," continued the artist, "rather than accept the popular definition. I painted myself into a fresh canvas and I got to choose the forms, the colors, the brushstrokes."

"Yes," said the doctor.

"And that's what gave me the power to paint the things I have, in the past, painted. The pieces that made my name for me. It's why people can look into my paintings and see things that run deeper than the de facto subject. Let's face it, if I paint a seascape it's not really a seascape."

"No."

"Instead of looking outward for approval or acceptance or kindness, like so many others like me do, I looked inward. I took my palette knife to the shadows, I cut away the weakness I saw in myself, I let myself embrace the horrors and *own* them." As he spoke, Destroyer's tone never got above a soft, sad, empty whisper. "But when Aztec left me this last time I realized something about myself that is a new level of horror."

"And what is that?" asked Velocity.

"I'm empty," said the artist. "My colors have dried out and my paint box is filled with dust. No, that's too cliché. My paint box is filled with dime-store watercolors, and everything I try to do now is rote, routine, rinse-and-repeat. God, before you got here, Vee, I was thinking about cutting my wrists or maybe jumping out of the fucking window. Really. And you know why? Because if I finish another goddamn painting, I know—absolutely *know*— that no matter how pretty it looks, no matter how much people oooh and aaah over it, there will not be one drop of real blood in it. All I have left is technique. Can you . . . can you imagine how much that terrifies me? To know that even if I continue to sell my canvases—and they *would* sell, let's face it—I would do so knowing that nothing I ever painted would be as good as what I've already painted. To an artist, that is more terrifying than anything I've lived through or imagined. It is to be dead. It's like being a zombie. Moving, walking, going through the motions but not really alive in any way that matters. Not to me and, ultimately, not to the people who are perceptive enough to know the difference. Not to the people who understand the art I used to be able to do, and who could see it for what it was."

The music changed again and this time it was a young woman singing "The Coventry Carol." Both men sat for a moment and listened to it. A woman singing to her sisters about their children slaughtered by King Herod to prevent the rise of the Messiah. There was such plaintive, desperate pain in her voice that it filled the room with sharp edges.

"That," said Destroyer, pointing to the closest speaker, "is exactly what I mean. That's what I lost."

"Ah," murmured Doctor Velocity. His eyes were filled with kindness and understanding, and there was a small smile on his mouth.

Destroyer looked at him. "What? Am I being amusing?"

"No, you're not."

"Then why the smile?"

He cocked his head to one side, lips pursed, considering. "Oh . . . I had a delicious little thought."

"Yes?"

"Well . . . I was just thinking . . ." He let his voice trail off into a smirk, watching as Destroyer slid forward until he clung to the very edge of his chair. "I was just thinking of something which would be nice to have—I mean, if such a thing were actually possible."

"Like what?"

"This is purely hypothetical, you understand," continued Veloc-ity, "but imagine what it would be like if you could collect the essence of spent lives and used incarnations, boil away everything but the emotions—*all* emotions, no matter how aberrant or mundane—and then contain this distillate into something like a pill. Think about it, Destroyer. It would be a roller-coaster ride of love, hate, agony, ecstasy, humiliation, triumph, degradation, exul-tation, boredom, excitement, sudden awareness, sexual discovery, first love, love lost: *all of it*. A pill such as that would catapult your mind through a lifetime's emotions in, let's say for the sake of argu-ment, three or four hours, and leave you with the emotional echoes that would have your senses tingling for days, possibly weeks. What a rush that would be."

"It would be terrifying," said the artist.

"Yes it would."

"It would be worse than a hundred haunted houses," said Destroyer. "It would be worse than being laid naked on a sacrificial altar to some dark god."

"You're in danger of getting poetic again," cautioned the doctor.

"No, I'm serious. I've read about human sacrifices and let myself go deep into the heads of the priests with the knives and the vic-tims waiting for that first touch of steel. To want to hold that knife, to believe that it is a pathway to a connection with God ... and to be the sacrifice, knowing that your pain is there to serve someone else's vision of the world. They say there are no atheists in foxholes, but I don't believe there are believers on altars. It's appalling. I was the priest and I was the victim, Vee. I *painted* it."

"Yes."

"This would be worse."

"It would," agreed Velocity. "And I bet you would give anything for a pill like that."

Destroyer came to point like a good bird dog, but soon sagged down with a heavy sigh. "Yes," he said, then flapped one hand in despair. "Of course I would. Who wouldn't?"

"Most people," countered the doctor. "For virtually everyone you would ever meet on the street what I'm describing is a horror story. It's nightmares and boogeymen and the clawed hand under the bed all at once. I mean . . . think about what it would be like to swallow a pill with all of Salvador Dali's dreams. Or those of Picasso."

"No," said Destroyer. "I've *had* those dreams. Surrealists, abstractists, cubists—who cares?"

"They were exceptional artists, surely."

"No doubt," growled Destroyer with annoyance, "but despite their famous eccentricities, I don't believe either of them was deeply afraid of much. They affected their quirks and oddness and used them to move like icebreakers through the chilly seas of high society. No. William Blake, maybe. I think he was seeing things that weren't there even when he was awake. Maybe Richard Dadd. And Frida Kahlo understood pain. But again . . . she was accepted, she had a circle of friends, of admirers. That was a buffer. I don't know that she was actually living in horror beyond that of her damaged body."

"So you wouldn't take a Kahlo pill or a Picasso tablet?"

Destroyer thought about it. "No. I don't think so, and I'll tell you why. I'd be afraid that I wouldn't be afraid. I'd be terrified of not feeling anything I haven't already felt. Let's face it, Vee, I'm a notorious eccentric myself. People *emulate* my weird habits, as people emulated Picasso and Kahlo." He shook his head. "No, I think taking such a pill would only sand the last few edges off what I have left. It would be too familiar a landscape and I wouldn't want to paint it."

"Just a thought," said Velocity.

"Oh, don't get me wrong, I can see why you would think that kind of pill would solve everything. Sure, if the right formula could be accomplished it would be so traumatic and overwhelming that it would sweep away any lingering ennui or apathy, but ... it's impossible, or at least improbable. And certainly no help to me."

"Mm, but think if it *could* be done," insisted the doctor. "Think of it, my dear Destroyer—the ultimate trip. Not a head trip, mind you, but a heart trip. Filled with real terrors so intense they would rip you open from head to heart to bowels."

"Please, Vee, I'm far enough out on the edge now. Don't make me ache for something like that. You're asking a drowning man to imagine a luxurious lifeboat."

Doctor Velocity relented and sat back, again brushing invisible specks from his pants leg. "Forgive me, Des, I was just thinking out loud. I was thinking that if such a pill existed, say a pill with the distilled emotions of someone like poor, mad, lonely, broken, brilliant, self-destructive, beautiful Vincent van Gogh—then wouldn't it be glorious?"

"Yes," said Destroyer hoarsely. "But please ... stop ..."

"Such a pill," continued Velocity softly, "might look something like this ..."

He held up a single small pill between thumb and forefinger. It sparkled like a bright blue sapphire.

Destroyer took in his next breath with a gasp. "What.... ?"

Doctor Velocity held the pill up so that it caught the glitter of Christmas lights from outside. Reds and greens and yellows seemed to dance along its seductive curves. "Lovely," said the doctor. "Isn't it?"

"No," cried Destroyer, his eyes bugging. Then he said, "Yes."

"Oh, yes, my friend," Velocity agreed, grinning a bright and conspiratorial grin. "Yes indeed."

The artist licked his lips and made small tentative movements with his hands as if he were about to pounce on Velocity to wrest the tablet away from him. He very nearly drooled, then he flinched as if stung and recoiled, shooting the doctor a harsh, accusatory look.

"You're being cruel," said the artist. "You're just playing with me to try and trick me out of my mood."

The doctor leaned closer, extending his hand. "I said I came here to give you your Christmas present," he murmured, "and here it is. All of the dangers of a dark mind, all of the dreadful emotions of a fractured soul. All for you, my dear friend. And all true."

Destroyer nearly swatted the pill from Velocity's hand. He nearly bolted and ran for the door. Or the window. Or to snatch up the palette knife and stab this smiling man.

He did none of those things.

Instead he stared at the glittering blue pill.

"Please . . . ," he begged.

"Take it," said Velocity, his smile as thin as a promise, his voice so very soft. "Take it and let it hurt you."

Still Destroyer hesitated. The song was reaching its mournful conclusion, and outside, the night sparkled with strange and alien joy.

"Open your mouth and close your eyes," coaxed the doctor.

After a long, long time, the artist complied, sticking out his tongue. His paint-splattered hands were shaking with the palsy of great excitement, his heart beat so forcefully in his chest that it bruised him, and he felt as if his ribs were ready to crack.

Velocity placed the sparkling blue pill on Destroyer's tongue.

"Just hold it in your mouth. Don't chew it, and for God's sake don't swallow it whole. Just let it dissolve."

Destroyer closed his mouth. His whole body was trembling with excitement and expectation.

It took exactly nine seconds for the effect to hit.

Nine.

Long.

Seconds.

Then Destroyer's eyes snapped wide and he stared with the goggle-eyed intensity of a person who was not seeing a single iota of his surroundings. Those eyes jumped and twitched as amazing vistas opened up within his mind. His mouth hung slack, his hands danced and wriggled in his lap as the first waves slammed into his mind. The horrors were all there, waiting beneath the surface of the black waters of madness. Monsters with long, wicked, sharp teeth. Monsters filled with madness and beauty. Monsters who needed to scream and could not manage to scream loud enough. Monsters who needed to feed and could never consume enough. And in the mind of that nightmare landscape crouched a tiny figure, a child born with bad wiring and the wrong chemical mix in his brain, but who possessed a light that struggled to shine forth. Struggled and struggled, and even though that child had left behind enduring masterpieces, he knew that nothing—*nothing*—he ever painted could match the things he saw inside the darkness of his head. As if the art was greater than the flesh of an artist could contain. It was truly and comprehensively terrifying.

The child squatted there, paintbrushes clutched in his tiny fists, and screamed and screamed and screamed.

And Destroyer screamed, too.

Cracks snapped jaggedly across the windows. The colors in his paint box writhed like worms. The canvas on which he had been working blackened to charcoal ashes and fell smoking to the floor.

2

Destroyer was not aware of Velocity as the doctor stood and smoothed down his clothes. Destroyer was looking into another kind of universe, and nothing of this exterior world existed. Not for now. Bombs could have gone off around him and not added one twitch to the waves of spasms that were shaking him.

Smiling, the doctor walked to the door and opened it. He watched the artist tremble and shake as year upon year of emotions surged over him with incalculable rapidity.

"Merry Christmas," said Doctor Velocity. He left before the secondary waves of one-eared Vincent's life's emotions crashed down on the soul of the artist. The screams followed him all the way down to the street.

YANKEE SWAP

JOHN McILVEEN

eaving already?"

Damn it! Kat cursed inwardly, cringing as if pincers had claimed the back of her neck.

Randy Oberlein was the personification of "insufferable." The son of affluent socialites, he was born with a silver spoon inserted so far up his ass he could stir his pancreas. It meant nothing to him that Kat was engaged and very much in love. *And pregnant,* she mentally added, although it didn't show yet.

As assistant division manager, Randy was her superior, which put her in an undesirable position as a subordinate. She was a pur chasing manager, a station she had been proud of ... until she'd actually started the job.

Randy wanted her—had for months—and as far as he was concerned, she was his right ... his entitlement. Evidently, "no" was a word he was not accustomed to and had difficulty acknowledging. She had considered reporting him, but he was as sly as he was arrogant, and the best offense she could present was a *he said / she said* scenario she feared would cost her her job. Her lack of action or reaction only seemed to encourage him.

Randy was the primary reason she had dreaded attending the holiday party, but she'd felt obligated to show up. That it was held in the DoubleTree Suites ballroom had made her more apprehensive. The smug bastard surely had a room reserved and expected her to throw herself upon the mercy of his unhinged whims.

Unfortunately, Kat's fiancé, Vernon, was in Singapore doing whatever it was field engineers did, otherwise he would have been here with her and for her and for their baby. Kat could envision him, with his rugged gunslinger's confidence and overprotective daddy-swagger, planting a size-eleven boot against Randy's forehead. She calmed herself but didn't look at the greasy bastard, instead focusing on the memory of Vernon's glowing smile when Kat showed him the two thick, pink lines on the pregnancy test. His eyes shone as he joked about trading in the Harley for a minivan and designer diaper bag. He had posed like a fashion model and asked her if she'd still find him irresistibly sexy with a baby in a papoose strapped to his chest.

"Leaving already?" Randy repeated, as if she hadn't heard him the first time.

"Yes. I'm not a fan of crowds or loud parties," she said, knowing it sounded like the bullshit it was and that he saw right through it. She remained composed. What she truly wanted to do was embed the pointy toe of her Franco Sarto pumps into his grapes.

"I've rented a top-floor suite. We could go there if you'd like to be someplace quieter."

Bingo!

"No. I really have to go . . . somewhere."

"Are you okay to drive? I can give you a lift."

"I'm fine," Kat said. "I didn't drink anything." She clutched her dinner purse tightly between her arm and ribs and headed for the door. As expected, Randy fell into step beside her.

You fucking fatheaded snake, she thought, and realized that was exactly what he reminded her of, with his large forehead that tapered down to sunken cheeks, and those black beady eyes. He was a dangerous, cold-blooded serpent. He was a cobra.

Shaking inside and out with fear and anger, Kat stopped abruptly, her eyes locked on the floor before her. "Stop—following—me!" she said, assertively enough that a few heads turned toward them.

Randy noticed, too. He held his hands up and took a step away from her in a show of harmless submission, but his hostile eyes promised she would pay for her defiance.

Kat rushed forward, through the ballroom doorway and away from him. She claimed her coat from the check, walked past a bank of elevators, and shoved open the heavy steel door that opened into the parking facility. She was taken aback by the painfully frigid winds that sliced through the garage, unhindered it seemed, from the Charles River. With her notoriously poor sense of direction, she naturally was disoriented. By the time she found her car, her face and fingers were in agony, and she cursed herself for not bringing gloves and a hat . . . mussed hair be damned.

The blow that caught Kat on the back of the head was sharp and unexpected. She had not heard anyone approaching, and her single thought before she lost consciousness was, *Randy.*

A rattling sound brought her around. When she tried to move her head, the pain defined her and owned her, radiating from the back of her neck, over the top of her head, and across her shoulders. A woman cried despondently from nearby, her sobs repetitive and shrill, piercing. Kat wanted her to shut the fuck up before the sound split her skull. She thought she might be in the hospital and tried raising her left arm to feel the small but reassuring swell of her belly, but something metal and unforgiving restrained her movement. She yanked and there was a tightening around the front of her legs, and her other arm was tugged downward.

She opened her eyes to nearly complete darkness, except for a small red light that blinked about every five seconds. Although bright, it seemed distant and offered little help. She couldn't see what bound her arms, but it rattled like heavy, steel chains. She panicked and yanked, ignoring the nauseating pain that flared up her neck and into her skull, driving her to tears. She was seated, her hands tethered to each by a chain strung beneath her chair. Any movement of one arm was countered by pressure on the front of her legs and a pulling on the other arm.

"Ain't no use," said a man's voice, originating from a few feet in front of her. "Just going to fuck your wrists up, is all."

Kat tensed. Her nerves buzzed with anxiety and she expected to be touched—or worse—at any moment and from any direction. *This is bad,* she thought.

"Randy?"

"No, ma'am."

"Who are you? What do you want?" she demanded with a fear-fueled bravado she wasn't feeling.

"I'm Shep. I'm not the one who did this to you, if that's what you're thinking," he said. "Or I wouldn't be sitting here chained to a fucking chair, either."

"Who did this? What do they want? Why . . ."

"Whoa there, cupcake. I don't know any more than you do," Shep said. "I woke up like this a couple hours ago, I guess . . . hard to tell. Head's splitting. Last thing I remember was closing up my office. Fucker said 'excuse me,' and when I turned to him, he popped me good on the head. Sounded like Richard Simmons, the twisted little prick who did this."

Shep didn't sound scared, which had Kat suspicious despite his words. She was terrified, her breathing elevated, and she teetered on the edge of hysterics, though not like the woman still blubbering miserably somewhere to her left. She was incoherent, but her deep, hoarse cries made Kat think she was a mature woman of fifty or more.

"Hey," Kat called to her, "can you give it a rest?"

"Yeah, don't bother. She's zoned out," he said. "And if she doesn't stop carrying on that way, I'll be going over the fucking edge, too. By the way, if he strung you up the same way he did me, you should be able to free a foot or more play for your arms by lifting your legs over the chain. It's work, but it's worth it."

It took Kat a couple minutes, but Shep was right; the small freedom was nearly blissful.

"Christ, I have to go to the bathroom," said a young woman at Kat's near right. *Or maybe it was a teen, or maybe a boy.*

"That there's Gwen," said Shep. "Name's about all I could get out of her; I think she's in shock."

A man to Kat's right released a contemptuous chuff, startling her. He sounded near enough to touch.

"Who's that . . . ? Is that him?" Kat sputtered, leaning away from where the sound had come.

"No. He's been fading in and out for a while, but that snort sounded like derision. It's dark as unholy fuck in here, but there are five of us, maybe six," said Shep. "I tried centering in on the breathing."

The man near Kat moaned in agony. *"Mierda,"* he mumbled, a word Kat was familiar with. Chains rattled softly, and then more determinedly. "What the fuck? What's with the chains, man? This some kind of joke or something?"

"No joke, hombre. Asshole's got a bunch of us penned up here in the dark," said Shep. "Took my phone. Reckon he took the rest of yours, too."

"What does he want?" asked the man.

"Fuck if I know," said Shep. "You Mexican or something? What's your name?"

"Miguel. I'm Dominican, but why the fuck does that matter?" he answered, and then said, "Come on, lady, shit's bad enough without you squealing like that, you know?"

"Please?" Kat said. It was getting on her nerves, too. The woman kept at it.

"How about you? What's your name," asked Shep, and it took a while before Kat realized the question was directed at her.

"Kat," she said. "Katrina."

"You got an accent, too," said Shep. "Fucked if I can tell where from, though."

"Philippines," said Kat. "You like that word, don't you?"

"What word?"

"The F word," said Kat.

"Fucking right I do."

She actually smiled, not that anyone benefited from it.

"Seems we got us an ethnic smorgasbord . . . a Philippine, a Dominican, a Texan, a Gwen, and by the sounds of it, a banshee," Shep said. "Maybe he's putting together some kind of collection. A set. Any of it make sense to y'all?"

"I'm black," said a nervous voice to Kat's right, somewhere between Shep and Gwen. "If he's collecting . . ."

"That you, Gwen?"

"No. I'm Delanna."

"That's a new one on me. Well, howdy, Delanna. I'd shake your hand, but that ain't in the cards right now. How long you been eavesdropping?" asked Shep.

"Fifteen minutes or so. Trying to evaluate the situation," she said.

"Any luck?" asked Shep.

"No," she admitted.

"HOLY FUCKING CHRIST, LADY, SHUT UP!"

The room fell into a dead hush; even the keening woman became silent. What was more unexpected than the sudden shriek was it had come from the one named Gwen.

"Amen," Miguel whispered gratefully.

They sat for an immeasurable amount of time, appreciating the quiet, when the room burst into blinding light. They all cowered, lowering their heads and covering their eyes as much as their fastened hands would allow. Although it seemed to Kat as if a bank of stadium light were turned directly on them, by the time her eyes adjusted, it was difficult to believe that only six standard incandescent lightbulbs on a wagon wheel chandelier, and two or three strands of Christmas lighting, could provide that brilliance.

They sat in matching chairs around a large, round, distressed-wood table. Each of them was equally distant from each other and the table, but all beyond reach due to their manacles and chains. The room was rectangular, with double windows on either side. An opaque material covered the glass, making it impossible to determine whether it was day or night. Kitschy Christmas decorations festooned the place, beneath which was a Southwest decor. Kat wondered how far they were from Boston and if Shep, Southern accent and all, was as innocent as he professed.

At the far end of the room was a door, but no windows. To the left of the door—behind Shep—was a sideboard with a lamp and a nativity scene, complete with baby Jesus and the full cast of characters. Beside the manger was the source of the blinking red light—a small desktop cam, the likes of which you could purchase from Best Buy for fifty bucks.

Kat looked at the five people who sat around the table and saw that they were all just as screwed as she was. Facing her from across the table, Shep was easy to recognize with his blue denim shirt and thick mustache on a weathered face that might have been handsome if he hadn't been so gaunt. Wholesome Delanna sat directly to Shep's left, staring back at Kat with frightened but intelligent eyes. She looked barely old enough for college.

Miguel, directly to Kat's left and across from Delanna, leaned forward, only his wavy black hair visible as he searched beneath his chair, trying to decipher the mechanics of his confinement.

"Son of a bitch," he said. "Chains trapped by the support rails. No slipping out of this, man."

He had intense black eyes, a rugged body, and thick arms, both of them sleeved with intricate tattoos. He intimidated Kat. Although she hated to admit it, he was the kind of man she would not meet eyes with in public and completely avoid in a dark alleyway.

The familiar, high keening emanated from the woman to Miguel's left. She lowered her head and managed to fan herself with one hand, a generous hammock of fat swinging loosely beneath her upper arm. Probably in her late sixties and easily two-fifty, Kat would have wagered a week's pay that the woman had twin teacup poodles named Mitzy and Fitzy at home that yipped incessantly at nothing in particular. Her eyes were red and swollen above bloated cheeks covered with a patina of tears and snot.

"Oh, don't fucking start that shit again," said the petite woman to Kat's right.

It was intriguing, such aggression coming from such a tiny woman with so adolescent a voice. If Gwen broke ninety pounds, Kat would have been surprised. Alabaster skin, hair dyed coal black—with matching black fingernail polish and lipstick—she was a teen Goth dream come true. Yet on closer inspection, Kat detected lines near her mouth and eyes that gave evidence of someone years older.

"Agreed," said Shep. "How about telling us your name there, Buttercup?"

The keening woman didn't answer, only carried on sniveling.

Fear dominated the table, but Kat saw something underneath the others' terror that kept her from dissolving into a hopeless, blubbering mess like . . . well, like "Buttercup."

Shep looked like a doer, constantly scanning the room for answers and a means to escape, as did Miguel, but Miguel also was a mover, pulling at the chair arms, trying to manipulate the chains. If they were to get free, Kat figured she would follow his lead. Delanna looked as confounded as Kat felt, though sentient, and Gwen just looked utterly pissed off.

Kat turned in her chair as far as the restraints would allow and looked behind her. A large Christmas tree, heavily swathed with lights and ornaments as generic and tacky as she had ever seen, stood to the right of another door. Beneath the tree, presents of various sizes lay across the floor in a haphazard offering. Further to the right, cornered with the windowed wall, was a small side table on which was set another camera that winked ominously.

"We're being watched," Kat said.

The far door slammed open, crashing heavily into the side-board. A figure leapt into the room and flung its arms skyward. "Correctamundo!" he blurted, and then took a moment to look at each one of them. "Oh, look at you all . . . so adorable!"

He wore a red mid-length jacket with a white fur collar, green tights, and a wide black belt that cinched his middle. On his head was a pointed red cap that bent to the left a third of the way down. The Santa's helper getup might have been cute and even disarming, if not for a hideous rubber goblin mask, which made the whole display terrifying. Buttercup crescendoed into a completely new level of wailing.

"What the fuck?" Shep said upon seeing this display.

"Oh, we're going to have so much fun!" The masked oddity skipped closer to them. "I'm Flea . . . get it? Backward it's A-E-L-F, a elf." He sounded proud of himself.

His voice was high and did have a Richard Simmons intonation to it, as Shep had mentioned, but Kat thought it sounded contrived.

"*An* elf," Gwen corrected, her lip slightly lifted in a sneer.

Flea's grotesque face snapped in Gwen's direction and he scuttled behind her.

"Oh, are we *an* English teacher?" Through unseen eyes, he watched her intently, swaying slightly. "No, honey, you're *a* tattoo artist and I'm still Flea, because I said so . . . so there."

He touched Gwen lightly on the head with his index finger and hurriedly moved around the table to beside Buttercup's side. He leaned close to her, their faces inches apart. His circus clown theatrics gave him unsettling stop-motion intensity.

"What's wrong, my blubbery, blubbering butterball?" he asked, his tone syrupy sweet.

Buttercup stared at the grotesque mask, quivering and sniffling, her fingers fumbling nervously among themselves.

"BOO!" Flea screamed in her face, and then pranced off, giggling maniacally.

Buttercup squealed childishly and managed to squeeze her girth deeper into the chair.

"Why are you doing this?" Kat asked.

"Oh, isn't that obvious? 'Tis the season, sweetheart." Flea spun, raised his arms in a less-than-impressive pirouette, and sang, "It's the most wonderful time of the year."

"Pardon me there, amigo, but what the fuck are you talking about?" asked Shep.

Flea stopped spinning and faced Shep. "Christmas, silly! It's the season for giving, and I've got gifts for all of you to open!"

He clasped his hands together and dashed to the Christmas tree, squatted, lifted three of the gifts, and carried them to the table. He set them neatly at the center and repeated the process.

"There! Isn't this fun! We're going to have a Yankee swap!"

He patted Miguel atop the head. Miguel recoiled, and Flea, unperturbed, skittered around the table. He situated himself behind Gwen, grabbed ahold of her chair, and slid her closer to the table. He repeated the process with the five remaining chairs and their occupants. To Kat, it seemed he moved Shep's, Miguel's, and Buttercup's chairs just as easily as Gwen's.

Stationing himself behind Delanna, he merrily clapped his hands together. "So . . . does everyone know the rules for a Yankee swap?" he asked and waited. "Come *on,* people, somebody answer me!"

"Fuck you," Shep muttered.

"Oh, I don't think so."

Flea quickly maneuvered behind Shep and ran a hand affectionately over his head. The Texan's eyes widened and his entire body began convulsing as a rivulet of drool ran over his bottom lip and fell to his shirt, forming a dark blue Rorschach pattern.

Buttercup amped up her squealing and Miguel let out a dismayed "fuck," trying to scoot backward in his chair. They all stared at Shep in dismay, and then at Flea, when he proudly displayed a black device to them.

"Nothing inspires cooperation like one of these . . . they're stunning, if you'll pardon the pun. Whether you want to or not, you're *all* going to cooperate." He put the stun gun in his coat pocket; his left one, Kat noted.

"Okay, sunshine, time to come back. You need to hear the rules," Flea said cheerily, as if speaking to a toddler. He slapped Shep's cheeks lightly. Shep groaned and glared at him. Flea cocked his head disturbingly to one side and then righted himself.

"Good!" he said dismissively. "So the rules *are* . . . the participants—that means all of you—draw numbers." Flea drew a handful of papers from a pocket on his jacket, removed his cap, and pushed them inside. "I *love* this! Okay! Whoever draws number *one* goes first and opens a gift from the pile. Number two then opens a gift. If he or she prefers the gift number one opened, he or she can *trade* for that one instead." He paused thoughtfully. "You know what? Fuck it, I'll tell you the rules as we go."

His masked face regarded each person seated around the table, moving from one to the next with a jerking motion that reminded Kat of a bird, especially with the black hollows of the mask's eye-holes that betrayed nothing of the man inside. The goblin face abruptly jolted and faced Kat, and with a flourish of the wrist, he pointed at her.

"You first!" he said. He bounced to her side and held the opened cap toward her.

Kat looked at the faces of the others seated around the table. In their eyes, she encountered terror, hatred, anger, and hopelessness, but not the salvation or inspiration she thought she'd seen earlier. That he had chosen her to go first was a terrible omen that seemed to validate her fear of not leaving there alive.

"Ka-at, pick a number," Flea said in a singsong voice, bisecting her name into two syllables.

She was frozen. She couldn't move or speak, but only stared at the collection of gifts centered on the table and Delanna's countenance in the hazy background, slowly shaking her head in fearful denial. Seeing no alternative, Kat slowly reached a shaky hand into the hat and pulled out a square of paper. The rest of them followed suit as Flea moved clockwise around the table.

"Okay, kiddies, unfold your papers and tell me who has number one." He rubbed his hands and shuffled around the table. "Who is it? Who is it? Oh, who is it, already, or do I have to get zap-happy?"

"I do," Delanna whispered.

"Ooooh, hooray!" Flea said with delight. He capered over to her and plucked the paper from her fingers. "Okay ... pick a gift!"

Delanna stared at the colorful packages, saying nothing.

"Come on!" Flea cajoled.

Silence.

"PICK A FUCKING GIFT!" Flea erupted. It started as a shriek and ended as a throaty growl. Everyone around the table started, and Buttercup recommenced her soggy sniveling. Kat heard insanity in his words, but they resonated in the back of her mind, as if they had awakened something familiar yet out of reach.

"The blue one," Delanna said, her voice no more than a whisper.

"Snowflakes or *Frozen*?" asked Flea.

"Snowflakes."

Flea grabbed the chosen package and tossed it to Delanna, who mechanically caught it, her chains rattling with the quick movement.

Half-crouched, rapt, and looking ready to bolt, Flea watched her. "Open it," he said with childish impatience.

Delanna cautiously pulled at a silver ribbon as if afraid it would explode. Within the wrapper was a small box. Delanna opened it and removed some tissue and a small prescription bottle.

"Whatcha get—whatcha get?" Flea asked excitedly.

"Pills?" Delanna said cautiously, sounding more like a question.

"Yes! Well, capsules actually, but not just any capsules ... those are special *Jesus* capsules. They'll take *all* your pains and worries away," said Flea. "And there are six of them, in case you're in the giving spirit. Sharing is caring! What a wonderful gift! I'll even open them for you."

He did so, setting the bottle and cap on the table before her.

"I really have to piss," Gwen said again.

"Me too," added Miguel.

"Be my guest," Flea offered amiably, dismissing them. "Okay, who's next?" After a short silence, he patted his left pocket. "Number two-ooo. Zap zap!"

"Yup," said Shep. He crumpled the paper and tossed it to the center of the table.

"I'm so looking forward to you!" Flea gushed, enthusiastically clapping his hands.

"I'm sure you are," Shep muttered.

"All right, cowboy, make a choice."

Shep sneered at their twisted host and said, "The flat one."

"Ooooh!" Flea brought the chosen gift to Shep and set it down. Shep slowly opened the package and from inside the slender box withdrew an old hacksaw with a black Bakelite handle and a rusted blue blade.

"Oh, what have we here?" Flea said. "It looks a little worn. I doubt it would cut metal, but in a pinch it could still work for you."

Flea grabbed the saw from Shep and dragged it across the man's exposed arm, leaving an angry red gash. Shep recoiled and hollered in pain. He pressed his wounded arm to against his abdomen, leaving a bloody streak on the denim. His jaw tightened and his face darkened as he defiantly tried to compose himself. Buttercup, in contrast, launched into another bout of squealing cries.

"Such a *handy* gift, if you catch my drift," Flea said.

Buttercup's wails escalated and Flea's head dropped and his shoulders sunk. He set the hacksaw down before Shep and walked purposefully around the table to stand behind the squealing woman.

"You are ruining our *fun*," he admonished her. There followed a high-pitched report, like the snapping of a dry branch. They all jumped and Delanna yelped in surprise at the gunshot. Buttercup's body went rigid as her right eye blossomed red, then she slumped to her side, silent and still. Eyes wide, mouth agape, Kat watched

Flea switch the small pistol to his right hand and pocket it. Despite her shock, she had the absurd realization he was left-handed.

"Why the fuck you do that, man?" Miguel demanded, disbelieving.

"She was such a party pooper," Flea said with embellished pathos. Recovering quickly, he clapped his hands. "Look at the bright side! We have an extra gift!"

Kat couldn't take her eyes off Buttercup. They had turned a corner. Reality shifted. She knew the potential of death was present, but she had wrapped herself safely within denial until then. A series of panicked thoughts scrolled through her mind and the awareness that they had never found out her name.

"So, cowboy, are you keeping your gift, or do you want to trade with Delanna for her capsules?" Flea asked.

Shep stared coldly at him. "I'm good," he said. His arm was still pressed against his shirt, but judging by the stains, he wasn't bleeding much.

"Now we're back on track! Who's number three-eee?"

"Yo," said Gwen, holding the paper loosely between thumb and forefinger, trying to appear unfazed. The fast rise and fall of her chest betrayed her terror.

"Yo-ho-ho, Gweno!" sang Flea. "Pick a gift, sweetie pie."

Something in the way he said her name troubled Kat.

Yo-ho-ho, Gweno!

Gwen's eyes shifted to the goblin face, and Kat thought she saw recognition in the other woman's eyes. *"Frozen,"* Gwen said, suspiciously watching the demon mask, searching.

"Adorable!" Flea clapped again, a frenzy of hand pats.

Gwen . . . Gweno, Kat thought.

Flea delivered the box to Gwen, his hip brushing Kat's arm. She recoiled impulsively, as if his corruption could leach through her clothing and flesh and contaminate her. Flea's head jerked toward her and Kat hoped he felt threatened, if only for two seconds. She sensed—or more so, smelled—a faint whiff of cologne. It was one she recognized . . . one she both loved and hated. It was so manly and stimulating on Vernon, so cloying on Randy, but downright nauseating on this piece of shit.

"Lacoste," Kat said.

"What?" Flea asked.

"Lacoste," Kat repeated. "Your cologne. You're wearing Lacoste Essential."

He froze for a moment and Kat knew she had shaken him and wished she could see his face behind the mask.

"Open your gift," he said to Gwen, a little less vibrant. She accepted the package, her frightened eyes never leaving the mask. He seemed to notice the scrutiny.

"Yes?" he asked her with a tilt of his head, his voice chipper yet wary. Gwen didn't answer. "Open your gift," he repeated, his voice deeper under the gravity of threat.

Gweno. Gwen the Ho, Kat thought. *Gweno . . . tattoo artist . . . Lacoste Essential . . . left-handed.*

Gwen opened the package and removed a small Igloo cooler, inside of which was a single box cutter that, like the hacksaw, had a rusty blade.

Flea, returning to form, gasped with glee. "Isn't the cooler delightful, sticking with the *Frozen* theme that way? And a box cutter! It would work great on those pasty white wrists of yours. Now all three of you have an easy way out . . . if you so choose!" He compellingly put his hands to his chest. "See, I'm not a bad guy. You can't deny there's an element of generosity here."

"Oh my God!" Kat said with a sob. "You're supposed to be in Singapore!"

Shep looked confused, and Delanna studied Kat like a scientist awaiting a chemical reaction. Kat's reality swooped and spun. The room seemed cavernous and then tiny, fading and sharpening, echoing and then stuffy, and Kat sensed she was on the verge of passing out.

"Excuse me?" asked Flea.

"You called her Gweno," Kat said. "Gweno the Ho. Gwench the Wench . . . the unfaithful ex. I know it's you, Vernon!"

"Vernon?" Gwen said in disbelief. A parade of emotions crossed her face starting with shock, then confusion, anger, disgust, and settling on fear.

Flea's shoulders fell and he pulled off the mask, revealing his handsome face. Delanna's eyes widened, but she remained silent. Somehow, she knew him, too.

"You miserable prick," Shep said.

"You always have to fuck things up, don't you?" Vernon said to Kat, his eyes cold and feral.

Gone were the elfin voice and ostentatious gestures and any sign of the tender man who had asked for her hand six months earlier, the man she had kissed in E terminal of Logan Airport four days ago. Kat felt as if she were detached from her body, trying to make sense of the unexplainable.

"Vernon. Oh, Jesus Christ, how could you?" Kat asked, her words choked with emotion and snagging on her confusion.

"I didn't get on the plane. I didn't go to Singapore, you idiot . . . I've never been there," Vernon said.

How could that be? He left for a week every two months, had been doing it since she met him more than a year ago.

"You fucking killed someone!" Gwen said, not comprehending. "You need help."

"She was a piece of shit. My asshole landlord. She deserved it." He gave a dismissive *oh well* shrug. "I planned to let one of you live. Not you," he said to Kat. "But since you let *this* cat out of the bag," he said, jacking both thumbs toward his chest, "no one's going home."

Disbelieving and fearful glances passed around the table, most pausing on Buttercup's still form. With surprising reserve, Shep asked Delanna, "So, what did *you* do to cross him, sweetheart?"

Delanna's lip curled as she spoke. "We worked at Hastings. He kept asking for a blow job. He tried to drag me outside one night. I started screaming and he got fired."

"Hastings?" asked Kat. As far as she knew, Vernon had never worked there, but it seemed there was quite a bit she didn't know.

"In Waltham. We make heat sinks," said Delanna.

"*Made* heat sinks in your case, you frigid bitch," Vernon said with a mocking laugh. "Should have just done it—you wouldn't be here. You're still going to give me one . . . maybe more."

"So this is a grudge-fest?" asked Shep. "Punish those who hurt your little pussy feelings?" His reckless defiance concerned Kat.

"Exactly. They might be little pussy feelings, but who has the upper hand now?" asked Vernon. "Not a thing even a piece-of-shit Texas lawyer like you can do."

"What the fuck I do, man?" asked Miguel.

"Sorry, guy, wrong place at the right time. I needed six players and you were convenient. Sucks to be you."

Players? Kat wondered. *This is all a game to him.* Who was this stranger? He was insane . . . evil. How had she planned a life with him? How had she slept with him, been intimate, and gotten pregnant by him and not seen this?

"I'm pregnant . . . with *your* baby!" Kat said.

He glanced at her abdomen and released a single, quick snort. "Number four," the man who looked like Vernon demanded.

"Are you fucking serious?" asked Gwen.

"Yeah, I'm fucking serious," mocked Vernon. "Number four. NOW!"

"I want to trade," Gwen said quickly, her scared eyes wide. "You said we could trade."

Vernon stared at her acidly. "Fine. With whom? How about Delanna's capsules? I'd love to watch you take one."

"Fuck your capsules," said Delanna. She flicked the bottle with the back of her hand, sending it spinning and scattering its contents across the table.

Rage contorted Vernon's face. He reached into his right pocket but stopped and forced composure. He smiled at his former coworker, and Kat could see it took every iota of his strength.

Disregarding Delanna, Vernon instructed Gwen to slide the box cutter to Shep, which she did. He then told Shep to slide the hacksaw to Gwen. Staring blankly at Vernon, Shep gave the hacksaw a quick push, and it caromed over the edge of the table. With barely bridled reserve, Vernon bent to retrieve it, his eyes locked on Shep's. Kat's eyes moved to the cutter.

"Watch yourself," Vernon said.

Kat wasn't sure if the warning was for her, Shep, or Gwen, but decided she'd rather not have any more of his attention than necessary. Vernon placed the hacksaw in front of Gwen and held her gaze. Kat saw the dare in his eyes, but they shifted warily and she thought, *He's scared, but he has to go through with this. He can't leave any of us alive, and he knows we're desperate.*

"Number four!" he demanded.

Staring blankly ahead, Kat set the paper face up on the table.

"Pick!" Vernon immediately responded, discharging the word like a bullet.

"The white box," said Kat.

Leaning close to Delanna, Vernon reached for the gift and slid it in Kat's direction. It fell over the lip of the table and dropped solidly into her lap. It was heavier than she had expected.

"Open it," he said impassively.

From inside she withdrew a wooden cigar box, the name *COHIBA* printed in thick black letters on the cover. A small metal latch held the box closed, and Kat preferred it that way.

"Go on. Open it," Vernon said.

Kat considered throwing it at him, but she'd never had good aim and it would only piss him off further. She slowly lifted the latch, opened the cover, and gawked at the box's contents. She quickly placed it on the table.

"That's a Ruger SR9C, but of course *you* wouldn't know that. It's also ironic *you* picked it, since you're too goddamned prissy to use it. For what it's worth, it's fully loaded, but I'm not concerned. How many times have you told me you'd never take a life, even to save your own? I guess we'll find out now just how honorable you really are."

She was confident he'd never give any of them a loaded handgun unless he was suicidal. He couldn't have known she'd be the one to pick that gift. But he'd already surprised her on a few accounts, so she couldn't really know. The bitch of it was that he was right. No matter her own shock and horror, she wouldn't kill. Couldn't kill.

"You're lying," she said.

"The clip holds seventeen rounds, check it out. Give it a try."

"Do it! What do you have to lose," hissed Miguel. "Shoot the motherfucker, man."

Kat couldn't. She didn't have it in her, but she could trade with someone who did. Maybe if . . . she again glanced at the box cutter.

"I want to swap with Shep," she said, and prepared to slide the box.

"Hold it!" Vernon said. Kat stopped and Vernon grinned. "Cowboy, slide the box cutter to Kat."

Kat's bleakness increased. She had planned to slide the gun over the edge of the table and divert Vernon's attention so Shep could use the box cutter on him, but Vernon was too attuned.

I'm so stupid! Kat thought. *Now I have a blade I'm afraid to use and Shep gets a likely useless gun.*

"Slide the box to the cowboy. Gently."

Kat did.

When Shep reached for the box, Vernon aimed the Beretta at him. "I'm watching your every move," he said. Shep slowly settled back, the chains rattling against his chair.

The gun might actually be loaded, Kat thought. Vernon's reaction seemed authentic. Vernon rounded the table and stood behind Buttercup's corpse, to Miguel's left. His eyes stayed trained on Shep.

"Two presents left, thanks to your neighbor, here," he said to Miguel. He patted Buttercup atop her head.

Kat looked at the presents and then saw Gwen to her right. She sat with her head slightly lowered, breathing rapidly as if she had sprinted up a series of stairways. Kat wondered if it was a form of meditation to alleviate the discomfort from having to piss, but Gwen looked up displaying the terror in her eyes.

"Oh God!" Gwen gasped and then snorted, desperate for breath. She tried to rise but the chains caught. She dropped back into the seat and started convulsing.

Is she epileptic? Kat wondered. A milky froth coated Gwen's lips and Kat understood what she had done. "No! Help her! She took the pills!"

All heads turned toward the struggling woman, and pleading voices rose. Kat's attempt to rise also succumbed to limits of the restraints.

Vernon walked slowly toward Gwen, watching her with profound interest. He squatted near her and studied her horrified eyes as she searched the room, her now shallow breaths creaking into and out of her.

"Not as quick and painless as you were hoping, is it?" he asked her impassively.

"Help her!" Kat said.

"Come on!" said Miguel.

Silent, Delanna watched Gwen, her eyes wide with shock.

"Nothing I could do if I wanted to," Vernon said, his eyes still searching Gwen's as if looking for some cryptic truth. Finally, gratefully, Gwen fell unconscious.

To Kat's right, Shep snagged the box from the table. Vernon sprawled to the floor and scrabbled behind Gwen as Shep wrestled the gun free of the box and clicked off the safety.

"Stupid move, cowboy!" Vernon said.

Shep aimed for Vernon's voice and the reemerging arc of his head as it maneuvered to either of Gwen's shoulders, popping up for a fraction of a second and then disappearing.

"He's got his gun out, bro!" warned Miguel. The words no sooner left his mouth when a shot snapped, and a red star blossomed on Miguel's left cheek. He jolted upright in his chair, as if posing for a portrait, and then slowly slumped forward.

"You fuck!" screamed Shep, steadying the Ruger with both hands.

Vernon feinted to the right and then lunged left, putting Kat between them. Shep tried to draw a bead on him, but Vernon repeatedly bobbed from left to right over Kat's shoulders.

"Shoot him!" Kat, sure she'd be the next to die, surprised herself by slapping hard at Vernon's gun hand. The little gun cracked a shot off before careening across the room and settling beneath the Christmas tree.

Taken off guard, his expression unreadable, Vernon stood with his hands slightly raised. Shep held the Ruger steady, aimed at Vernon's head, and pulled the trigger, but no shot rang out. Instead, Shep yelped in pain, threw the pistol to the ground, and brought his hand to his mouth.

A smile spread across Vernon's dementedly handsome face. He walked toward Shep and stooped to pick up the gun. Holding it with the handgrip toward the ceiling, he pressed the trigger, and a silver needle protruded from the handle directly behind the trigger.

"I'm proud of this one ... an old trick, making the trigger a syringe, but I machined it myself." He patted Shep on the shoulder, though keeping safely behind him. "You're in store for an ugly, painful death, cowboy, which really kind of pleases me after the screwing you gave me. Ever hear of an Eastern Brown Snake? Australia has the best critters. The venom is available on the black market, if you're willing to cough up the cash. I was willing, so you'll be dead within an hour." He set the Ruger on the table.

Gwen's body released a shuddering paroxysm, and Kat hoped it was her last, for Gwen's sake.

"Three dead. Soon to be four. Two to go," Vernon said.

"They'll find you," Delanna said. "They'll make the connections."

"No, they won't," Vernon said.

His smug confidence disgusted Kat. She couldn't believe she had once found it appealing. She recognized the certainty of her death, but she couldn't accept the unfairness that her child would be cheated of a life. When she had told him of her pregnancy three months earlier, he had seemed so pleased and comforting. Beside her, Shep jerked in his seat. A fine sheen of sweat had formed on his brow.

"Won't you help him?" Kat asked.

"Nope."

"And you're willing to let your baby die?"

Vernon gave a scoffing laugh. "That's the reason you're here ... well, it was the final straw. I don't want no fucking kid, and I know you wouldn't let me walk away, like I wanted to. You'd demand money and other shit and make my life miserable, like the rest of these pricks have."

"Who are you?" Delanna said, the thought contorting her face. "You evil bastard. I hope you burn in Hell forever."

Vernon snorted. "Maybe if I believed in Hell."

"So you feel nothing," said Kat.

"Nada." He gave a sarcastic *sorry* shrug.

"And for me?" Kat asked.

"Especially not for you," Vernon said.

"Prove it," said Kat. "Kiss me."

"What?" asked Delanna, unbelieving.

"I can't even stand looking at you, why would I want to kiss you?" asked Vernon.

"If you really don't love me, kiss me and prove it has no effect on you. You know you still care."

Vernon searched her sad eyes and looked behind him. Gwen was no threat. Shep sat across from them, staring blankly forward, his chest rising and falling rapidly. On the table, out of either Shep's or Kat's reach, were the Ruger and the box cutter.

"Fine," Vernon said, too arrogant to refuse the challenge.

Vernon pressed his lips to Kat's and she spit heavily into his mouth. She simultaneously dropped her left hand and drove her balled right fist into his throat. Even though the chains enfeebled the blow, it worked. Vernon stumbled backward, the impact of her small fist causing him to swallow both her spit and the little capsule she had popped into her mouth.

Vernon recoiled, shocked, disgusted, and clutching at his throat. He collided with Gwen, swerved around her chair, and staggered away from Kat, trying to cough. Leaning his left hand on the back of Gwen's chair, he glared at Kat, who was spitting repeatedly onto the floor, praying she would be able to get rid of at least most of the residual poison.

Vernon reached to gain his balance, but Shep, rattlesnake quick, grabbed his wrist and yanked, pulling him onto his lap. The Texan wrapped his arms tightly around Vernon, trapping him.

"Can either of you get to the blade?" Shep asked, his face contorting with the effort, his body shaking.

"Just hold him! He swallowed cyanide!" Kat said.

"No shit?" Shep asked, managing a grin despite his struggle.

"He's reaching for the stun gun!" Kat warned, noticing Vernon's fingers working at his jacket pocket.

Shep clamped his teeth into Vernon's shoulder and bit down hard. Rewarded with an agonized wail, he clenched harder and held Vernon until his breath became labored, his limbs twitched, and ultimately his body went limp. Shep let him slide to the floor.

"How in the hell did you pull that off?" he asked.

"I was counting on his ego and that he'd look to see if he could reach the box cutter, and he didn't disappoint. That's when I popped the pill." She spat on the floor again.

"I think you'll be okay. Those were capsules and the poison's inside," Delanna said.

Kat looked at the inert form of her fiancé sprawled on the floor and spit again. The betrayal, the emotions, and the utter horror of what had transpired finally grabbed hold of her and she burst into tears.

"Shep, oh my God, are you okay? Is it starting to affect you?" Kat asked, guiltily pulling herself out of her grief and back to the present.

Shep flexed his hand. "Got the nervous sweats and a little burn where the needle bit me, but feeling no worse for wear. I'm thinking Vernon got played by his black market friends. Either that or I'm nastier than that old snake. 'Course, he said an hour, so maybe it just hasn't set in yet."

Kat pitched forward, bouncing her chair and herself toward the table in diminutive increments.

Shep watched her for a moment, then asked, "Where you off to?"

"The hacksaw," Kat said. "Might not cut metal, but if it'll cut a bone, it'll cut wood. We got to get out of here and get you to a hospital."

The saw lay on the table in front of Gwen's slumped form, but at the rate Kat was moving, it would remain there a while longer.

Shep took up after Kat's lead, bouncing forward in small hops toward the table.

"Don't! You'll speed up your circulation!" Delanna warned him, and started bouncing toward the table, too, but Shep was quickly within reach of the box cutter and Ruger. Delanna and Kat both stopped bouncing.

"I'm going to try to knock the saw closer to you," Shep said to Kat. He took aim and slid the box cutter across the table. It careened off the side of the hacksaw, only managing to nudge it closer to Gwen. Delanna rolled her eyes, and despite the nightmare they had endured, Shep laughed aloud.

"Well, that wasn't worth its weight in shit," he said. "Hang on."

"You the one needs hanging on," Delanna said.

"I'm good," Shep said. He repeated the process with the gun, which again missed the mark. "Fuck!" he shouted as the Ruger shot across the table, knocking the hacksaw even farther to the left.

The gun plunged over the edge of the table, but Kat hooked the trigger guard with the tip of her ring finger in an impressive display of athleticism. She was saved from tumbling to the floor by the arm restraints, but not without a substantial dose of discomfort to right herself. Shuffling a bit closer to the table, she set the gun flat, aligned her sights, and pushed. The gun hit the intended target squarely, and the hacksaw ricocheted perfectly into Shep's waiting hands.

"Show-off," said Shep.

———

The saw was indeed dull. By the time Shep made the four cuts necessary to free him from the multiple binding points on the chair, his arms and hands shook and throbbed, and a clammy sweat covered his brow. He sat back to rest a moment.

"Still feeling all right?" Kat asked.

"Yeah." He flexed his hand again. It felt weak and was still vibrating, but he attributed that to the sawing. "Maybe Vernon's venom was a dud, after all."

"Clearly, after exerting like that," Delanna said. "You're a lucky guy."

Shep rose, flipped his chair, and freed the chain. Fighting a bout of vertigo from rising too fast, he gathered the restraint over his shoulder and asked, "Who next?"

"Forget that! See if you can find a phone," Kat said. "Call the police."

"Maybe there's a better saw around here somewhere, too," said Delanna.

Shep looked at them and huffed. "Smart ladies," he said.

He headed for the kitchen; if there was a phone, it would be in there, he figured. Legs numbed from sitting too long, he stumbled through the doorway and scanned the room, which was cluttered in a haphazard way that was indicative of intrusion, not of residence.

A computer backpack lay open on the counter beside an opened laptop. To the left of the laptop, near the door, a landline phone was mounted to the wall, and to the right, two open clamshell containers, one of them still half full of Chinese takeout food, an empty bottle of Corona, and a mostly full bottle of Diet Coke. Shep found this especially disconcerting.

Dinner for two.

He stood silently still and listened for evidence of another soul, then decided the best action was to get help as quickly as possible. As he reached for the phone, a sudden dizziness washed over him. He staggered to the counter, knocking the laptop's mouse to the floor and awakening the computer display to a disturbing split-screen image of the dining room from either end, one facing Kat, the other facing Delanna. The cameras were black-and-white, which gave everything an ethereal, indistinct hue. The women's eyes shone silver and Shep was taken by their vulnerability, chained to the chairs as they were.

With a shaking hand, Shep lifted the handset, which slipped through his numbed fingers and fell to the countertop. His left leg defied him next, folding beneath him and dropping him to his knees in front of the laptop. The strength in his legs had diminished with unsettling speed, but it wasn't his legs that stopped his effort to rise.

On the small computer screen, Shep watched as a monochromic Delanna stood before Kat. Short lengths of untethered chain dangled from both of Delanna's manacles, dragging across the tabletop as she picked up the box cutter.

Shep corralled the phone handset closer to him and jabbed the break button. Once he heard the dial tone, he managed to depress 9-1-1 with barely responsive fingers.

Ringing . . .

On the screen, Delanna moved toward Kat. Shep's chin hit the counter, and as he fell to the floor, awkwardly clutching the phone to his ear, Kat's screams emanated from the dining room. He heard a voice that sounded miles away.

"911, what's your emergency?"

HONOR THY MOTHER

ANGELA SLATTER

Snow is falling and Agnes is sure she can hear it whisper through the air and land with the softest of sighs on tree branches, cars, outdoor furniture, and on the layer of flakes already deposited on the ground. She loves how it looks, loves that there is a season that can be relied upon. Christmas in Salem will always be white.

Everyone is here this year. She insisted. In the past, one or other of her sons would make the call, sheepish and apologetic: *This time we'll be with Jill's family—or Amy's or Rebecca's. Next holiday season, Mum, we'll come to you and bring the kids. We'll stay a whole week, I promise, you'll see.*

And in truth that one generally kept his word, but then another would fall by the wayside, calling while his wife waited in the background, not saying anything, but glaring, Agnes knew, as her boy's voice faltered, made excuses. She wondered if her sons drew straws: Who would it be this year, freed of duty to Mother, so another could be done to Wife?

Agnes peers out the tall window into her front yard. The blocks are large in this neighborhood, the houses vintage and venerable, all of them dragging their history through the centuries. It's Salem, it's always a witch: a witch lived here, a witch lived there. One appeared in the bedroom of this home, yet another disappeared up the chimney of that. This parlor was infested by dozens of glowing blue jellyfish, in that barn a spectral woman sat astride the beams and laughed as she rained nails down on the head of a man who'd offended her.

Agnes's house is conspicuous by its lack of witchy history. That's why she chose it: without a past that's both picturesque and grotesque, an abode garners no great interest from tourists; no one wants to see a place where neither witchcraft nor murder occurred. Others feel it as a lack—Agnes knows several of her neighbors have made up their own stories, and there's a man in Boston, a fine forger, who's happy enough to create "historical" documents to support their claims—but she's never wanted anyone to knock on the door and ask to be shown the bewitched kitchen or spectral outhouse. She likes her privacy, knows it's integral to her safety; her husband used to joke that if she could have got away with it, she'd have put a plaque on the front fence that read, "Nothing ever happened here."

The building is First Period, in the Chestnut Street District; on the outside it's tidied and maintained in proper architectural style so no busybody can complain that she's had it painted hot pink or added Gothic gables or an Italianate balcony. On the inside, however, it's been renovated to within an inch of its life for maximum comfort; the decor is modern and she doesn't care what anyone else thinks. Agnes has no love for antiques, finds them uncomfortable things to have around, and the chairs and lounges impossible to sit upon for long periods; forget sleeping in those beds! Such things gather too much dust and she's got no love of excess house-work. She's seen the pinched lips on her daughters-in-law when they catch sight of the La-Z-Boys scattered through the house, but she doesn't care; comfort above all. Agnes has always had her idio-syncrasies, and her late husband—she does miss him sometimes—was smart enough to give way in most things, which was probably why they got along so well.

It doesn't take night long to fall, and the sky has gone from pale blue to icy gray to black while she's watched. Now there are just the tasteful luminous Christmas decorations (which strikes her as a contradiction in terms) on facades and in trees, and the expensive light fittings inside the houses across the street, which are dimmed, for she seems to be the only person in the neighbor-hood who likes them bright at night. She likes the darkness kept at bay. Mood lighting is, she thinks, the correct word for it; it puts her into a mood all right.

In the front sitting room, she's curled in an ungrandmotherly fashion in an armchair by the hearth. The Christmas tree, with mounds of presents beneath, is in the corner, far enough away to avoid a similar meltdown to the one that had occurred forty or so years ago, when she and Phips were young, newly married, and inexperienced in the ways of tree placement. It had been a much smaller tree—they couldn't afford much, having stretched them-selves to buy the house, and she was only twenty-four hours away from giving birth to Brian—but, Lord! Didn't it go up quickly? She chuckles at the thought of how fast Phips had got the damned thing out the window and into the snow.

Then, the room was filled with acrid smoke from the presents that had been scorched; now there's the scent of pine and wood smoke. The angel on the top of the tree scrapes the ceiling, and Agnes looks at it with fond mockery. The outfit is all wrong, she thinks. Flowing fabrics, buttons and bows: imagine flying in *that*. Besides, the wings are too small by far.

From the kitchen at the back of the house comes the sounds of her daughters-in-law preparing a Christmas Eve meal, talking among themselves, whispering things they think she can't hear—and she shouldn't be able to, either—holding their little gathering of bitterness and bile. Complaining of how *she'd* won this year, how they'd much rather be with their own families; the irony of telling each other how much they didn't want to be with each other was apparently lost. Agnes had got them here by abdicating her reign over the feast: she was an old woman, tired and alone, wouldn't her good *daughters* come and help? Amy's turkey will be dry, Rebecca's fruit cake insufficiently alcoholic, Jill's mashed potatoes lumpy and her sprouts bitter, but it doesn't matter. The family is in full attendance: Brian and Adam and Bailey, little Walter, baby Phips, Adeline, Sarah, Abigail, Mercy, Talbot, and Erin. She likes the little ones, they're still quite sweet, not yet soured by contact with their parents. They're all here, she thinks.

All those bearing her blood, and some who don't.

All those for whom she gave up everything.

All here.

"Mom?"

Bailey's standing in the door frame; he's her favorite, though she'd never say it aloud. Not because he reminds her of his father, because he doesn't, but because he reminds her of herself. There's something so very light about him, from the way he walks to the way he talks. Phips used to sneer *effeminate,* which was curious given that he'd tell her during their worst fights that she was *masculine*—or perhaps not so curious. Yes, they fought; mostly he gave in, but sometimes resentment would rise up from somewhere deep inside and he'd spew forth an acidic fury few folk would have believed him capable of. Then he'd rage and shout and throw things—not *at* her, he wasn't that stupid—but at the things around her, so it was like he was trying to hit the pedal to dunk her in a tub of water, trying to find the trigger that would make her hurt. Phips's heart was tender.

It never worked.

"Mom?" Bailey was softhearted, too, though his father never saw it. That's why he'd named his youngest "Phips," even if the old man wasn't around to see it anymore. The little boy is strapped to Bailey's chest, and his was the heartbeat the child would know best, of that Agnes was certain.

"Yes, honey?"

"Are you comfortable like that?" He nods at her crossed legs, at the lotus position she habitually adopted when she was on her own, when there was no one around to see how she never moved like an old woman unless she was in company. Her flesh had declined, yes, but beneath it she was ageless. She just had to hide it most of the time, that was all.

A deception she's finding more frustrating by the day.

"Oh. Sometimes I forget," she says, and smiles, uncrossing her legs and letting her feet touch the floor beside her house shoes. He'll tell the others I'm getting demented, she thinks. "How is that little one today?"

Bailey comes over, unstrapping the child. He hands his youngest to Agnes, who rocks Phips gently as the blue, blue eyes stare up at her in awe. She wonders if perhaps the littlest ones can see better than the others whose minds have filled with so many mundane things they can no longer perceive what's uncommon. Small fingers reach up to touch her face, get caught in the furrows of her cheeks. It makes her heart ache, although not enough to stop her.

Bailey kneels at her feet, just like he used to when he was a toddler and his hair was so blond and curly. It's cut short now; he looks like a soldier, but he's an accountant. "Dinner will be ready soon, Mom. Amy asked me to let you know."

"How kind. I am looking forward to some of her turkey," says Agnes. It's always been her gift, to sound sincere even under the most trying of circumstances, the driest of Christmas turkeys. She rubs noses with the baby, thinks *Good-bye*. No need to get too attached.

"Mom, have you thought anymore on what we talked about? At Thanksgiving?"

Thanksgiving, when all she'd got were calls. Thanksgiving, when her best boy thought the subject he'd broached was a conversation to be had on the phone. Then again, she reminds herself, that was the price of Christmas. Didn't stop her from feeling annoyed about being alone then. But Christmas was better, Christmas fit the bill. She smiles and Bailey thinks it's for him.

"I know it's hard, Mom, to think about leaving. You——we——have so many memories here." He sounds sad; perhaps he really is. But not sad enough to do the right thing. To respect his mother's house, her wishes, her memory. They've mistaken her for a little old lady, which, she supposes, is understandable; that's what she's been—— appeared as——for so many years. "But you'll like the new place. It's full of people your own age, they have clubs, movie nights, knitting circles——"

"I'm sure it's delightful, Bailey darling, but I'm not going."

"Mom, you said you'd think about it——"

"And I did, but that's not the same as agreeing," Agnes says, a hint of steel in her voice. When had her sons decided she was feeble? Open to being bullied? That they were young eagles who could tear at her belly? Was it just their bitch wives who had pushed for this? Were her sons so without intestinal fortitude——without balls——that they'd agree to anything their spouses suggested? She leans forward, hisses into Bailey's face, "If you think you're going to ship me off to God's waiting room that smells of piss and shit and boiled cabbage, Bailey, you've got another thing coming."

Her son recoils in distaste. They'll take that, the cursing, as a sign of dementia. *Why couldn't she get pleasant dementia?* she imagines Brian complaining as if she's already got the other kind, as if she's not in full control of her faculties, as if she couldn't still think rings around him. Her oldest has always hated that he's never been able to win an argument with her, never been able to put one over her. Agnes saw right through him from the day he was born. He's only ever submitted to her will because he was too stupid to think his way out of it, too afraid to try to intimidate her. He's afraid of his wife, too, sharp-eyed Jill, so he cheats on her regularly and thinks *she* doesn't know. Thinks his mother doesn't know, either, thinks she can't see into his head and heart.

Adam, her quiet middle boy, is smart but sly. He'll store away all the little behaviors that can be made to appear *aberrant,* start making notes. He's a doctor, he'll be the one to get her declared unfit, asking his roster of medical friends to sign off on the required documents. She imagines them, a cabal of professionals: *You scratch my back, I'll scratch yours;* legions of elderly parents consigned to places they shouldn't be just because their children can't be bothered to be grateful. He'll be estimating how soon they can sell the house so he can use his share to pay off the gambling debts he thinks no one knows about.

But Bailey, sweet Bailey, believes he's doing the right thing. He's taken her silences, her melancholy, for signs of a decrepit old age; thinks she's drifting. Thinks his mother needs company, needs to be somewhere she's watched twenty-four hours a day as if that's something to be desired! As if she no longer requires her privacy, her independence. That's why the family sent in Bailey, her baby, her favorite: so his credulity might convince *her.*

Agnes is missing her old life, true, but not the one her boys or Phips shared. The weight of grief doesn't lessen, she's found, even when the loss is one you yourself occasioned by fleeing. She stares down at the baby in her arms—honestly, she'd almost forgotten he was there. She looks at Bailey and returns the child to his father's trembling hands.

All she can think is, *With such divine blood in their veins, how did they get so* mundane?

She wonders if it would be different if she'd had daughters: would she have hesitated if she'd produced girls? They have such power, after all, so rich and full of life. But the daughters-in-law are *not* hers, she shares no blood, no link with them. Her sons are as weak with their spouses as their father was with her; she shouldn't be surprised to find them so easily dominated.

Bailey is back in the kitchen, reporting his failure. She can hear them clear as a bell, clear as she can hear the snow falling outside, clear as she's always been able to hear everything in this house. In the street, too; even farther if she'd but let her powers loose. But to do so would have been to draw attention. Agnes has no doubt she's still being looked for. She's seen enough of her brethren over the years, sitting in trees, on rooftops, in the belfries of nearby churches where they can siphon off the adoration, get drunk on it. Junkies, she'd once have thought, for it wasn't something she indulged in; she wasn't that kind of being, although judgment was long her stock-in-trade. One of them, but not the same. Set apart; so far apart, really, that at the time it was easy enough to decide she didn't want to be there at all. Didn't want to be in the nest with the rest. She was a cuckoo, no matter that she looked the same. A cuckoo in her heart and mind, a cuckoo with a silver sword etched red by blood—a substance of which she'd grown so very weary.

She can hear Brian now: *If she won't go quietly, then we'll force her out. She can go kicking and screaming.* My, how brave he sounds when she's not in sight, when he thinks she's out of earshot. Adam now: *I'll talk to some of my colleagues. It's not that hard, to get old people declared* non compos, *not really.*

Oh, you little shit, Agnes thinks. Did she deserve them? Were her sins really so great? In her heart, she knows the answer. That's why her self-imposed exile has begun to hurt so much. Even though she thought herself different, distinct, *apart,* the Heavenly Host was her first family, her true family.

She wants nothing so much, she now knows, as to go home.

When she fled the Heavens, denied her Father and refused her name—Azra, Azrael—she was hunted, sought out, constantly discovered until she'd at last hidden herself thoroughly in humanity. When she wrapped her sacred flesh in the ordinary stuff of mortals, when she lived a life as one of them, when she almost let herself forget who and what she'd been, then she'd been free. The angelics sitting in trees, on stoops, disguised as beggars, no longer looked at her twice. Perhaps she'd sunk so truly into being *other* that when she gave birth none of her divinity could pass to her sons. How else could they be so fucking *ordinary*? So disappointing?

She'd found Phips so soon after she'd fled, he seemed to be what she needed, a good disguise, a mostly easygoing mate—but with him gone she thinks more and more on the old days, recalls with nostalgia being something different entirely. Inside the aging flesh she remains what she'd once been. Always been. Unlike others who chose to fall, who'd begged their departure from the powers that be, she had asked no permission. Doing so would have meant she'd have to have given up her memories, her uniqueness, her *wings,* and that was something she wouldn't countenance.

Quite apart from anything else, the Lord God had no interest in letting its Angel of Death go lightly. It was not a forgiving God, no matter what the propaganda said. A simple apology would not suffice.

It did, however, love a good sacrifice.

"It's time," Agnes says, and stands. She smiles at the pink marble of the fireplace that she selected long years ago, because she knew it had a dampening effect; because she knew it would camouflage what she hid there. The old woman makes a fist, knows this will hurt, for the human meat is vulnerable and fragile, but there's a different core underneath that will shine through soon enough. She draws the fist back, concentrates, and then rams her knuckles into the stone, *through* it, feels the broken rock tearing the muscle, breaking the bones, ripping at the skin. Agnes doesn't hesitate, repeats the blow, does so again and again until there is a good-size rectangular hole. She reaches in with her broken, bleeding right hand, feels around, finds the cloth wrapping with a tiny relief, retrieves the bundle, and unwraps it.

The light from the fire picks out the red engraved along the silver blade, so it looks like pulsing veins. The sword will draw *Them* down, she knows. Even now she can hear its song, so high that only dogs and angels can perceive. Her family won't hear. They won't know anything until the last moment. She'll do them a greater kindness than they'd have done in deserting her in a single room in some low-rent care facility, wasting her days in despair and fear.

The hilt is warm in her palm. Its touch speeds up the process of unbecoming: the broken skin and flesh peel back from her fingers, her hand, up her arm, across her shoulders, down her back to her heels, up her neck, over her head, down her face, throat, chest, stomach, thighs, knees, shins, ankles, and feet. It sloughs off as a snake's might, taking her gray hair, red dress, and black stockings with it, to reveal the bright shining substance beneath. Flesh like white opal, limbs long and muscular, a warrior's garb and breastplate in a dove-gray leather whose sheen is glorious to behold. And at her back . . .

. . . at her back, the wings. They scrape the ceiling; with a spite-ful swipe she uses one to knock the angel from the top of the tree. In the kitchen is the laughter of her children and grandchildren, of her daughters-in-law with their malicious giggles, plotting what they'll do with their share of the sale proceeds. Agnes thinks of the grandchildren, of their innocence, then shrugs. The Lord God *does* love a good sacrifice, and innocent blood will buy more than what flows in her sons' veins. Agnes thinks how wonderful the red will look on the white of the snow, like a beacon to those above.

Help me. Take me home. I'm ready.

Flexing her wings, Agnes heads for the kitchen.

HOME

TIM LEBBON

The man woke up hungry again. It was the same every morning, and he didn't think things would ever change, but that didn't prevent him from mourning his lack of food. Nor did he ever stop feeling the intense cold, suffering from pains in his bones, or hearing voices in his head because outside was so silent, still, and desolate. Sometimes he believed that dwelling upon the wretchedness of his existence was the only thing keeping him alive.

He rolled onto his back. The ice that had formed over his one thick blanket crackled and broke, and as he sat up he heard the familiar sound of his bones doing the same. He took in a deep breath. It seemed to stall in his lungs, heavy and cold, and his heart felt like a lump of ice. He sighed, and his meager exhalation misted ice crystals in the air before him. They drifted and settled on the inner surface of the small tent. He wasn't certain how long he sat and stared. Time had lost all meaning.

Eventually he reached for the flap. He sensed that the sun was up, and once outside the tent he would perform his usual morning rituals. Sometimes they took him all day.

Today, he would ensure that they did not. He was almost there.

Standing, stretching, the beauty and horror of what he saw struck home as it did every single morning. "Look at that, Old Bob," he said. "There's the end of the world, just as it was yesterday, and just like it'll be tomorrow. And only you and me left to witness it."

The dawn sky was smeared red, pink, and purple, like an open wound or the sickly tint of spilled insides. The sun hung above the eastern horizon, piercing the heavy atmosphere yet still undefined. Soon it would disappear as heavy clouds began to build toward the midday blizzard, but he was pleased to see it, for a while at least. It was the first time in seven days.

He had camped beside a rocky outcropping on top of a hill. By the time he'd pitched the tent and buried Old Bob, it had been too late to check for dangers—icy outcroppings, frozen ledges, the chance of the tent being swept down the hillside in the grip of an avalanche. He'd crawled into the tent not really caring. One day he would be taken, and as he suspected he was the last man standing, that event would come as a blessed relief. He did not court danger, but neither did he expend every ounce of energy and brainpower avoiding it. He wandered, camped, backtracked, searching for nothing, staying nowhere. He was like a breath of wind that would never find a home. It didn't make him sad. He remembered too little to be sad.

With each day the same, it was easy to forget how many had passed and awful to consider how many would follow. Few days threw up anything different enough to differentiate them. They were dictated by his search for food, water, and shelter. They were uniformly cold, usually with a blizzard around midday and a rapid descent into a clear-skied, blood-freezing night. He only rarely saw living things, and over the past few years—or maybe a score of

years, he had no way of knowing for sure——there were so few creatures left alive that seeing one marked a day as unique. Seventeen
days ago he'd seen a bird spiraling high up, so high that he could
not make out its species. He'd watched for a while, then followed
as it drifted eastward, spending hours kicking through fresh snow
and hauling Old Bob behind him, finally losing sight of the creature
as the day's snow began. More than fifty days prior to that, he'd
found a mouse half-frozen into the cracked bark on the side of a
rotten tree. He'd plucked it from the tree and tucked it into his
pocket, planning to cook it later if he could start a fire. But later
it was gone, escaped through a hole in his jacket. He was glad. He
hoped it was still alive somewhere, if only because seeing it again
ten days or a hundred into the future would make a day special for
him once again.

And today, down in the valley is . . . he thought, frowning at the
idea that there would be anything down there other than what
he'd seen everywhere else. He sometimes had these brief flashes of
expectation, as if there was a separate consciousness within him
constantly searching for something new. Searching for hope.

He knew there was no hope. Walking to the edge of the steep
drop-off and looking down into the snow-smothered valley only
confirmed that.

The valley sides had once been heavily forested, but the trees
were now stiff, stark shards, angular spikes pushing up from the
deep snow. Leafless, most branches gone, many of the remaining
trunks were rotten. A heavy wind would topple some. The relentless passage of time would take the rest. There had been no new
trees for a long, long time.

Wending along the valley floor was a river. Ice floes drifted from
east to west, and here and there they clogged the river and formed
dams. Several small lakes had widened and broken the banks.
Waterfalls tumbled. Mist rose, freezing and falling back onto the

water's surface. It might have looked beautiful if it weren't for the small town the river flowed through.

He caught his breath. "Old Bob!" he called. "Come and see! We didn't know how close we were."

I knew, he thought, *I always know.* That internal voice again. He recognized it as his own, yet he did not understand the words. Perhaps it was madness stalking him.

Old Bob did not reply. It was too early.

The town was not large, perhaps three hundred homes and other buildings splayed either side of the river. Two bridges spanned the waterway, both fallen. A handful of buildings might once have been tall, but their upper floors had fallen or been blasted down. He could discern little detail from this far away, mainly because of the blanket of snow blurring the landscape like a hazy memory. But he knew what he would find when he made his way down. He'd seen it all before, everywhere else, and he would see it again.

Shattered buildings. Rotten, dead trees. Countless signs of destruction, and no evidence of rebuilding. There would be bodies, the skeletal remains of those who had once called this place home. Sometimes, some of those bodies would be piled up, the remnants of great bonfires. Occasionally he would find their sad bones hanging from trees, sacrificed by those few roving survivors who had come and gone following the great fall.

There was no plant growth. Very few animals, and most of those that did still exist were vicious hunters, changed over time from whatever they might have been before to single-minded monsters—hunt, kill, eat.

He was surprised he hadn't gone the same way.

"Come on," he said, turning to pack up his tent and collect Old Bob. "We're here."

He had no idea where here was, or why he had come. That internal voice had urged him this way. It was a whisper on the breeze, and at night when he slept and dreamed it was more insistent. He took down the tent and folded it, tying the frayed lines and forming it into a roll he could carry slung beneath his backpack. As he worked, he heard the crackle of breaking ice to his left. Old Bob was waking.

A crust of ice broke and angled up. The sound was loud in this silent landscape. He existed within a great white silence that he was familiar with but had never become used to. Somewhere in his past—long lost now, little more than suspicion and rumor, barely even there in his dreams—he thought there was noise and laughter and singing, and that trace memory made the silence he now lived with heavy. He sometimes sang, although he knew no songs. He had to make up the tunes and words. Sometimes he tried laughing, but the sound of his laughter echoing across plains of snow and ice and decayed forests frightened him more than anything.

"Good morning," he said.

A hand protruded up through the snow. Naked, clawed, wrinkled, the skin a deep brown like old, old leather, the fingers slowly unfurled as if the faint touch of sunlight thawed tendons and muscles. The claws tipping the fingers were long and blunt. The middle finger was missing, leaving only a stump.

The hand and forearm lowered down across the snow and pressed, heaving the body below up into sunlight. Old Bob emerged naked and shriveled, groaning as he crawled from the hole he had slept in. His head was hairless, ears small as if worn away, eyes deep-set and a deep, glimmering black. His nose resembled a gnarled knot of wood, and his mouth was lipless, parted as he drew breath to reveal two rows of sharp teeth. His skin was mud brown and lined so deeply that he looked like a mosaic creature, a composite of many parts held together by some invisible means. The man often thought that if he dropped Old Bob he might well

break apart. But Old Bob was tenacious and strong. He had survived much more than being dropped.

"I think we're almost there," he said, and Old Bob's eyes glimmered even more. He writhed on his side, eager to be hoisted onto
the trap the man pulled behind him everywhere they went.

With camp broken and the trap secured to his belt, the man
started walking toward the drop down into the valley. To begin
with, the weight tugged at his hips, but he was used to it, and the
trap was well made. It slid efficiently over the frozen snow. He
could hear Old Bob's labored breathing behind him. He had never
heard Old Bob speak but suspected that the inner voice might
belong to him.

Though the man wandered this landscape of desolation and
destruction, and witnessed the palette of apocalypse painted
across the sky, he had no memories from before. They were like his
recollection of song and laughter—mere rumors, like forgotten
whispers echoing in the most hidden corners of his mind. He knew
that there must have been a before, but it was so long ago in time
and experience that his mind had blotted it out. A few snapshot
recollections flashed at him on occasion—inspired usually by the
waft of a smell, or a blink of déjà vu in the falling of a snowflake
or the shape of a cloud—but they were rarer than ever nowadays.
He was content with wandering, scraping a meager meal from
dying soils, sleeping, and waking again to a brand-new day that was
exactly the same as the last.

Now, though, something had brought him here. It didn't feel
mystical or even mysterious, but he was aware that his random path
had been steered toward this valley, and this ruined settlement.

Starting down the hillside, the weight of Old Bob on the trap
threatened to push him down. He dug in his worn boots, easing
down the slope slowly. Old Bob breathed harsher behind him. The

wizened naked thing had been with him for as long as he could remember. It never ate or drank, never defecated or pissed, and he had never heard it speak. Still, it provided a shred of company in this empty land.

It took a while to reach the valley floor. He stumbled a few times and rolled in snowdrifts, and the layers deeper down were gray and stinking, as if even the snow carried rot. He often thought it was the case. People were gone, and now the world was slowly dying.

Approaching the first huddled ruins at the edge of the small town, he saw that it was something far different from what he'd first believed.

"This is no town," he said to Old Bob. "It's a compound."

Old Bob groaned, breathed heavily, rolled so that he could see.

The man started circling the ruined place. Here and there were the remains of a heavy fence, and strung up on its rusting steel sheeting were skeletons. Many of them had fallen apart, but some were whole. Skulls betrayed fractures from weapon impacts. Ribs were splintered. Spines severed. They had been tied high on the walls as a warning, but now there was only the man to heed it.

"It didn't work," he said. "This place fell as well."

Old Bob grunted. The man glanced over his shoulder and down at the ancient creature, whose origins he still did not know. Maybe he pulled a monster behind him. Perhaps an angel.

"*Every* place fell," the man said. "So why have we come here?"

Old Bob ceased twitching and writhing and stared up at him. It was rare that they made eye contact, and if they did, it was fleeting and almost embarrassed. Now Old Bob glared right at him, his oily black eyes unreadable and mysterious. He placed both hands on the trap's framework, and the man saw muscles twitch beneath his leathery skin.

"Do you want me to go—" he began, but then Old Bob heaved himself from the trap and into the snow.

The man held his breath. Old Bob landed on his feet, the snow up to his knees. He swayed a little, like a tree in an unseen breeze, hands swinging back and forth by his side.

Then he ran.

The man gasped. He'd only ever seen Old Bob stumble a few steps before falling, but now he bounded through the snow, too fast to catch. He fumbled at the straps securing the trap to his belt, drew the sharp knife from his boot, and took off after his strange companion.

"Wait!" he shouted. "What about me?" It was a strange thing to say, but the man knew where it came from. It was fear of being left alone.

Old Bob reached the fence, dived through a gap behind a fallen panel, and then he was gone.

The man stood there in silence, breathing heavily, shivering as sweat cooled on his body. As his shock faded and he started running toward the compound, an intense rush of memories bit in and he—

—was running toward the compound, his belt rubbing his right hip, left boot leaking, a fallen tree to his left leaning against part of the perimeter fencing, fencing that must have been built to keep something out—

—*Or keep it in,* he thought, and then he reached the fence. He looked through the gap where Old Bob had disappeared, scanning for movement. There was none. Buildings lay beneath a blanket of snow, some of them reduced to rubble, others with parts of tumbled walls still standing, slumped roofs visible.

Old Bob's footprints disappeared between these ruins, and the man slipped through the narrow gap in pursuit.

Something screamed.

He froze to the spot, breath held and mouth open. The sound faded to nothing, vanishing so quickly that he wondered whether he had heard it at all. He looked around, searching for the source of the scream, yet hoping not to see it. The cry had scored his soul.

Silence hung over the deserted compound.

The man moved on, following the disturbed snow, wending left and right between buildings and feeling with every step that he had been here before. The familiarity was a distant thing, like scenes from a past life. A waft of smoke caught in his nostrils, though he could see no fire, and the smoke carried a mouthwatering hint of cooking food. A snatch of laughter rose and fell, the combined joy of many voices. None of them were real, but all of them might once have been.

Rounding one of the larger buildings fallen to ruin, he came to a wide-open space, at the center of which stood the stump of a tall tower. It must have been a grand sight once, but it was now a broken spire. There was no way of saying how tall it might once have been.

Old Bob stood close to the tower's base, staring up.

"Old Bob," the man said. The wizened shape, no taller than his hip, gave no indication that he had heard.

The screech came again, louder this time, and it was taken up and carried from other mouths in different directions. The man turned left and right, wielding the knife. His heart hammered. Blood pumped. He could not remember ever feeling this warm before, but it was the heat of terror.

Old Bob turned to look at him just as the first of the shapes darted at them from between the buildings. It scampered across the surface of the snow, spiked limbs flicking up showers of ice behind it as it came. It moved incredibly quickly, and the man struggled to make out what it was.

It was only as it slowed to confront Old Bob that the man saw.

Old Bob grabbed the smaller version of himself, swung it

around, and ripped its serrated jaws wide open. It whined, then fell into the snow, squirming its last and bleeding black into white.

"What the hell . . . ?" the man asked, but Old Bob gave him no easy answer. His shriveled, silent traveling companion was preparing for more attacks, and as the man crouched with his knife held wide, they came.

Two rushed in from the left, skittering across the snow. One went for Old Bob, the other for the man. He swung his knife, catching the ravenous creature a glancing blow. There was something painfully human about its cry of pain, but there the comparison stopped. It was even less human than Old Bob, a spitting, snarling thing spilling blood as it came at him again. Its hide was thick and knotted, features vaguely human but blurred by disfigurement and mutation. Though their origins were unknown, the creatures' aims were clear.

The thing the man had cut jumped up and leapt for his leg. Its teeth clamped on tight, jaws sawing as it struggled to bite through his thick clothing. It was only the old animal hide material that saved his leg from being bitten right through, and three hacks from the knife parted the creature's head from its body.

Panting, staggering, the man drew closer to Old Bob. His companion had killed the other attacker with his bare hands, and now three of them lay dead upon the snow. Their blood was so dark it was almost black, and so hot that it melted down into the snow and out of sight.

"What are they?" the man asked.

For a moment he thought Old Bob was going to reply. The creature looked up at him with obvious intelligence, dark eyes shining, but he said nothing. Instead he started across the square away from the tower, moving slower than before so that the man could keep up. He had always believed that he was leading the way, and Old

Bob allowed himself to be carried along. Now he was following Old Bob.

They entered a low doorway to one of the buildings that still remained half-standing. Inside, several bodies were piled in one corner, the smaller creatures' features evident. There was a faint musty smell, but any stench of rot had long since vanished. These things had been dead for years.

Old Bob passed them with hardly a look, threaded his way through a series of corridors and small hallways, and the man followed, realizing that Old Bob knew just where he was going.

And have I been here before? he wondered. There was something about the compound that seemed familiar. A sense of being inside, while the outside was a different place. The idea that whatever happened beyond that fence belonged in another world, and that the world within would survive.

That hadn't worked out so well.

Old Bob paused by a broken doorway, a stairwell beyond leading down. He sniffed at the air, tilted his head to one side as he listened. The man heard nothing.

"What is it?" he asked.

Old Bob glanced at him before jumping down the staircase. One moment he was there, the next gone. The man followed him down the staircase with caution. Even though by his reckoning they were headed underground, there was still some form of illumination coming from ahead. Listening for any sign of those fierce things, hearing nothing, he reached the bottom of the staircase. He was in a small hallway with several doors leading off, but only one was open. He walked to the doorway and peered inside.

Every time I come here, he thought. *Every single time I see this for the first time, and for the thousandth, and maybe the millionth, because everything here is as familiar as my own hand.*

Beyond the doorway was an expansive basement area. Lit by glowing windows set in the high ceiling, the place was a mess, with smashed furniture and equipment strewn across the floor and piled into corners. There were two more bodies close to the door. These were fresh, their blood still seeping, and he saw Old Bob hobbling toward a pile of refuse to the left, dragging his heavy clawed hand on the floor beside him.

"Old Bob?"

The creature glanced back, then carried on walking. When it reached the pile of rubbish—heavy furniture broken and smashed, and other mechanical items ripped and rusted—it sat down with a sigh and started sorting through some items.

The man looked around the large underground area and heard singing, and laughter, and he smelled food roasting. When he blinked he was back in the ruined room.

"Where are we?" he asked. The small shriveled creature ignored him. He seemed immersed in this new activity, no longer alert to dangers, away from this world and into another.

The man sat on a fallen storage unit. It was made of wood, and sitting upon it he could see how intricate the carvings on its surface were, even though a spread of gray mold smothered most of them. It gave slightly beneath him but did not come apart. He tried to make out what the carvings depicted, but saw only random patterns and symbols that might once have meant something more.

"We should go," he said. "It isn't safe here. There might be more of those things." Old Bob ignored him. He was doing something with the items he'd found, twisting and folding, using shards of metal to scrape and screw, and the activity seemed to change his whole aura and appearance. Still wizened and old, there was a fluidity to his movements that belied his deep age. Still wrinkled, his leathery skin shone with a vitality the man had never seen before.

Never seen and remembered, at least.

I'm so old, the man thought. *Sometimes I can't remember yesterday, but I have a past so deep.* He watched Old Bob working and felt like he had done so many times before. It was like breathing—he couldn't recall any breath he had taken in his life, yet he knew he had taken millions. Soon, Old Bob had finished his task. He carried a small object with him and darted around the large room, searching for something. The man remained seated, letting him look. The room was silent and empty but for the two of them, and those ghostly memories pricking at the edges of his consciousness.

At last, Old Bob seemed to find what he was looking for. He approached the man with a strange reverence, and perhaps that really was a smile on his face. He held out the object for the man to take. It was the size of his fist, wrapped in a shred of folded, holed cloth, and with a loop of discolored plastic circling it both ways, finally tied in a neat bow.

"For me?" the man asked, and he had asked countless times before.

Old Bob nodded, again.

The man slipped the knife into his boot and took the gift, and déjà vu struck again, rich and full as—

—he opened the gift, scratched his finger on some of the coarse wrappings, remembered countless other times like this all bleeding into one—

—and Old Bob had fashioned him a model of a reindeer out of a piece of charred wood, some wires, and several shards of sharp metal. It was basic. It was beautiful.

"For me," the man said, and he nodded his thanks at Old Bob. The creature smiled, shy, and held out his hand. The man took it and, still holding the model reindeer, let Old Bob lead him across the room.

With light bleeding down from translucent ceiling tiles, he could make out some of the piles of refuse they passed. And with each ruined thing he built up a picture of what this place had been, an image layered upon countless forgotten layers from the past, like an oil painting gradually emerging from a blank canvas.

It was a workshop. Some of the rotting junk was the remains of tools and benches, stools and boxes, and mixed in were raw materials that had once been formed into something less raw.

"Old Bob?" the man said, because he had a question. But however many times he asked, the creature he called Old Bob would never be able to reply.

Instead he steered the man across the workshop to another door at the far end. The door was closed, and Old Bob took the key hanging around his neck and unlocked it. He pushed it open and urged the man inside.

This place was much smaller, also lit by daylight filtered down from above. Many years ago it might have served a different purpose, but now it was something else. Something personal, and revealing, and not so much of a shock as it might have been.

He knew that he was very, very old, after all.

One entire wall of the room was lined with shelving, and on those shelves were hundreds of model reindeer, all of them similar to the gift he held in his hand. The man scanned along the shelves, and he knew that every one had been made by Old Bob. He knew also that he had placed each gift here, a safe place to leave it, protecting them all from the dangers outside.

"Thank you, Old Bob," the man said, and he wondered what the creature's true name was. If he was a younger, fitter man, perhaps he might remember, but even then he doubted it. All that was so long ago. There were at least three hundred model reindeer on the shelves, maybe more.

He moved slowly forward, chose his place, and put the model down. *That's another year gone by,* he thought. *Same again next year. And the year after. And . . .*

"And forever," the man said, shrugging his heavy old red jacket tight. His vision filling with eternity, he closed his eyes, readying himself for their journey back into the dead, cold world.

HIKING THROUGH

MICHAEL KORYTA

Anytime you end up in trouble in the night woods with snow falling and a cold wind blowing, it was probably a trip that started in the sun. It might be hard to remember by then, but I'm convinced it's true. Stories like that don't start in the dark.

They just end there.

What I saw on Christmas Eve—or maybe it was Christmas morning by then, because time got hazy on me there in the snow and the dark—actually began on a sunlit summer day. I was working maintenance for a camp in western Maine and training for my thru-hike of the Appalachian Trail, my last gasp at putting off adulthood for one more year. There were plenty of people looking at me sideways by then, because I was five years out of Bowdoin and hadn't found anything approaching full-time work. But I knew plenty of twenty-seven-year-old slack-asses with Bowdoin diplomas on their walls and their feet up on coffee tables, checking their social media feeds and writing wry, disaffected posts about the state of the world while their trust funds kicked over solid monthly payments. At least I was swinging a hammer. That's better, right? Unambitious, maybe, but not *coasting,* not freeloading. Just getting by.

At least that's what you tell yourself until one of your Bowdoin buddies invests those trust-fund dollars into a start-up that's making a fucking water filter or some shit and they end up grossing a billion dollars *and* saving lives in Sudan. Then the hammer doesn't feel quite so pure, and you remember the way the world really works—it's money, honey, we all know that—and saying that you don't need it is just a haughty way to defend laziness. *I don't care for material possessions; I am one with the wilderness.*

But, hey, call it what you want, that summer I didn't care much for material possessions and I was working hard on being one with the wilderness. I pulled four-day shifts, then had a three-day weekend, and each weekend, rain or shine, black flies or mosquitoes, found me on the trail. I was trying to get to the point where I could do fifteen miles per day easily. My plan was to walk the Appalachian Trail in reverse, leaving Maine in the early fall and heading south. Most people who walk the whole two-thousand-mile show do it the other way, arriving at Mount Katahdin weary and spiritual, approaching the place like pilgrims. Most of us probably think we are just that, to be honest. People don't hike the A.T. just to get away. They're looking for something.

It was June and there were still traces of snow in some of the shadowed rocks when I first heard about the witch. It was a dumb story, but I filed it away, because by nature I'm not the most extroverted guy and on the trail you're always meeting strangers, so you need material to break the ice, or at least I do. The story about the witch was a good one, to my mind, because you could tell it any way you wanted to; you could adjust for the audience. You could make it campy and cheesy and go for the laughs, or you could bring in the tragic truth of Geraldine Largay, who'd died just off the trail in the Maine woods, surviving for a month while searchers combed the area but never found her. A couple years later, they found her body in a tent, and journals indicating just how long she'd survived. Everyone who walked the A.T. in Maine knew about Geraldine Largay, which meant you could spin the witch story into a commentary on the types of assholes who would create a story like that in the wake of a tragedy. You see what I mean? It was a flexible story. Versatile. And with the right crowd on the right night, all the necessary elements present, you could make it scary. Yeah, I was pretty sure of that. There was a way to spin it for chills.

The first place I heard it told was at one of the lean-tos just north of the New Hampshire border. It was a Saturday night and I'd covered twenty-six miles in two days and I was bone tired. Maine is rugged. A lot of people don't believe that, particularly your southwestern hombres who ration water and your Boulder microbrew bros who think altitude is all that matters, and God forbid those people who fly somewhere exotic just to walk briefly around with their backpacks on, out in Argentina or Thailand or whatever. If you say "Maine is rugged" to those types, you'll get an eye roll, I guarantee you. Because it seems too *settled* in their mind's eye, a part of the friggin' East Coast, and what is lamer and less rugged than the East Coast? They'll grant you that it's cold, they'll nod about the tough winters, but what they won't truly believe is how hard the hiking is. Not enough altitude, not enough elevation change, whatever. But before you roll your eyes, you ought to look at a map. Go ahead, pull up a map of Maine.

Part of the East Coast, are we? Well, check out that Atlantic Seaboard, my friend. We're jutting way up and out there, aren't we? Farther from New York City than you remembered. Farther from Boston, even. And what about all those blank spaces? So many of them on a simple map, not so much as a single town in an entire quadrant, or series of quadrants. Go ahead, scroll, zoom in, do what you'd like—that map is staying blank. Makes Wyoming look populated; makes Nebraska look downright cosmopolitan. Then remind yourself that this state had numerous settlements as early as the 1600s, centuries before Lewis and Clark set out, centuries before the California gold rush ... so why isn't that Maine map filled in? Why are all the towns huddled along the coast like they're clinging to the rocks, and why aren't there any highways at all in the northwestern portion of the state? There's just the one interstate, and 95 starts on the East Coast, heads north, and then bends back east like it's running away from something, like it's in a hurry to get to New Brunswick—and who in the hell was ever in a hurry to get to New Brunswick? On the other side of 95, the western side, you'll see there's not a whole lot going on in our quaint, summer-people state. They've had four hundred years to turn this particular paradise into a parking lot, and they've done a damn good job of that work in most of the country already. So why hasn't it happened in Maine?

I already said the word: rugged. It's no joke. You think about all that the next time someone tells you that Maine is rough country, dangerous country, and you're ready to roll your eyes. You think about how early the Europeans found their way here, and then about all those blank spaces, and ask yourself why they've stayed so blank for so many years.

Twenty-six miles in two days in Maine is fucking *earned,* you'd better believe that. I was in good shape and had good boots and an ultralight pack, but the night I came to that lean-to where a group from Tennessee already had a fire going, I was sporting blisters and bruises and I was punch-drunk tired. The group from Tennessee had just crossed over into the state. Not thru-hikers, but summer hikers, working slowly and patiently from New Hampshire and toward Baxter State Park, a very slender cut of the A.T., but a difficult one. None of them had ever been to Maine before, and since I was genuine local product, born in Bangor, educated at Bowdoin, and currently swinging my hammer in Rangeley, I was a bona fide tour guide as far as they were concerned. They had the questions you're used to from summer people if you grew up here—how cold is the winter, how much do we pay for lobster rolls, who has the best lobster roll, have you seen a moose, have you eaten a moose, have you seen a moose eating a lobster roll, and if so, how much did the moose pay for it?

All of this Q&A was easy enough for conversation and surely made me feel better about enjoying the warmth of their fire and sharing in the dehydrated pasta and smoked sausage they offered. I had my own food in my pack, of course, but they were offering, and, hell, I was the state's official welcoming committee on this night.

And on that night, like pretty much all nights when hikers met on the Appalachian Trail in Maine in the summer of 2016, the conversation found its way to Geraldine Largay.

Because that was the year they'd found her bones.

Geraldine's story had given the whole country chills. You didn't need to have ever lifted a backpack to your shoulders for that one to make you shudder. She'd been walking the A.T. with a friend for a couple months, and then the friend bailed out for a family emergency, and Geraldine decided to keep at it. She did not have a compass, and she was scared of two things: being alone and being in the dark.

A few hours after leaving a lean-to much like the one the Tennessee contingent and I were enjoying, she left the trail for a bathroom break.

She never made her way back to it. She was alone in the dark by sundown.

In the month she survived, she never saw another soul, so far as anyone knows.

The search for Geraldine Largay was the largest and most expensive in the history of the Maine Warden Service. They canvassed the woods, sent up choppers, brought out bloodhounds. Everything you could think of to do in a search, they did that and brought a plus-one to the party, and when they found her body three years later, she was less than two miles off the trail. Less than two miles, and still they hadn't been able to find her, and she'd never heard the searchers.

Remember what I said about rugged country?

When they called off the search, the rumor mill was jammed up with theories, but the professional opinion was that she'd have died within a week in those conditions. Then they found her body, spring of 2017, and found her journal, which told the world she'd approached death with stronger spirit and more grace than most of us could hope for—and that she'd survived alone in the woods for nearly a month.

There were five in the group from Tennessee, three girls and two guys, and it was—inevitably and indubitably—one of the guys who brought up the witch. His name was John and he had an acoustic guitar with strings that glimmered near-silver in the firelight and I'd been wary of him from the first, because there's nothing scarier at a campfire than an amateur armed with an acoustic guitar. All this time I'd been afraid he was going to play something, probably an off-key Neil Young or Dylan cover to start, and then, God save us, he'd say, "I actually have a few of my own if anyone wants to hear them . . ." and I'd start rethinking my hiatus from marijuana in one hell of a hurry.

Instead, he never so much as glanced at the guitar, just said, "Some of the people we met hiking south? They said there are legends about a witch up near here. An old woman alone. Always alone, and always walking. They say she doesn't talk, but just keeps on hiking through, even if you scream in her face. You can do anything, but she doesn't break stride. She's an older woman, grayhaired, with a single hiking stick, nothing modern and fiberglass or whatever but more like something carved out of an old dead tree, and she'll look at you as if she wants help, but if you ask what she needs or try to talk to her, she won't stop, won't so much as slow. It's like she can't stop walking, you know? She wants help, or wants guidance, maybe, but she can't stop long enough to find it."

The girl closest to him, a pretty brunette named Liz, made a sour face and slid a few inches away, as if physically repulsed.

"That's an awful thing to make fun of," she said. "What that poor woman went through, she deserves better than that."

"Well, to be fair to the people who told us about it, nobody was pretending that it's Geraldine's ghost or anything like that," John said. "At least not in the group we talked to. I agree, that would be pretty terrible."

"Talking about an old woman walking around lost and looking for the trail, after what happened with Geraldine, is nothing but a cruel child's joke," Liz said, unconvinced.

John nodded, as if in total agreement with her, though I think he was just trying to preserve notions that he might not have to solo in his sleeping bag that night. So that was both the first time I heard the story, and the first way I understood how it could be told, how it could land with one kind of audience. *Isn't this awful,* that was one option. Then John pivoted nicely and promptly showed me the second option.

"Tell you what I think," he said. "Do you remember the guy that had the camera?"

The others in the group nodded.

"You saw his goatee, you heard him talking about PBR like it was the nectar of the gods. He couldn't just say 'Man, I want a beer,' he had to say 'Man, I want a PBR *so damn bad.*' And nobody has ever wanted a PBR that bad. It is not a beer associated with passionate desires, and I can speak with full knowledge on this matter. Not once in history has anyone done anything but *settle* for a PBR."

That drew some smiles, and he'd managed to shift Liz's mood back toward the warm side, which I think was his intent.

"Now," John said, "there is the hipster exception, of course. The kind who find that pisswater beer worthy of ten or twelve dollars a can. That goatee, and that apparently unquenchable thirst for a PBR leads a wise man like me to suspect that he was, in fact, a hipster—perhaps from Park Slope but more likely an imposter from someplace more Cincinnati or Indianapolis in nature, and a wise man like me further observed that he was not only telling stories about a witch but *carrying a camera.* So I observe all of these things and put them together for my deductions, and do you know what I fear?"

The second guy in the group was a big boy named Wade, one of the fatter men I'd ever seen on the trail, and he had a rich, deep voice like a blues singer. He said, "Heaven help us, John, you fear we have an aspiring filmmaker on the trail—and even worse, one who has not yet seen *Blair Witch,* or *Blair Witch 2.*"

It wasn't a great line, but his delivery, in that mellifluous bass voice, somehow sold it, and suddenly we were all laughing our asses off like it had been a true howler of a joke. It's not uncommon; I've never laughed as hard in my life as I have around a campfire. Every emotion is heightened at night in the woods, but none more than humor.

Well . . . maybe fear. Sure, fear runs high, and that's probably why the humor does, too. We all laugh harder around a campfire, because we don't want to acknowledge that some part of us is deeply concerned about what's out there just beyond the reach of the firelight.

But that night it was humor that won, and the big boy with the B. B. King voice had given us the giggles and it took a while for them to taper off, with everyone throwing in a line or two of their own, either imitating this hipster with the camera giving art direction or quoting lines from *Blair Witch,* or, at its most effective, blending the two together, and we all had a hell of a laugh.

So that was the second way I saw how the story of the witch could be told. It could be offered as something awful and cruel, a real woman's tragedy used for sport, an example of the very type of human behavior that you'd come to the trail to escape, or it could be parody material, done for laughs. I thought then, as I enjoyed their company and considered my many months among strangers once I set out on my thru-hike, that it was going to be a useful story. You'd have to assess the crowd, but it would work with either the serious types or the slapstick types.

Of course, I hadn't heard the third version, yet. I had not heard anyone go for the goose bumps.

In fact, I don't think I even considered the option that night. In the campfire light, surrounded by friendly people, with sure knowledge of where I was and with only four miles left to do in the morning before I was out of the woods, I don't think fear ever even entered my mind.

That happened later, when I was alone.

I didn't put so much as a mile of my thru-hike on the board that fall. Don't worry, it wasn't because I got a job—it was because I fell in love.

In late summer, a girl from Florida joined the staff at the camp in Rangeley. I'd had instant crushes before—shit, who hasn't?— but this one, this was more than a crush. The sight of Gina Garcia seemed to envelop me, soak through my skin, and crawl through my bones. She was five feet nine inches of sculpted Cuban beauty, with hair that shone like oil on water and a smile that reduced me to a stuttering fool.

And, for some reason, she saw past that. For some reason, Gina Garcia was willing to give me a chance, and my dreams of long weeks on the Appalachian Trail vanished in a blink. The idea of being anywhere other than Gina's side for hours, let alone months, suddenly seemed laughable. What thoughts of the future I did have were all wrapped up in what we could be, and what she wanted, but truthfully I didn't think much about the future at all. I'd never been so content with the present.

Except when it came to the idea of summer ending, and Gina leaving. *That* made me think of the future. And it scared me more than any horror story ever had, or could. I started pricing apartments in Fort Lauderdale, where she lived, and scouring job sites online, looking for anything that could keep me close to her. Then, on Labor Day weekend, laying on a blanket beneath the pines and a million stunning stars, Gina Garcia told me that she'd fallen in love with Maine in the way she'd fallen in love with me, that because I was in Maine, she would be in Maine.

And for three months, she was. For three months, it was as good as life can get when you're twenty-seven. I was with a gorgeous, intelligent girl, in a beautiful place, and we had enough money to get by with the kind of life we wanted. For three months, I couldn't have imagined being any happier.

Then came November, and Gina made a trip back to Florida to see family. She would be gone a week, she said. I drove her to the airport in Bangor, got her luggage out of the trunk, and kissed her good-bye, blissfully unaware that it was the last time I'd ever see her.

She called a few days later—the one-week visit was going to have to be two, she explained. There was some family drama, there were old friends to catch up with, and, she added with a laugh, the Florida weather didn't seem all that bad after leaving Maine in November.

Maybe I should have been smart enough to have a bad feeling then. I didn't, though. I just told her how much I missed her and told her to keep having fun.

After two weeks, she informed me that she'd decided to stay until January, and get her affairs in order before moving back to Maine permanently. I wasn't clear on what affairs needed to be ordered, but it sounded like a funeral process, and in a way it was. I had the first sense of disaster during that call, so I suggested I come down to visit for a week or so, meet her family, meet her friends.

When she responded to that offer by saying she didn't want me to waste my money on a trip like that, I knew how things were going to end. The writing on the wall, as they say. I kept up the pretense, though, kept lying to myself and those around me, saying she'd be back by the first of the year, and back for good.

It was on Christmas Eve that one of her friends posted a photo of Gina kissing another guy under mistletoe hung from a fucking palm tree. There was some text accompanying the photo, something about how great they were together, how friggin' adorable they were as a couple, but all I could focus on was that picture. I'd known it was over for a while, had understood that she probably wasn't coming back, but it's one thing to sense a situation like that, and another to see it.

I was supposed to be at my parents' house that night, to do the family Christmas Eve festivities and wake up in my childhood bed on Christmas morning. That was the plan, and no matter how impossible it seemed to bear, I started the drive with good intentions. Or pointed in the right direction, at least, numb and hollowed out. As the miles went by, though, the reality of having to go through the Merry Christmas charade landed on me, and that photo of Gina Garcia and her nameless but oh-so-adorable new boyfriend danced before my eyes, and I knew I just couldn't do it. I called my parents and told them I had the flu, and then I exited the highway and took the back roads, driving without purpose, driving with tears stinging my eyes and the pines a blur.

It was an hour or so before I decided that I needed a drink.

It took a while to locate a bar that was open on Christmas Eve, and then it was, as you'd expect, a real dive. But that felt right. That felt perfect.

I drank beer first, and then whiskey, and at some point a grizzled old bastard with yellow teeth bought everyone a shot of something milky and sweet, and then I think I had some more beer. My skull was feeling high and tight and the room had a little spin to it when I heard someone talking about the Appalachian Trail.

"Dumb bastards hiking it right now in the snow," he was saying. "Only a few inches are down, sure, but what in the hell would anybody want to be out there in December for?"

"Was it a couple?" I said, turning on my stool. The guy and his buddy stared at me.

"I mean, were they, you know, dating or married or something?"

"How would I know? And what the hell does that matter for?"

"Romance," I told him, working hard to present a sober voice and failing miserably. "That's what they're doing it for—romance. It'll give them a story, someday. The romantic Christmas hike in the snow. They want the story, don't you see?"

"I got plenty of stories, and I ain't hiking in the fucking snow to find them," he replied, and his buddy laughed and so did I, and then they moved on in their conversation and pointedly left me out of it. I turned back to the bar, thinking about what it would have been like to hike in the snow on Christmas Eve with Gina, make love under the stars in a sleeping bag, and somewhere along that train of thought a subtle dilemma occurred to me: I had nowhere to stay the night. I was in a dive bar in the middle of nowhere, I'd canceled on my parents, and I was hardly in shape to drive far looking for a hotel. I did have a sleeping bag in the trunk; I always kept some loose camping gear in there. But if I was going to sleep in the cold on Christmas Eve, I sure as hell didn't want to do it in the parking lot of that shitty bar. Wake up with a headache in a parking lot next to a Dumpster—Merry Christmas, right? But there'd once been a place that got my heart right, there'd once been a goal for the year, back before Gina Garcia had come along. I'd tossed the goal aside for her the way she'd tossed me aside for the guy in Florida, but that didn't mean I couldn't get a night of it back.

"You say the A.T. crosses near here?" I asked the two old guys, who took this fresh interruption in with less patience than they had the first time.

"Less than a mile down the road."

"I might take a walk," I said. "A walk in the snow on Christmas Eve. That's a nice thing to do, right?"

The guys gave me a long look, and then one of them said, "Son? In your condition, if you go out walking in the snow tonight, the Warden Service will be looking for your body soon enough."

"And finding it," his buddy put in.

I laughed like they'd been joking.

They didn't join in.

The road seemed to have four centerlines, but when I closed my right eye and drove with only the left eye open, the four centerlines merged into two that stuck fairly close together. No cars passed, which was good for me—and for them. The best thing for everyone would have been if a state trooper had come up behind me, but it didn't happen. It was just me and the dark night road and the blowing snow.

On Christmas Eve, everybody has someplace to be.

I still found the trail crossing, though. Even drunk and even in the snow, I recognized the gap in the trees. I'd spent a lot of time down here, pre-Gina. A lot of preparatory hikes for the dream journey I'd given up on the first time she'd so much as smiled at me.

I pulled the car off to the side of the road and killed the engine. There was a moment, right then, when I thought about staying there and sleeping it off. The old-timers at the bar hadn't been entirely wrong—it was bad weather for hiking even if you were sober, and if you were *in my condition,* as they'd termed it, it could be damn near suicidal.

Three things talked me out of staying in the car, though: I was experienced in the woods; I didn't mind the idea of dying there in the snow because I hoped the vision of my frozen corpse might haunt Gina the way that cute little Facebook picture was haunting me; and, most critically, I needed to piss.

There was no reason to go far. Hell, there was no reason to close the car door. But the moonlight on the snow gave the trail a sort of blue luminescence that looked like a tunnel. It drew you toward it.

Drew me, anyhow.

I went maybe a hundred yards along before I stopped, and then I stood like any good drunk and watched the steam rise off the snow where I'd pissed as if it were a fascinating natural phenomenon, worthy of deep study. When I finally looked up again, the trail around me was the same—bare limbs weaving in a light wind and silvery moonlight—but there was an addition to it that I didn't understand yet, only felt. A shift in energy, like the air had been infused with a low electric current.

Then I heard the noise. Soft at first, very soft, and in two pitches, one a bit higher than the other. Two different whispers. I stared down the trail in the direction it was coming from—deeper in the woods, not back toward the road, and didn't see a thing. The volume changed, though. The whispers got rough around the edges. *Pop, crunch, pop, crunch.*

Someone was walking my way. I understood that from the sound before the shape even became visible. Then the silhouette appeared and I finally understood the sound—the first tone, that soft *pop,* was a walking stick plunging through the crust of the snow. The other sounds were the footsteps following it. Crunching toward me.

"Hey there," I said, just to make some sound of my own, blurt something out in the way you do when you're nervous.

No answer. Not words, anyhow. Just that *pop, crunch, pop, crunch.* Closer. Not a hurried pace, just steady. And relentless.

"Hello?" I called, and once again, I received no answer.

I remembered the story about the witch then. That summertime story, the one that had been told around a warm campfire on the eve of a blue-sky day.

You always start these trips in the sun.

As the figure crunched on toward me, closing the gap steadily, I had an urge to run, and I think I might have, I think I could have gotten all the way back to the car and the hell out of there, been at my parents' by Christmas morning after all, because I'd gotten a little more sober with each second, each footstep. I really believe I could have done that . . . if I hadn't already called out. There was something about breaking the silence in the moonlit snowfall that seemed to anchor me. Like I had to wait for a response now, whether I wanted one or not.

The figure came closer, and I could see her face. She was lost between beauty and years, with traces of what she'd been and promises of what she'd become. Gray hair down to her shoulders, no hat even in the cold, and the snow didn't seem to stick in her hair, it just passed through it. The clearest thing in the moonlight wasn't any of her features; it was the walking stick. A polished and knotted piece of hardwood, like the railing at an old-time general store. Too big and too heavy for hiking. Or for hiking comfortably, anyhow.

She was about twenty paces from me when I tried again.

"I thought I'd be alone out here," I told her. "Christmas Eve, and in the snow . . . I figured it would just be me."

Pop, crunch, pop, crunch.

"Or maybe it's already Christmas," I said, realizing how damn late it was, and how far out in the middle of nowhere I was. "I bet it is by now."

I laughed awkwardly into the silence. She was ten feet from me. "Merry Christmas," I said.

She looked right at me. Not through me, but *at* me—it was absolutely a gaze of awareness, of acknowledgment, but her expression didn't change, and she didn't say a word, or break stride.

I'd been scared, but all of the sudden I got angry, too. That's how I'd always been with fear, even as a little kid. I lashed out like anger was courage.

"Hey, what the fuck is your problem? I'm not asking for a fucking gift, I'm just saying hello! It's *Christmas,* damn it."

Looking back, I think the word *gift* mattered. I've had a long time to think about it, and I'm pretty sure it mattered a lot. It seemed like there was little light in her eyes then.

At any rate, she stopped. For the first time, she stopped.

Still she didn't speak. She just held out the walking stick.

I should have known better than to take it. Any fool would have known better. But it was the first recognition she'd shown, and the way she extended it to me was with this sort of deep relief that I couldn't ignore. It was like a drowning woman's hand reaching for you out of the water.

I took the stick. It was smooth and cold and very heavy, like it was carved out of lead rather than hickory.

That night, at least, it was heavy. I've gotten not to mind it so much.

She never did speak. She left the walking stick in my hand and went on into the moonlight and through the snow toward the road, toward the place where I'd come from not that long before. The sound was different now, just the crunch of her footsteps, no longer the pop of the walking stick, and she moved a little lighter, more fluidly, more naturally.

I just stood there and watched her go. I didn't try to call after her, even though it would be a little while before I realized it wouldn't have mattered if I did.

It took them about six months to make me the star of the stories. The winter was long and lonely, of course, because there weren't many people around after the search parties were gone. Then spring came and the snow melted and the first bands of thruhikers began to appear. They don't seem to notice me when they travel in groups. They have to be alone. Even then, most of them don't try to speak. Not beyond a muttered greeting, at least. Anything beyond that is rare. There's something primal about me now, I think, something that warns them a little.

A few times, people have yelled at me, annoyed as I passed silently by, but nothing anyone has ever said has made a difference. I just get pulled on, like it's not a trail under my feet but one of those conveyors at the airport, and I've got no choice in the matter. Then whoever tried to engage me falls behind, and I'm gone, hiking on, alone again.

They do tell good stories, though. I've heard plenty of versions of my fate by now. Some of them are mean, sure, but sometimes they're sad and even a little sweet. A lot of the time, they're funny. What they say to each other, out there around the campfires, doesn't matter at all. What they say to me might. I'm not sure, but I think for it to matter, I'll need to find one of them alone, and then they'll need to say the right word.

I think they'll need to say *gift*.

Like I said, I've had a lot of time to consider it by now.

This fall I heard a girl ask an interesting question. She was one of the sad/sweet types, not one of the mean ones, or the funny ones. She was taking it very seriously, wondering about me and how it had ended and how bad it had been, and then she asked the one in their group who'd seen me—he was a college boy who'd yelled at me, as a matter of fact—if I'd looked hungry to him.

He said he wasn't sure. He sounded uneasy with the question. Even if I could have argued with him, I wouldn't have. Because I don't *feel* hungry.

Yet.

THE HANGMAN'S BRIDE

SARAH PINBOROUGH

Don't you worry, young Alexander," the old man said, looking up from the fire that crackled in the grate beside his chair. "In a day or so your parents will be here for Christmas and Mrs. Carmichael shall cook a fat goose and once we've eaten our fill we will sing carols and open presents. Their ship has already docked and this weather won't keep them away."

The boy stood by the window staring out at the dark afternoon and the thick snowflakes that gusted out of nowhere and died in their hundreds against the glass as the wind whistled once more, dashing around the huge house and darting down the chimneys. The boy flinched and glanced over his shoulder. The old man didn't blame him. The house was large and, when only half the gas lamps were lit, full of shadows. Even when the weather was fine the walls and floors creaked and groaned like the old man's stiff bones.

"It's natural to think of ghosts at midwinter," he said, reading the child's mind in his nervous tics. "The dead walk close in where there is more dark than light in a day. But there are no spirits abroad in this house, I can guarantee you that." The boy looked at him then, small in his smart trousers and shirt, his eyes doubtful. He looked younger than his eight years, and the old man smiled. "But I can tell you such a winter's tale, if you'd like? It's about a little boy, not very much younger than you." Alexander was a naturally curious young soul, and despite his tremors at the raging weather, not overly fearful, and he looked up with interest.

"Come and sit with me by the fire," the old man said. "And I will tell you the story. It will fill the time before Mrs. Carmichael comes to take you off to bed. It hasn't been told for a very long time, and I think you will like it."

As soon as his grandson had taken his place on the rug before him, the old man stared back into the hypnotic flames of the warming fire. He listened to the spit and hiss from within for a moment, before starting to speak, and the boy listened, rapt, to his story.

It was sixty years ago or so, almost to the day, but the world was a harder place then. There were no carols or Christmas trees, and for most the approach of Christmas was simply a breath of something intangible. A dream that belonged to others who had warm beds and full stomachs. A day for those who could afford a whole day to themselves. Most had other concerns. The simple business of staying alive.

Winter was bitter that year. A fog coated the city like darkness personified, and within a month or so, the ice in the river would be so thick that a fair would be held there, but such frivolities were in the future, and throughout that December there was just the icy cold and drifting snow filling the streets.

The boy was found by his dead mother's side, still wrapped in her frozen arms where he had been pressed against her for a warmth now long gone. She had been singing to him when she died and he couldn't remember hearing her stop. He was sure she still sang, whispering out the tune—*lavender's green, diddle, diddle, lavender's blue. You must love me, diddle, diddle, 'cause I love you*—even as she froze solid and cold beside him, the tune she'd always shared when he was frightened, perhaps when she was frightened too. He was so close to death that when the man emerged from that awful fog, top hat and tails over his greasy hair and thin frame, the barely conscious boy thought it was the final undertaker, Death himself, come to carry him to his grave. He found he didn't mind so much. But the suit was worn and frayed and an inch too short on the leg for its current host, and as he pressed the boy into his chest, all the child could smell was smoke.

To a passerby this might have looked like an act of Christian charity, the master sweep saving a poor urchin from his imminent demise, but in fact the sweep, one Mr. Arthur Crockett, was thinking of his business. He'd just lost one boy, Tom, and needed another to replace him. This happenstance would save him the cost of apprenticing one from the workhouse. So yes, he held the boy close to keep him warm, and yes, he nursed him back to health with a warm bed and hot soup, but only so that once he was well, he could put him to work.

When that day came, the boy found himself standing, morning and night, so close to the kitchen fire that he was sure he would be set alight, and the sweep's wife would scrub brine into his elbows and knees until he thought he would scream at the pain of it. Unlike the others of Crockett's chimney boys, however, the small boy did not cry nor make a single sound as they worked on hardening his skin. In fact, he barely spoke at all, and when he would not give up his name, Master Crockett declared he would be called Tom, the name of the boy who'd gone before him.

At night, when gathered under dirty blankets on their beds that were sacks of soot and before exhaustion sent them quickly to sleep, the other boys would tell tales of the Tom-who-died and how he'd cried when he'd become lost in the flues and then burned to death coming down into the wrong hearth in a panic. There were other stories too, of pins in feet, and fires lit under them, and they all laughed at these as they spoke, but under the laughter, black as the soot they slept on, was fear. Occasionally the other boys would huddle and whisper and talk of things they did not share with Tom and he did not mind this. He still felt somewhere between life and death, the soot like grave dirt, just as he had since his mother breathed her last in that freezing alley, and in many ways it was a relief to him when they forgot he was there and he could drift in his memories of her.

The days fell into a routine. Rising well before dawn, following the master sweep as he called out in the streets, and then hours of cleaning chimneys until his skin bled and he could barely breathe, before hauling back the sack of soot upon which he would collapse and sleep. Time passed in something of a dream, not exactly a life, but an existence that sat between the burning black heat of the hearths and the freezing cold of the streets in between, until a fortnight and an eternity had passed since the boy's recovery.

One morning, however, there was a great excitement in the town, everyone from the wealthiest to the poorest rising and breakfasting early in anticipation. This was an event that all could attend, a moment to feel entirely alive, whatever position luck gave you to be born into in this world. It was still dark when people began to gather, but the streets were noisy with chatter, and Arthur Crockett had his boys out early to be well-placed to pick up business once the main event was done and the well-to-do were filled with thoughts of warm fires in their grates. He sent some toward the back of the gathering horde, but kept Tom and two others close by as he weaved his way toward the front. The mist was thick and even in the crowd people appeared dismembered as they drifted in and out of the boy's sight—a leg, an arm, a leering face—and he tried to keep his eyes on the master sweep's tails for fear of losing him. This life might be hard, but it was better than the workhouse or freezing to death on a street corner, or forever being lost in this blinding fog.

Arthur Crockett paused at a pie stall and bought himself breakfast, and he must have been in a fine mood, for he bought another for the boys with him to share. Tom thought he'd never tasted anything so good and would happily have walked up to the noose himself for another bite—but Crockett would never have allowed that. Chimney boys needed to be thin, and even Crockett's favorite boys—those now devouring the biggest chunks of pie—were never far from starving.

The master sweep eased them into a position where he at least could see the wooden gallows erected in front of the grim prison building. "They say it's the Gentleman Hangman today." His eyes were shining with glee. "He don't take no payment for his services, that's what they say. All he asks is that he can study their faces after. Sometimes he sits with them for hours, just looking." He paused and his shiver had nothing to do with the bitter cold. "Especially at those of the dead women."

"A gent? A proper one?" Harry asked, licking his fingers clean of gravy. Harry had come from the workhouse more than a year before and like Tom was small and agile. If any of them were thought of fondly by Arthur Crockett, it was Harry. Harry did the chimneys of all the best houses. Harry was one of the boys who whispered at night.

"A proper one. Rich beyond anything we can imagine," Crockett said ruefully as if he too bled from the knees morning and night and cried as brine was burned into his skin. As if he too had to shimmy up naked into that black hell for hours. "His father ran ships to the East. Built up a trade there. House full of treasure, that's what the Chinamen down at the docks tell me. Godwin's Shipping, that's them. He was a proper businessman. Traveled the world. Until two years or so ago when suddenly he took up the hanging." His voice hushed. "Make sure you don't find yourselves at the end of a rope, boys. I won't come to try to save you." Although he winked at Harry, his expression was grim.

Tom's mind drifted as the proceedings started. Death had been too ever present in his short life, and he had no desire to watch a life snuffed out no matter what their crimes might have been. Thankfully, being as small as he was, all he could see were the bodies of those around him. The fog having lifted somewhat, like a stage curtain on the action, Crockett hoisted Harry onto his shoulders, and Tom was glad it wasn't him who saw the sobbing man being led to his death. He dozed on his feet, enjoying the slight relief from the cold that so many people pressed together could bring—a clammy almost-warmth that at least protected him from any gusts of sharp wind, and the catcalls and gasps from the crowd of hundreds were just sounds that drifted through him until the final gasp and thud of the drop.

Even before the unfortunate criminal had finished twitching, the master sweep was about his business, dropping Harry so suddenly that he stumbled and was nearly caught underfoot in the dispersing noisy crowd. Crockett's voice was deep as he called out, "Sweep, oh! Sweep, oh!" expertly keeping close to the broadsheet sellers, following in their wake, knowing that many housekeepers and butlers would be eager for such salacious—and more than likely false—confessionals.

The housekeeper who *did* stop the sweep, however, had not purchased such an item but instead, strode with purpose, directly to Crockett. She was not exactly as one would expect a housekeeper to look in such a winter's tale as this, as she was neither austere nor forbidding, but instead comfortably stout in body, firm in bosom, and with a ruddiness in her cheek that exuded warmth. In many ways, she looked more like a cook than a housekeeper and if it wasn't for Arthur Crockett's obsequiousness, Tom would have thought her quite ordinary.

"It's time some life returned to the house, and I'm determined we shall all be merry this year," the woman said, as she and the master sweep turned to face the boys. "And that requires lit fires whether they like it or not. Between his moodiness and her peculiarities, I'm fit to burst with irritation. Enough is enough."

"Tomorrow morning first thing it is, Mrs. Pike," Crockett said. "I'll bring Harry here, he's my best boy—and you'll find—"

"That one." Mrs. Pike pointed a gloved finger at Tom. "He's smaller. The chimneys at Thornfields are a maze and God only knows how narrow they get. I want the house full of heat and good cheer, not screaming boys stuck in a flue." She said this with a smile, as if it were simply jesting, but all Tom could think of was his faceless namesake, the boy who'd burned, and how awful that must have been.

"And clean him up first, please. He can be as filthy as you like leaving, but I can't have Mr. Godwin or Miss Darkly seeing him crossing the threshold like some black devil." She pulled a coin from her purse. "For your trouble." And with that, she turned her back on them and bustled away.

"Until tomorrow, madam!" the master sweep called after her, his face alight with a wolfish grin. "Until tomorrow!" He looked down at Tom with fresh enthusiasm. "You know where you're going tomorrow, lad?" He clapped a hand on Tom's shoulder in a way that made Harry's face tighten with envy. Tom shook his head.

"You're going to the house of the Gentleman Hangman himself. Oh what a day we shall have." His hand tightened uncomfortably on Tom's scrawny shoulder. "Time for you to learn the *real* business of the day. Harry, that's down to you. Explain it well, and you can have young Tom here's bathwater when he's done tonight, and some bread with your broth if you're lucky."

And so it was that the next morning, Tom, scrubbed pink and wearing clothes that, if too big and close to rags, were at least clean, followed the master sweep as they walked out past the edge of town and across the wetlands to the hangman's house. It was still so dark that Crockett carried a lamp to guide them, and the only sound was the crunch of their feet on frozen earth. The journey took more than an hour, Tom pulling the sweep's barrow behind him, and by the time they reached the heavy iron gates that signaled their arrival, his feet were numb and his hands scalded raw with cold. The metal creaked too loud in the darkness, and then, when they clanged ominously shut behind them, and the austere building at the end of the drive hove into view, only then did thick white flakes begin to fall, the gentle heralding of a blizzard to come.

"You know what you've got to do?" Arthur Crockett muttered, his foot tapping, as they waited at the servants' entrance tucked away around the back of the house. Tom nodded. "Don't mess up, boy." The mutter turned into something of a snarl. "Because if you do, you're on your own. You got that?" Snow landed on his dark-suited shoulders, thick as volcano ash, and there was a stillness in the air that whispered of a wind to come. Crockett sniffed and stared at the door with a hungry longing. "They say all the treasures of the Orient are in this house. Hidden away in rooms no one uses. Do your job right and this could be the first visit of many, so work hard and make them think you're an angel. I'd tell you to keep your mouth shut but too much talk's not a problem you have, is it? Cat ate most of your tongue in that alleyway, I reckon." Some of his teeth matched the black of his suit as he grinned, the rest a raggedy line of yellow. "Now, what's the rule, boy?"

"Take something small and forgotten." Tom forced the words out. Harry had explained it to him while they'd shared the barely warm bath the night before. 'The big houses don't have many chimneys, but they have lots of fireplaces,' that's what Harry had said. 'So you start cleaning one and then use the flues to come down into another room. See what you can get from there. If anyone's in the room, you just pretend you got lost. Crockett'll beat you for that though, and there won't be no supper. Don't take anything big. Just something simple. A chain maybe. Silver. A teaspoon. An ivory comb. Something he can sell to the Chinamen.' A few items like that gathered in a week could make a difference to the wily master sweep's finances, and his mood, and Tom hadn't seen the worst of his moods, Harry had whispered, but the Tom-who-died had.

It was barely past seven in the morning, the sky still dark outside, but the household, such as it was, appeared to be awake, as Mrs. Pike led them into the heart of the building. "Not much sleep goes on here," she said as she took them into the vast wood-paneled hallway. Huge portraits hung on the walls leading up the sweeping staircase, and a large model ship sat on an imposing side dresser. Everything shone, spotless, and even the walls smelled of polish. Tom had never seen anything like it. Away from the warmth of the kitchen, however, the house was so cold Tom was sure that he could see the ghostly smoke of his breath. Mrs. Pike, looking somewhat more formal in her dark housekeeper's dress and with her chatelaine hanging from her waist, wore a thick shawl around her shoulders as she directed them toward one of the drawing rooms. "You can start in there," she said, nodding the master sweep forward.

Tom, trailing behind with the sheets and sack and brushes,

passed a door that was slightly ajar, and with the curiosity of a child, he peered in. Although there was no discernible change in temperature, he could see a small fire burning in the grate of what appeared to be a library. Stacks of various books and papers were piled on shelves, but as if abandoned, and a long strip of silk hung with strange black shapes on it. It was Japanese, but Tom couldn't possibly know that. He couldn't read or write in English, let alone translate the intricacies of such a foreign language. For him it was just a strange art, and in itself something beautiful. A chair was turned in, toward the fire, much as mine is now, and a man's hand was resting on the arm. As if the occupant could hear Tom's shallow breath, he twisted around and peered back. A somber face, mouth downturned and lips pressed tight together as if holding back a thunderstorm of rage. For a moment their eyes met, the hangman's and the chimney boy's, and Tom recoiled. The chill that possessed Thornfields could have come from the coldness radiating from that expression. Tom had never seen the sea, but those eyes were as black as he imagined its depths.

"Mrs. Pike," the hangman said. "A word, please." He didn't shout, but his voice carried on the waxy air, well-spoken and yet gravel rough, empty of any expression.

"One moment, Mr. Godwin, sir," she answered, not pausing as she walked, even though his voice made Tom want to crawl into a corner. He scurried to catch up to the familiarity of Arthur Crockett, and soon the drawing room door was closing behind them.

"There are guests coming to Thornfields for Christmas, and so make sure you clean up after yourselves. I don't want any muck left behind." She gave the master sweep a stern glare. "You've a good reputation, Master Crockett. Don't disappoint me and should all go well we may retain your services into the new year." She turned and bustled out, heading no doubt to answer Mr. Godwin's questions.

"You hear that, boy?" Crockett smiled, his rotten tombstone teeth on show. "We're in. Now get to work."

Tom's stomach tightened. The fireplace was dominated by a huge painting hanging above it, of a ship on a tortured ocean as a vast creature, tentacles spreading out from his bulbous body, rose from the black depths to suck it back down. Tom found the enclosed spaces of the chimneys terrifying enough without the sense that he'd be climbing up into those depths.

He wanted to stay in the vastness of this room and browse the books on the shelves, only ever having seen one book before and that being a Bible, and do as Crockett was, while covering the largest items of furniture with sheets, perusing all the knickknacks and ornaments that gave the room at least a little life. A ship's compass. A decorated china egg. A white vase painted in blue with strange-looking women and the same odd writing he'd seen on the wall of the library. This room alone was a fascination to Tom, and he found it hard to comprehend that the house was filled with what seemed like hundreds more, and he wondered how so few people could need so much space.

Being a good boy, however, and fearful enough of his master, he took off his clean shirt, leaving on the trousers with the secret sewn-in pocket, and hung the heavy sheet as he'd been taught to do from the fireplace. Armed with his brush and scraper, he was about to take a deep breath and start his shimmy into the darkness, when a gasp from the doorway stopped him.

"What on earth are you doing?"

A woman stood there, frozen, eyes wide in horror. Her dress was dark, a midnight blue that served to highlight the lines on her gaunt face, and hung, ill-fitting, from her thin body. Her face was pale as was her hair. At first Tom thought she must be of Mrs. Pike's age, but when she stepped in closer, her hands worrying at her nails, the skin there was smooth and young, like his mother's had been, and her hair wasn't silver but the lightest blond.

"Cleaning the chimney, ma'am," Crockett said, nodding to her. "Mrs. Pike—"

"There can be no fires." The hands fluttered to her throat. "No, no. no. Not in these rooms. Not where I go. I read in here. I—I cannot have a fire in here. I cannot."

Her speech and breath came more rapidly and Tom was sure she would faint or scream or whatever else hysterical women were wont to do, when Mrs. Pike returned. She took in the scene before speaking, at once no-nonsense and yet also warm.

"Breakfast is served in the dining room, Miss Beatrice."

"But Mrs. Pike, these people—they—"

"Mr. Godwin is already at the table. You should hurry. You know how he doesn't like to be kept waiting."

The mention of the hangman's name silenced the breathless, fluttering woman, and she gave Tom one last horrified glance and then contained herself, her back stiffening. "Of course," she said, as quietly as snowfall, and then left the room.

"Don't mind her," Mrs. Pike said. "That's Miss Beatrice Darkly. Mr. Godwin's adopted sister, taken in when she was small. She has had some recent troubles. Nothing to concern yourselves with but I'd rather you didn't engage her in any conversation. She is prone to flights of fancy."

Arthur Crockett nodded, but Tom could see that despite the wealth around them, he thought the household as unsettling as Tom did himself. He had never imagined that he would yearn to be on that cold sack of soot in Crockett's basement, but he longed for the hours between to vanish and for it to be night and this day done. Of course, before then, he had to clean these flues and commit a crime that could get him sent away on the convict ships or to prison or worse. There was no escaping it. He was the chimney boy and this was his fate. Resigned to it, and with a tremble in his knees, he pulled back the curtain of the sheet and clambered into the hearth.

All thoughts of prison and crimes had evaporated within ten minutes of starting the job. The flues of a house such as this were like a maze, and they grew tighter and tighter as Tom scuffed his knees and elbows wriggling through them, pausing to scrape at tar and free soot from their walls. His lungs were filled with the now familiar taste, the dust lining them as if meaning to drown him, and with each turn there was no sight of the chimney up above.

Some walls were hot to the touch, giving clues as to where he might be in the house—above the library or the kitchen perhaps—but it was so dark, and in many places the soot was packed hard, narrowing his movement so that he could barely squeeze through, that he soon became disoriented. Worrying about his imminent crime had distracted him from keeping track of which turns he'd taken where, and his fear of Crockett's wrath was being overtaken by his fear of becoming the next Tom-who-died. As his panic began to rise, all he wanted was to reach the fresh air of the rooftop, but he was trapped in the endless twists and turns of the flues. His whole body ached and he knew his elbows, half-hardened as they were, had started to bleed. Upward. He had to keep aiming upward. Soon there would be a crack of daylight or some drifting snowflakes. There had to be.

And then he heard it. A scratching. His small body froze, and he tilted his head as far upward as he could manage, peering into the darkness for some hint of daylight. Was it a bird? Up by the chimney? It came again.

Scratch, scratch.

Slightly closer this time as if something was working its way toward him. A rat, he thought, even though he knew it was unlikely. Rats live in the streets, not on the chimneys. A rat was too agile to tumble down a chimney. Birds' carcasses could be found, but not rats. Birds and dead boys. But still, his imagination and fear took hold, and he was sure that a giant fat rat with sharp, hungry teeth was edging toward him to feed on his face. He scrubbed harder at the walls, trying to fight his panic with hard work. There was nothing in here with him. There couldn't be. Nothing else would fit.

And yet the scratching came again, and this time he was sure he heard a short sigh of breath with it. He very slowly tilted his head sideways, to peer down the angled flue where two chimney pipes met and where he hoped to find more space than the cramped flue he was nearly trapped in at present. Soot drifted over him like the snow outside.

Was it his imagination or had it turned colder? Goose bumps pricked on his hot skin.

Scratch, scratch.

A shuffling closer. His heart thumped hard against his bony chest and within that awful darkness, a different black shifted. Something he couldn't—his eyes widened as a flash of something pale behind it made the foreground clearer.

Hair. Long dark hair, dull and dead. Hanging down in thick strands in front of a face.

At first he could not move at all, frozen with both fear and confusion, trying to comprehend what he could barely see, and all he could think of was his dead mother and how pale she'd been before she'd died, and that here was a dead woman pushed into a flue, and maybe her hair wasn't truly a hellish black but she had been up here so long the soot had turned it that way. All these thoughts turned and tumbled in terrified Tom's head, but still the air froze around him, and now he really could see his breath before him, and then, and then—

Behind the matted strands of hair, a bloodshot eye, black at the core, opened.

Tom twisted and let out a cry, the brush banging hard against the walls and, with the beating of his feet as he tried to scurry backward, his only thought to flee this horror, the soot above him dislodged, raining down over him, an avalanche of choking darkness that filled his eyes and nose and lungs. He fought to breathe, forcing himself back down the flue, sure that whoever—whatever—was hiding behind that black hair, was coming and if they touched him every drop of blood in his veins would freeze and he'd be trapped here forever.

Having spent so much of his short life on the verge of death, he was filled with the panic of the relatively healthy when faced with the reality of a sudden, possible demise. His frame was suddenly stuck, one knee at his chest as one leg dangled free below, and like dirt thrown on a corpse, he was drowning in soot. Stars began to form at the edge of his vision as his lungs burned. He was going to die here and he would be the new Tom-who-died and no one would ever know the name his mother gave him.

Scratch, scratch. The scrabbling was coming from below him this time. As his breath wheezed in desperation, his terror forced him to look down. An ivory-white hand was reaching up for him. Black, rotten nails on grasping fingers, a bony wrist emerging from the sleeve of a pale nightdress. Farther down, that awful sheet of black hair, one terrible eye open behind it.

He tried to scream. He tried to kick away. As the icy fingers finally brushed his ankle, a weightier darkness took hold, one that started inside him, and as he sunk into it, his final conscious wish was for his mother, but there was no sign of her in that inner night as he became one with the void.

The light was so bright behind his eyes that he thought he might be in heaven. At first he had no idea who he was or where he was, or whose blurry faces were so huge as they leaned over him, Crockett, Mrs. Pike, and Beatrice Darkly, and then all thoughts were overtaken by the wheezing sound coming from his chest and the buzzing in his ears as he tried to breathe.

Strong hands had rolled him onto his side and were beating at his back and he coughed hard, a cloud of soot erupting from his lungs and, at least partly, allowing the passage of cool sweet air. His throat was raw and his nostrils clogged, but he could breathe again. A figure stood up behind him and he knew it was the hangman himself.

"What made him scream?" Beatrice Darkly muttered.

"He got stuck. They do sometimes, the new boys," Crockett said. "I pulled him out, though. Grabbed his ankle."

Scratch, scratch. Black hair. That terrible cold. Not Crockett's hand. For a moment Tom was back in the darkness and couldn't breathe all over again.

"His lips are still blue," Mrs. Pike said.

"He'll be all right," Crockett replied. "He'll be back up the chimney in a few minutes, won't you, Tom?" It was a growling threat.

"Don't be ridiculous," Mrs. Pike said. "The boy's half-dead. He needs to recover."

"I'll take him home."

"He won't make it to the end of the drive in that condition." The hangman's voice was as cold as Crockett's was angry. "I've cut down men from the rope with more life in them than the boy had just then. Put him in the old nursery, Mrs. Pike." Mr. Godwin paused for a moment before looking at the master sweep. "Come back tomorrow. The job can wait until then."

"Mark my words he'll be punished." Crockett was gruff.

"I'd say he's been punished enough," Mrs. Pike said. "And Christmas is a time for charity, after all. And as such, there'll be no docking of your fee for this inconvenience, Mr. Crockett."

"You're too kind, Mrs. Pike. Tomorrow it is. Thornfields will be warm by suppertime." Crockett leaned in, his hot breath sour, and whispered fast in Tom's ear. "You'd best get something good after all this, boy. Or else you'll get a beating the likes of which you won't believe." He got to his feet and Tom thought he should try to do the same but his skinny limbs were like lead. He could barely keep his eyes open, and the voices around him melted together into a drone he couldn't interpret. He was exhausted and his skin was hot. It took all his energy to turn his heavy head sideways to look back at the hearth. The sheet was down, no doubt torn out of the way when Crockett had pulled him free, and the fireplace was empty of everything but soot and ash.

As he started to lose consciousness again, his eyes met Beatrice Darkly's. She was staring at him with a grim intent, and one hand fluttered at her throat as if expecting the pull of a noose. And then, once again, he sank back into the nothing.

The next time he opened his eyes, he was in a bed. He had vague memories of hot water and sponges but they were like delirious dreams. He was clean, though, and the mattress under him so soft and the covers so warm, that he couldn't imagine why anyone would leave such a place once they were in it. The room was big, an old cot in the corner alongside a rocking horse, both pushed aside and forgotten, and Mrs. Pike was lighting a fire in the grate.

"Ah, you're awake," she said with a smile as she finished her task. "There's some warm milk by your bed. I put one of my grand-mother's herbal tinctures in it to help you sleep and ease your fever." She touched his forehead. "Although I think that's fading already." Tom tried to murmur a shy thank-you, but his lungs and throat ached and his arm felt impossibly heavy as he reached care-fully for the glass she was proffering. "You had a fright, that's all."

The warm drink was soothing, yet Tom still shivered at the memory of what he'd seen in the chimney. But had he really seen anything at all? Perhaps he'd been coming down with a fever and between that and his fear of becoming the next Tom-who-died, his imagination had gotten the better of him.

"What you need is a good sleep." Mrs. Pike said. "You'll be right as rain by tomorrow. A hardy little chap like you." Almost on impulse she leaned in and kissed him on his forehead, as if now that he was scrubbed clean and tucked up in bed she saw him as human boy rather than some monstrous urchin. "It's nice to have a child in the house again," she said softly, getting to her feet and drawing the curtains against the evening. "There should have been more. Now sleep. It will make you feel better." By the time she'd reached the door, Tom, his eyes heavy, realized he was exhausted.

Although he did sleep heavily for several hours, he was unused to such comfort, and indeed such rest, and as soon as his immediate exhaustion had lifted, he became fitful and restless, too aware of the quiet away from the bawdy streets of the overcrowded slums.

The first time he woke fully was with the sound of his door opening. Rolled onto one side, his instinctive thought was that it was the master sweep come to rouse him, but there was no shouting and noise and this was no sack of soot he slept on. The door clicked shut, and behind his lids a shadow with a delicate tread darkened the glow of the firelight. As he carefully listened to make sure that the clicking footsteps were not close by the bed, Tom opened his eyes just a sliver, expecting to see Mrs. Pike perhaps, checking on him before going to bed herself.

But it was not the housekeeper, and the darkness the fire cut through was that of the dead of night, the witching hours. Tom recognized the straight, narrow back of Miss Beatrice Darkly, as she stood, facing away from him, staring into the fire. After a moment, she lifted the wash bowl she held and hurled water onto the dying flames. With an angry hiss the fire died instantly, but loudly enough to make her spin around to check whether the noise had woken Tom, and he quickly closed his eyes. He didn't open them again, even after she'd tiptoed back out to the corridor, leaving him alone in the dark. He didn't know what to make of it. Was this what happened in big houses? Did someone put the fires out each night? But surely it would have been a servant? As it was, he preferred the room cooler. Coldness he was used to and there was too much luxury here for him to sleep.

He woke once more, not long before dawn, when the black of night had turned to a deep blue, and even this deep in winter, the morning began to battle for its claim. This time, however, he was immediately filled with a terrible dread.

Scratch, scratch.

He held his breath, his toes curling as he pulled his knees up under his chin. It couldn't be, it couldn't be. That had just been his imagination. There had been nothing in the chimney. He'd just been a cowardly boy. And yet it came again, a small sound, but persistent. And it came from the fireplace.

Scratch, scratch.

The temperature dropped, his nose stinging in the sudden cold, and although the scratching did not return, there was a whispering of ash from the hearth as if something moved there. Terrified of looking, but more afraid of *not* seeing, he forced himself to sit upright as fast as he could and his eyes flew open, sure that this was when he would suck the last breath into his damaged lungs.

There was nothing in the gloom. Aside from the wet ashes, the hearth was empty. He stared at it, his vision grainy and his chest burning as he panted hot bursts of air, relief rushing through him. Nothing. Just his imagination. It must have been the remaining traces of his fever. His mouth dry, he drank what was left of the now cooled milk and waited for his heart to stop racing.

Although he had been sure after that second waking that he would not return to sleep, his body made a liar of his thoughts, and a lifetime of tiredness and the heaven of the cotton sheets meant that he was soon once again lost to the darkness and this time he sunk deep. When he finally awoke properly, it was with the ever bustling Mrs. Pike saying his name as she pulled open the curtains. He stretched, blearily.

"It's nearly three o'clock. You'd have slept all through another night if I'd have left you, I warrant. Perhaps my tincture was too strong for a scrap of a thing like you."

The sky outside was an off-white wash turning to muddy gray, a dull deadened shade that still had a kind of brightness even though it was leaning toward dusk. A snowstorm sky. As his eyes adjusted, Tom could see that heavy flakes were indeed still falling, dancing around each other in the freezing air. He thought of Harry and the others who would already have been up from the soot sacks they called a bed for nearly twelve hours. That thought led to the master sweep and the task he'd set Tom, and the boy's heart sank, but as if she could read his mind, Mrs. Pike said, "Not that there's much reason to rush. Mr. Crockett hasn't made it back to Thornfields today. And he won't in this weather. You'll be staying with us until at least tomorrow by my reckoning."

Tom didn't have time to bask in the joy of his temporary reprieve before the housekeeper went to light a lamp on the wall and as she turned back, her face fell in surprise. "Well, what have you been up to in the night?" She looked up at him from glancing at the floor. "It's on your face too."

Confused, Tom looked down at the bedsheets and his stomach turned to water as he saw long cobwebs of black dust trailing on his covers. He stared at the thin lines. As if strands of sooty hair had been dragged across them. "And look at my clean floor too." Mrs. Pike tutted. Tom peered over the side of the bed, a growing sense of dread filling him. Ash footprints from small, bare feet. His eyes followed their path. They came from the fireplace. He swallowed hard. As if someone had crawled out of it and come to lean over him as he slept.

Beyond the fog of his fear, Tom was aware that Mrs. Pike was complaining about the dampness in the hearth, that she was questioning him about sleepwalking, or whether he'd thrown his jug of water onto the fire and why on earth would he do a thing like that when it was so cold a night, but her words were muffled as if she was far away, and he kept staring at the footprints and hearing her words—*It's on your face too*—and all he could imagine was the thing from inside the fireplace standing over him as he slept.

"I suppose it will clean up well enough," Mrs. Pike sighed, standing over the footprints and bringing Tom's attention back to her. "Maybe you've still got a fever." She touched his cheek, unconvinced. "There's some fresh clothes on the chair. Some of Mr. Godwin's from when he was a boy. There's a belt too for those old breeches." She turned away. "Get yourself dressed and come down to the kitchen where it's warm when you're ready. There's some stew and bread there."

"Thank you," he said. His mother had always taught him to be polite and Mrs. Pike was the kindest woman he'd ever known other than her. "Have you children, Mrs. Pike?" he asked from nowhere, the badly strung together words merely a thought spat out from his rusty tongue. She paused in the doorway and for a moment that cheerful face was awash with an old sadness. "I did have a son. A long time ago. He died before his life got started. But Mr. Godwin and Miss Darkly are my children. I love them as if they were my own. Can't help it, can you?" She was wistful, her words snowflakes, beautiful and yet so fragile. "When you're around them growing up. You always want the best for them."

It made Tom want to cry—a small moment of self-pity. He had

no one who wanted the best for him. Not anymore. He was entirely alone in the world. "Now enough chatter. Get yourself dressed," Mrs. Pike said, back to her practical self as she closed the door behind her.

Tom kept his head up as he clambered out of the side of the bed, not wanting to look down at those disturbing footprints, and as he yanked the nightshirt over his head he rubbed his face clean of sooty trail marks on the cloth.

Scratch, scratch. He didn't want to think of that. Not now, not in the dying daylight. Neither did he want to linger in this room too long. Perhaps, if he was to stay tonight in this room as well then he could ask for the fire to remain unlit. Maybe the flames woke it, whatever it was. He doubted the people of Thornfields would want to waste their coal and wood on the likes of him anyway. Now that he could stand and was almost healthy again, the hangman would probably make him sleep in the cellar or some such, just as Mr. Crockett did. Beds weren't for boys who by rights should have frozen to death by their mother's side.

It took him some time to negotiate himself into the clothes Mrs. Pike had laid out, and when he was finally buttoning up the shirt, he went to the window to look out at the snow. The snow was his respite. Despite the fireplace and the fear, he still had the master sweep's theft to commit before he returned. But if he stole a thing, where would he hide it without his special pocket? Under the mattress perhaps? It would have to be a small item for sure. But what? What would be enough that he could escape Crockett's wrath but not enough to be noticed by Mrs. Pike? His heart was heavy. He was a good boy and he didn't want to commit any crime, even if he did find this house and all its occupiers—with the exception of the housekeeper—quite strange indeed.

The snow still fell heavily, and the icy wind was making the window rattle, but the vast garden was not empty. The hangman, the master of the house, Mr. Godwin, was standing still as a statue in the sea of gray white, his hands thrust into his overcoat pockets the only indication that he was feeling the cold at all. An old man—Tom wondered if he was Mr. Pike and indeed he was—was clearing the falling snow from on and around a large tree stump. It was this cut-down tree that was the focus of the hangman's attention, the great wooden circle all that was left from what must once have been a towering oak, now just a tombstone to that life, roots no doubt rotting deep in the frozen earth.

The hangman's face wasn't visible, but he stood with such a stiffness in his spine that Tom found it hard to take his eyes from him. The boy and the man might have stayed in their places all morning were it not for another figure hurrying out across the snow and breaking the moment. Mrs. Pike. She did not so much as glance at the tree stump, but instead spoke briefly to the hangman, who, his reverie broken, turned and followed her inside. As they passed under the window, Tom caught a glimpse of his face, all dark scowling rage, and it filled him with such fear that he wished he hadn't looked out at the snow at all.

Once dressed, he stepped nervously out into the corridor. The walls were wood-paneled and gloomy, only one candle sconce—no modern gas lamps then—spluttering out a pale yellow light farther down, and he realized, with some disappointment, that the nursery was quite far from the rest of the house and he'd probably spent the night—apart from his visitors—quite, quite alone. There was a set of empty rooms near his bedroom, which he presumed must have been for a nursemaid at some time, but like the nursery itself, they had a forgotten air, and as he peered inside, Tom was sure the creak of the door was a moan of sadness for their lost purpose.

He turned his back and scurried toward the main staircase that cut down into the vast hall and linked the various wings of Thorn-fields. He kept close to the walls, and darted around the upstairs, his small hand quickly gripping each cold door handle and twisting. Most were, as the master sweep had said they would be, locked. Others were empty bedrooms, in one of which he spied a dressing table where a small mirror and hairbrush sat among various other mysteries of womanhood such as combs and small items of jewelry that told him the room must be Miss Darkly's. The air that greeted him was cold as ice and the bed was hidden beneath a mountain of blankets. There had clearly been no fire lit in that room all win-ter. Tom wondered if he should perhaps take a ring or necklace from her table—she seemed strange enough that she might not notice—but he could not bring himself to step farther inside. He had an awful feeling that if he did, the door would slam shut behind him and some awful thing—*scratch, scratch*—would suck him up into the chimney and keep him there forever.

Downstairs, his heart in his mouth, he discovered more rooms locked. Were they filled with treasures or just unused? He saw no servants—although there must be some—and he couldn't escape the feeling that the whole vast building was simply some kind of mausoleum. How could anyone live here, he wondered. Such lux-ury and yet no warmth. There had been more comfort in his dead mother's arms than could be found in this great house.

As he crossed the hall toward the servants' stairs, he heard voices coming from the library. A man, low, gruff, and angry, and a woman, distressed. The door was closed but the words carried through in the quiet, muffled and deadened. It was the hangman and Beatrice Darkly.

"You were in the chimney boy's room last night, weren't you?"

"I put the fire out, that's all. I could not sleep thinking of the fire and—"

"You were by his bed. Looking over him. Mrs. Pike said there are footprints there. In ash."

"I didn't, Theodore. Teddy, I didn't, it wasn't me. I just—the fire—"

"Do not call me Teddy, Beatrice. We are not children anymore. That warmth is long gone now. You stay away from that boy. You don't touch him. Don't whisper your wickedness to him."

"It was the fire. I only put out the fire."

The pause that came after was long.

"Two years today. Two years." His voice was a heavy sigh. "I will never forget the things you said, Beatrice. Everyone would laugh at her. No one would accept her. You were full of so much scorn. You, who should have been happiest for me. We never had the chance to find out whether she would have been accepted, did we? Did you say those things to her when she came here? Did you taunt her to her face?"

"I cannot remember. I did not—I cannot—you know I cannot—"

"You were a monster then, Beatrice. Are you still a monster now?"

When she spoke next, her voice was like the frost outside, cold and sharp. No longer pleading.

"Why don't you just put me out, Theodore? Why don't you just let me go if you despise me so much? A prison could be no worse than this life."

The hangman laughed; an unpleasant sound that made Tom flinch.

"If I were to send you anywhere, it would be to a madhouse."

"Don't you say that, Theodore! Don't you ever say that to me! Not to me!"

"I would. Don't doubt it. Just give me more reason like this business with the boy, and I swear to the God almighty who damns you, Beatrice, it's to the asylum you'll go."

Tom backed away, his eyes wide. He didn't know what they

were talking about, but he could hear the anxiety and anger in their voices and it made him feel sick. What happened two years ago? Why did the hangman hate Miss Darkly? Why did he want her to stay away from Tom? The footprints by the bed. Had that been her? Heels clipped against floorboard in his memory, and as they did so the library door swung open, and he was caught in the sudden light.

The hangman loomed large in the doorway, his broad chest nearly filling it, while behind him the nervy figure of Miss Darkly shrank back into the walls.

"Boy," he said, abruptly stopping in his stride. "You're awake. What are you doing here?"

"I'm going to the kitchen, sir. Mrs. Pike told me to." His throat was still raw. "I heard what you said, sir." The words rushed out. He didn't like Miss Darkly—she made him think of witches somehow—full of bitterness and bile like in the stories his mother would tell him when he was very small, but neither did he want her to carry the blame for something she hadn't done. Beatrice Darkly had been wearing shoes when she came into his room last night, but the footprints had been made by bare feet. "And it's my fault, it was me. It was me who trod in the soot. I did it in my sleep, sir. I'll clean it up, sir."

It was a lie, but what else could he say? That he thought there was a ghost in the fireplace? Something terrible and terrifying and it came out and watched him while he slept? No. He could not say that. It would be him the hangman wanted to send to the asylum if he told a tale like that. But neither could he let someone else take the blame, because his mother, God rest her soul, had done her best, despite their poverty, to raise him to be honest and good.

"Go down to the kitchen, boy." The hangman's voice was cold. "I do not wish to see you."

Tom nodded, whispered a final apology and almost ran to the servants' stairwell. He hated this house. He hated the hangman and

Miss Darkly. He hated his fear of the thing he'd seen in the chimney, his fear of everything. And he hated the master sweep. Oh, in that moment how he wished he'd died with his mother, and not been left all alone in this awful existence.

In the kitchen there was no sign of Mrs. Pike, but the old cook, a stooped woman with a hunch growing in her back and a dour face, ushered him silently to a stool next to the open range where various pots simmered. The heat immediately enveloped him, blasting away the freezing cold of upstairs. She ladled a thick, meaty stew into a bowl and handed it to him, alongside a rough hunk of bread. "Mrs. Pike says I'm to give you this," she said. "And don't spill any on those clothes. A boy like you shouldn't even be in them."

A servant girl leaned against the table watching Tom. She was like a street cat, thin and alert. "You choked in the chimney?"

Tom nodded slowly, concentrating on spooning the delicious food into his mouth.

"Get back upstairs, Elsie," the cook said. "Those floors won't scrub and polish themselves. Mrs. Pike wants them gleaming."

"Those la-di-da guests probably won't even be able to get here in this weather." The girl had barely moved from where she stood. "And I don't see why they'd want to come at all."

The cook scowled at her. "You don't know what this house used to be like, back in happier times." She glanced up to a small painting balanced on a shelf, its gilt frame out of place in the earthy common surroundings of the kitchen. "They'll come, all right. Well loved, the Godwin family are, and you'd do right to mind that." The cook shuffled into the pantry, muttering to herself, and as he chewed his food, Tom looked at the painting. Two children—a young man and a younger girl—sat in the boughs of a vast tree, looking at each other and laughing in the sunshine. It was not a very formal painting, Tom thought, for a house as grand as this, but it was full of warmth and love.

"That's mad Miss Darkly and the master of the house when they were young," Elsie said. "He wanted to burn it, that's what Cook says, but Mrs. Pike brought it down here instead. For her and Cook to have. To remember how things were." She pulled up a stool and sat opposite him. "Were you at the hanging yesterday?"

Tom was still staring at the painting. "What happened two years ago?" he asked. "Why is the house like this?"

Elsie shrugged. "I've only been here three months. They don't talk to me about all that. They don't like me. They say I chatter too much. But I do know this"—she leaned forward, all bright and alive—"whatever it was, it started him with the hanging."

"Is it true that he studies their faces?" Tom whispered. "After they're dead?"

"No one will say. Mrs. Pike'd sack me for asking, that old witch." Elsie dropped her own voice, the pair of them conspiratorial. "But he doesn't come home for hours after. And when he does, his mood is even darker than normal. Even Mrs. Pike stays out of his way. He sits in his study and just stares out the window, at the place that big old tree used to be." She sat back. "They're all mad here, that's what I reckon." Tom saw it then, the little shiver of fear under her confidence. "You just make sure it don't catch on you, little chimney boy." And with that, she grabbed her brushes and pail and was gone.

"You can't stay here all evening," the cook snapped at him once she returned, bursting his bubble of hope that he'd be allowed to remain in the warmth and help her with any tasks she'd see fit to give him. "If you've finished, then get back upstairs and find Mrs. Pike. She'll find some use for you."

"Where will she be?" he asked.

"You've got eyes. Use them. Try the dining room. If guests are coming, the silver will need polishing."

Silver, Tom thought, his head filled once more with the shadow of the master sweep. A teaspoon perhaps.

"Now shoo."

And so Tom reluctantly returned to the gloom and desolate cold abovestairs, and with no real idea of the layout of such a large house, all he could do to find the dining room was keep trying different doors on the ground floor and whispering the housekeeper's name as he went. He was about to explore a shadowy corridor that ran off the central hallway when Miss Darkly rounded the corner. Her fingers picked at the skin around each thumb, tiny frantic actions. Her eyes widened when she saw Tom.

"You!" she said. "I was looking for you." Tom's skin crawled under her gaze and he was sure the temperature dropped slightly.

"I was in the kitchen," he whispered, backing away.

She darted forward, hunching over so her face was level with his and gripping his shoulders in her clawlike hands. "You saw her, didn't you?" she hissed at him, a fine spray of sour breath and saliva hitting his cheek. "You saw her in the chimney. She was by your bed in the night. I put the fire out, but it was too late. She knew where to find you."

Tom said nothing but stared, terrified, at her eyes that darted here and there, lost in her own thoughts. "She torments me," she continued. "I feel her watching me. She would reach for me when I saw her. And I knew, I know, that if she touches me I shall die, I know it. Even now, with barely a fire lit in the house, I can still feel her. She'll never let me rest. She wishes to take vengeance on me. I cannot tell them again what I see. They say I'm mad and wicked, like my mother. They'll send me to an asylum. They'll say it's bad blood. That it was all just me. But you," she focused on Tom once more, "if you see her too, then we cannot both be mad, can we? It's all I need. To know that I am not mad."

"I didn't see her," Tom squealed, although the lie screamed in his mind in flashes of that awful eye behind a veil of black hair. *Scratch, scratch.* "I don't know what you're talking about. Let me go, please!"

"But you did!" Beatrice Darkly wailed, as frightening to Tom as whatever was in the flues. "I know you did. And she came to your room. What does she want with you, chimney boy? I know what she wants from me, but what can she possibly want with you?"

"Let him go, Beatrice." The hangman and Mrs. Pike had both appeared as if from nowhere, he holding a large glass of brandy. Miss Darkly did not take her eyes from Tom's, but she did release him and straighten up. She smiled too brightly, the expression both tragic and terrifying.

"Then let her come for me and be done with it. I can take no more. I cannot."

"Now, Miss Darkly, don't go upsetting yourself." The house-keeper tried to take the young woman's arm, but she stepped out of reach.

"We shall have fires in every room, Mrs. Pike," she said, laughing, almost hysterical. "Burn the wood. All of it!" She spun around, into the center of the hallway. "And I shall dance and dance whatever dance she wants of me, and it's done." She paused, breathless, and only then looked at the hangman, who stood, his face dark with loathing, watching her. "Perhaps I shall dance at the end of a rope. Yes, perhaps I shall choose that waltz to end it all. Perhaps that is what she wants. Is it what you want, Theodore? Would you like that? My brother of sorts? My beloved?"

"Don't you talk that way, my dear," Mrs. Pike said. "We have guests coming and we will close a door on the past. There has been enough gloom and mourning." She shot a look at the hangman then, and Tom, mouth half-open with it all, wondered at her bravery to speak so to the master and mistress of the house. "Now go to your room, Beatrice dear, and I'll send Elsie up with tea and some soup. You don't eat enough. There's nothing of you."

"I'm so tired of it," Miss Darkly muttered as she began to wan-der up the stairs. "I'm so very, very tired of being afraid. Of feeling so guilty. Let her come and be done with me." She weaved her way to the top and then disappeared into the gloom.

"What did she say to you?" the hangman asked Tom when Mrs. Pike had hurried away. The boy had hoped to be ignored until the housekeeper returned, but that was not his luck.

"Nothing, sir."

"God does not look kindly on liars," he growled, "and neither do I."

"She asked if I saw her." Tom's voice was small.

"Saw who?"

"I don't know, sir. Someone in the chimney." He swallowed hard, before saying the word aloud. "A ghost, I think."

"There are no ghosts." He stared up to the empty hallway above. "I would there were ghosts. She is driven mad by her guilt. And to think," he muttered softly, before taking a long drink of his brandy, "I once believed I loved her."

"More wood, Mr. Godwin, sir." The voice, dry as twigs itself, made Tom jump, and he turned to see the old man from outside holding a large basket of chopped logs. "I took the liberty of bringing a wheelbarrow full in. Left them downstairs. Thought you might need more given this weather. I'll put them in the library, sir." Snowflakes were rapidly melting into his dark coat, and his face was lined and old, his back hunched over, and as he headed toward the door, he dragged one leg slightly behind him as if its weight was greater than the load he carried.

"Thank you, Pike," the hangman grunted. "How much more of it is left?"

"Still plenty."

"Then the boy should clean the chimneys. Now. Tonight. Let Mrs. Pike have her fires. Burn it all for her warmth. It's only because of my affection for your wife that this farce of visitors has even been entertained."

"I'm well aware of that, sir." Mr. Pike nodded. The hangman looked down at Tom, fiercely angry, as if without Miss Darkly in front of him, the chimney boy would do well enough to take his rage out on. "He can work through the night if needs be. He's rested enough. I have no time for workhouse children in my house. I am not my father." He spat the words out and stormed away, down into a dark corridor that had not so much as one candle lit.

"Take this, boy." Pike gave Tom the wood to carry, the weight of which strained his thin arms until they were screaming, and he hurried into the library and put it down by the fireplace. The old man came in after him, unscrewing the top from a hip flask that had appeared from his pocket.

"Don't mind Mr. Godwin," he said. "He's got a good heart. Or at least he used to. Still in there somewhere."

Tom picked up one thick chunk of wood. It was solid. Ancient. He could almost feel all the life it once held humming on his fingertips. "Is this the tree from outside? I saw it in a painting downstairs."

Mr. Pike nodded and peered more closely at Tom. "You speak nice for a chimney boy."

"My mother used to be a ladies' maid before . . ." His words trailed off, his eyes still on the wood. Before him. Without him she'd still be alive. Still be working in a fine house in the town. She used to call him her joy and sing to him, but she can't really have thought that. Not really. Not when she was freezing to death in an alley. "She said it would serve me well to speak well."

Pike half laughed at that. "And look at you now." He held out the flask, but Tom shook his head. The old man sniffed and took another swallow. "I need it for my leg. It's no good in this weather." His eyes darkened. "In this house. This miserable house."

Tom stared at the flames in the grate, remembering Miss Darkly throwing water onto his in the night. "Why did you cut the tree down?" he asked.

"Too many memories for him. He stared at it all the time. Him staring, Miss Darkly refusing to look at it. It had to go. Mrs. Pike thought it would help." He took another drink. "But now Mr. Godwin just stares at where it used to be."

"Memories of what?" Tom kept his voice small and barely moved a muscle where he was by the hearth. Mr. Pike was talking to himself as much as Tom and perhaps now he'd find out why the hangman hated Miss Darkly so.

"She hanged herself from it," Mr. Pike said, curt. "Two years ago tonight. There was a blizzard like this. Icy it was. She was like a tiny awful doll hanging there in the morning. I cut her down myself when we found her. Will never forget the sight of it. That black hair all fallen forward in front of her face. Her neck frozen tilted at that awful angle. Still, it meant no one else had to see her face. I did, though. I'll always be seeing it."

"Who was she?" Tom whispered. Black hair over her face. Pale, cold skin. There was a long pause with only the crackling of the fire, just as ours crackles now, in the silence. The old man lowered himself onto a footstool, his bad leg stretched out in front of him, and he sighed.

"In the east they call ghosts *Yurei*. I learned that when I was on old Mr. Godwin's ships. Before my accident." As he leaned forward to rub his leg, Tom saw a strange tattoo on his forearm, odd letters in a vertical strip, like those up on the wall. "He gave me a job here when I couldn't walk properly. Me and Mrs. Pike. I was glad of it too, by then. Our boy had been born and died without me even holding him. That took my sea legs from me more than any limp could ever do. It gave Mrs. Pike a purpose again, to have a grand house like this to work in, and young Master Theodore and little Beatrice, the ward, to raise. I'd have worked for nothing just for her to have that. But still, I sometimes dreamed of the sea, and in those dreams it always carried me east, to those magical, mystical places with their strange ways. Brutal and beautiful all mixed up together. And the women"—he let out a sigh—"they were the most magical of all of it. So different. I've seen many men enchanted by them, but I never expected it of Master Godwin when he sailed away on his father's business. That I did not expect." He paused, his face darkening. "The worst of the Yurei, they used to say, are the *Onryo*."

"Who hanged from the tree?" Tom asked, his small stomach filling with dread. Mr. Pike continued, oblivious to the boy's question.

"None of us expected him to fall in love. Not in the east. Not with one of their women, enticing as they were, because we thought he was in love here. He was to marry Miss Darkly, you see, and they were happy. As they'd grown, their relationship had changed and any fool could see they only had eyes for each other. Thornfields was a house full of joy then. Warm. But, when that ship sailed, Theodore was a boy, and he came back, a year or so later, as a man. She knew straightaway, did Miss Darkly, clever as she is, that something had changed. He couldn't look her in the eye, but he told her he'd met a woman in the east, Yuki, fallen in love and married her. He would send a message to the port where she waited, halfway to England, once things were straight with his father—never less than respectful was Theodore then—and she would follow him. But he'd wanted to tell Miss Darkly himself and give her time to adjust before his new wife was among them. But Miss Darkly, poor heartbroken soul, did not adjust. She raged. She was bitter. She said terrible, terrible things to Master Theodore. Called him a laughing-stock and worse. Old Master Godwin—who was quite infirm by then and would die before the night that darkened this house—felt pity for her, even though she was behaving like a banshee, perhaps like her mad mother who'd died in that asylum, a crazed murderer. We all loved Miss Darkly, see? Even young Master Godwin still, in his own way, kept her in his heart. But she could not compete with his eastern beauty. Yet he could have forgiven her, her words, I think. Had events not turned out as they did."

"What happened two years ago?" Tom asked, his voice barely a whisper. The secrets of Thornfields were tumbling from Mr. Pike, and he didn't want it to stop. He thought perhaps he might be less afraid if he were to know what had trapped these people here in this melancholy.

"It's hard to say. Miss Darkly says she can't remember. She had a fever—the madness of her mother gripping her perhaps—and had been that way, on and off, since he'd told her about the marriage. But she was the only person here when Yuki arrived. Master Godwin was in Liverpool, Mrs. Pike had gone to her sister's for the night— Miss Darkly had insisted she go—and I was away delivering some business papers. What happened that night? All I know is that Miss Darkly had wanted the new bride dead, had raged about it, and the next morning she had her wish. Yuki had hanged herself by the silk cord of her dress from a sturdy branch of that old tree. Mrs. Pike found her and I cut her down. Couldn't let the young master see her like that, and it would have been days before his return anyway, the snow being thick and the ground treacherous, and we couldn't keep her that long. She might have been beautiful in life, but death, and such a death, can do terrible things to a person's face. It etches itself into the skin. She was no beauty then under the curtain of hair that covered her. I took her straight to the churchyard and she was buried." He took a long drink from his flask. "That's why Mr. Godwin became a hangman. To look at their faces. To see how they suffered. How she suffered. All to punish himself for not being here. For not saving her. Trying to understand why she would do such a thing after coming such a long way—to think what Miss Darkly could possibly have said to her that would make her doubt his love. How she would believe a scorned woman over his own pledge."

"What do you think Miss Darkly said?" Tom asked.

"I've got the boy's own clothes here." A shadow fell across the door and both boy and old man looked up to see Mrs. Pike in the doorway, carrying a single candle and Tom's now washed rags. "If he's going back into the chimneys, then he's not doing it in those breeches."

"People will do terrible things for love," Mr. Pike said to Tom before turning his attention to his wife. "I'll sort the boy out. It don't matter much if my clothes get soot on them."

"Don't you stay up late with him," his wife admonished. "You've got a chill." She looked softly at Tom. "And don't you pay no mind to what Mr. Godwin said. Don't work all night, there's no call for that. I'll put an old blanket in the drawing room and some bread and cheese. You can rest in there when you think you've done as much as you can, and then you can finish in the morning when the sweep gets back. Mr. Crockett won't make it here before nine or so, I warrant. Not in all that snow. Just you make sure you clean up as you go. I need to tend to Miss Darkly before bed." She left his clothes behind and disappeared off with her candle, and with the hangman nowhere to be seen, it felt as if the house had swallowed everyone up and there was just him and the old man left.

"Why are you telling me all this?" he asked.

"It's like trying to spit a poison out, I suppose. No one talks about it. Not even my wife." His eyes slid off to one side and his voice lowered. "I think you lied when you said you saw nothing in the chimney. I think you saw the Onryo." His brow furrowed. "But I don't know why she would show herself to you. Perhaps this is it. Perhaps she is finally coming for Miss Darkly. And if so, there is nothing we can do to stop her except pray that she chooses to leave the rest of us alive, for an Onryo has no empathy. It is pure vengeance and will wreak its will on any who come into its path."

"There's no such thing as ghosts," Tom whispered, even as the sudden draft from the chimney sucked up his words, as if something there were mocking him.

"They say an Onryo has the power to kill anyone instantly. To stop their heart with fright. But they prefer their chosen victim to live in torment and suffering. To be haunted. Sound familiar? Don't you think Miss Darkly is suffering? I think she's in the wood we burn, Yuki's vengeful spirit, and now she's in the flues and the fireplaces. Whatever Miss Darkly did or said that night, in death it invoked her wrath. There is nothing to be done if an Onryo marks you. There is no escaping that terrible fate."

Tom stared at the old man, his eyes wide. Why would Mr. Pike say such a thing? Was it some cruelty to frighten him knowing he had the chimneys to clean that night, alone in the dark? Was it to make him get the job done quickly?

"So if you see it," Mr. Pike continued, "try to stay calm. She doesn't want you. She might be curious but that's all. She wants Miss Darkly. If you know what's good for you, you'll stay out of her way. Pretend you don't see her at all and maybe she'll leave you alone." He got to his feet, his knees creaking, and in obvious pain.

"Have you ever seen her?" Tom asked.

The old man shook his head. "I'm haunted by her enough. I saw her face that morning. I don't need to see her now."

And so it was that as darkness fell outside and the windows were shuttered against the cold, Tom found himself back in the clothes Crockett had given him, hanging a sheet across the chimney he'd nearly died in, thinking of vengeful ghosts, murderous women, and looming over it all was the shadow of the master sweep's grasping greed and his cellar of soot and the hidden pocket in his trousers to hide a stolen object in.

At least Mrs. Pike had left two small candles lit, but with his brush gripped in his hand, Tom trembled at the thought of going back up into that darkness. Ghosts don't exist, he told himself, but the thought was hollow. After the tale Mr. Pike had told him, he knew that what he'd seen in the flues was Yuki, the hangman's bride, her vengeance come back as some inhuman malevolent spirit.

The thought of her waiting there for him made his breath freeze in his chest and when the drawing room door creaked open behind him he jumped, startled, half expecting to see her there watching him from behind that awful veil of hair, but instead it was the hangman himself. He came into the room, awkward, as if he didn't belong there, gripping a lit candelabra in one hand and a small handbell in the other.

"Take this with you." He handed the bell to Tom as he spoke curtly. "Ring it if you should find yourself in trouble. But only if that is the case. Disturb me just for childish jitters and I'll have you beaten soundly, do you hear?" He spoke the last as if his kindness embarrassed him, gruff and fierce, although without the wolfish bite of Crockett's threats. Now that Tom had heard the history of the house, and being a sensitive boy, he could see the pain and grief behind that hardened face and he found his fear of the hangman waning slightly. He murmured a thank-you and tucked the bell into his belt, and the man left without another word, leaving Tom alone with only the flues and what might be lurking inside them, for company.

He took a deep breath and steadied himself. He had no choice but to climb. He was, after all, a climbing boy, and if the Onryo didn't kill him, then Crockett surely would. Once again he felt entirely alone in the world and for a moment just wanted to cry, but then he thought of his mother—not her face, he somehow couldn't picture that—but of her voice and her song, and then crawled behind the sheet and to whatever awaited him.

As he climbed his mother's song kept him company and he

whispered along with her voice, so sweet in his head, the song going around and around and never finishing, soothing him in the dark as he worked.

> *Lavender's green, diddle diddle,*
> *lavender's blue.*
> *You must love me, diddle diddle,*
> *'Cause I love you.*
> *I heard one say, diddle diddle,*
> *since I came hither,*
> *that you and I, diddle diddle*
> *must lie together.*

And so, despite a constant ball of terror in the pit of his stomach, he climbed and he scrubbed, and let the cold and dark envelop him and surrendered himself to fate to decide if he was to be the next Tom-who-died. He kept his mother's song in his head and his eyes firmly fixed only on what was in front of him, and with the hangman's bell tucked into his waist he didn't feel quite as alone as he should have. As the cold faded with his exertion, he could, for a while, keep his fear contained.

The hours passed. He had come down through the narrow flues into a few of the many locked rooms in the house, but they were all either entirely empty or so sparsely furnished that Tom knew he would find nothing in any dresser drawer or cupboard to take, but then, just as a clock ticked over to midnight, he clambered out of a large hearth and knew he had arrived somewhere special. After carefully wiping the soles of his feet with the inside of his shirt—which although already filthy, did knock the excess dust away enough that he would not leave obvious footprints on the wooden floors or rugs—he stood up and cautiously walked forward, his mouth a small O of wonder. The walls were covered with vast maps and charts, and paintings on silk of strange trees and seas and women with dark hair and strange clothes. There were cabinets and tables and cases displaying painted china vases and bowls and animals carved from green stone and all manner of treasures the likes of which Tom couldn't even have imagined in his life of grime and starvation on the streets of the city where everything that might have once been bright was caked in mud and dirt.

Tom could do nothing but stare for a moment. Even aside from its contents, the room was the largest he had ever been in, two imposing fireplaces, one at either end, and it seemed to Tom that an endless magical world sat between the two. Art was not for the likes of him, and he had never seen so much beauty in one place before, and even dulled in the darkness, each item seemed to sparkle to the boy's eyes. Breathless, he walked forward. He had no mind to steal from this room—although he was sure that at some point Crockett would demand it of him should they return to Thornfields in the future—but he wanted to drink each item into his memory and store it there to savor later when sore and aching and with an empty belly on a bed of soot in Crockett's basement. He pulled the small bell from his trousers and left it on the corner of a table to stop it jangling as he walked, and then wandered the room, lost in his studies of the pieces of jade or china, eyes wide on the maps that showed a world so vast his mind couldn't even comprehend it. In one painting a beast with water spouting from its head erupted from the roiling sea to ensnare an entire ship in its huge jaw and Tom wondered, once again, how anyone could think to go to sea if such monsters could live in it.

He was so absorbed in everything around him that he paid no heed to how far into the room he had wandered, and as he stood in the middle of that ocean of wooden floor and rugs, admiring a tiger painted on silk, he didn't at first hear the soot dust falling from the other chimney, the sound not much more than a whisper as it sprinkled onto the flagstones.

Scratch, scratch.

Tom froze.

Another flurry of soot scattered out of the chimney, this time like hailstones against glass, and he slowly, so slowly, turned his head. Black hair hung down from the chimney, almost touching the grate.

Scratch, scratch.

One pale hand, clawed, with black nails at the end, gripped onto the chimney breast brickwork, feeling its way down, the cuff of a white shift visible against the blue white of dead skin.

Tom squeezed his eyes shut. She wasn't there. She couldn't be there. There are no such things as ghosts. His eyes were playing tricks on him. His breath panted out cold, the temperature dropping once more, making a mockery of his thoughts, and although he wanted to heed Mr. Pike's words and stay calm and still so she wouldn't see him, as more soot rustled in the grate, his terror was too great. He had to look.

He opened his eyes, and it took all he had to swallow his scream. She emerged from the fireplace, crablike, her arms and legs moving unnaturally, and as she crouched there on the wooden floor before him, her head tilted forward on her damaged neck so that her hair still hung long over her face, she looked up at him with that one terrible eye.

The Onryo. Yuki, or what was left of her. And she had seen him.

Slowly she unfurled, a series of awful jerky movements, unfolding a stiff puppet from a box, until she was upright. Despite having emerged from the flues, just as Tom had, her white shift was clean and the mottling of her skin stood out against it. She shuffled forward, as if her legs weren't used to walking, and with each step, her black, furious eye stayed fixed on Tom.

Only when she raised one arm and reached for him did the moment break. His heart in danger of stopping in his chest, Tom turned to flee. The door, he knew, was locked. There was only one way out. The way he came in. Through the other fireplace. He raced across the rug, no longer cautious of leaving footprints behind, and only as he fell to his knees, hard enough against the stone to make him want to yelp and reached up to climb, did he risk a look back, expecting her to still be making her slow shuffle across the room.

But she was there, only a foot or so away from him, sitting back on her haunches, her feet planted wide, that one arm stretched out, thin fingers grasping for him. She let out a long hiss and scuttled forward.

Tom didn't hesitate but climbed as if he was born for it, hurling himself back into the darkness, scraping his knees and elbows in his panic, shimmying up with no regard to the dust that filled his lungs and made him choke. Every moment he expected to feel her grip on his ankle as he had before, but nothing came, and only when the urge to cough overwhelmed him did he finally pause. She had not followed him. He was alone. There was no dark hair or scratching hands behind him, and he could feel her absence in the air that while cold no longer had that freezing chill about it.

Pressed tight in the flue, he allowed himself a few moments' tears as he trembled, his terror slowly easing. He wished he'd died with his mother, he wished Mr. Crockett had brought Harry here instead, and he wondered if perhaps the Tom-who-died was the luckiest of them all. He was free. He did not have to steal for his master or face ghosts or listen to terrible stories of a woman driven mad. He did not have to exist in a world which had not time or care for him. He was dust. He was nothing.

Tom, however, as he dried his eyes and took a long, shaky painful breath, had learned in his short life that wishing for things did not make them happen. He was still here, and he still had to steal for the sweep. But he would do that one thing and then leave the rest of this dark madness until the morning. Crockett could beat him for not finishing the job, that he could take. It would be nowhere near the beating he would receive if he had no special item for his master when they left the house.

He stared at the filthy blackness that had become his world and let it be a blanket around him as he made his decision. Miss Darkly's room. He would go there, steal a comb, and then return to the drawing room until dawn. It was all the bravery he had left. His hands still trembled as he climbed through, and in his head his mother sang to him and he once again clung to her words.

The air was biting cold and Beatrice Darkly's thin figure was barely visible under the heap of blankets and linen on the somber four-poster bed. As Tom crept out of the fireplace, if it wasn't for the sound of her breathing in the silence he would not have been sure there was another soul even in the room. On the side table, next to the unlit candle, he could see a cup and hoped it contained something from Mrs. Pike to calm her into a deep sleep.

After the pitch black of the flues, Tom could see well enough in the gloom to make his way to the small dressing table near the windows. He felt sick with what he was about to do, and knew his mother would be so disappointed in him, but if he had to steal, he decided, then wasn't it best to steal from a madwoman who had driven another to suicide? And maybe this would go some way to appease the Onryo? Perhaps it would leave him alone?

A brush, a comb with pearls on it, and various other pins sat on the surface. He was about to take the smallest item when he noticed a small bowl filled with broaches and earrings, items perhaps from happier times but now covered in dust. The combs she would use. These were clearly forgotten. He picked up a silver broach with a red stone at its heart and slipped it into the hidden pocket of his trousers.

"I'm so sorry, I'm so sorry." The whisper, frantic, cut through the darkness, echoing his own regret for the crime he was being forced to commit. Startled, Tom turned to see Miss Darkly suddenly twisting and turning in her bed.

"Better sister. Should have been a better sister." The woman had pushed her covers away and her hands rose, as if pleading with someone in her sleep. "I didn't . . . I don't remember . . . I'm so sorry. No more. I can't . . . no more." The last came out in a wretched sob.

Fearful of moving in case the woman awoke, Tom could do nothing but watch as she trembled in her sleep and tossed from side to side, obviously in some dreaming torment. It made him feel worse for what he had taken, and he wanted to get as far away from her as possible in the hope that he could forget.

Something shuffled in the shadows beside the bed, and Tom froze as the figure came forward, emerging from the soot shadows of the night, movements sharp and unnatural, until her dress touched the side of the mattress. *Yuki.* The Onryo. Tom's heart almost stopped in his chest as he watched her bend over the restless woman and start a strange almost rocking that brushed her jet-back hair against the sheets. Backward and forward she tilted, and slowly Miss Darkly quieted.

The Onryo stepped back all angles in its movement, and then, suddenly, in one instant, she raised one grasping hand, flicked her tilted head sharply toward Tom and hissed. As her fingers flexed, the cup by Miss Darkly's bed fell to the floor, and Tom, terrified, darted toward the door, ready to flee from both the insanity of the ghost and the living flesh of the madwoman who would surely now wake.

The Onryo turned and her arm stretched toward Tom, and for a moment, as he glanced back, his terrified eyes met her dark glare, and he caught half a glimpse of the face beyond the hair.

He stopped, assailed by a memory that until this moment, he had forgotten. His mouth dropped open. His mother. A memory of his mother. He was back in that alley in the city, unsure if he was dead or alive. Being swept up into the master sweep's arms from his mother's frozen ones. The rough feel of Crockett's coat against his painfully cold skin. He was barely living but he saw her for the last time over the sweep's shoulder. Her face. Not like her face at all. Distorted. Misshaped by death. Pale and yet blotched, her blood sunken after death. That monster was not his mother—*lavender blue, dilly dilly*—and he'd shut the awful image out from his mind.

But she had been his mother, he thought as he stood between the fireplace and the door, watching as the Onryo stretched her arm out toward him. She had been his mother and he had loved her, and she had loved him. Yuki had loved the hangman. Yuki had not been a monster.

He glanced at Miss Darkly, still restless but calmer than she had been, and still sleeping. He thought of the white hand pulling him free from the choking soot. He thought that if the Onryo had wanted him dead, he would be so by now. He looked at the cup on the floor and her outstretched hand. Was she trying to tell him something? To share something?

He breathed crystals of icy breath and took a tiny step forward, sure that as he did so, the Onryo let out a sigh that sounded like the howl of a winter wind. He thought of her reaching for him. Always reaching. That's what Miss Darkly had said too. That she was trying to touch her.

She wants to be touched, he realized, as they stood there in the dead of the night, on the longest night of the year. She needs someone to take her hand. He saw her stance for what it was now—pleading.

Without allowing himself time to change his mind, Tom took a deep breath and lifted his own arm, reaching out toward hers. He wrapped his warm small fingers around her icy pale ones.

And then she showed him.

They moved through the fireplaces to different places and times, a whirlwind of images that left Tom unsure if he was him or her, so immersed was he in the scenes that both held him for an eternity and threw him back into the darkness in an instant. He had no sense of what minutes were passing, and all he had to anchor him to the corporeal world was the cold grip of her hand in his. His spirit was somewhere other as she filled him with her story. Wood rocked beneath him as he sailed the oceans, heart full of happiness. The talismans she'd brought: wood wrapped in silk. Arriving in freezing England, another note waiting for her. Going to the inn dressed as an Englishwoman, fascinated by her own appearance. Waiting, waiting. Finally, in her own clothes and coming to Thornfields at night. The conversation. The fireside. The silk around her neck. The ending. And then, finally, the last image, a terrible thing that had not yet come to pass.

It may have been hours, it may have been minutes, but Tom could not tell. When she was done, he was a husk that needed to be filled again, and the darkness blurred into nothing. But he understood. He knew.

The hangman found him, as night was turning to dawn, sitting out on the wooden stump that was all there was to show of the tree where the man's beloved had hung and where he had played so happily as a child. Tom, once again half-frozen to death, was barely aware of him as he rushed across the snow, and swept him up in a coat, holding him close. He didn't hear him shout for blankets and a fire, and barely felt it when he stumbled in the snow. And yet he saw it all, as if from above. He was there and yet not there, once again, for a short while, hanging in the balance between life and death.

"How long has he been out there?" Mrs. Pike fussing around him.

"I do not know. I saw him from my window. I was . . ." The hangman didn't finish his sentence, but Tom knew. He'd been looking at the tree stump as if it could surrender answers to mend his heart.

Tom tried to speak. His mouth moved but no words came out,

although life began to tingle in his burning fingertips and toes. He had to survive. He had to tell Yuki's story.

"We need to get those clothes off him," Mrs. Pike said, already tugging at his frozen rags. "Get a blanket around him." She stopped suddenly as she tugged at his trousers. "Well, I never. Where did you get this, boy?" she asked, all care gone from her voice.

"If it's a bell"—the hangman threw more wood onto the fire—"I gave it to him."

"This is no bell."

Tom tried to sit up, his limbs screaming. The hangman turned as Mrs. Pike held up the broach fallen from the hidden pocket of his trousers.

"My mother's," the hangman said, his eyes widening. "My father gave it to Beatrice."

"And this little bastard has stolen it. Look. Tucked into his trousers. It was there."

The hangman loomed over him. "Is this true, boy? Have you abused our kindness and hospitality?"

Tom knew he should deny it, or at least try to explain, but his mouth was dry and there was only one thing he wanted to say. The hangman leaned forward and shook Tom roughly by the shoulders. "Is it true? Is this who you are? A common thief?"

"He should go on the ships," Mrs. Pike said. "To think I was soft on him. Looked fondly on him."

"I saw her." Tom finally managed to spit the words out, heaving himself up onto his elbows. "Yuki. I saw her. I touched her. I know."

The hangman recoiled as if Tom were poison personified, his face full of disbelief and disgust. "I will hang you for that lie, boy, and I will make it a slow death. But first I shall make sure your master, who will no doubt be here soon, knows of your crime. Let him beat you for your wickedness!"

Tom was barely listening. Although still dark outside, it was in fact the early hours of the morning. Once again the witching hour. The time that Yuki swung from the tree outside two midwinters ago, and the time that—

"Miss Darkly!" Tom's cry was hoarse as he pushed himself upright. "We must save Miss Darkly. Yuki showed me . . . she showed me . . . it's happening now . . ." With a strength that perhaps was not his own at all, he wriggled past both Mrs. Pike and the hangman, and despite their curses and calls after him, he fled the bright warmth of the library and ran up the stairs on numb and frozen legs. They could not be too late. They could not. He could not.

The hangman thundered up the stairs behind him at a surprising pace, with Mrs. Pike following behind loudly exclaiming she had no idea what on earth was going on as she breathlessly came after them.

"Tom?" Another voice bellowed up from the bowels of the house. "Boy? What mischief are you making?" Arthur Crockett, the master sweep, had arrived, Elsie leading him up from the kitchen. His presence only made Tom run faster. In that moment he cared not what happened to him, whether he would be beaten or thrown into the ships or hanged by Godwin himself. He was driven by the visions that Yuki had shown him. The terrible injustice that had been done. He may now be a thief but he could still make his mother proud.

He slid along the polished corridors and just as he felt the hangman's grip on his bare arm, he pushed open Miss Darkly's door.

She was balanced on a chair, the cord tied round her neck and attached to the unlit chandelier above. Her eyes were red-rimmed and her hair hung loose around her thin shoulders, strands hanging over her face and down onto her white nightdress, all a pale echo of Yuki's ghost. "I'm sorry, Theodore," she whispered, as she saw them. "I'm so sorry."

She kicked the chair away.

"Beatrice! No!" The hangman thrust Tom aside, sending him

crashing hard into the wall where he hit it headfirst, and ran into the room, grabbing Miss Darkly's legs and holding her up to stop her from choking.

"Let me die, Theodore," she said softly. "Please let me die."

Stars spun in Tom's vision, as if the two once-lovers were being sprinkled in glittering snow, and then the stars and darkness overwhelmed him and he was once again lost to the world.

When he came to, he was not in the warm comfort of the nursery bed but in the cold cellar, laid out on some old sacks, with one cast over him as if that could in any way keep the chill out. His head throbbed and in the candlelight he could see Crockett, top hat still on, sitting in the corner of the room, his wrinkled face full of venom.

"You fool," he said quietly. "Getting yourself caught like that. You think they were going to keep you, boy? In a nice house like this? You're on your own, you know that?" He unfurled himself from the chair and leaned over Tom, his face close, hissing anger at him as he took one of the boy's ears and twisted it hard. "I told you. I told you I would take no part in this. And don't even think of telling them otherwise. I'll strangle you myself if I hear so much as a whisper——"

"Mr. Crockett."

The hangman stood in the doorway.

"Mr. Godwin, sir," Crockett took off his hat to reveal his thick greasy hair. "I was just——"

"I can see what you were doing, Mr. Crockett. Mrs. Pike has prepared some food for you in the kitchen. Go and eat. I wish to talk to the boy."

"Do you think that's wise, sir? A wicked boy like this deserves just punishment."

"Mrs. Pike is waiting, Mr. Crockett." It was a voice that would brook no argument and despite his reluctance to leave the two alone, the sweep was wise enough to know he had no choice. With a final, withering glance backward, which left Tom in no uncertainty of his fate should he incriminate his master, Crockett left the room. The hangman closed the door. He took the empty chair and stared at the boy huddled on the sacks.

"Is Miss Darkly . . . ?" Tom was afraid to finish the question. Dead? Alive? Hurt?

"She's resting. She's emotionally exhausted but otherwise unharmed." A moment's silence passed before the hangman spoke again. "That was my mother's broach," he said. "A ruby broach."

"I'm very sorry, sir. I truly am. My mother would be ashamed of me." Suddenly Tom felt the urge to talk, to share a personal truth before trying to explain things he could not possibly know to this man who held his fate in his hands. "My name is William, Mr. Godwin, sir. Not Tom. He called me Tom after a boy who died in a chimney. I didn't want to share my name with him. I liked the sound of my mother calling my name. I didn't want him using it."

"I found the bell. You left it behind in my maps room. Were you looking for something to steal there?"

Tom nodded slowly. "It was all so beautiful. But it was too beautiful. I needed to take something small. Something that wouldn't be noticed."

The hangman stared at him for a long while, thoughtful. Troubled. "How did you know?" he said eventually, as if the theft were inconsequential. "What Beatrice was doing? You could not have seen her, for you were half-frozen outside. That broach was stolen hours ago, it was like a block of ice itself."

"She showed me that it would happen." The boy looked up and hoped the hangman could at least see the sincerity in what he said. "Yuki. She showed me everything. It's what she's been trying to do with Miss Darkly. She wanted to show her."

"Show her what?" he growled.

"That it wasn't her fault. That they are sisters. They both love you. That Miss Darkly had no part in Yuki's death."

"I think the others are right," the hangman said. "I believe you must be an evil boy to talk such wickedness of ghosts and stories and blame." He got to his feet, kicking the chair away, the boy's talk of his love tearing the scars open again. "You are a thief and a liar."

"I am a thief, although I never wished to be, sir. But I am not a liar!" Tom, for we shall continue to call him that for the sake of clarity, young Alexander, said. "She brought two wooden charms with her. Small and wrapped in tiny silk purses. I think one was for you and one for her."

The hangman turned back, his eyes narrowing. "Omamori," he said quietly.

"If that is what they are called. She wore them around her neck to keep them safe. Near her heart." He swallowed hard, for now he had to risk more anger with the truth he'd learned. "They are around Mrs. Pike's neck now."

"What devilment is this? What accusations do you throw? Mrs. Pike raised me after my mother died. She raised us both, Beatrice and I. She loves us. Perhaps more even than my own father."

It was Mr. Pike's words that found their way out of Tom's young mouth as explanation to the angry man. "People will do terrible things for love."

Without a further word, the hangman seized Tom's shoulder and dragged him out of the room and into the heat of the kitchen. Arthur Crockett sat at the table, shoveling hot stew into his mouth and his eyes widened, but it was not he the hangman glared at but his housekeeper. Mrs. Pike was by the fire checking the boots that Elsie was polishing.

"Whatever is it now, Mr. Godwin, sir?" she asked. "What has the boy done this time?"

"Do you wear any jewelry about your neck, Mrs. Pike?" he growled, thrusting Tom down on a stool and filling the doorway with his own broad frame, casting a long shadow on the flagstones.

"What kind of question is this? I have my crucifix as you can well see." She bristled, pulling her squat, strong body as tall as she might. "I am a godly woman, sir. Mr. Pike can assure you of that."

"Do you wear any other jewelry about your neck? Under your clothes. Any talismans or keepsakes?" His voice had calmed but there was no hiding the urgency.

"I don't see why you should—"

"She does!" Elsie cut in, sudden and excited, alive in the mischief of it all. "I've seen it. When I took sick and stayed for the night. I saw her in her nightdress when she cared for me. They hang round her neck. Two small colored bags."

Mrs. Pike's hand fluttered up to the high collar of her housekeeper's dress. "I found them in the grounds. I knew they would upset you, so I kept them. I couldn't bring myself to throw them away. I didn't see any harm—"

"Give them to me." The hangman's voice was cold, and Tom shrunk back against the wall slightly as Mrs. Pike glared at him. She turned her back to them while she undid the top of her dress, and then she pulled the cord around her neck free.

"There." Her voice was small as she handed them over.

The hangman stared at the two beautifully embroidered bright silk pockets. "Enmusubi," he said softly. "We chose them together when we pledged our love. She kept them until we were reunited."

"She must have thrown them away," Mrs. Pike said, her chin high. "When she did what she did. I should have given them to you, I know. But you were so devastated and I thought it best to—"

"She took them." Tom's words were but a whisper, but the weight behind them carried. He stood up and let the heat of the fire burn his knees. Unlike in Crockett's house, this time he drew strength from the pain. She was in there somewhere, Yuki, and she was relying on him. One good thing. He could cope with his life, whatever might be left of it, if he could do this one good thing. "She took them. After she killed her."

Crockett was out of his chair and around the table, as Mrs. Pike gasped. "How dare you say such a thing? How dare you!"

As punctuation to her words, Crockett slapped Tom so hard around his face that his teeth rattled, but the boy stood his ground, even as the earth spun and he saw the master sweep pulling his arm back for a second assault. A strong hand stopped him.

"You do not hit a child in my house, Mr. Crockett. Not even a thief. My father would turn in his grave."

"He's a wicked liar," Mrs. Pike said, clutching a handkerchief to her eyes as her body trembled. "Possessed of the devil."

In reply the fire in the hearth suddenly spat and raged, and the candles that lit the room blew out as a gust of icy wind came down through the chimney. In the sudden gloom, Tom saw the crone-like cook, hovering by the pantry, make the sign of the cross against her cowed bosom.

"She's in the wood you burn from the tree where she died," Tom continued. "She's in the fires."

"Not only a liar, but mad," Crockett growled. "I heartily apologize, Mr. Godwin, sir——"

"I want to hear him," the hangman said, as if Crockett did not even exist. "I do not say I believe him, but I want to hear him." He looked at Tom and nodded. "Speak, boy, if you have something to say."

Tom swallowed hard and the room hushed, even Mrs. Pike ceasing to protest, all fascinated in the firelight as to what this chimney boy could possibly know of their secrets.

"You were right when you said Mrs. Pike loves you and Miss Darkly," Tom started. "She does. Too much. It's why she did what she did. She wanted you to get married as you promised. She wanted her family to be happy with no new wife from a strange land coming to make a mockery of you in society. She didn't go to her sister's that night, although I'm sure her sister will say she was there if asked. But she was not. I know because Yuki showed me. Mrs. Pike had planned it all long before that final midwinter night."

The housekeeper dropped into a seat as if her legs wouldn't hold her weight any longer and the hangman raised one hand to stop her protests. "For the love of God, boy, do not hesitate, but tell your story."

And so Tom did. He put into words what the dead bride had shown him. He told the hangman how his housekeeper had sent a letter, in his name and in a hand identical to his own, to Southampton for when Yuki's ship landed. There was money too, and the young bride was instructed to buy herself some new dresses of the English fashion and that there were rooms booked for her at an inn, the White Horse, five miles from Thornfields, and she should lodge there until he sent for her when problems at home were resolved. She should not contact him directly but could send a letter to his housekeeper once she was established at the inn. She was alone and in a strange city, but being a loving and devoted wife, she did as the letter told her, presuming that old Mr. Godwin was sick or that there was perhaps some other trouble with the family, and she waited, patiently, until finally a letter came telling her to come to Thornfields, late that night.

She dressed in her finest kimono, and made herself beautiful for her love, and then she came, lured into Mrs. Pike's trap. Mr. Godwin was away on business, Mr. Pike to London with letters, and Mrs. Pike had induced a fever in Miss Darkly over the previous few days—her grandmother's tinctures ever useful—and then gave her a sleeping draft before claiming to go to her sister's for the night as Miss Darkly insisted she went. The cook had already gone, having left a cold plate out should Miss Darkly want anything, and so it appeared that the young woman was entirely alone in the house—which of course Mr. Godwin would never have allowed, but in his absence Mrs. Pike knew she could get away with it and plead forgiveness later.

But Mrs. Pike did not leave. She came back, and waited, and when Yuki arrived, she brought the tiny exotic beauty into the kitchen and sat her by the fire with a hot drink to keep out the cold. Yuki had used her time apart from her husband to learn English, and she chattered about their future together and the children they would have and told Mrs. Pike of the two omamori that they'd chosen, blessed to give them protection and the promise of a long and happy life. She took them from around her slim neck to show the older woman, and she was so happy, so excited to soon be reunited with her husband, that she didn't notice how drowsy she was feeling until she began to slide from her stool, and by then it was too late.

Mrs. Pike undressed her down to her shift and then lifted her slight body into the wheelbarrow Mr. Pike brought wood to the kitchen in, added her clothing, and then took her out into that midwinter blizzard. She hung her from the branch of that strong, old tree with the silk obi of her kimono the rest of which the housekeeper laid out on the ground to appear as if Yuki had removed it herself.

She watched as the young woman choked and twisted and her eyes started to pop and her tongue thicken, and when she could not take anymore, she grabbed the slim legs and pulled down hard to snap her neck. She went back inside, allowing the snow to cover her tracks, and stayed hidden until morning, when she claimed to have made the gruesome find.

She did not know, however, that Miss Darkly, in her drugged fever, had heard the doorbell that night, and come to the top of the stairs and had caught a glimpse of Yuki, and heard her chattering, before deliriously wandering back to bed. When she recovered, and there were accusations against her of doing or saying something to drive Yuki to suicide, she was overwhelmed by guilt and uncertainty. She wished she had thought more kindly of her rival. She was afraid that she was mad like her mother and perhaps she had done something that night. She blamed herself for all of it, and that is why, when the chopped wood from the old tree began to burn in the fires and she saw Yuki's haunted spirit, she believed she had come for vengeance, rather than to help her see the truth.

"It is all lies," Mrs. Pike spat when Tom had finished quietly telling what he'd seen. "What a ridiculous story. How can you possibly consider trusting a thief? A street urchin with no mother and no morals?"

"I did steal," Tom said, avoiding the black, threatening look Crockett gave him. "But I am no liar. I have no cause to lie about this, sir. Yuki would never have taken her own life. She loved you. She had faith in you. You should send to the White Horse. They will remember."

The hangman, his face full of pain, looked at him long and hard, and then down at the omamori in his hands, and was about to speak when the door burst open and Mr. Pike came in pushing a barrow full of wood from the shed. "The blizzard has come again, sir," he said, for a moment oblivious to the tension that filled the dark room. "No one is leaving Thornfields tonight."

And so it was that poor Tom was locked back up to lie awake all night in the dark on the cold sacks, and Mr. Crockett was given a room above the stables away from the main house, which he knew better than to grumble about, and perhaps, given the tales of ghosts and murder, he was pleased to be somewhere away from the flues and the chimneys the hangman's bride lurked within.

The hours passed and Tom sat in the cold with no fire to warm him as the blizzard raged, but he knew that he had done what Yuki wanted. It was as if he could feel it in the very bricks of the house itself. Upstairs, the hangman sat by Miss Darkly's bed, the two omamori in his hands, lost in his own thoughts and regrets.

Eventually, Mr. and Mrs. Pike went to bed. Mrs. Pike convinced that Theodore Godwin, who she had raised since he was a boy, loved her dearly and would dismiss any suspicions the chimney urchin could throw on her, especially as she had paid the innkeeper handsomely for his discretion those two years before.

The long midwinter night passed, and finally, finally, the snow stopped.

It was Elsie who found her. The poor girl screamed and screamed, and the cook could not calm her for hours, so awful were the contortions of terror on Mrs. Pike's face. She lay, twisted, on her bedroom floor, as if she'd been trying to flee. The only clue as to what may have caused her fear were small footprints of soot that came from the fireplace. Mr. Pike, however, had slept through it all, and only woke when the poor servant girl's hysterics served as an alarm bell for the entire house.

The hangman had fallen asleep in the chair by Miss Darkly's bed, and when the cries roused him, he found that the two omamori he'd been holding had moved. One now hung around his neck, and the other around that of the sleeping woman he had watched over in the night, Miss Beatrice Darkly, his once love. His anger at her had vanished after the chimney boy's story, and in its place was something else. A peace. A regret. A need to make things right.

He released Tom from the cellar, and all three—the boy, Miss Darkly, and the hangman—watched as a weeping Mr. Pike laid his wife out on the bed. None of them spoke. They all, even the housekeeper's husband, knew that the Onryo had come for her now she had no omamori to protect her. They all knew that in its own way, justice had been done.

Outside, the sun shone with a beautiful winter brightness and the snow glittered on the lawns and bushes. It was Miss Darkly who saw her first, standing as she was, so close to the window.

"Look," she said, breathless. "Come and look."

The hangman and the boy joined her and followed her gaze to the stump of the old tree. Yuki stood upon it, her head still hanging forward, hair blocking any sight of her face. Slowly, slowly, her neck straightened, the strands of hair falling back, a gloss shining on them as they did so, and as she looked up, she smiled, radiantly beautiful, before vanishing into the sunlight.

"And what happened after that?" Alexander stared up at his grandfather, his eyes wide, lost in the story. The old man smiled. "What happened to Tom? Did he get sent away on the ships?"

"Well," the old man said, leaning forward and smiling cheerily. "The secret pocket in Tom's trousers had not been the brightest idea of our greedy Mr. Crockett. It was clear to all, that surely Tom—William—hadn't sewn it there himself, and that the master sweep was the orchestrator of the theft. But he wept and begged forgiveness, and after all the anger and hangings and bleakness that had been his life for the previous two years, Mr. Godwin didn't have any more punishment left in him. He sent Crockett away, but with a promise that he must treat his boys well and feed and clothe and pay them, and a warning that Godwin would be checking up on him. Which he did, and surprisingly it seemed that being forced to become a better person actually turned Crockett into one. Harry became like a son to him, and eventually took over the business, which had grown quite large by the time Crockett retired. And what of Tom, you ask? Little William found frozen on the streets? Well, he stayed at Thornfields, where Mr. Godwin and Miss Beatrice Darkly became, after a cautious courtship during which they found that old love could blossom again, husband and wife and adopted him as their son. They changed the name of the house to dispel the last shadows of the past, but stayed there, and they lived long and happy lives together."

"And what happened to William when he grew up?" Alexander asked, stories of children always far more interesting to children than those of adults.

"Ah, he went into business too, and was very successful at it. He kept his mother's name, which the hangman, who did no more hangings after that night, thought was fit and right, and he stayed on land, always still fearful of those monsters of the deep, but he built on the Godwin business, and became very rich." The old man paused, savoring the last he had to say. "William Charters was his name."

The little boy at his feet gasped, momentarily confused. "But, Grandfather, that is your name."

"That it is, young Alexander." He smiled. "And that is how I know there are no ghosts in this house. For I laid them to rest a long time ago."

A few minutes later, Mrs. Carmichael, who like a housekeeper had with a charge a long time before, loved young Alexander as if he was her own, came to take the boy to bed, leaving the old man alone with only the crackle of the fire and the falling snow for company.

Tomorrow, perhaps, he thought as he stared into the flames, he would take the boy out into the garden and show him the old stump, where each midwinter he never failed to go and say a prayer for the woman who died there. Yes, he thought. Perhaps he would.

He gazed into the flames, lost in his memories for a while, and then, after touching the talisman that sat under his shirt, threw another log onto the merry, roaring fire.

ABOUT THE AUTHORS

Kelley Armstrong is the *New York Times* number one bestselling author of the Women of the Otherworld series, the Cainsville series, *City of the Lost, Forest of Ruin,* and many other bestsellers.

Christopher Golden is the *New York Times* bestselling author of such novels as *Snowblind, Tin Men, Of Saints and Shadows,* and *Dead Ringers.* Christopher Golden is also the cocreator, with Mike Mignola, of two cult favorite comic book series—Baltimore and Joe Golem: Occult Detective. As an editor, his anthologies include *The New Dead, Seize the Night,* and *The Monster's Corner.* As a general rule, he frowns upon editors including their own work in an anthology, but for this project, he's making an exception. (Once he came up with the idea for a story called "It's a Wonderful Knife," he couldn't help himself.) (He also generally frowns upon people talking about themselves in the third person, but there is a protocol for these sorts of things, after all.)

The author of fourteen cross-genre novels, Elizabeth Hand has received the World Fantasy Award (four times), the Nebula Award (twice), the Shirley Jackson Award (twice), and the James Tiptree, Jr. and Mythopoeic Society Awards. She is also a longtime critic and essayist for *The Washington Post,* the *Los Angeles Times, Salon,* and *The Village Voice,* among others. Her latest novel is *Hard Light,* part of her Cass Neary crime thriller series.

Michael Koryta is the *New York Times* bestselling and award-winning author of such novels as *Those Who Wish Me Dead, The Ridge, So Cold the River,* and the upcoming *Rise the Dark.* He has won or been nominated for the Los Angeles Times Book Prize, the Edgar Award, Shamus Award, Barry Award, Quill Award, and International Thriller Writers Award, among others.

Three-time Bram Stoker Award–winning author of such novels as *The Missing, The Keeper,* and *Audrey's Door,* Sarah Langan is also an American Library Association Award winner and is on the board of directors for the Shirley Jackson Awards.

Edgar Award–winning novelist and a unique voice in American literature, Joe R. Lansdale is the author of dozens of novels across a variety of genres. His work has been adapted into the films *Cold in July* and *Bubba Ho-Tep,* and the recent Sundance TV series *Hap and Leonard,* with other adaptations on the way.

Tim Lebbon is a *New York Times* bestselling author of more than forty novels. Recent books include *Relics, The Family Man, The Silence,* and the Rage War trilogy of Alien/Predator novels. He has won four British Fantasy Awards, a Bram Stoker Award, and a Scribe Award. The movie of his story *Pay the Ghost,* starring Nicolas Cage, was released Hallowe'en 2015. *The Silence,* starring Stanley Tucci and Kiernan Shipka, is due for release in 2018. Several other movie projects are in development in the United States and the United Kingdom. Find out more about Tim at his website, www.timlebbon.net.

Author of *The Three* and *Day Four,* Sarah Lotz has quickly become one of Stephen King's favorite horror writers. A novelist and screenwriter, she lives in London, England.

The *New York Times* bestselling author of the Joe Ledger and Rot & Ruin series, Jonathan Maberry is also a five-time Bram Stoker Award winner, a popular comic book writer, and a frequent lecturer at writing and publishing conferences around the world.

The author of the breakout horror hit *Bird Box* and *Black Mad Wheel,* Josh Malerman is also the lead singer and songwriter for the band the High Strung.

Both under her own name and as Mira Grant, Seanan McGuire is the highly acclaimed author of the Newsflesh series, the October Daye series, and many others. She received the John W. Campbell Award for Best New Writer in 2010, and among her many other honors, she is the only writer ever to appear five times on the same year's Hugo Awards ballot.

A relative newcomer to the horror scene, John McIlveen's first novel, *Hannahwhere,* was shortlisted for a Bram Stoker Award. The best of his short fiction is collected in the groundbreaking work *Inflictions.* McIlveen works at MIT's Lincoln Laboratory, but the government won't let him tell you what it is, precisely, that he does.

The acclaimed author of the Seven Forges epic fantasy series, James A. Moore cut his teeth on horror fiction, first as one of the primary writers behind White Wolf Games and later as the Bram Stoker Award–nominated author of such horror novels as *Blood Red, Deeper,* and *Under the Overtree.*

The *New York Times* bestselling author of *Behind Her Eyes,* acclaimed horror and thriller novelist and British television writer Sarah Pinborough also received the British Fantasy Award and nominations for others, including the World Fantasy Award, for such novels as *The Death House, Mayhem,* and *The Language of Dying.*

Winner of the World Fantasy Award, the British Fantasy Award, the Ditmar Award, and six Aurealis Awards, Angela Slatter is the author of *Vigil* and numerous short stories and novellas, including *Of Sorrow and Such* and tales collected in *The Bitterwood Bible and Other Recountings,* among others.

Scott Smith is the *New York Times* bestselling author of *The Ruins* and *A Simple Plan,* both adapted for film, the latter of which won him an Oscar nomination for best adapted screenplay.

Thomas E. Sniegoski is the *New York Times* bestselling author of *The Demonists, Savage,* the Remy Chandler series, and the Fallen series, which was adapted as a trilogy of TV movies starring Bryan Cranston. His comic book and graphic novel work includes *The Raven's Child,* Mike Mignola's *B.P.R.D.,* and *Stupid, Stupid Rat-Tails,* a spin-off from Jeff Smith's *Bone.*

Everything you need to know about Jeff Strand can be found in the name of his website, Gleefully Macabre. Strand is the author of dozens of novels, including *Graverobbers Wanted (No Experience Necessary), A Bad Day for Voodoo, Single White Psychopath Seeks Same,* and *Sick House.* His latest novel is *How You Ruined My Life.*

PERMISSIONS

"Absinthe & Angels" by Kelley Armstrong, copyright © 2018 by Kelley Armstrong. Printed by permission of the author.

"Christmas in Barcelona" by Scott B. Smith, Inc., copyright © 2018 by Scott B. Smith, Inc. Printed by permission of the author.

"Fresh as the New-Fallen Snow" by Seanan McGuire, copyright © 2018 by Seanan McGuire. Printed by permission of the author.

"Love Me" by Thomas E. Sniegoski, copyright © 2018 by Thomas E. Sniegoski. Printed by permission of the author.

"Not Just for Christmas" by Sarah Lotz, copyright © 2018 by Sarah Lotz. Printed by permission of the author.

"Tenets" by Josh Malerman, copyright © 2018 by Josh Malerman. Printed by permission of the author.

"Good Deeds" by Jeff Strand, copyright © 2018 by Jeff Strand. Printed by permission of the author.

MEDDLING KIDS
by Edgar Cantero

In 1977, four teenagers and a dog—Andy (the tomboy), Nate (the nerd), Kerri (the bookworm), Peter (the jock), and Tim (the Weimaraner)—solved the mystery of Sleepy Lake. The trail of an amphibian monster terrorizing the quiet town of Blyton Hills led the gang to spend a night in Deboën Mansion and apprehend a familiar culprit: a bitter old man in a mask. Now, in 1990, the twentysomething former teen detectives are lost souls. Plagued by night terrors and Peter's tragic death, the three survivors have been running from their demons. When the man they apprehended all those years ago makes parole, Andy tracks him down to confirm what she's always known—they got the wrong guy. Now she'll need to get the gang back together to find out what really happened in 1977, and this time, she's sure they're not looking for another man in a mask.

Fiction

HAUNTED NIGHTS
Edited by Ellen Datlow and Lisa Morton

Sixteen never-before-published chilling tales that explore every aspect of our darkest holiday, Halloween, coedited by Ellen Datlow, one of the most respected genre editors, and Lisa Morton, a leading authority on Halloween. In addition to stories about scheming jack-o'-lanterns, vengeful ghosts, otherworldly changelings, disturbingly realistic haunted attractions, murderous urban legends, parties gone bad, and trick-or-treating in the future, *Haunted Nights* also offers terrifying explorations of related holidays like All Souls' Day, Día de los Muertos, and Devil's Night.

Fiction/Short Stories

THE APARTMENT
by S. L. Grey

Mark and Steph have a relatively happy family with their young daughter in sunny Cape Town until one day when armed men in balaclavas break in to their home. Left traumatized but physically unharmed, Mark and Steph are unable to return to normal and live in constant fear. When a friend suggests a restorative vacation abroad via a popular house-swapping website, it sounds like the perfect plan. They find a genial, artistic couple with a charming apartment in Paris who would love to come to Cape Town. Mark and Steph can't resist the idyllic, light-strewn pictures and the promise of a romantic getaway. But once they arrive in Paris, they quickly realize that nothing is as advertised. When their perfect holiday takes a violent turn, the cracks in their marriage grow ever wider, and dark secrets from Mark's past begin to emerge. Deftly weaving together two complex and compelling narrators, S. L. Grey builds an intimate and chilling novel of a disintegrating marriage in the wake of a very real trauma. *The Apartment* is a terrifying tour de force of horror, psychological thrills, and haunting suspense.

Fiction

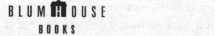